WRATH AND WRAITHS

CHRONICLES OF THE DAWNBLADE BOOK 4
ANDREW CLAYDON

Wrath and Wraiths

By Andrew Claydon

Just because you're chosen, doesn't mean you want to be.

Finally home, all Nicolas Percival Carnegie wants to do is sit quietly for five minutes and figure out who he's becoming after his latest adventure...but his plans are destined to be foiled yet again – because he's about to discover how terrible wrath can be.
Nicolas and his companions have meddled in the schemes of a powerful foe three times now, and that is one time too many.
Unleashing one of his most fearsome servants, the Maestro is bent on Nicolas's destruction.
But fate has something different in mind.
Finding himself somewhere he never dreamed he'd end up – even with his overactive imagination – Nicolas is instead thrust into the middle of a war whose outcome doesn't just impact life itself, but the afterlife too.
Cut off from his companions, he needs to try and survive as enemies old and new surround him with a single goal - to make sure the only place he ends up is the grave.
At least amongst the legions of the undead he may discover the answer to a burning question:
Why *does* nothing in Etherius stay dead anymore?

For my son Alex, who continues to earn my wrath with his never ending
stream of – arguably witty – bald jokes.

And to everyone who loves a good adventure.

'Across the various cultures that make up humanity, there is a great deal of conjecture on the exact nature of the Underworld.
Some describe it as a fiery pit, filled with demonic creatures and their various spiked implements. Others believe it to be a bleak and desolate world, where those you wronged in life haunt your every step. There are even those who claim the place itself has no true form of it's own, and that your own consciousness manifests the realm from the darkest fears your own mind can conjure, in order to ensure the best punishment for your sins.
Despite the range of theories on offer, there is one thing that all of the theorists can agree on:
None of them want to end up there.'

Etherius, A Travellers Guide – Dieter Von Ostric

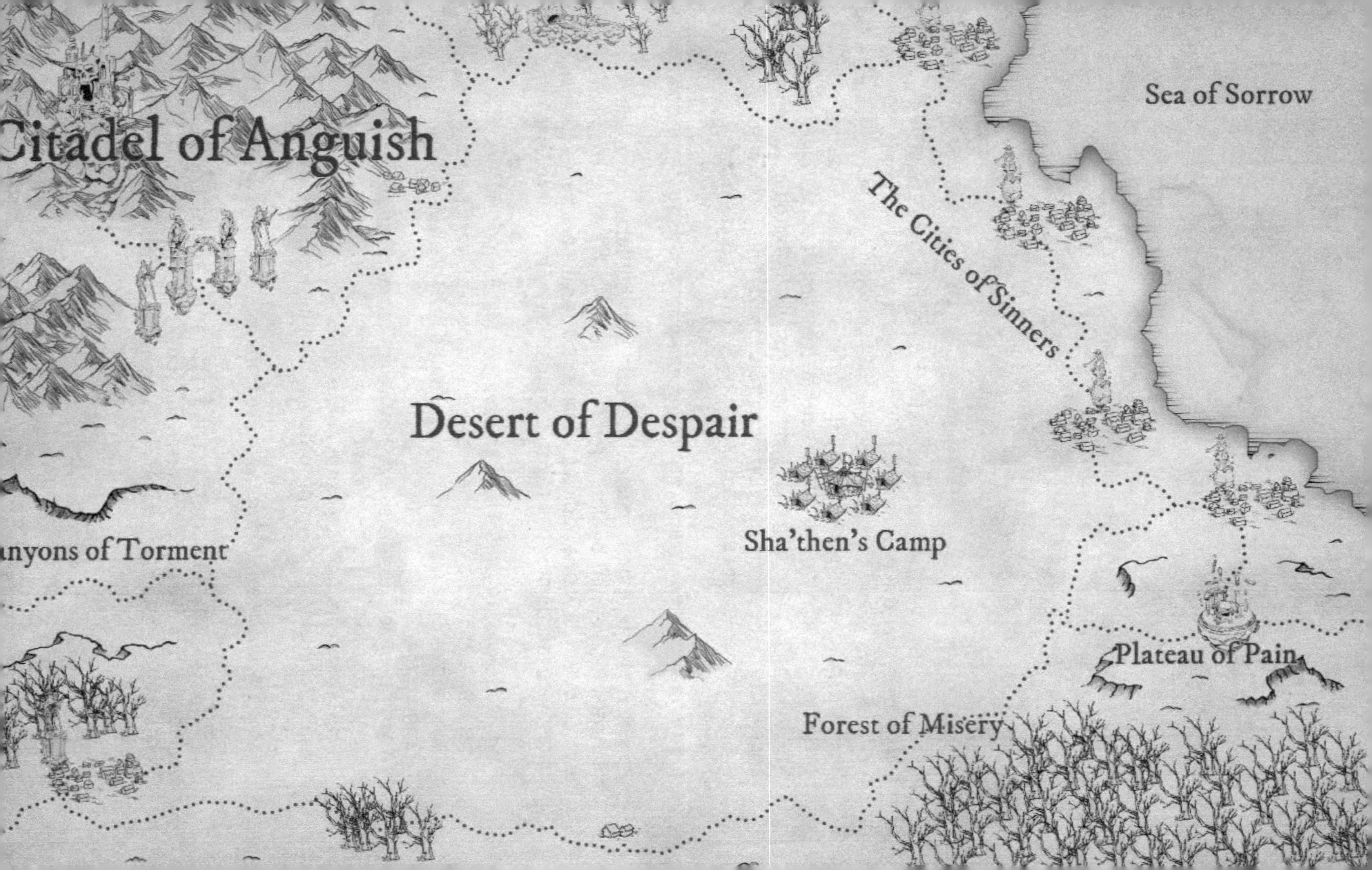

Citadel of Anguish
Sea of Sorrow
The Cities of Sinners
Desert of Despair
Sha'then's Camp
Canyons of Torment
Plateau of Pain
Forest of Misery

CHAPTER 1

Nicolas Percival Carnegie rubbed his face, hoping to banish the ghosts that were haunting him, though it was a wasted effort. They—well, he—would be gone for minutes at most, only to reappear the moment he let his guard down, like in the bottom of a tankard after he'd drunk its contents. The faun's face had the habit of appearing in the most random of places. He'd already seen today it reflected in a tavern window and in the centre of a flower, surrounded by lovely yellow petals. Last night it had even appeared on the back of his father's hand at the dinner table.

I need a break, any break…before my mind breaks. Assuming it isn't already broken.

Using all his will, he banished the little horned bastard for a few moments, locking him behind a reinforced door in his mind that was guarded by a troll with a poor temperament. The only problem with his success was that he now had to focus on the festival being thrown in his honour.

Maybe I should just let him out again and go fully insane.

This whole thing was insane. People around him were dancing and drinking and making merry as they celebrated him, of all people.

It's a farce.

When he looked up, his stomach sank at the multicoloured bunting that crisscrossed the main street of the village square.

That should be my hanging noose. I am a murderer.

Instead of making him want to dance, the jubilant music nauseated him.

It should be the beat of a drum as I'm led to the gallows and hung…because I'm a murderer.

Each person who passed smiled and congratulated him, and he had the audacity to smile back and say thank you.

They should be standing around me chanting, murderer! Murderer! Murderer!

Quickly, he brought one hand up to his mouth to stop himself from shouting the word aloud. When he was sure he wasn't about to bellow a confession across the square, he quickly checked his hand, turning it over to ensure there was no blood on it. As usual, it was clean.

Then why can I still feel his blood on my skin?

Shaking his fingers, he put his hand under his leg, where it couldn't bother him for a few minutes.

'Well done, hero!' Billy Bagrad, the tavern owner, shouted as he passed by, raising his tankard in salute.

AAAAAARRRRRRRRRGGGGGGGGGGHHHHHHHHHH!

'Thank you.'

Though he relived what happened in the cabin of that freighter daily, in reality, it had been two weeks since he'd killed the faun, Ro. The memory didn't ever seem to fade. If anything, it became clearer each time; The faun's hands around his throat, staring down at him with bloodlust-filled eyes, trying to choke the life from him. In his hand, he could still feel the wooden stake he'd picked up off the floor. *Stab. Stab. Stab.* The faun's eyes grew wide and then vacant as what passed for a soul—if the child-snatcher had one at all—left his body. The spark of life had been extinguished. By him.

Murderer.

There was all the justification in the world for what he'd done, of course. The faun had murdered royalty, kidnapped a princess and numerous children, tried to start a war, attempted to kill Nicolas and his companions multiple times, and was an all-around lowlife piece of scum who'd needed killing. Not to mention the obvious reason: he'd been defending himself. There was no way a nice chat would've taken the hands from his throat, and anything he'd attempted to say at the time would have come out as a hacking noise anyway. Yet none of the justifications helped.

Oh look, he's back, in between those dancing girls. And he's come back as a blood-covered corpse this time.

As he closed his eyes, a bead of sweat ran from his forehead to his cheek. The pressure inside his head was immense, the guilt building up as the confession demanded to be released so that everyone would know what he really was. He certainly wasn't this *hero* the people of Hablock kept banging on about.

I need to be punished. So why can't I own up to it?

He'd tried, repeatedly, since his return to Hablock not a few days back, but the words vanished each time he opened his mouth.

A killer and *a coward. What a man I'm becoming.*

Part of him wanted to walk up to the stage now, stand in front of everyone and announce to the world that he had blood on his hands. That voice was much louder than the little mouse-like one telling him he'd done the right thing. In his mind, he tried to picture some of those he'd helped—the freed slaves, the princess, the saved children. Within seconds, each of them became the faun. Yet Ro never said anything; he just stared at Nicolas blankly.

If I'd just minded my own business.

And he'd been so enthusiastic. Another adventure. On the seas, no less. *'You can do this,'* he'd stupidly told himself. He'd even allowed himself to start enjoying it. And look what that had led to.

That was why he'd fled from his companions. Before leaving the village to deliver a message, he'd never hurt a fly. In fact, he'd gone to great lengths not to. Now he'd fought and killed. He'd needed to get away before the damage to his soul became irrevocable.

If it isn't already.

Coming home, he'd hoped to escape what he'd done, to find a semblance of himself again. But like it or not, his deeds had followed him, though in a stranger way than he'd have thought. By the time he'd returned to Hablock, everyone knew *everything*. They knew about the vampires in Yarringsburg, how he'd saved the King of Sarus, and his role in averting a war in Merida. And he hadn't the foggiest idea how. Naturally, the stories had come to Hablock using the stupid name that dogged him everywhere he turned: *Nick Carnage*, master adventurer turned murderer. But it hadn't taken much for the locals to put two and two together.

And so I get a festival in my honour.

His parents—well, his mother—had been the architect of this little affair. They'd been so pleased to see him home, once they'd gotten over the shock of the state of him, and so proud of his achievements.

Good job I had plenty of time to heal from the worst of the beating Ro gave me hitching wagon rides here.

'If only I could heal my mind,' he muttered to himself with a harsh chuckle.

The party didn't help his fragile mental balance. Right now, it was as if this was all happening to someone else. Which would've been nice. Suddenly the music muted, the outdoors somehow enclosing around him as conversations became whispers. Feverishly he looked around, waiting for the people to turn on him in judgement for his crimes.

'Did you hear about my aunty over in Tavlock? Poor dear died the other day. Old age. Well overdue, if you ask me. And her. She's been waiting to go for what must be five years now. Anyway, she croaks...and then rises again a day later as some kind of undead creature. At her own funeral, no less. The priest and Uncle Harold had to finish her off with a shovel and— Oh, there he is, the man of the hour. Well done, Nicolas, we're all so proud of you.'

Their pride was pulling him into a pit. With every piece of praise heaped upon him, a little more of his mind eroded as the guilt and shame consumed it.

'Deities, Nicky boy, I know you don't like being the centre of attention, but you do recall this party is in your honour, right?' A tankard was thrust under his nose. 'You know it doesn't do for the guest of honour not to have a drink?'

If I drink, my lips will loosen. Maybe then I can be man enough to confess...

'Nicky.'

The poke that accompanied the name made him start, and he accidentally slapped the tankard held in front of his face aside, spilling its contents to the ground. The man who'd been holding it looked at the puddle in a bemused manner.

'You're lucky none of that got on me, or I'd have to ruin your honouring day by kicking your ass.' Potter raised his fists and boxed the air around Nicolas playfully.

You're just lucky I didn't kill you.

He looked up at his friend, and his mouth dropped open. The bald head, beard, and roguish grin he knew were gone, replaced by a horned head with a smug smile.

He's finally come for me.

The faun leaned in close and whispered in his ear, 'This is the part where you say, *'But spilling ale on your tunic would only improve it.'*

What?

Shaking his head slowly, Nicolas struggled to bring himself back to reality. Potter clicking his fingers beside his head helped, giving him something real to focus on so he could wake up.

His friend looked down at him, stroking his beard. 'You look like you need this more than me.' He offered Nicolas his own tankard, which he'd placed on the bench beside him. 'Maybe then you'll lighten up a bit. You're the single thundercloud on a sunny day, Nicky boy.'

He wanted to grab his friend by the collar and shake him until Potter could explain, in very precise terms, how he could lighten up after what he'd done. Instead, he took the tankard, mumbling thanks. Drinking now didn't seem sensible, but had anything he'd done of late been sensible?

He raised the tankard to his mouth, the foam tickling his top lip before the warm liquid poured down his throat. It didn't refresh him in the slightest, though he had half an idea that with enough of it, he could drown the guilt for a few precious hours.

'That's better.' Potter grinned, sitting on the bench beside him.

After a second, Nicolas realised his friend was watching him inquisitively. 'What?'

Potter waved an admonishing finger at him. 'You've been holding out on me, Nicky boy.'

By the Deities, he knows. But how could he...

The truth was on his tongue, ready to be spoken aloud. All it needed was a single prompt, the right prompt.

'C'mon.' Potter laughed. 'I've heard all the stories. Yarringsburg. Sarus. Merida. You've done some amazing things, Nicky boy. I can't quite marry up the person I know with the things I've heard. I'd refuse to believe any of it if I hadn't seen you jump on the cow-dragon that attacked the village a while back.'

Nicolas looked up into the air around the square, precisely where that event had occurred.

'And now look at this,' Potter said, fanning his arm around to encompass the celebration. 'A party in honour of the one person who hates attention.' Nicolas furrowed his brow. 'Don't deny it, everyone knows you hate this sort of thing. Why do you think all the maidens are leaving you alone when all of them want to ask for a dance...and probably for you to sire a few of their future offspring?' A sly elbow to the side accompanied the remark.

'They wouldn't if they knew.' The comment left his lips before he could catch it.

'Knew what?'

Taking a second, he fought back the rising panic brought on by the images of the judgement and repercussions if he told all. 'That it isn't as much fun as the stories make out,' he mumbled finally. 'It's actually quite scary.'

Why can't I just confess?

Potter laughed. 'Well, it needn't have been if you'd taken me with you.'

'What?' *I didn't even want to go.*

Part of him would gladly have traded places with Potter, except in reality, he wouldn't have. He'd had the opportunity when Potter offered to take his place and deliver that fateful message, and he'd refused.

How different my life could've been if not for my ridiculous sense of duty.

'You should've come and gotten me before you wandered off to Sarus.' There was a hint of accusation in his friend's voice, of bitterness, but it quickly picked up a dreamy quality as Potter stared off into some distant horizon in his mind. 'Imagine the team we could've made. Wandering the world, righting wrongs, making our mark.'

'That's your dream, not mine.' He sighed. 'I just got caught up in it all. But I'm sorry, if that helps.'

'Hey, I was only saying.' Potter seemed almost offended by the apology. 'Besides, you'll know for next time.'

Nicolas scoffed so loudly several people near him turned to look. 'There won't be a *next time*. I'm done with that life.'

Potter's brow furrowed and his lips pursed, as if he were struggling to understand. Just the way someone would if a baby dragon materialised before him and shat a gold brick. 'You what?'

'That life...' There was so much he really wanted to say right now. 'It just isn't for me.'

'Oh, I see.' Potter leaned forward, running his hand over his bald head. 'Gone out and made your mark, got your glory, so it's time to hang up your sword whilst the quitting's good. Nicky boy's the big man of the village now. Got his glory.'

'I beg your pardon?' The speed at which his fists balled up scared him. 'What exactly do you know about it?' Shaking his head, he gestured around him. 'Do you seriously think I want any of this? I just want the quiet life.'

Potter let out a derisive breath. 'Easy to say when you've got it all.'

Got it all? What do I have that's so special? The memories of things I can never unsee, the scars that won't ever heal, the nightmares that plague me, the relentless, never-ending guilt? All of that for...a party and some fluttering eyelashes from the local maidens?

'You don't understand anything. You say you want to go out and do all these great things, yet I haven't seen you take one step beyond this village,' he snarled, his guilt becoming an anger that was barely controllable now that it had someone to be directed at. 'If you acted as big as you talked, they'd probably have a statue in your honour in the capital by now.' Nicolas had a yearning in his fist, insistent and loud. *Throw the punch.*

Potter was taken aback, before he got angry too, his face darkening. 'And who'd look after my sick mother if I go prancing off on adventures? Some of us don't have the opportunity to just up and leave when we fancy.'

The wind was instantly knocked out of his sails. Forcing his fingers apart, Nicolas put his hand back under his leg. 'I'm so sorry.'

See what that life was making me? Would I have murdered him too, out here in front of everyone so they can see exactly what I am?

After a moment, Potter smiled warmly. 'No harm done, Nicky boy.' He chuckled. 'You're not wrong. I can't imagine the things you've seen or had to do. I shouldn't have pressed on whatever wound you got.' That was an understatement. 'Besides, when I do go out in the world, I'll do such great deeds that the festival they throw me will piss all over this little party of yours.'

Despite himself, Nicolas laughed.

Potter wrapped his arm around him, coming in close and whispering conspiratorially, 'What that little outburst tells me is that you need a party. Well, my friend, there just so happens to be one right here.'

Maybe he did need this? He didn't deserve it, but maybe he could numb the guilt with drinking and dancing. It would come back anew in the morning, but for a few precious hours of peace...

It'd be a shame to miss out on dancing. I've done that once recently already.

CHAPTER 2

The sky was fully dark by the time his father half-carried, half-dragged him through the door of their home. Blearily, he registered his shoulder banging against the door frame. His head lolled to the side as he looked back and mumbled a curse at the wood. He wanted to look up, but his head wasn't listening to his commands. Nor were any of his limbs, for that matter.

His body was hovered over a chair and lowered. At the last second, he spasmed to the side and nearly fell. But strong hands hoisted him back up quickly, putting him on the chair. The room was swaying more than his worse days at sea aboard the—

No. Don't think about that. If you do—

'Here, drink this.' A cup was pressed into his hand.

Ooooh, more ale.

Raising the cup to his lips took serious concentration and effort. A couple of misses later, which left his hands quite wet, he finally managed to take a sip. Instantly removing the cup from his lips, he stared at it with disappointment. It was water. Plain, boring old water. A sensible voice in the back of his head, most likely awakened by the cool liquid, told him that what he needed right now was refreshment, not more ale. Greedily, he guzzled the rest of the drink, pouring a fair bit down his chin in the process. Between the cold water going down his throat and the cold water he'd decided to have an impromptu face wash with, he was more in the room than he had been.

'I think somebody enjoyed having their own celebration day.' His father chuckled, sitting beside him.

'Maybe a little too much.' His mother's tone was equal parts admonishing and playful.

Nicolas found it hard to speak, even slowly. From organising the words in his head to actually uttering them, the whole process was like wading through quicksand. 'Jus...just getting in the spirit.'

That word. *Spirit*. It conjured an image of someone in his mind. Wincing, he pushed it away before it could form properly. If he thought about him, then he had to think about...

'Am...am I a good person?' His gaze was focused on his cup, but it wasn't the cup he was talking to. Instantly, he was aware of his parents' intense gazes.

'What makes you ask that?' his mother asked, worry evident to him even in his current state.

Well, he wasn't about to admit the truth, so he simply shrugged. 'Just asking.'

'Odd question.' When he looked up finally, his father was squinting at him suspiciously. They'd both seen the state he'd been in when he arrived home, and had tended to his injuries but asked no questions. That didn't mean they didn't have plenty of them.

'What if I'm not...good?' Half of him wanted to confess. The faun was in the corner of the room, waiting patiently for it.

'Are you saying the things we heard, the things you did in Sarus and Merida, aren't true?' His mother sounded as if she might be scared of the answer.

'N-no...I did those...things.' Why was it so hard to talk properly? Was it the ale or the guilt? 'Bu...but what if I had to do some bad things to do them?'

When his mother's hand touched his, he nearly pulled it away in surprise. 'You did some amazing things, Nicolas.' Her voice was warm and tender. 'You saved so many lives. I don't know what you had to do to achieve that, I'm not sure I even want to imagine it, but it's...I don't know. If good came out of your actions, can they be bad?'

Yes...maybe...I don't know.

'I wish you'd tell us so we'd know for sure,' his father interjected. 'But we don't. Judging from what we heard, you're a hero.'

Now he did pull away, so sharply that his mother gasped. His indignation rising, he stood too quickly, causing him to stumble until he ended up against the nearest wall. He deserved that title no more than he deserved their love. The faun smirked in the corner.

'*No!*' he cried, waving his arms in the air as if trying to swat away a persistent fly. 'No hero. I'm...I'm no hero. Heroes don't do what I did. No. No hero.'

Both of his parents rose from the table, ready to come to him. Why would they do that? If they knew, it would be different. But he was too scared to tell them. He'd already imagined their reaction, seen the judgment and disappointment in their eyes, the disgust. His mind created a vivid picture, and he couldn't handle seeing it in reality.

'No.' Waving them away, he made for the stairs, his uncooperative legs taking him the scenic route across the house. Why were so many pieces of furniture suddenly in his way? His shin connected painfully with a table. 'Dammit!'

When he made it to the stairs, he climbed them on all fours. They were moving from side to side too much to trust it to just his legs. Why were they doing that?

'Nicolas.'

Turning back, his head moving as if through water, he looked at his mother. She looked worried. They both did. And they were right to be; their son was a murderer.

'We will talk about this in the morning,' his mother said softly. 'But whatever happened, we know you're a good person. We love you, Nicolas.'

'I don't deserve it.' The admission brought tears to his eyes.

He didn't so much put himself to bed as stand over his bed, sway several times, and pass out. His last memory before sleep was of the faun's face, laughing.

****

His eyes shot open, and he sat up, frantically brushing the back of his head. There was no dagger or arrow sticking out of the back of his skull, so what accounted for the stabbing pain in his head?

Too much ale.

Closing his eyes again, he groaned in pain. His brain pounded angrily with the footsteps of a running giant. And why wouldn't it? He'd done his absolute best to drink it into submission and wash away the memories, which—

And there's the faun's face, right on my pillow staring at me.

Grabbing the pillow, he struck it, jostling and folding it until the face was gone. His violent reaction to his dead enemy's face only served to feed the guilt, so he put his head into that same pillow and screamed.

Can't this all be someone else's fault?

Despite feeling like a horse was continually kicking him in the head, a notion struck him. There *was* someone else to blame. The Deities-damned Oracle. If not for him, Nicolas would never have left home, never adventured, never...

If only I could go back in time and snap that bloody choosing stick.

It'd ruined his life. But maybe he could stop it ruining anyone else's. He could find it, snap it, and save generations to come. The sensible part of his mind informed him that the stick itself was generic and replaceable, but it's logic came too late. His mind was set on a course. Though right now wasn't the best time to enact his plan, when he was drenched in sweat with an inexplicable rug covering his tongue.

From the corner of the room, Ro smirked at him and his ridiculous plan.

'Leave me *alone*,' he hissed, careful not to wake his parents. 'Just go away. You were a bad person, and killing you was the right thing to do. It was self-defence.' The words were hollow even to his ears, so he doubted the faun gave two shits about his reasoning.

Putting his head in his hands, he was about to sob when he stopped suddenly. Something was wrong, but he couldn't immediately see anything amiss. Still, there was an insistent niggle in the back of his brain.

Danger.

'No,' he whispered, blood draining from his face.

Not here. Not in his home, with his family.

It's not in my home...yet.

He turned slowly towards the window. Though it was covered in unseasonable frost and he couldn't see through it, he knew there was someone outside. Someone bad.

They won't stay out there forever.

But what could he do about it? Forcing his head to turn, he looked at the one thing in his room he'd ignored since returning: the *Dawn Blade*. He hadn't used it to kill the faun, but it was still an implement of death. Why had he even kept it? Could he use it again?

His gaze rested on the wall separating his room from his parents'. His mother and father. Rising, he grabbed the sword and secured it to his belt. Maybe just the threat of it would be enough?

'Not my home,' he muttered, steeling himself. He had no real idea what he'd do, but what he wouldn't do was sit here and let whatever was happening go unchallenged.

His every survival instinct told him to get back in bed, pull the cover over him as if it were a magical protection barrier, and stay put. Yet he walked towards the door of his room, opening it carefully lest an errant squeak of a hinge gave him away, and ventured downstairs.

Briefly, he glanced at the faun stood by the door. 'You must be loving this, you bastard.'

Moving was tricky. Between the dark and the after effects of drinking too much, he had to be careful. Still, he smacked his shin against a table, most likely the same one as earlier. Stifling a cry, he looked towards the stairs. There was no sign his parents had heard him.

Good.

Reaching for the door handle, his hand froze, just the way it had after he'd returned home from his first adventure and been haunted by images of vampires. He wasn't entirely sure if it was fear of what lay beyond, of what he'd do to it, or a precarious mixture of the two. With sheer force of will, he grabbed the handle and turned it, slipping outside and closing the door behind him with a soft *click.*

The sky was it's usually dispassionate blanket of black with numerous twinkling lights. As soon as he saw his breath in front of him, it occurred to him that the chill in the air, like the frosted glass, wasn't entirely natural. Menace wafted around him like a gentle breeze, not harsh or obvious, but present.

By the well was a shadowed figure. Drawing the sword, more for confidence than a will to use it, he approached. With each step forwards, his mind told him to run like the wind in the opposite direction. How he ignored the strong urge was anyones guess. The closer he got, the stronger the aura of menace was.

Then his eyes adjusted to the darkness.

What in the Deities is that?

He gasped, nearly dropping the sword outright as a spasm of terror clenched his bowels.

It was a man, but at the same time, it really wasn't. The limbs were at the wrong proportions, even to each other. The clothes it wore were torn from muscles bursting through cloth too tight for it. Horns made of bone sprouted from random parts of its body. Atop its head were two antlers, which intertwined like some terrible crown. But the face... The skin of the head had extended and broken as a goat-like skull protruded from its face. The patchwork monstrosity regarded him with empty eye sockets. The creature stood idly, but the raising of the hairs on Nicolas's arms told him there was mighty power in it that could be unleashed at any second.

I can't fight this. I haven't a hope.

'Greetings, Nicolas Percival Carnegie.' The voice was a whisper, but an odd one, like multiple voices saying the same thing at the same time, all overlapping each other.

Of all the times people got his name wrong, this was the single worst time for someone, something, to get it right. The fact that the creature knew his proper name made it all the more terrifying.

I'm going to die tonight.

'Wh...who are you?' he asked. The voice that came from his mouth was a meek whisper.

The goat-skulled head inclined itself slightly. 'I am Koth,' it whispered. 'From the tales I had heard of you and your companions I expect-ed...more.'

Nicolas looked down at himself. Scrawny normally, he was a stick compared to the creature.

'He who commands me sent me here,' Koth continued.

'Why?' It was a stupid question. He knew he was going to die tonight.

'I am a fixer,' the creature explained. 'I take care of problems for the Maestro. You have become such a problem.'

Maestro? He'd heard that name before. The cursed faun had used it. That meant...

Oh Deities, I'm actually *going to die tonight.*

'Thrice, you have interfered in his works,' Koth explained. 'There will be no fourth time.'

Three times? It was all connected then. Fat lot of good that information would do him now.

'There won't be.' He was acting in desperation now. Truthfully, there was no talking his way out of this. 'My adventuring days are done. You can tell him that. Tell him I won't be a problem anymore.'

Koth seemed to intake breath sharply. Or was it a laugh? 'I cannot take your word for that,' the creature told him. 'And this is as much punishment as anything else. You must suffer.' The monster paused. 'And those you may have told must remain silent.'

What?

His nose picked up the scent of smoke, and he looked to his left. Between the trees, he could make out the rolling fields of Hablock, and multiple torch fires bobbing amongst them. The air picked up a faint scream and carried it to his ears.

'*No,*' he whispered, stunned, both because of what was happening and the knowledge that it was because of him. 'What have I done?'

'This is the will of he who commands me,' Koth said. 'You must suffer, and those who may know must be silenced. Only a couple left now.'

At the implication of the creature's words, he looked back towards his home.

Mother. Father.

Suddenly, the sword in his hands was raised again, defiantly. He was going to die, but he was also the only thing standing between this creature and his parents. He'd never beat it, he could tell that with a casual glance, but he wasn't about to just stand by and let Koth kill his family. Looking at his reflection in the blade of his sword, he came to a resolution. *Fight.* If he could just wound it, or tire it enough so that it was too weak to hurt his parents. Maybe he could make it die laughing at his attempts to fend it off? If he could...

'That is a futile gesture,' Koth explained levelly. 'But if you must.'

'I must,' Nicolas said grimly. Taking the blade, he drew a line in the dirt before him then returned to his guard position.

The skulled head inclined again. 'Brave. Pointless, yet brave.' And yet Nicolas didn't move a muscle. The creature grew silent, appearing to study him. His soul itched, as if Koth was gazing directly into it. 'I see now what you are, human. I will make this as quick as I am able.' A bead of sweat ran down Nicolas's cheek. Maybe it was a tear? 'Does that make you feel better? Humans like to be made to feel better.'

'No,' he cried. 'Not even slightly. It would make me feel a whole lot better if you just buggered off.' *It's going to kill me anyway, might as well say what I want.* 'But you're not going to, are you?'

'No.'

He tightened his grip on the blade, making his stance a little firmer. 'Then come at me, monster, and taste—'

His body shuddered violently, a sharp, piercing pain flaring in his chest. The world vanished suddenly, to reappear a moment later. There was a numbness that he couldn't account for. Lowering his gaze, Nicolas stared incredulously at the arrow sticking out of his chest, a patch of red expanding across his shirt from the point of impact.

That's not sporting.

He made to raise his dangling arm, to try and fight, to defend his family. He blinked several times at his empty hand.

Where's my sword?

He began to topple backwards. It felt like he was being slowly lowered to the floor, but he knew that wasn't the case. Hitting the ground heavily put his perception and time back in synch. He couldn't breathe properly. With a hacking cough, his chin became warm and wet with blood. The stars were dancing and twinkling in the sky above him as he lay on the grass, dying.

I've failed. I couldn't stop him.

The stars vanished as Koth loomed over him, tilting his monstrous head.

'You...cheated...' he spat at the creature.

He wanted to say more, to curse the monster, to beg for his parents' lives... But the numbness passed and his body became wracked with pain. He spasmed, and cried out.

Koth reached towards him and put a giant half-bone hand on his chest. His body spasmed again at the touch, burning energy flowing through his veins as freely as blood. His teeth clenched in pain, stifling the scream he wanted to unleash.

'You suffer,' the creature whispered. 'This is the will of he who commands me.'

There was a concussive force, and Nicolas felt himself being dragged downwards as his eyes closed and his head lolled to the side.

Darkness shrouded him.

CHAPTER 3

With an audible huff, Shift stopped abruptly and spun on their heel.

And lo, the others are still well behind me. How can two reasonably fit people and a spirit who doesn't get tired do such a piss-poor job of keeping up with me?

'Why am I the one leading when I don't even know the way?' they called back impatiently.

'Maybe because you're marching ahead like a solider on their way to battle?' Auron suggested with a shrug.

'Of course I am,' they scoffed. 'We have to check on Nick. Besides, you all told me what a great cook his mother is, and we missed breakfast.'

'Because you insisted on leaving before we could eat,' Silva remarked, as dryly as everything else the stoic warrior said. Her sentences were a desert with not even a mirage of a lagoon.

'You shouldn't be so excited,' Garaz remarked tartly. 'I doubt we'll get a warm welcome.'

The comment was repaid with an instant glare, but as usual the orc's yellow eyes avoided theirs.

Yeah, you revert back to sullen silence.

It was fair to say that things had been tense all round since the freighter, but they didn't want to dwell on that. There was no point now.

'I know.' Shift smiled sarcastically. 'If I turn into a snail, I can keep pace with the rest of you without a problem.'

'Look, Garaz is right,' Auron said, sidestepping a branch he could've easily walked through. Maybe a reflex from when he was alive? 'The kid won't be happy to see us.'

'He's had two weeks to calm down.'

Auron arched his eyebrows, his pupilless eyes wide as he tilted his head to the side. The expression said it all. *'You think that's long enough?'*

'I thought the whole premise of this trip was because we were sure he wouldn't have calmed down yet,' Silva said as the others finally caught up to Shift.

That was true enough. Around two weeks ago, Nick had killed a faun then thrown a massive wobbly about it and run off. No matter that the faun had been a fiend of the highest order and trying to kill him at the time. Because this was Nick. Logic withered and died in the face of his anxiety.

In truth, the others would've been on his tail a lot faster, if not for an angry captain and an overly officious officer of the law. The captain of the freighter on which they'd travelled to the port city of Arida had been quite animated about the damage to his freighter, which really amounted to a single door. He'd demanded compensation for that, cleaning costs and his *emotional trauma,* which itself came with a specific price tag. Eventually, being bitten by a zombified faun that'd been killed on his ship by them was also added to the bill. Shift had tried to reason with the captain, but he'd summoned the law. The group had been detained whilst their story about being the ones who'd saved Merida from war were confirmed, and *then* Shift personally was detained even longer. Apparently, they looked similar to someone called *Saraya,* who'd undertaken the theft of a freighter company payroll in the city, amongst other things. Obviously a mistake. If only the captain hadn't been such an asshole about the whole thing.

May the pox riddle him furiously.

It had left them with no money for horses, forcing them to hitchhike all the way here, having to listen to various folk stories about the dead rising all over the place.

When did not staying dead become fashionable?

'Yes,' they confirmed levelly. 'I know how badly he'll react. But I'll flash a smile at him, make fun of his whining, and we can then talk him down.'

The notion was all well and good, but none of them wanted to admit the reason they were *really* here, to check that he'd actually made it home okay. He'd been badly beaten when he'd run off into the night. Home was the only place he would've gone, but the question was: had he made it?

Of course he did. I don't know why I'm doubting it.

Maybe because Nick was naïve and would probably accept a lift from passing cannibals without realising it...even if they were sat on the wagon munching on someone's leg right in front of him.

Mentally, they wafted those thoughts away. He was home, waiting for them to go and talk some sense into him.

Easier said than done.

It'd actually surprised them, the level of denial Nick could manage. He'd killed a vampire outright, been responsible for the death of an unknown number of gangster's minions and probably several pirates...yet apparently none of that *counted*. Silly boy.

Boy.

Shift chuckled to themselves. Nick might not be as worldly as the rest of them, but there was a sweetness to his naivety, and more often than not it was bloody entertaining.

'Are we actually sure he went home?'

Urgh. Why is everyone else so downbeat? I've just had to dispel this doubt myself.

Silva caught the look they were giving her and shrugged. 'I am not wrong. We have no real evidence he came back here.'

'Still, can you imagine him going anywhere else?' Auron chuckled. 'The kid isn't exactly the *wander the wilderness* type. And we took the most direct route here. We would've found the—'

Shift's look stopped the spirit from finishing the sentence.

Besides, Auron wasn't telling them anything they didn't already know. Shift prided themselves at being able to read people—a required skill for someone who stole and conned their way across Etherius. Despite the growing casualness between Auron and Silva, they could still see the tension clearly. It'd probably never go. Shift couldn't imagine having to travel around with someone who'd murdered them. At least Auron wasn't trying to get her killed anymore, and by extension endangering the rest of them.

We certainly don't need that.

Shift's eyes flicked quickly in Garaz's direction, looking for his usual dose of wisdom. The orc said nothing, defaulting to the silence that had become the norm since the fight on the freighter.

These bloody people. 'He's home,' Shift said with confidence. 'And we'll find him, talk sense into him then...we get him back on the road.'

Almost slipped up and said you *then. I can't give it away so soon.*

'So this one time...' *Oh Deities, no.* 'I knew this guy from the Heroes Guild who had this obsession about hunting and killing a gargoyle. Think his name was Da-something, or was it Xan-summit? Anyway, for years he would go on about killing a bloody gargoyle. Then the guild gets word one is terrorising a temple, so we all say *'Go, live your dream,'* and off he trots. Really, we were all hoping he'd just shut up about it. Anyway, he finds it, and they fight, but turns out, the bow staff he used can't kill stone monsters...gasp.' Auron shook his head with a chuckle. 'So the gargoyle says, *'Tell you what, if you can tell me why I shouldn't terrorise humans, I'll stop.'* Fancying himself a debater, D...Dav...Dan...or was it

Xan...X...whatever, sits down and uses his reason. For two days, he and the gargoyle went back and forth on the subject of right and wrong.'

'Is this going somewhere?' *Because Nick is imminently going to die of old age waiting for us.*

The spirit pursed his lips in annoyance but kept talking. 'Turns out, you can't reason with a gargoyle. Eventually it killed him and just continued doing what it was doing.'

'And the point of that was?' Shift sighed.

Auron held up a couple of fingers. 'Twofold. Be careful what you wish for, and you can't talk sense into a stone.'

Closing their eyes, Shift rubbed the bridge of their nose. 'I don't *wish* to see him, I just want to check he's okay, and Nick isn't a stone.'

'And yet he can be as difficult to reason with at times,' Silva remarked.

'Can we please go now?' *Please.*

'Not just yet,' Auron said firmly. 'Once the gargoyle killed the other guy, I was called in. I waited until day, when the gargoyle was just a stone statue, and pushed it off the roof of the temple it was sleeping on. Job done.'

Shift faux clapped. 'Fantastic. Well done. I'm sure you found someone nearby to bed afterwards. Can we *go?*'

Finally, the group pressed on, painfully slowly in their opinion. Were the others even really bothered about Nick? But they had to be.

I need to know the group is together and strong before I leave.

'At least we're almost there,' Auron said, looking at the trees around them. 'This is familiar.'

'Then can we please pick up the pace?'

'Don't worry.' Silva sighed. 'We will see him soon.'

Worried? I'm not worried. He's fine. It's all fine. And once that's done, I can be on my merry way and get back to doing what I'm good at.

The decision hadn't been an easy one. Part of them liked being with the others, but...it was just time. They had to face it: this wasn't their life. They'd gotten the bug and done a couple of good deeds. Now it was time to go back to what they were supposed to be doing, the life they were built for. The only thing keeping them here now was how fractured the group had become. Nick had run off, Garaz had reverted to a moody youth, Auron was one bad day away from getting them all killed to get vengeance on Silva, and Silva was just borderline crazy. Shift couldn't leave them in that state, and was determined to do something about it before they left.

The image of a toad-like creature briefly flashed before their eyes.

Sort Nick out, get the group back together, then vanish into the night and find some valuable stuff to pinch.

It was a good plan, and they were comfortable with it. They were also comfortable not bothering with goodbyes. They were hard, and tedious, and Nick would probably cry. Briefly, they touched their pocket. The note they'd written was still in there, ready to go.

Slip it into his pocket and off I go. It's the best way.

They crested the next rise, the valley lying below them. Fields of farmland rolled as far as the eye could see, interspersed with the occasional forest and the hint of mountains on the horizon. It would've been picturesque if not for a single column of smoke trailing into the sky that told of a fire that had raged furiously.

Shift might not have known exactly where they were, but it didn't take a scholar to guess where the smoke was coming from.

'No,' they whispered.

CHAPTER 4

His eyes shot open, and he went to sit up but realised quickly that he was lying on his front. Pushing himself up instead, Nicolas got to his knees. His mind was flooded with incoherent images, as he gasped for breath. He stopped suddenly. Then he tentatively opened and closed his mouth a few times.

It doesn't feel like I'm taking in any air.

Closing his eyes, he tried to shake off the disorientation, to figure out what had happened to him. All he got for his efforts were a jumble of incoherent images.

There's a hand on my chest.

Scrabbling with his shirt, he pulled it forwards. There was no hand. Of course there wasn't. As off as he felt, he was sure he'd notice if someone was stood in front of him touching his chest. In amongst the tingling that marked the outline of this fictious hand, there was a single point of discomfort, yet he could see nothing amiss.

What happened to me?

Rising, he checked himself over. Everything appeared to be attached to everything it was supposed to be.

He looked around. His head darted from side to side as he tried to comprehend what he was seeing. Closing his eyes, Nicolas bent over, putting his hands on his knees. 'I've done this already.' He sighed. 'I have already *done* this. It's happened. Why, for the love of the Deities, is it happening again?'

Straightening up, he took in his surroundings. It was a vast step down from the island he'd been stranded on. The ground in all directions was featureless, dark and ashen. Numerous cracks split the dry earth. There was a slight breeze that occasionally picked up flakes from the ground and sent them spiralling into the air like a poor man's snow. What vegetation he could see was blackened and dead. It was not, in any way, shape, or form, Hablock.

'This is taking the piss,' he said as he put his head in his hands. 'I have already woken up somewhere I don't know. I did it a *few of weeks ago*. How in the Underworld does the same thing happen to the same person in such a short period of—'

His ranting came to an abrupt halt as he looked up. There was no sky, just a rolling black cloud, dense and impenetrable. And somehow vaguely familiar.

'How did I even get here?'

Parts of his memory were a blur. Putting his fingers to his temples, he forced his thoughts into coherence.

'Oh no.'

Koth. The monster. An arrow.

With a scream, he ripped open his shirt, running his hands over his chest. There was no arrow nor sign one had ever been there. Just the tingling.

That's odd. I definitely remember being shot with an arrow.

Yes, that was right. He'd faced down Koth to stop the creature from getting to—

'My parents!'

No. Nonononono.

Panic gripped him fiercely. With him wherever he was right now, they were undefended.

Not that I mounted much of a defence.

That wasn't the point. Somehow, he had to get back home, *now*. His parents' lives depended on it. Desperately, he looked around for some sign of civilisation, someone to talk to…ideally, a wizard who could teleport people.

His eyes came to rest on a set of ruined buildings of the highly ominous variety. Frowning, he traced a line of footprints in the ash that seemed to originate from them. They turned out to be his. Above the ruins, the endless cloud was broken slightly, a shaft of grey light spilling through it. But even as he watched, the opening was closing.

Maybe there are answers back the way I came.

In all honesty, the collection of ruined buildings looked foreboding, but there wasn't a direction in which things *didn't* look foreboding. Terror kept poking him on the shoulder, trying to get him to take notice of it, but for now, he was refusing.

Really, I do have all the reason in the world to give in to panic right now. But that isn't going to help my parents. Who could be…

That was all it needed. Suddenly, his mind filled with images of death and pain as his stomach clenched violently. Putting his hands on his knees again, he tried to steady himself as the world blurred around the edges.

Calm down. Calm down.

The only thing that would really calm him was information, to figure out where he was so he could figure out how to leave. And like it or not, the most likely source of said information was in those buildings. Even from here, they didn't look like they'd been inhabited in a good long time. But maybe he could find something.

A sword, map and compass would be ideal.

The slim hope was enough to help him collect himself. Taking a deep breath, which still didn't feel right somehow, Nicolas trudged back towards the buildings.

The closer he got to them, the slower he walked. They'd obviously been abandoned for many years, though he guessed they used to be a farm of some kind, with a two-story main house, several stables and some sheds. Not one building had four complete walls. The stone was dusty and covered in dark black vines. He really wished he had a sword right now.

And a set of stalwart companions. Doing this on my own is much worse.

But they weren't coming. He'd forsaken them, fled from them. So he was alone, and it was up to him. There was no room for doubt whilst his parents were still in danger.

Reaching the edge of the buildings, he was glad to be partially shielded from the biting wind, even if he didn't feel any safer. He was half tempted to call out, but he wasn't sure who or what would answer. Going around shouting in ominous ruins was a sure way to end up dead.

Peering around the chipped and holed wall, he saw a courtyard littered with debris. In its centre, there was a large crater directly under the nearly sealed hole in the clouds.

I'd best be careful around that. It'd be pretty stupid of me to fall in.

Not that anyone would be around to see it if he did. But he'd know, and he was as good at reminding himself of his embarrassing moments as Shift was.

The faun's grinning face was on the spur of a broken wheel in the courtyard.

'You made it then?' He scoffed. 'I don't have time for you right now.' He continued carefully around the debris. The face just moved onto a nearby rock instead.

The prospect wasn't one he relished, but he'd have to search these buildings, though with every passing second it seemed less likely that he'd find something useful. Still, hope was all he really had right now—along with the drive to get home as quickly as possible.

His ears pricked up suddenly. A noise. Shuffling of some kind. Nearby. Zombies.

Don't be ridiculous. Why even think of that?

In his mind, a ship's corridor appeared, and there was groaning and movement in the dark. And then it was gone.

That's the memory I need when I'm walking around the ruins of a strange land alone.

The shuffle came again. As much as he detested the idea, he'd have to check it out. As he moved along the wall of the building, his gaze rested on an old broom handle discarded on the floor. He picked it up and took a couple of practice swings with it. The handle was light, but if he put enough effort into it, he could do some damage.

As long as I don't kill anyone.

Instantly, his brain replayed what he'd done. He nearly dropped the handle for fear of what he could do with it, but like it or not, he needed it. Yet the urge to avoid a fight for what it might lead to was...imperative.

It's not like I ever had a choice in the past.

Pushing his doubts aside for now, and emboldened by his stick, poor weapon though it was, he edged to the end of the wall and peered around the corner.

Two figures stood a little way from him, backs to him. He couldn't make out much detail, save the rusty armour they wore, with shreds of torn cloth hanging from it that occasionally flapped in the breeze. Initially, he thought them dead, but their spiked helms moved side to side, so they were alive.

Part of him wanted to watch and wait, but with every second, the urgency to get home and save his parents grew. This wasn't going to get any smarter the longer he waited, so he stepped out from behind the wall.

Politely, he coughed to get their attention. 'Good day, uh—' He wanted to introduce himself, but this wasn't the place for over-formality. 'I was hoping you could help me. I appear to be lost and...'

Slowly, the figures turned around.

They are *dead.*

His jaw dropped as the pair of skeletons looked at him intently, a slight glowing light emanating from the middle of their otherwise empty eye sockets. The implication that he was stood before a pair of walking skeletons stunned him into inaction.

Without a word, the skeletons advanced towards him.

He dropped his club.

****

Running as fast as they could, Shift grunted with frustration at the fork in the road ahead of them.

'Left,' Auron shouted from behind, doing a better job of trying to keep pace now.

Shift was fast, whether on two legs, four legs or wings. Numerous frantic getaways had taught them to be quick when they needed to be. This, again, left them well ahead of the others, but thankfully Auron was happy to yell directions.

Barely slowing as they turned, Shift pelted down the dirt track, flat-out refusing to stumble or trip on the numerous stones and potholes marking it. Part of them wanted to turn into a panther and bound on faster, but sudden panic was impairing their ability to think straight, never mind change form. Every so often, they were tempted to glance back and see how far behind the others were, but it might slow them down—and they were *not* slowing down for anything.

When they rounded the next turn, the treeline broke, and there was a building ahead.

It used to be a building anyway.

It looked like the remnants of a house and mill, though fire had taken its toll on the structure. The smoke from the flames wafted lazily in the air in satisfaction at a job well done, like a skilled lover taking a pipe after sex.

'No,' they whispered, their heart clenching at the sight of the destruction and the knowledge that this had to be Nick's home.

Their legs demanded rest but were instead driven harder as Shift charged towards the buildings. The closer they got to the charred shell of the home, the more residual heat warmed their face. Shift wasn't pious, it wasn't a quality thieves generally had, but as they approached, they prayed to every Deity individually that Nick was alive and well.

Skidding to an abrupt halt, they nearly toppled forward and fell. Shift's heart threatened to turn their ribcage to mush, pounding against it furiously. Part of them wanted to stay put. At the moment, they didn't know for sure either way, but if they approached the body lying by the well with the arrow sticking out of it, they might get an answer they didn't like.

He's not dead. He needs help.

Forcing their numb limbs into action, Shift closed the gap quickly, sliding to the floor beside Nick, barely registering the small crater he lay in.

'Nick?' Their hands hovered over him.

What can I do? I'm no healer. Should I pull the arrow out?

Turning back towards the treeline, they did the most useful thing they could think of.

'*Garazzzzzzz.*'

Okay, the healer's on the way. What now?

Nick looked so pale, practically white. Putting their hand on his chest, they waited for the rise and fall of breathing. None came.

Probably me doing it wrong. I'm no healer.

Grabbing his head, they cradled it, stroking his matted hair. 'Nick?' Why were their eyes watering? '*Nick. This has gone far enough. It isn't funny, so get up.*' No response. '*Get up!*'

Nick wasn't rude, so he definitely wasn't ignoring them, but if this was a game, it was in very poor taste. Angrily, they swiped their cheek as the stupid tears tentatively slipped out.

'*Garaz!*'

Why is he being so still? This is ridiculous.

They tapped his cheek. 'Wake up.' Grunting in annoyance, they slapped him. 'Wake up.' Grabbing his collar, they started to shake him. '*Wake. Up.*' Nothing.

'Oh Deities,' came a startled voice behind them. 'Kid? No.'

Fine, you want to play games? I'll slap that stupid facial hair right off your face. Let's see how funny you find that.

But when they raised their hand, their wrist was grabbed, and they were hauled up. Turning, ready to fight, they were shocked when Silva firmly hugged them. It surprised Shift even more when they started sobbing, smacking the warrior on the arm, vaguely aware of Garaz kneeling beside Nick, checking him over.

When they pushed themselves off Silva, the warrior's face was set in stone, unreadable save for the emotion in their eyes. Beside them, Auron stared at Nick.

Why does he look so despondent?

'Nick won't answer.' Shift gave a choked laugh. 'He's being an idiot.'

Auron's pupilless eyes flicked to theirs then back to Nick. It was only then they realised that Garaz had stopped working.

'Hey,' they snapped. 'Why aren't you taking the arrow out? You can't just leave it there. Get on with it.'

The orc looked up at them, tears staining his green cheeks. His mouth opened and closed, but nothing came out.

This doesn't make sense.

They stomped over to the orc and grabbed Garaz's cloak, getting right in his face. 'Heal him,' they snarled.

Why is he shaking his head?

'It will make no difference,' Garaz said quietly. 'He's dead.'

'Bullshit.' Shift turned and kicked Nick. 'Get up...'

They were about to do it again when Silva grabbed them, securing their arms to their waist and hauling them away. 'He's gone.' The warrior's voice betrayed the emotion her face wouldn't show.

'Get off me,' Shift snapped, bucking and kicking in Silva's firm grip. 'You're all idiots. He's not dead and neither am I. He's alive.'

Why am I the only one who sees it?

CHAPTER 5

After stooping to pick up his club, making sure he didn't take his eyes off the skeletons for an instant, Nicolas backed away slowly, the creatures matching him step for step.

'There...well...there appears to have been some kind of misunderstanding,' he said with a polite but extremely nervous smile. 'So I'll just be on my way.'

What am I doing? Am I really trying to have a conversation with skeletons?

Talking was all he could do right now. He highly doubted the old handle he had would do much against armour and bone. Besides, they were both carrying swords *and* shields.

I really am cursed to meet every single form of undead creature in Etherius.

Every time he thought he was getting used to this kind of thing, something new was thrown at him. Today, it was skeleton warriors.

'See you later then,' he added nervously, the skeletons watching him silently.

Why did I even say that? I don't want to see them ever again.

Unsure whether the creatures could reply, he started to back away just a little faster. Still, he kept his eyes on them. Who knew how fast whatever dark magic animated the creatures had made them?

There was a problem with backing away. Yes, you keep your eyes on the advancing evil monsters, but you miss all the debris on the ground behind you. Catching his foot on a piece of wood, Nicolas toppled backwards, club falling from his hand again as he flapped his arms to stay upright. The lance of pain shooting up his spine as he hit the floor was the punctuation mark on his failure.

Note for when...if...I get out of this situation: tie a piece of rope around the handle and my wrist if I keep insisting on dropping the damn thing.

But getting out of this became much less likely as the skeletons saw their chance. Stooping and raising their shields, the pair closed on him faster. He grabbed his club—more by accident than design—as he scrabbled back into the courtyard across the bumpy rubble. The hope was to find somewhere to hide. It wasn't the greatest plan in history, but he was in a strange land with only a broom handle to defend himself, so he could forgive himself for not coming up with anything better.

As he scurried back across the rough terrain, his eyes wide with fear as the skeletons got ever closer, time somehow managed to slow to a crawl so he could contemplate every possible fate in store for him.

They could stab me to death. They could beat me to death with their shields. They could gnaw the flesh from my bones. They could—

His thoughts were cut short as he went tumbling down into the crater in the centre of the courtyard, throwing up rock dust and grunting in pain as he struck every single jutting-out rock on the way down. When he finally rolled to a halt at the bottom of the crater, he tried to rise quickly, but dizziness kept him in place as the world around him continued to spin. The only thing he knew for sure was that his hand was empty again.

Dammit.

Holding his head in his hands and willing the scenery to stop moving, he managed to get to his feet. His attempts to find his weapon proved pointless as it'd been snapped in two during the fall. Neither piece was serviceable as a club.

Maybe the skeletons will die laughing at my stupidity?

Except they were already dead.

I really hate it here.

The noise of falling dirt made him look up quickly. The skeletons were at the lip of the crater, staring down at him. In lieu of a handy discarded axe or sword, he grabbed a rock, raising it threateningly.

'You two be good undead monsters and stay put. If you come down here, I may have to use this.'

'*May*' *have to? For goodness' sakes...*

Maybe all hope wasn't lost? Yes, he was stuck at the bottom of a crater facing two skeleton warriors, but he had a rock and the will to defend himself. Thanks to Silva, he was okay in a fight, though he'd much prefer the two undead monsters to not be armed. Maybe he should...

There was a shuffling noise behind him.

Sighing and lowering the rock, he turned around.

'Oh, come *on*.'

Looming over the lip of the crater behind him were four more skeleton warriors. They were spaced out well enough to cut off any potential escape route. None of the skeletons spoke; they just watched him. Why were they after him? Was he just in the wrong place at the wrong time, or did they have a master who wanted him? If they did, then the master must be evil. No decent person would use skeletons as soldiers.

If Auron was here, he'd be telling me how he got out of a situation just like this. Something about how he'd fought his way out of a pit of ogres armed with only a quill? Garaz's fireballs might also be handy right now.

But there was only him, and he had to accept that. He was about to draw another, figurative, line in the dirt when...

'Ah-ha, there you are.'

At the edge of the crater appeared someone who wasn't a combination of walking bones and poorly kept armour. The man regarded him with interest, stooping most likely due to the large hump that protruded from beneath the tattered grey robe he wore. What parts of the man he could see were covered in sores and boils. He had a pig nose overshadowed by a thick brow. What hair he had left was patchy and straw like. All in all, he was quite repulsive, but there was no way Nicolas intended to say that aloud. In his stubby arms, he lovingly cradled a large and aged book, which was chained to his wrist. The cover had gold filigree around it and a gaping skull on the cover. His terror, for a moment, was overcome by his curiosity.

'You know me?' Nicolas asked, really hoping the answer was no.

The hunched figure looked taken aback. 'Of course I know you,' he scoffed in a rasping voice. 'I know everyone here. You're...' He flipped through the pages of the book. '...You are...' The page turning became more intent as the figure's brow knitted first in concentration and then frustration. '...you...' Finally, he slammed the book shut. 'Who the bloody Underworld *are* you?' he snapped at last. 'You aren't in the book. How can you not be in the book?'

How do I even respond to that?

The figure let out a loud, derisive snort. 'Well, come out of there, and we will get this sorted.'

'No.'

The hunched man clearly wasn't expecting any sort of answer, much less a negative one. 'What do you mean, *no?*'

He picked up the rock and held it aloft again. 'I'm not going anywhere with a strange man who has skeleton soldiers. You're obviously a bad guy, and I have somewhere extremely urgent to be. So I'll just stay here whilst you leave and then be on my merry way, if it's all the same to you.'

'It isn't.' The figure sighed, before turning to the nearest skeleton. 'Take him.'

Moving as one, the skeletons advanced down the lip of the crater, weapons raised. Internally, he sobbed as he prepared for what was sure to be a desperate last stand doomed to failure.

Still, better than just letting the creepy librarian take me, I suppose.

Though without him, who would defend his parents? He readied the rock.

They're skeletons. It isn't killing. They're already dead. I can do this.

A thudding sound repeated itself several times before something came to rest at his feet. It was the head of one of the skeletons.

Do they just randomly fall off like that?

They did not.

As the rest of the skeleton crashed to the ground, the man who'd beheaded it looked on his work with a self-satisfied smile. In fact, *self-satisfied* was a good general description of the fellow. He was blatantly a warrior of some kind. There was a vague familiarity to him, along with a nameless quality that made him instantly dislike the guy. Mind you, the sword with a grinning demonic hilt didn't make him seem the friendly sort.

The other skeletons turned towards the newcomer as the hunched librarian let out an unmanly *eep*. Not that the man cared, he was still too busy admiring his handiwork, tracing the lines of his neatly tended goatee with two fingers. Finally, he looked up, as if he'd finally deigned to notice the other creatures. Turning to look behind him, his long ponytail swished through the air.

'Am I having *all* the fun here, lads?'

The air filled with whoops and cheers as more warriors, mostly clad in furs or leather armour, charged forwards, brandishing an array of weapons. The skeletons moved to meet the challengers, apparently unconcerned that they were outnumbered. Soon the battle was in full swing, but it was painfully short, with the bone warriors lifelessly decorating the floor of the crater within moments.

The hunched man made to scamper away but was quickly apprehended by two of the warriors. The creepy librarian cradled his book in his arms as he was dragged back to the edge of the crater, his whole body shaking with fear.

Turning, Nicolas nearly let out an *eep* of his own; the ponytailed warrior was directly behind him.

I wish I'd made it down the crater half as quietly.

The warrior looked him up and down appraisingly, before grinning broadly and offering him a gloved hand. 'Vargas Quell, nice to meet you,' the man said with false sincerity.

Carefully, he took the hand and shook it. 'Nice to meet you.' Again, the urge to share his name out of politeness was repelled. The less this Vargas knew about him the better.

'You sure? Because you don't look happy to see me.' The warrior pursed his lips thoughtfully. 'Actually, you look like someone I've heard of.'

Wracking his addled mind, he tried to think where he may have met this man. Coming up with nothing, he shook his head feebly.

Nicolas jumped as Vargas suddenly clicked his fingers and pointed at him. 'You wouldn't be *Nick Carnage* by any chance, would you?'

'No,' he answered honestly and a little too firmly.

'Oh, I think you are.' Vargas chuckled. 'And if you are, I know someone who wants a word with you.'

Eep.

****

Yes, Nick wasn't moving. Yes, he had an arrow sticking out of his chest. And yes, Garaz, the healer, had declared him dead.

But he isn't dead. We are all alive.

It was just a truth they knew, simple as that. It was as obvious to them as the fact that there was sky above their heads. So why exactly was Garaz claiming different?

What kind of healer can't tell the living from the dead?

Unless he was lying. Since the incident on the freighter, there'd been a marked change in the orc, one that'd caused their trust in him to waiver. In the Thieves' Guild, trust normally leads to your stash *'mysteriously disappearing'*, with the potential addition of a knife in the back, so it was given dubiously and removed quickly.

But why would Garaz lie?

Uncaring, they stared directly at the orc, trying to discern some motive for saying that Nick was dead. Garaz finally caught the look, breaking eye contact as soon as he'd made it.

Why is he acting so strangely around me? I know what he did on the freighter, I couldn't miss it, but...

Shutting their eyes, they pushed the image of the toad-creature away. Right now, they had more pressing concerns, such as convincing everyone that Nick was alive.

Beside them, Auron let out a harsh laugh. 'I don't know what to do.' The spirit seemed aghast, surprised and angry all at once. 'I've *always* known what to do. Even as a gh...spirit, I found my usefulness. But now the kid's—'

'Don't say it,' they growled threateningly.

Silva was kind enough to finish his sentence for him. 'Dead.'

From beside Nick's still-alive body, Shift sprang up, getting themselves nose to nose with the warrior, or near enough, with the height difference. Their breathing was fast as adrenaline poured through their veins and into their clenched and shaking fists. When the punch didn't come, the energy instead moved to Shift's mouth.

'Happy?' they asked petulantly.

Silva moved closer, her face set in a scowl.

You don't intimidate me. I can scowl just as hard. In fact, I can turn into you and copy your scowl.

'I beg your pardon?' the warrior asked, each word spoken with slow menace.

Shift allowed themselves a half smile. 'Well, you've tried to kill Nick a few times. Job's done now. So I asked if you're *happy*.'

Within a moment, Silva's arm was drawn back, ready to strike.

Shift didn't even flinch. Part of them welcomed it, and that surprised them. Maybe they were just baiting Silva to hit them, to distract themselves from the body behind them.

Not the body. Nick. He's alive.

A large green hand engulfed Silva's fist gently.

'This is unproductive,' Garaz said softly.

'You would say that,' they spat at the orange-haired orc.

'Meaning?' The orc's face looked neutral enough, but there was intensity in his yellow eyes that couldn't be disguised.

'Or maybe you wouldn't say it?' they continued theatrically. 'Who knows anymore? I thought I knew you, but I clearly don't. Since the freighter—'

'That will do.' Garaz massaged the bridge of his nose firmly. 'I do not wish to discuss it.'

'Perhaps some of us do,' Shift shot back. Not that any answer the orc gave about his behaviour would keep them travelling with these people any longer. What had happened to Nick was only helping to justify their decision.

'*Enough!*' Auron's aura rumbled like thunder, veins of red lacing what used to be his skin as his white eyes blazed. 'Nick is lying there dead, and all you can do is pick fights. I get that you're hurting, we all are. But grow up!'

Why is everyone talking such nonsense today?

Shift's nose wrinkled slightly as a foul odour suddenly penetrated their nostrils. But they were too riled up to pay it any heed.

'Goblin crap,' they spat. 'He's alive. Garaz is wrong.'

'I am a healer—' the orc began.

'Who is wrong,' they interrupted firmly, causing Garaz to make a series of offended huffing noises.

'Actually, you're both right *and* both wrong.'

Shift spun around in surprise, same as the others. They didn't need to look to know that Silva had drawn her sword. A shabby-looking man knelt over Nick's body, his hand on their companion's chest. He looked like a vagrant, with tattered robes and long knotted hair, beard included. It was only then that Shift really noticed the foul stench coming from him. They blinked rapidly as their eyes watered.

'Hello?' Garaz said finally, cloak to his nose.

There was no answer. Instead, the man continued looking Nick over. How could someone say something as vague as that then not follow it up? In fact, it was like he'd completely forgotten they were even there.

'What...'

The man held up a silencing finger, complete with dirty brown nail. Shift's initial reaction was to give him a mouthful of abuse for the gesture, but despite his outward appearance, he had a certain commanding presence.

Finally, with great effort and the considerable aid of his knotted walking stick, the figure rose, joints clicking as if giving him a round of applause for managing it. Turning to Shift and their companions, he rested on his cane, staring at them uncomfortably. Every instinct told Shift that this was a man of poor temperament.

I would be too if I smelt like that.

'As I said just now,' his near growling voice began, 'you are both right *and* wrong.'

'What does that even mean?' Garaz had blatantly taken offence at having his diagnosis challenged again.

Good.

The old man pursed his lips as if trying to keep his temper. 'It means, orc, that he is really neither alive nor dead. He is in a strange...between state.'

Shift was surprised by the sudden glimmer of hope. They hadn't even realised they needed it, being sure Nick was alive and all.

'As much as I want to hope, I don't think we should be listening to a wandering tramp,' Auron said, shaking his head sadly.

'*Hey*,' the old man shouted, pointing a bony finger at Auron, 'Respect your elders, especially when they're the damned *Oracle*, you undead piece of cloudy crap.'

'You can see me?'

The old man looked to both sides theatrically. 'Well, I'm looking at you, and talking to you so maybe...hmm...*yes*, I can bloody well see you. Did you leave your brains in your physical body?'

Wanting to get back to the matter that required their urgent attention, Shift inserted themselves into the conversation. 'What do you mean about a *between state*?'

'Speak plainly or die.' It was nice to have Silva's support, even if it was overly aggressive.

'It is difficult to explain,' the old man said, caressing his beard and ignoring Silva's threat as he addressed Shift. 'And so far, none of you are impressing me with your brains, so I'm not inclined to go into much detail, lady.'

Pleasant fellow, this one.

'I'm not a lady, *old man*,' they replied through gritted teeth. 'You'd think an *oracle* would be able to tell the difference between a *she* and a *them*.'

His lip curling in annoyance, the old man gave a theatrical bow from which they barely managed to rise. 'Humblest apologies. I'll endeavour to correct my poor behaviour,' he replied dryly. 'But as we are getting titles correct, I'm not *an* Oracle, I'm *the* Oracle.'

'I'll call you whatever you fancy if you can save Nick,' they retorted flatly.

'That's what I'm trying to do.' The Oracle sighed, looking back at Nick's body. 'But none of you are making this any faster. Now, get the mean-looking lady to put her sword away and help the orc who can't tell whether people are alive or dead to load this arrow-stuck boy into my wagon.' Briefly, the Oracle glanced at Auron. 'And you can go haunt something.'

'You believe you can save him?' Garaz asked, raising an incredulous eyebrow.

'If you lot can stop holding me up with your incessant questions,' the Oracle snapped. 'Because if we don't hurry up, young Nicolas may well end up completely dead.'

Shift looked at the others, who shared their worried look. But this strange old man could be Nick's only hope, and they weren't about to let that pass. Carefully, Shift helped Silva and Garaz lift Nick's body from the ground and make for the approaching wagon.

The driver sitting atop it—a man maybe as old as the other with straw grey hair and a narrow face with a stony complexion—looked almost as cheery as the Oracle.

CHAPTER 6

On the plus side, he was out of the crater now, but Nicolas knew he was in a tricky situation. Yes, he'd been saved from the skeletons, but those who'd done the saving didn't look at all savoury.

They're looting the corpses of skeletons, for Deities' sake. Do skeletons even have loot worth taking?

Maybe one of the skeletons was wearing a mass of gold chains or hiding a priceless family heirloom under their rusted armour? Despite appearances, some of Vargas's men must've found something, because he heard several shouts of triumph over the background noise of the hunched man's cries as several of the ruffians shoved him between them, laughing like the pathetic schoolyard bullies they were copying.

I can't believe I'm feeling sympathy for someone who travels around with skeletons.

How could he not? The creepy librarian looked truly wretched with tears in his misshapen eyes as he stumbled from one push to another, the book swinging on the chain as he did.

'What a great prize.' Vargas smirked as he watched. 'We actually got the big guy's chief adviser. I mean, that was the plan, but still...he's going to be happy with me.'

Taking his attention away from his ruffians, Vargas turned back to Nicolas, who was very aware that whilst he wasn't a prisoner, necessarily, there were two men in close proximity to him to make sure he didn't go anywhere. Vargas studied him, rubbing his beard with one hand, and caressing the hilt of his sword with the other.

Must he do that so...tenderly?

'So, I take it from your stunned silence that you're aware of my significant reputation?' The warrior closed his eyes as if waiting to bask in an awe, or fear, filled response.

He wasn't a good liar, and his ability to think on the fly was so-so at best. Nicolas opted for honesty. 'Um, no actually,' he replied meekly. 'Sorry.'

Vargas's eyes shot open, his face contorted by rage for a moment, before the easy smile returned. The annoyance at not being recognised reminded him of a certain deceased hero...

'Look,' the warrior began, putting a hand on Nicolas's shoulder, 'If you are who I think you are, and I'm rarely wrong, then I know who you travel with, and he *must've* told you about me. We both know he loves his stories.'

'I'm not travelling with anyone.' Right now... *Not exactly a lie.*

'I know you travel with Auron of Tellmark. I was told.'

An idea formed in Nicolas's mind. Was Vargas's boss this Maestro he'd heard about? But why would Koth shoot him with an arrow and send him to a strange land just to have him taken by another of this Maestro's minions? Something was awry here, and he really couldn't put his finger on what.

Now Nicolas had noticed it, it was odd how like Auron this man was. There was a similar style to the warrior, as well as an ego big enough to comfortably house a dragon's gold hoard. Plus, the silly hairstyle. For reasons Nicolas couldn't fathom, he let out a chuckle.

Suddenly, the hand on his shoulder clamped down, forcing his knees to buckle as he gasped with pain.

'I didn't say anything funny,' Vargas said with thinly veiled menace, showing the obvious difference between him and Auron. 'What I did was ask you a question. Auron of Tellmark, did he mention me?'

The pain was intense enough that he couldn't speak so he shook his head. He exhaled hard as the grip was released. It still didn't feel like air was coming out.

The warrior searched his eyes intently. 'But he still tells stories all the time, right?'

Nicolas nodded.

'And he never mentioned me?' Vargas scoffed. 'Not once?'

He was in a very precarious position, with a wrong answer likely to part his head from his neck, but an answer was expected, so he shook his head again.

Vargas's eyes widened as his pupils dilated. His arm shook as his hand went from caressing the hilt of his sword to gripping it tightly.

Nicolas's vision narrowed to the hilt of that sword, trying to prepare his body to move out of the way the minute it was drawn.

Instead, the warrior did something far stranger. Screaming in annoyance, Vargas ran around, kicking any object that happened to be near him on the floor. As the scream continued, he found an old sack, which he stomped on repeatedly, throwing a cloud of dust into the air. Finally, he grabbed rocks from the ground and hurled them at the nearest wall, still screaming. The old stone wall became pitted with dents where the rocks struck. It was all a little...pathetic. Like a child throwing a tantrum. Not that he was about to point that out.

As the warrior stopped and turned, whole body shaking, all his men—who'd been watching the display—suddenly became busier with other things. Vargas's eyes locked onto Nicolas, and he winced, ready for the wrath about to be unleashed on him.

'That son of a *whore*. All the stupid stories he tells, and not one of his nemesis,' Vargas raged. 'All our battles, and he just forgets me as soon as I'm gone. Are you sure he never mentioned me? Not once?'

Nemesis? That's a new one. Auron doesn't have a nemesis...does he?

Wait...what does he mean gone?

The warrior took a step forward, and Nicolas took a step back, very aware how close he was to the edge of the crater, his heels almost dangling over it.

'I'm sorry, but he never mentioned you,' Nicolas pleaded, holding his hands up in front of him. 'I don't even know where I am, and I'm terrible at lying so...sorry.'

The demon-hilted sword was drawn.

'Please, I really don't know you. I don't, I swear.'

'Um, boss,' one of Vargas's men began tentatively, 'don't we need to take him back...to the master?'

Nicolas cried out as the blade flashed, and the ruffian's head and neck were permanently parted. He watched in horror as the head fell away from the body, expecting fountains of blood. Instead, the body and head turned to black smoke, which faded away into nothing. Nearby, the hunched man gasped in fear, holding the book over half his face as if it were some kind of shield or might make him invisible.

Where am I?

He'd been so intent on the scene of the strangely dying man that when Vargas suddenly snapped his sword back into the hilt, he started...and fell back into the crater. The same scene of rolling and pain played out. When he finally came to a halt, he pushed himself up from the ground, coughing up dust.

'You know what, I actually believe you.' Vargas stood at the edge of the crater, his easy smile returned. 'Someone as scared as you would've talked.'

Part of him didn't want any more of the warrior's attention, but the uncertainty, the not-knowing was driving him insane. 'Please, where am I?'

Vargas let out a single laugh. 'You didn't give me a satisfactory answer so I'm not going to give you one.'

Nicolas got to his knees and let his head hang as he desperately fought back the despair threatening to consume him. How could he find a way home if he didn't even know where he was? What was Koth doing to his parents in the interim?

'Grab him and let's go,' Vargas said to his men.

That didn't help.

****

Again, the wagon jinked hard as its old wheel passed over a pothole. Shift scowled at the hole, though they'd thankfully missed biting the inside of their mouth by a hair's breadth. Looking back at the road—dirt track would be the more apt term—they realised how many holes it really had in it. Apparently, road maintenance wasn't a priority for the people of Hablock. At least on this road to their mysterious destination, anyhow.

Maybe it's a decoy to ward off unwelcome travellers? Maybe because there's something valuable there?

Either way, there was plenty of greenery on either side of them to be studied. Normally, Shift wasn't one to take a keen interest in the scenery but having Nick's body lying by their feet made them suddenly intrigued by the venation pattern of every single leaf they passed. It was either that or cover Nick up, and doing that was a step closer to admitting he was dead.

Which he isn't. The stinky old man confirmed it. Maybe if the orc *took a few less baths, he'd be a bit more insightful?*

Briefly glancing around them—but certainly not at the floor of the wagon—Garaz looked as grim as Auron and Silva, each staring off into some distant place of woe. The Oracle was currently picking his nose...

And he just wiped it in his beard. Lovely.

Why were they all so forlorn? Shift had no time for their negativity, just like none of them had had time for Shift's smugness when the Oracle confirmed that Nick was alive.

Sort of. But he also said he was sort of...

Not wanting to follow that train of thought to the dark place it led, Shift decided to amuse themselves with the other method they'd used to distract themselves on the journey so far.

'So, do you have other duties, or do you just drive this wagon up and down this crappy track?'

Upon boarding the wagon, the driver, a surly fellow to be sure, had greeted them with the barest of grunts. And that made Shift want to get him talking. It turned out to be a challenge, which they were enjoying immensely, especially with the driver's barely contained annoyance at their attempts. Each failure only egged them on further.

'So, driver,' they asked as they stretched their arms high. 'Are you his personal driver, or are you more of a local service?' The man turned just enough so they could see the glare he was casting from his peripheral vision. Shift smiled to themselves. 'Because I have a birthday coming up, and I'm throwing an affair, of sorts, to celebrate.' They patted the edge of the wagon. 'I'd love to book this wonderful conveyance for—'

To their right, there was a deep sigh. 'Will you just leave Cuthbert to drive the sodding wagon?' the Oracle snapped. 'If your poking isn't annoying him, I can assure you it's thoroughly pissing me off.'

Good. What a good pair you two make.

According to Auron, this *Oracle* received messages from the Deities themselves then picked some village boy to go and deliver it to a hero. Strange to think that was why they'd met Nick in the first place. At some point, he must've made this same journey. Stranger still that the Deities would entrust their words to some mangy old git. Shift would've picked someone with more people skill, as they'd be dealing with...people.

But for now, they let his rudeness go unchecked. If he could help Nick, they'd take a few curt remarks and bite their tongue.

But when Nick's better, you are getting a sizeable piece of my mind, old man.

That'd be the last thing they did before going on their merry way.

It was funny to think of everything they'd experienced since meeting Nick. There'd certainly been some adventures. Shift chuckled to themselves as they remembered their first meeting, in a vampire's lair. The silly boy had gotten down on one knee and made some weird knightly gesture. Had he really gone all that way just because he liked the way they looked? It was oddly flattering. Though, they would've saved themselves anyway, whether he'd turned up or not. But it was nice to have company when fleeing from vampires, they couldn't deny that. It had been fun for a little bit, a curious sidestep to their normal life. Helping people had been good and all, but Nick was a reminder of one of the things that could happen when you got too close to people and walked a dangerous path. They'd had a few close calls already, like when Nick had gotten them caught by the dwarven gang...

There's certainly been a near death experience or two and...

Stop it! You're reminiscing like you're at a funeral. And he isn't dead. Nobody is. Enough.

'Where are we going?' Garaz's words thankfully pulled them back to the present.

I suppose he has some uses.

Since meeting the Oracle, they'd been sort of swept along without any specific explanation. The group had just blindly put Nick in his wagon and followed dutifully, with only Auron's assertion that he was a good guy—though his manners spoke to the contrary. The few times they'd asked questions, they'd been told to be silent, a wrong that would be righted as soon as Nick was back, with interest.

We're probably going to some mystical tower or something. Isn't that where Oracles ought to dwell?

'To my home.'

And that was all the information they were getting, judging by the cranky old man's face.

Maybe a distance or time frame would be nice? His home *could be on the other side of Etherius. By the time we get there, we might be raising a zombie, not Nick. Though apparently raising the dead is no problem in Etherius these days.*

That was a good point. With all the rumours of the dead rising, why was Nick not up and about, groaning for some yummy flesh?

'Don't worry about specifics, Nick's only half dead.' Their petulant mumble earned them a glare from the Oracle. They met it with one of their own.

Oh, the joy when I finally get to tell you what I really *think of you.*

Auron stroked his chin thoughtfully. 'The Tower of the Oracle,' he whispered. 'I never thought I'd get to see it.'

Ha. I knew it was a tower.

'Perhaps you'll be a bit more forthcoming about it than *him*.' They were quite pleased by the sideways glare the old man gave them. As much as they held their tongue, it didn't do to make everything too easy for the miserable old goat.

'The Tower is where the Oracle, who you referred to as *him* with such distaste, lives,' the spirit began with an impressed half-smile. 'There are plenty of myths and legends surrounding it, and him. Though I can see the '*dignified and wizened*' description was an exaggeration.'

Hardly a shock. Shift didn't want to admit that they'd ever even met, and they'd not been in his company for long.

'Yeah, at least I'm alive, smoke boy,' the old man snarled through the few yellow teeth he had.

What was worse, his attitude or his smell?

'Judging by the others wrinkling their noses, I'm actually glad I'm dead, you miserable old codger.'

They nearly choked at Auron's retort, as much as at the wide-eyed expression of the old man.

Well done, Auron.

Hopefully, it didn't get them tossed out of the wagon.

'How can you see him?' Garaz asked, smirking himself at Auron's remark. The orc was never fond of vague answers. He liked facts.

'I'm the Oracle.' The old man was sour now, the wind taken from his sails. *Good*. 'I receive messages from the Deities themselves. This gives me a certain...*different way* of viewing the world around me. Apparently, one of the benefits is that I get to see every cocky ghost who crosses my path.'

Auron bristled. He hated the word *ghost*, preferring to be referred to as a spirit. It was...better or something. Yet he gave no response. If they hadn't known better, they would've sworn the spirit and the Oracle just shared a look of mutual respect. If it took being insulted to earn the old man's respect, he'd best be ready to respect them. Whatever the look had been, it was broken by a grunt from Cuthbert.

'We're here,' the Oracle informed them.

The trees on either side of the road broke into a large open clearing that was bright and lush. Part of them resented how beautiful it looked when something so terrible had happened so close to it. Then their eyes were drawn to the centre of the clearing and what stood in it, and for a moment, all other thoughts were forgotten.

'That crappy cottage is the *Tower of the Oracle?*' they scoffed, their illusions of a large stone tower emanating majesty and power shattered in an instant.

'Don't refer to my home as *crappy,*' the Oracle said with a glare.

What better word was there? The place looked so rundown and uninhabitable they were surprised it was still standing at all. Debris encircled the cottage—discarded items and broken tools, like the worst moat in the history of Etherius. When they looked at the others to try to figure out if this was some kind of weird jest, Garaz was pulling his cloak around him as he did when he was somewhere he deemed unclean and didn't want to touch anything. That time in the brothel, it was funny. Here, they wanted to join him.

Quickly, they ran their eyes up and down the old man, regretting every gross detail they saw. Still, him living in a place like this made sense.

Cuthbert turned the wagon in an arc until the back was parallel to the door of the cottage. Then he jumped down and walked to the back with yet another grunt and a sharp nod, suggesting it was time to vacate the vehicle.

Hopping out of the back, they gave Cuthbert a broad smile. 'Thanks, driver,' they said in a faux sweet voice. 'This has been a lovely journey, and I'll recommend you to all my friends.'

Cuthbert glowered at them as their companions disembarked.

The Oracle was the last to get off. Rising from his seat with a barely contained groan, he shambled on his stick to the edge of the wagon. As the old man teetered on the edge, Cuthbert offered his hand, only to have it slapped away.

'I can do it myself, dammit,' the Oracle told the driver in a surly tone.

Cuthbert looked like he wanted to return the slap.

Despite the urgency of their mission, Shift found themselves stopping to watch. The old man getting onto the wagon had been pretty amusing. He'd blatantly needed help but waved his stick at any who tried. Shift had thought he was going to have a heart attack the way he'd puffed and panted as he mounted the wagon. He'd nearly fallen twice. This should be much funnier...though if he did have a heart attack, who was going to help Nick?

Tentatively, the old man took a step down, his leg too short to reach the floor. Problem was, he'd already put his weight on it. Slowly, he began to topple forwards until the driver caught him and lowered him down. The Oracle looked apoplectic at having to be carried down. Once he was on the ground, he violently shook off the driver's hands.

'Let's get him in the house,' the Oracle commanded, paying the driver no heed as he pointed at Nick.

As they went to help, Cuthbert passed them, muttering under his breath in a voice thick with sarcasm, '*I can do it myself, dammit.*'

CHAPTER 7

Marching down the dirt track with a nice slice of bleak landscape on either side of him, Vargas made no pretence now that Nicolas was anything other than a prisoner. Guards flanked him and the hunched man, urging them on with enthusiastic jabs of their weapons and curses about their families or their fondness for lying with livestock when they slowed. For him, it wasn't so bad, but the hunched man had more difficulty. His legs were stumpy and different lengths, causing him to struggle to match the pace of their captors.

I am in so much trouble. First the strange place and skeletons and now this. How does Vargas know me? Who is his master? How can I get home and save my parents?

He tried not to dwell on how long he'd been here and the implications of that. What he needed was information. Auron always said that knowing your enemy was a step in the right direction.

'Excuse me,' he asked the guard to his side, 'but who's your master?'

'Me, but you'll meet our liberator soon enough,' Vargas called from the front as the guard cuffed him around the head, nearly making him fall to the ground.

Liberator?

Rubbing his head and trying to be casual, he looked around. Even if he could outrun the guards, where would he go? They'd be able to see him for miles.

'You clumsy idiot!'

He turned at the guard's cry. The hunched man had tripped on a rock and fallen forwards. Thankfully, with his height, the trip to the ground was a short one, certainly shorter than his shriek had suggested. The guard's foot tensed, ready to deliver a kick up the backside that would do absolutely nothing to aid the situation.

Stopping and bending over, Nicolas reached out towards the hunched man. 'Here, let me help you up.'

The bulging eyes blinked at the offered appendage several times, before the creepy librarian slowly put his hand in it, testing it as if it were a steel trap that might snap shut on him and remove his hand at the wrist. Straining, he helped the man to his feet.

'Thank you.' The rasping voice was overcome with emotion. He probably wasn't used to kind gestures. Then he shouted with pain as the guard smacked him around the head.

'Get moving,' the ruffian bellowed.

'Very altruistic.' Vargas chuckled as he stood by the road, watching them pass. Suddenly, the warrior's lips pursed, before he clicked his tongue. 'Is it true that Auron died with his pants around his ankles, taking a shit?'

He didn't need to answer. As usual, his face said it all.

'Ridiculous way to go for such a *great hero*.' Vargas's face hardened, his mouth becoming a fierce scowl as he looked into the distance. 'It should've been me. I should've been the one to finish him. It was *my* right as his nemesis. Mind you, I suppose there's a certain poetic justice that it was Silva who killed him. Maybe I should take comfort in the fact that I set in motion the events that *led* to his death.' Vargas mimed stabbing the air. 'Still, to stick him myself and watch the life drain from those arrogant eyes...' His voice trailed off as he apparently lost himself in the fantasy.

What does he mean by that?

'Shame you'll never have vengeance for him sending you down here,' Nicolas's fellow prisoner muttered loudly.

There was a sharp crack as Vargas's fist struck the hunched man's face. The convoy stopped as the creepy librarian crashed to the floor. The warrior stood over his victim, hand on the hilt of his sword. 'Auron of Tellmark did *not* send me down here,' Vargas snarled. 'He tried to, many a time, but every time, I cheated him. I bet it rankled him to be cheated of the satisfaction of finishing me off for good?'

If the hunched man knew the answer to that, he had the good sense to keep it to himself.

Why do they keep saying down here?

The creepy librarian was about to push himself back to his feet, but for a moment, he hesitated, eyes fixed on the ground. Nicolas could've sworn he caught a brief flash of a smile on his wart-covered lips.

'Does it matter how you were finished?' The hunched man shrugged, but his tone was more defiant now. 'A ghost is a ghost.'

With a snarl, Vargas hauled the librarian to his feet and then into the air by his collar, bringing them face to face. 'Let's get this straight,' the warrior snapped. 'I am not some kind of common ghost. I'm a *wraith*, an avenging spirit able to put my enemies to the sword even after death.'

What?

Letting go of the collar, Vargas dropped the hunched man to the floor again and turned to his troop. 'What are we, boys?' he called, putting a hand to his ear as he awaited the response.

'*Wraiths! Wraiths! Wraiths!*' his men chanted in unison, raising their weapons high.

Ghosts? Wraiths? What in the Underworld is going on here? Are these men dead? Do I add wraiths *to my undead creature list?*

'Not for much longer,' the hunched man muttered. The slight grin on his pudgy face was quite unnerving, so much so that Nicolas's body trembled.

No. That wasn't my body. That was the ground.

Judging by the sudden silence and wary glances around, he wasn't the only one who'd felt it. Soon there was a second tremor then a third. Weapons were readied as the party formed a defensive circle. The only one who appeared unbothered by the occurrence was the hunched man. In fact, he looked quite pleased. There was a fourth tremor, fiercer than the others.

Deities, I wish I had a sword right now.

His body tensed as the shaking became constant and quickly worsened, being everywhere and nowhere at the same time. His legs struggled to keep him upright as the world around him blurred, his ears filled with a deep rumbling. Suddenly, he longed for a weapon in his hand.

I'd settle for the broom handle again, in a pinch.

Vargas was miming commands to his men, who kept their positions and readied themselves. The warrior looked as excited as a child waking up on his birthday.

As the shaking became more violent, Nicolas looked at the hunched man, who was staring at Vargas with the smile of someone who believes revenge is imminent. As many questions as he had, he doubted he'd get any straight answers from the strange fellow. Right now, the only thing to do was stand in this circle of very bad men and hope for the best. Though he found himself inching towards the hunched man. Standing by the man who looked like he possibly knew what was going on might increase his chances for survival.

His very bones shook as his head darted this way and that in panic, fervently searching for the source of the increasingly violent disturbance.

An earth-shattering crack drew his attention. On the road ahead of them, the ground bulged upwards, as if something were pushing from beneath it, trying to be born.

Oh shit.

The analogy proved accurate as a great maw burst through the earth, spraying dirt and ash in all directions. He raised his hands to cover his eyes then wished he'd kept them there once he lowered them again. With two giant legs on either side of the hole it'd made, the creature heaved itself from the ground. It was immense, a giant four-legged beast—possibly a dragon once, but now just a bone monstrosity.

How does it move with no muscles or skin? How come it doesn't just fall apart?

Shaking off the last of the dirt, the fanged skull slowly looked down at those below it. Rearing back, it let out a feral roar that blew Vargas's ponytail around. Suddenly, he no longer cared about whatever dark magic animated this monster and all the other skeleton creatures that ran around this terrible land. All he cared about now was not getting eaten by it.

****

'You know this is all preposterous,' Garaz said firmly as they manoeuvred Nick's body through the cottage door. 'I want him to be alive as much as anyone, but it just isn't so, and I don't think going along with this farce is—'

'Do you know what I think's preposterous?' the Oracle interrupted sharply. 'A healer who can't tell who's alive or dead.'

Maybe the old coot isn't so bad after all?

Even if they didn't know for a fact that Nick was alive, which they did, they would have hope that he could be brought back. Necromancers did that sort of stuff all the time. They were just doing it *before* the months of decay set in.

Or maybe I hoped too soon?

Their mouth dropped open at the sight of the interior of the cottage. It closed again quickly once they took a gulp of the festering air.

And lo, the inside of the house of the Oracle is just as disgusting as the outside.

He could raise the dead, but not do some dishes occasionally? Could a man who lived in such a slovenly way *really* help Nick? The problem was, they were out of crazy old wizards who could try, and their *healer* was being less than helpful.

'There, on the table,' the Oracle snapped as he closed the door, leaving the words *please* and *thank you* outside in the wagon.

Shift looked at the table and then at the others, who were all equally flummoxed. There wasn't a table not covered in books and junk and some cringingly large bugs.

Behind them, the Oracle huffed. 'That one there,' he bellowed as he pointed a clawed fingernail at a table near the centre of the room. 'Just toss the crap on the floor.'

Giving Garaz and Silva a second to adjust to the redistributed weight of their charge, Shift did as bade and swept the assorted rubbish to the floor—pulling their sleeve over their hand first, of course.

When Nick survives the arrow, the infection he gets in here might finish him off. Or maybe the large scuttling things will gnaw on him while we sleep?

They shuddered at the thought of the creature disappearing into the shadow of a cabinet. Normally, they weren't so squeamish, but it was bloody big.

Garaz scowled at the table for a moment before finally laying Nick on it gently, with Silva's help. Then the orc pulled his cloak around him tightly, eyeing everything with thinly veiled disgust. Shift took in the sights of the room too, rather than look at Nick. The more they did, the closer they might come to admitting he was dead, and that wasn't happening.

Though someone really needs to do something about that arrow now.

Silva was more detached, as usual. Once Nick's body was down, the warrior moved to the window of the cottage. None of them could over-look the fact that Nick's home had been attacked, the whole village maybe, and that those attackers were almost certainly still at large. Despite their current priority, danger might be nearby. So, Silva dutifully stood guard. Being nearer fresh air was probably a nice bonus.

Despite Silva's closed exterior, when you travelled with someone long enough, you picked up ways to read them. Currently, if Shift was right, the warrior was mentally punishing herself for not being there to protect Nick as she had sworn. Well, really, she hadn't sworn; it was just kind of *understood* that she would. As clearly as they saw that, some of the warrior's motivations were still difficult to pick up on.

Is she upset about her tarnished honour?

Did Silva have any? She'd done some bad things before they met, and some after as well. Their first experience of the warrior had been a fully armoured Silva knocking them unconscious with the shaft of a spear, before offering Shift up as a tribute to a group of vampires. Nick said that he trusted her now, but that was Nick. Their trust wasn't so easily given. Silva was close to earning it, though. Not that it'd matter once this was done.

Around the warrior's shoulder, the hilt stroking her short blond hair when her head turned, was Nick's sword, the *Dawn Blade*. Shift couldn't look directly at it. Not because of grief or anything, but because they'd instantly remember all the times he'd dropped it, and this was no time for laughing.

'So, do we get some answers now?' Auron asked impatiently.

Waving away the question, the Oracle shambled over to Nick and scrutinised him intently. As they watched, he allowed his hands to hover above Nick's body and closed his eyes. For a second, Shift assumed he was humming, but eventually they picked out words. He was chanting under his breath. The Oracle's brow furrowed, and he scrunched his face up several times in a way that did not inspire hope. The wait was almost unbearable.

With a sharp exhale, the old man opened his eyes again. 'Yup, just as I thought.'

'Well?' Shift asked after the pause became too long for their liking.

'Your friend here has been preserved at the very point of death.' Something on Nick's collar seemed to catch the Oracle's attention, and he fiddled with the top of his shirt. 'He is in limbo, neither alive nor dead, but stuck between both. His physical form, anyway.'

What does that mean?

They were about to ask when Auron cut in. 'How could that happen?'

The Oracle spared the spirit a brief glance. 'Happened to you, didn't it?' He didn't wait for an answer, instead pulling open one side of Nick's shirt. 'I imagine it has something to do with *this*.'

Suddenly, the arrow wasn't the most prominent feature of Nick's chest, nor was it's utter hairlessness. What drew the eye were the parts of his skin that were blackened, but in a very specific way—a handprint, and not a human one. It was too large, for starters, and possibly had three fingers instead of four, though one looked like two combined, with a large claw extending from the tip. The pulled-back shirt also revealed the pink scars around Nick's shoulders, where harpy talons had penetrated his skin.

His back is worse.

That whole adventure was nearly worse for all of them.

'I don't recognise that type of print,' Auron said, studying it thoughtfully. The ethereal hero looked questioningly at Garaz, who shook his head, as did Silva and Shift when he turned to them.

'Whatever it belongs to is pretty damn powerful,' the old man said, leaning in and sniffing the print. Getting that close to Nick's chest without being blinded by the whiteness of the untainted parts of his skin was almost impressive. 'It pushed his soul from his body and somehow petrified him whilst doing so. At the moment, he is in both states and yet neither until his soul is restored and things can conclude one way or the other.'

'So it wasn't the arrow that...left him like this.' A pang of sympathy hit Shift as they saw the way Auron stared at the arrow. His life had been ended in the same way, save for the fact that Nick was still wearing his breeches. Seeing it happen to Nick too must be terrible.

'It did most of the work,' the Oracle said as he sat on a nearby stool. 'But it didn't have a chance to finish the job.'

'But why go to all the trouble of trying to kill him just to then...pause? And why leave his body out in the open to be found?' Silva asked.

The Oracle shrugged. 'Don't ask me to try to explain the logic of evil. My guess is that someone wants him to suffer. Maybe the petrification was an unintended side effect?' There was a sad pause from the old man. 'I knew something bad had happened. I had a premonition. That's why we were out, checking the local farms. The people, they're gone. Taken, I guess. The boy was the only one we found, but I think the rest was a by-product. *This* is the epicentre of it all. Someone wanted young Nicolas dead—'

'And to make sure that anyone he may have talked to would remain silent,' Auron finished grimly.

'Exactly. Maybe not all your brains stayed in your mortal remains.'

Shift shook their head, trying to come to terms with what they'd been told. 'So someone came here for Nick and just...took the whole village? Why not just kill them?'

'That again falls under *the mysterious ways of evil*.' The Oracle shrugged.

'It seems we have made a powerful enemy on our travels.' Garaz's face was set in stone.

'Which means we are also targets.' Silva drew her sword, and her watch out the window became more intent, the warrior pressing herself to the wall and peering out.

The sheer scale of it was insane, making an entire community vanish. But then, in the last few months, they'd seen a lot of '*insane*.' The group had surmised that it might all be connected, but this confirmed it, as well as the fact that they were in danger too.

Another reason to set out on my own. We've all come too close already.

Yet they couldn't dwell on that now. Not with Nick lying there. As they opened their mouth to speak, the Oracle held up that silencing finger again.

How does it not cramp from overuse?

'His soul isn't hanging around here.' How had the old man known exactly what they were going to ask next? 'Whatever put its print on him pushed his soul out of his body. Until it's restored, he will stay like this.'

Thank the Deities. I thought it'd be more difficult.

'So,' they began cheerily, 'find his ghost and stuff it back into his body. We can do that.'

After that, me and Nick are going to have a long *talk about him scaring me like this. Not too long, mind you. Longer I hang around, the harder it's going to be to go.*

Their smile dropped as the Oracle's face darkened. 'It won't be as easy as that,' the old man said solemnly. 'As far as I can tell, his soul has been banished to the Underworld.'

Nick? The Underworld?

That couldn't be right at all.

CHAPTER 8

hy is Vargas hooting in delight?

There was literally a giant monster in the road, and he was happy about it? With no skin or muscle, it should've looked frail and fragile, but instead it was powerful and immense...immensely terrifying, anyway.

Regarding the group of people before it, of which he was one, the creature let out another bestial roar. For something without windpipes, it made a lot of noise. As Vargas's men formed a line, Nicolas found himself backing away.

'If the big pale moron thinks he can trap *The Notorious* Vargas Quell, he has another thing coming,' the warrior cried—nearly howled—as he raised his sword high.

He really should be scared. How can he not be? Is he that *good with his sword? There's no—*

Did he just refer to himself as The Notorious? *Wow.*

The rhythmic stomping of boots interrupted his train of thought. Emerging from the ground, using the sizeable hole made by the bone monster, were ranks of skeletons armed with a variety of weapons. As the wall of rusted armour and bone advanced, Vargas burst out laughing.

I really don't see anything funny about any of this.

Not that the skeletons cared. They didn't appear to care about much except getting to Vargas and his men as they clacked forward as one, with unfeeling faces. And once they were done with them...

I need to get out of here.

The thought that maybe they would all just kill each other crossed his mind as Vargas's men readied themselves. But no way was he that lucky, especially in this place.

Auron would tell him to use a distraction to escape. And here he had a very large distraction, accompanied by a host of smaller ones.

'Wait for the right moment,' he whispered to himself.

Beside him was the hunched man, having been thrown to the ground roughly by the ruffian with the axe who stood behind them both to ensure they didn't try anything.

As much as he didn't want to, he didn't have a choice; he *had* to try something. It was the only way he was going to get home. And he needed to take the creepy librarian with him—he had answers.

'When the fight starts, we run,' he muttered quietly.

The hunched man gave a slight nod of agreement, indicating he'd heard. If he was happy to flee, he couldn't have unshakeable faith in the cohort of undead warriors—something the hunched man and Vargas seemed to have in common.

'Who's up for a fight then, lads?' Vargas asked, as casually as a husband might ask his wife *'do you fancy dining out tonight?'* His easy manner and confidence riled his men up into a frenzy as they raised their weapons and cheered raucously. Vargas swung his demon-hilted sword from side to side.

What is that? A warm-up?

Everything was done slowly and deliberately, as if there wasn't a giant skeleton monster and accompanying army right in front of him.

Oh, and now he's posing.

After stretching his neck, Vargas wielded his sword in a number of different poses: at his side two-handed, switching to a horizontal one-handed pose then raising it slowly above his head, and so on and so forth. Nicolas couldn't see the warrior's face, but he didn't need to. The *smug git* emanating from the man was as obvious as the bone monster in the road.

Finally, holding his sword point forwards, he broke into a charge, his men joining him with a fierce battle-cry.

How outnumbered are they? Three to one? Four to one?

Within seconds of the battle starting, it was clear that the skeletons numerical advantage counted for naught. The number of disembodied skulls flying through the air made that clear. The clashing of blades and battle cries mingled into a din that was becoming all too familiar as the melee began. The skeletons were slow and unwieldy compared to the warriors, but they still exacted a toll. Twice, he saw figures turn to smoke and vanish as their heads left their necks. At least it was preferable to blood and guts being strewn everywhere. As he watched, one of Vargas's men was plucked from the ground by the monster and bitten in half, but he didn't turn to smoke, just a flailing torso that fell to the ground.

Who are these people?

It was very clear who Vargas was: a warrior. Whenever his sword swung, a skeleton fell. But the pageantry and arrogance with which he felled his opponents was irksome, like he was almost bored.

Just how I imagine Auron fights. Without looking like such a dick, of course.

Still, the distraction was in full swing. Time to make his move.

Using his peripheral vision, he looked at the man guarding them. Knocking him down might be a monumental task. But he had to. The ruffian's eyes were fixed on the battle. He was practically licking his lips to run and get involved. Vargas must be a powerful man for him to rein in that urge.

The battle wouldn't last forever, so Nicolas drove his elbow backwards into the guard's stomach. The man stumbled back a step or two, but he wasn't winded like Nicolas had expected.

Shit.

By the time Nicolas knew his plan wasn't going to work, he was already fully committed to his follow-up punch, which was grabbed mid-air by a meaty fist. The guard drew himself up to his full height and growled like an enraged animal. Desperately, Nicolas tried to wrench his arm free, but the grip was only released when the guard drove his fist into his chin. He was destined to fall back and have another sharp meeting with the floor, but the man grabbed his collar before he could, leaving him hovering like a rag doll as he lined up his fist again, savouring the moment.

A large book struck the guard on the back of the head. Dazed, the man fell forwards, dropping Nicolas backwards, the pair ending up on the ground. As he fell on his bottom, Vargas's man landed on all fours before him, shaking his head rapidly in a bid to right himself. Nicolas grabbed two rocks and hit him on both sides of his head simultaneously, robbing him of that chance. Vargas's man collapsed to the floor.

That did the trick.

He gave the man a single guilty glance as he rose. But he had a thick-looking head, so he must be alive. Besides, he'd just seen a man bitten in half, and he was still on the ground over there, shuffling towards his disembodied legs.

'Thank you,' he said, turning to the hunched man.

'We need to go,' the creepy librarian rasped. 'Our chance is getting slimmer by the minute.'

True enough, the battle wouldn't last much longer, though the lizard skeleton monster ought to buy them a few minutes.

Within moments, the pair were fleeing down the track, the battle still raging at their backs. A cheer erupting behind him caused Nicolas to turn, nearly stumbling as he did so. The giant bone creature collapsed, as if whatever magic held it together had vanished and gravity reasserted itself. A dust cloud rose from the ground, making Vargas, his men, and the skeleton warriors vanish.

They can all stay gone, as far as I'm concerned.

****

Auron was, generally, not someone they associated with rage. The only time Shift had seen him really angry was around Silva, which was hardly surprising. So the way the spirit marched around the Oracle's cottage ranting and raving was unnerving. And just in case that wasn't enough of a tell that the spirit was mad, the glowing red veins clawing across his aura were a dead giveaway.

Unless you're Nick. Then you may need some other clues.

'The Underworld? The *Underworld*?' Auron raged, white eyes wide in shock and fury. 'The Kid? Absolutely ridiculous. How is his soul damned? Can someone explain this to me?' The spirit looked around the room expectantly but didn't wait for an answer, so maybe it was rhetorical. 'He saved a city...*two* cities. He stopped a war. He's rescued numerous people. He helped restore a Deity's power, for Deities' sake.'

Shift let out a low whistle at the curse words that followed.

They agreed with their companion completely. Nick, of all people, in the Underworld? He was about the most decent person they'd met. So decent it was damned infectious, or Shift would've happily been robbing their way across the Eastern Kingdoms by now. A fact they would soon remedy. Okay, he was naïve, and so very whiny...but he was also sweet. Funny, though not by choice. Handsome, maybe, if you liked that sort of thing. But the most important thing was that he was good...to his core. They didn't know anyone else who'd flap like a distressed bird when killing someone who actually deserved it.

Stop it! You're listing his finer qualities like you're writing a eulogy. And he's alive, so cut it out.

A pang of anxiety stabbed them in the gut. If Nick could go to the Underworld for practically nothing, what would happen to them? They'd done *a lot* of stealing over the years, not to mention cons and the occasional piece of highway robbery. What awaited them after they finally died of old age and...?

Oh no. If Nick's there, he's being tortured.

Bringing their hand up to their mouth quickly, Shift stifled a gasp, before making sure the same hand removed any potential tears from their eyes before they were shed. That couldn't be right. People just said you got tortured there. No one really *knew* because no one ever came back and they hardly had organised tours.

No one comes back...

'He does not deserve such a fate.' Garaz's voice was a hoarse whisper, his face gaunt and lined with emotion as he leant against the wall, maybe due to the shock. 'How could someone so decent fall in such a way?'

Silva kept her vigil out the window, saying nothing but her face saying everything. The warrior rubbed her cheek as if warding off one of the many flies in the room, but Shift recognised the motion. She might be trying her best not to show her emotions openly, but pain radiated off her like the odour of mouldy cheese off the Oracle.

He sighed loudly. 'Well, he doesn't belong down there, does he?' The old man grunted, rummaging through some parchments on the far side of the room. 'That's why I said he's been *banished* there. Use your ears properly or I'll stop talking to you all.' A cloud of dust enveloped him as his rummaging continued. 'Nicolas is a little...shall we say, cowardly, but he seemed decent enough.'

Cowardly? Seemed?

Shift slammed their fist on the table, and the Oracle turned slowly, his expression suggesting someone had let out a large fart rather than abused his furniture. As if one extra fart would matter in this room.

'Yes?' the old man asked.

They had a lot they wanted to say to him, but still...Nick's only hope. 'We have to do something.'

The Oracle raised a bushy eyebrow. 'And what exactly do you think I'm doing over here? Tidying?' The fact that he actually acknowledged the state of the place was kind of surprising, but also beside the point. 'Seems to me that as his body is in a state of limbo, we should be able to pop the soul back into it.'

'As easy as that?' Shift raised their fist from the table, rubbing it on their breeches once they saw the layer of dirt on the bottom of it.

'I don't recall saying it'd be easy at all,' the Oracle griped. 'Especially as there's one matter to attend to.' Pursing his lips, the old man looked at Garaz. 'You, orc. You're supposed to be a healer, right?'

Garaz was riled in an instant. '*Supposed*?'

'Well,' the Oracle said as he went back to his parchments, 'you can't tell who's living or dead, so are you really surprised I asked?'

The orc's face darkened as he rose to his full height, pointing an accusing finger. 'Now you listen here—'

'No,' the Oracle interrupted. 'You listen. I don't intend on putting young Nicolas's soul back into his body when there's still an arrow sticking out of it. Are you planning on removing it in the near future?'

Garaz looked at the arrow, opened and closed his mouth several times then simply said, 'Yes.'

I wonder what he was going to do just then?

The pang of doubt surprised Shift. But the orc had been acting in an uncharacteristic way of late.

'With that *finally* taken care of,' the old man said as he picked up and unfurled a parchment, blowing the dust from it with one breath, 'we need someone to go and find his soul and guide him back to his body.'

'I'll go.' The look on Silva's face was one of fierce determination.

'Love the attitude, my dear, but no,' the Oracle replied. 'Living people can't just go to the Underworld like you'd pop to the tavern for a pint. You need to be dead to cross the veil, and for you, it'd be a one-way trip.'

The determination in Silva's eyes didn't flinch for a second. 'So?'

'As noble as that is, and as much as I'd like to see you dead, I think we have a better option.' Auron looked equally determined as he gestured to himself with both thumbs.

'And that, dear boy, is why I was finding this exorcism spell,' the Oracle confirmed, holding the paper in his hand aloft. 'But like I said to her, it'd be...'

'Yes, I heard,' Auron shrugged. 'I can make my peace with that. The kid deserves nothing less.'

How exactly did I end up with a group of people so ready to sacrifice like this?

It was certainly different to their time in the Thieves' Guild. Anyone there who was nice to you wanted your purse. A hug meant you were getting your pocket picked. A kind word was the setup to try to sell you timeshares in a troll cave or something. Confusion clouded Shift's mind for a moment as they realised they'd opened their mouth to volunteer too.

What are these people doing to me?

The need to leave was becoming more and more imperative. Yet they were going nowhere until Nick was whole again. But that wouldn't take long. Not only did they now have hope, they had a plan. Things were getting better. Though Shift hoped they didn't have to lose Auron to get Nick back.

I think I'd actually miss his stories.

'Are you sure about this?' they asked him hesitantly.

Auron turned and gave them a half smile. 'Never surer.' The spirit seemed to see something in their expression. 'Don't worry, I'll bring him back. It'd take the entire army of the Underworld to stop me.'

'I doubt the Underworld is a very *'army and war'* type of place, but good to know.' They smiled.

The spirit leaned in close, lowering his voice, 'And when I return, you and I need to talk about your half-assed idea to up and vanish.'

Shift locked eyes with Auron. How had he known? They weren't easy to read; they couldn't be. It was a matter of professional pride.

Before they could ask, the Oracle shuffled over to the table and placed the paper on it, beginning to read it with a knitted brow. 'Seems like I need to exorcise a ghost then. As I doubt you're destined for the Underworld yourself, I'll have to make some adjustments, but it's doable.'

Auron's face was unimpressed as he spoke slowly, 'I. Am. Not. A. Ghost.'

The Oracle nodded in faux agreement. 'And I'm a young virile man.'

CHAPTER 9

Running was something a body could have enough of very quickly, even when trying to get away from madmen who turned to smoke when they died. Still, they hadn't gotten far enough for his liking. Part of that was due to keeping pace with the hunched man, who was considerably slower, his stumpy legs pumping hard as he tried to run *and* keep hold of the oversized book. But like it or not, Nicolas couldn't leave him. It wasn't all to do with needing an ally and some answers in this dark place; on a very basic level, leaving the slower man to his fate seemed just plain wrong.

Nervously, he checked behind him for the hundredth time. In the distance, there was still a dust cloud from the battle, and the odd faded clang of metal reached them even here. He had no doubt Vargas would win, just as he was sure the warrior would come after him as soon as he was done with the skeletons.

'I can't go on,' the hunched man cried weakly. 'We need to stop.'

He could hardly argue; his legs were nearly spent too. Hopefully, Vargas would throw himself an impromptu victory party after the battle and delay pursuing them for an hour or two. Seemed like something he'd do.

A week or two would be nice.

'Okay,' he replied. 'Down there.'

One side of the trail sloped downwards into a ravine, of sorts, filled with rocky outcrops. An ideal hiding spot.

Carefully, the pair slid on their sides down the slope. Still, it was treacherous and the danger of tripping and rolling down the rest of the way loomed over them both. But Nicolas must've been due some luck, because they made it. Quickly, the pair pressed themselves into a shadowed outcropping.

Instantly, his legs became numb, to the point he wasn't sure he'd ever get up again. Though if he saw Vargas coming, he could probably push some more out of them. Usually, he would've been panting now, with burning lungs to accompany it, yet he wasn't.

'Okay,' he said, steeling himself for the response. 'Who are you? Where am I? What is this place? Who are those people? Why are the dead walking? Why don't I appear to be breathing? And generally...what's going on?'

The hunched man's brow furrowed as he studied him. 'That's a lot of questions.' He snorted. 'But I have a more pressing one. How are you here? You shouldn't be here. Not at all.'

'That's on my list.' It would be at the top, but there were so many questions vying for the spot, it was hard to choose a clear winner.

'But to answer that,' the man said. 'I need to figure out *who* you are. Which this should tell me.' He tapped the book emphatically. 'If you're here, then you should be in *here*. I don't know why I couldn't find you before. But I will.'

'Why am I in the book? What is the book?'

Why am I getting more questions, not fewer?

'Introductions first.' A gnarled hand hovered in front of him. 'I'm Allius Geldheart,' the man slurred, approximating a grin. 'I'm The Tallyman. But most call me Shambles. Please don't, though. I don't like it.'

Nicolas respected not wanting to have a nickname forced upon him. Either way, he took the hand and shook it. 'Nicolas Percival Carnegie. And I really hope you can help me get out of here.'

There was a look on The Tallyman's face that he didn't care for. One that suggested he was never leaving.

Allius licked his lips with a wart-covered tongue. 'Let's find you in the book first then sort out the rest, shall we?' With that, he reverently opened the book and leafed through the pages. 'If you're here, then you're in *here*,' he repeated, mumbling to himself. 'Should be simple now I have your name.'

All he could do was watch as Allius thumbed page after page, brow furrowed in concentration, and fight the urge to scream at him to hurry up.

'Ah-ha,' the hunched man exclaimed finally, his finger tracing a passage in the book. 'Here you are. Nicolas Percival Carnegie.' Allius grinned. 'You were in an appendix.'

I didn't even make the main book?

The hunched man tapped the book lovingly. 'See, I told you. If your soul is in the Underworld, you are in the book. You were just—'

'What did you say?' he asked slowly. 'Did you say *'Underworld?'*'

The hunched man nodded.

'As in, the afterlife, where the dead go to be punished for their crimes during life.'

'There isn't another one.' Allius shrugged. 'But, and this is quite fascinating, all souls come here briefly when they die. Here, their souls are weighed and measured before they...'

Nicolas could see Allius's lips moving but couldn't hear a word he said as he stared blankly, trying to come to terms with what he'd just been told. He was dead. In the Underworld. His soul was amongst the damned.

To his side, the faun appeared on a rock, laughing.

'Murderer,' he whispered to himself.

But it wasn't just the faun, was it? Apparently, the vampire *had* counted. And the others as well...and his family. The last wall of denial that he could somehow get back and save his parents crumbled to dust. They were dead. Probably long dead as he walked around this terrible place. Not only them, but all of Hablock. His friend Potter amongst them. Koth would've killed everyone, and that was a fate *he'd* brought down on them.

How can I be surprised that I'm down here? All those deaths I caused. All that suffering, because of me.

Suddenly, he didn't want to be near himself anymore. He wanted to rip his soul out of his body and run as far from it as he could, leaving all the horror and shame with it. Not that his soul was even in his body anymore; it was in a realm of despair built for people like him.

Because I'm as much of a monster as Koth. And because I'm dead.

Disorientated, a thousand thoughts vying for his attention at once as a storm of guilt raged within him, he rose, flailing his hands as if trying to swat away the truth before falling to the ground again to stare back at the black clouds above.

'Are you okay?' Allius asked. The voice was an echo, the man looking to be at the end of a long tunnel.

How did this happen?

He'd been doing the Deitie's work, for Deities' sake, delivering *their* message. And it had led to *this* carnage. *Nick Carnage.* Everyone he'd saved, and he'd still ended up damned.

'How? How? *Hoooooooooow*!' he cried, his voice echoing through the ravine. 'How did I end up here?'

'Those you may have told must remain silent.' That was what the monster had said. His swanning around trying to help had led to this. And now he'd never see his parents again, his mother's bushy hair and his father's broad shoulders, neither of their smiling faces. He'd never see Potter's roguish grin or listen to him brag about what a good archer he was and his plans when he finally went out into the world.

Allius coughed politely, though it was a hacking sound. 'If I may—'

'No,' he cried, scrabbling to his feet and backing away. 'Stay away from me. I'll get you killed. Or kill you.'

'If you'd just—'

'I'm evil.' He rose to his feet with a choked sob. 'I'm in the Underworld, where I belong. People die around me.'

All because of him, as sure as if he'd put the knife to their throats himself. His only hope was that it'd been a quick death.

'I'm so sorry,' he whispered to them all. He would do anything to take it back, to go back to that bloody bridge and look the other way when the wagons passed him, maybe to just let Grimmark kill him. In the long run, it would've saved his whole village. That was a sacrifice worth making.

But I'm here now, and I'm going to be made to pay for every soul taken in my name or by my hand.

'So it's torture for me then.' This new knowledge was already torture, but he was sure that Sha'then, Lord of the Underworld, had something special lined up for someone like him.

'Well, you see—'

A random thought crossed Nicolas's mind. 'Why did Vargas's men turn to smoke when they lost their heads?'

'Well...' Allius paused for a moment. 'Ah, you're going to let me speak. That is what we call the *true death*. Down here, the body feels pain, as in life, but can regenerate from even the most grievous wounds. It wouldn't be very good torturing people who die easily.' The hunched man let out a chuckle. 'But if you get beheaded, you're done. Your soul vanishes into nothingness.'

Nothingness sounds appealing. Much better than carrying this guilt. Much better than Sha'then's torture, or whatever Vargas's master has in store for me.

And if he stayed here, there'd be an eternity of it. Maybe it'd already begun? Was carrying the guilt his torture or just the appetiser? His eyes stung from tears that wouldn't come. Wanting to cry and not being able to, another form of torture. This whole place was torture.

'Nicolas?' the voice of the robed man persisted. 'Are you okay?'

No, he was confused and terrified and alone. And now he felt the death of every single person he'd known as sure as if he'd done it himself. Which according to the cosmic scales, he had. There was a pressure in his mind, as if it were a dam ready to burst. He couldn't live like this. But what else could he do? Go and find his torturer and offer himself up? Wander these wastelands for all eternity, haunted by the ghosts of those he'd slain through his actions?

Or maybe there was another way. *Nothingness*. He could just end it, forever. He wouldn't have to carry this terrible guilt, to have it eat away at him, and he would finally pay for his crimes.

But he couldn't do it himself. So how?

Vargas's men would be looking for him by now. If he found them first, it shouldn't take too much to goad them into killing him—they were angry killers, after all. Yes, better to simply cease existing than live in...*this*.

Slowly, he got up and walked back up the slope to the main track.

'Where are you going?' Allius asked impatiently.

He half-turned his head. 'Stay away from me. I'm going to die.'

'You *what?*' the robed man scoffed. 'No, wait. You don't understand...'

Allius kept talking, but Nicolas wasn't listening. Instead, he trudged to the top of the slope and headed back towards the battle. In his peripheral vision, he caught sight of the homestead he'd first awoken by... Ruined, just like his soul.

Beside him, the faun danced, playing his pipes as Nicolas marched to oblivion.

****

Confidence, wit, looking unbelievable in tight-fitting clothing—these were just some of the many amazing qualities they possessed. Patience, though, wasn't amongst them, especially with something *this* important. Shift huffed aloud for the third time as the Oracle continued to shamble around his cottage as if he had all the time in the world. The old man half-turned towards them and scowled. In response, they folded their arms impatiently. It might not actually make the old man *hurry up,* but it was good to at least be doing *something*.

At the start, they'd offered to help the Oracle in his preparations multiple times, which had received either a curt '*no*' or a glance suggesting they were too stupid to help and how dare they even ask. Fair enough. But if he didn't want their practical help, they'd settle for hassling some extra speed out of him.

'You need to let him work,' Auron said at their side.

'He needs to work *faster*,' they retorted. 'Nick's stranded down there, and he's taking an age drawing something on the floor that I probably could've finished in minutes.'

'But would you have done it right?' the spirit replied. 'This is deep magic we're talking about, not some random etching on a wall, and I don't fancy getting sent to a demonic pit by accident because you didn't cross a rune properly.'

'But—'

'We all miss him, and we all want him back,' Auron cut in. 'But there are some things that need to be done properly.'

'He could be being tortured down there,' they whispered, as if saying it any louder would make it real.

'I know,' the spirit replied, his mouth a thin line. 'But let the man work. Between him and Garaz, we'll have him back in no time.'

No time was too long in their opinion, yet frustratingly, the spirit was right. They knew that. And at least Garaz was working hard to ensure that Nick had a serviceable body to come back to, provided decomposition didn't set in with the Oracle's snail's pace. The orc had once removed an arrow from Silva and saved her life, so Nick was in good hands, despite the earlier misdiagnosis. Already, the shaft was out, and Garaz was closing the wound. They trusted him to do that, at least.

'How did you know?' they whispered to Auron.

The spirit looked at them levelly. 'That you plan to leave? An educated guess. Beyond the boasting and storytelling, I'm pretty savvy, don't you know.'

He says boastfully.

'Look—'

'Not now,' the spirit said firmly. 'When I return. Talking some sense into you will give me something to get back for. And you need it, because your idea is ridiculous.'

'Is it?'

'Yes,' Auron scolded. 'You're doing it for all the wrong reasons. You don't even really know *why* you're doing it. You're overreacting. Just like someone else I know...'

Straightening himself with an audible bone crack that made Shift wince, the Oracle looked over the chalk design he'd drawn on the floor. It was made up of several concentric circles. The outer ones were filled with what looked like a load of random squiggles and dots. The centre circle contained a large pentagram. Something about the design made their skin prickle if they stared at it for too long.

'Candles,' the Oracle barked at them, pointing with his bony finger at a pile of yellow wax candles on one of the tables. 'If you want to make yourself useful, place them in equal distances around the circle and light them.' All the times they'd offered to help, and when he did finally ask, it was in the most impolite way possible.

Swallowing their sassy retort, Shift grabbed the candles and placed them as the old man had said whilst the Oracle lowered himself into a cross-legged position in the centre of the pentagram. Deities, did he have any bones that *didn't* creak?

As they put the candles down, they briefly looked at *him*, lying on the table as Garaz worked, looking pale but peaceful.

Maybe while he sleeps, I can shave that thing off his top lip.

It wasn't like he'd miss it. He'd surely only grown it to try to look a little older and more proper. *Nick Carnage* didn't have a moustache; he was more of a rugged stubble type. The idea of Nick looking like that made a chuckle slip out, which drew a glare from the Oracle.

Your glares get less withering with overuse, you cantankerous old git.

'I said *equal* distance apart,' the Oracle snapped. 'Concentrate on what you're doing if you want your friend back.'

Okay, so they *had* lost their concentration for a second, but it had only been an inch too close. No need for such an offensive tone. It was hard enough to concentrate this close to his odorous aura, anyway.

They moved the candle into the proper position. 'Better?' Shift made no attempt to hide the venom in their tone. Let him be warned that he was on thin ice.

The Oracle nodded.

Finishing the placement, Shift lit the candles one by one. Looking up again, they could see Silva through the cottage's grubby window. Kind of. The warrior was standing guard outside. Unable to be of use in here, she'd positioned herself where a fight was most likely to be. And with the thunderous mood she was in, woe betide any assassins who came knocking. If they did, Shift would make sure they were out there with Silva, so they could turn into a troll and squeeze their heads until they *popped*.

You took your coward's run at Nick when he was alone. Let's see how it works out when you come after the rest of us.

Though it was so close last time...

I'm not Nick. I can look after myself. Always have, always will.

Their work done, candles lit, Shift stepped away from the circle.

The Oracle beckoned Auron to him. 'You ready?'

The spirit gave off a palpable aura of determination as he nodded and stepped into the circle.

'Do you think you can find him?' It wasn't that they didn't believe he would; it was just nice to check.

Deities, it's like Nick's talking, not me.

But they had to assume that the Underworld was pretty vast—unless being cramped was one of the tortures—so how was one spirit supposed to find another in a place full of spirits?

'Nicolas was the first person to see you, right?' The Oracle acknowledged Auron's nod before continuing. 'Then there's a bond between your souls. If I do this right, you should appear not far from where he did.'

'I'll find him,' Auron said firmly. 'Judging by how out of place he normally is, it shouldn't be too hard.'

Despite the gravity of the situation, they laughed. The spirit wasn't wrong. For someone who allegedly didn't like to be the centre of attention, Nick often stuck out like a sore thumb.

'Fair point, but what about actually getting him back in his body again?'

They both looked at the Oracle, and the old man shrugged back at them. 'Don't ask me. I'm just facilitating the journey. Everything else you need to improvise.'

That shook their faith in the plan slightly, but Auron gave a confident half-smile. 'Improvising is what I do best.' The ethereal hero pursed his lips for a moment. 'So this one time—'

'Not now,' they interrupted. 'If you want to tell a story, you can tell the one about rescuing Nick when you get back.'

Auron gave a theatrical bow.

'Good luck.' They put every ounce of their soul into the wish.

The spirit looked like he didn't need it. In fact, he looked almost excited. 'Adventure time,' he declared with a wink.

Beyond the pair, Garaz had stopped working for a moment to watch what was happening, curious as usual about any form of magic. He needed to finish healing Nick's body, not gawk at his first exorcism.

The Oracle seemed to share their opinion. 'If you don't heal him before rigor mortis sets in, you may end up with a zombie when he returns,' he snapped tartly at the orc.

'I have ointments and spells that can slow the decay,' the orc replied. 'He will be ready for his return.' If the orc managed that, it'd definitely go a little way to restoring their faith in him.

With an unconvinced *humph*, the Oracle closed his eyes and muttered under his breath. Quickly, the air around them became warm with energy as the room brightened...or was the chalk glowing? The Oracle's muttering quickened, —they caught a few words, but they weren't in a language they understood. The heat in the room grew until it was almost oppressive, and they found themselves undoing the top buttons of their tunic as sweat ran from their temples.

With a moan, the Oracle's eyes shot open. There were no pupils in them; they were just empty white orbs, like Auron's. The room continued to brighten, forcing them to squint firstly, then use their arm for shade. Part of them wanted to look away, but they didn't want to miss anything.

Time passed. And passed. Shouldn't something have happened by now? Even Auron looked at them and shrugged uncertainly. Then the whole cottage shook, a single violent spasm accompanied by a thunderclap that dislodged straw from the ceiling to rain down on them. Within seconds, Silva had kicked the door in, sword in hand, Cuthbert at her side, also armed.

The walls and ceiling rumbled as the Oracle's face showed signs of extreme exertion. His several teeth were clenched in a grimace as thick veins appeared on his sweat-covered temples and across his face and arms. The old man's body trembled in time with the building, the whole room was becoming charged with energy. Auron had the same *'oh shit'* look on his face they were sure they had. Garaz put himself between the pentagram and Nick's body.

For reasons they couldn't fathom, they backed away from the scene. Almost as if they were being pushed by some unseen force. The chalk circle reverberated with energy—they could almost see it, a vibration in the air cutting those in the circle off from the rest of the cottage. Items fell from table tops, the world blurring around them as the shaking increased. Nausea rose in their stomach. From what they could see, the Oracle looked as if he might explode at any second, his mouth open and screaming, even though they heard nothing.

There was a blinding flash, and a blast of energy exploded through the room, throwing them back over a table to land in a pile of something they assumed wasn't sanitary, the wind driven from their lungs. Panting heavily, they used the table to pull themselves up, ears ringing and eyes filled with dancing ghosts of lights. Trying to blink them away, and finally rubbing their eyes, they smelled the burning before they saw it. The whole pentagram was a charred mess burnt into the floor. In its centre, the Oracle lay prone, smoke rising from his clothes.

Quickly, they ran over to him. Silva and Garaz beat them there, and Cuthbert was faster than all of them. The man's odour was now cooked and assaulted their nostrils brutally. They were thankful when Garaz put his hand on the Oracle's chest. Not that they wouldn't have, but touching that old, stained robe wasn't something they were keen to do.

'Get your damn heavy hand off me, orc,' the Oracle groaned weakly. *He's being rude. He's okay.* 'And the rest of you, give me some damned room to breathe.'

The old man attempted to struggle into a seated position but was clearly too weak to do so. Grudgingly, he allowed Cuthbert and Garaz to help him up, though he scowled the whole time. They brought him some water, which he took without thanks.

After taking a long gulp, he coughed several times. 'That,' he exclaimed finally, 'was a lot harder than it should've been.'

Looking around, they couldn't see Auron. 'Did it work?'

The Oracle looked hesitant to answer. 'I don't know,' he said finally. 'It was like there was a wall I had to punch through. All I know is, he isn't here.'

He'd be there. It was Auron. *He'd be there.*

CHAPTER 10

Nicolas had made a decision. Half his mind thought it was a ridiculous one, but the other half was at peace with his choice. The realisation of what he'd done was already eating him from within, and he'd only just discovered it. Besides, he was already dead. This would simply be a matter of putting the final nail in the coffin, so to speak. Part of him wondered if he should stay here and accept his fate, the eternal torture, but he couldn't do it. He just wanted to stop existing.

Vaguely, as he trudged back down the road, he was aware of Allius calling after him. The man had tried to follow him up the slope, but Nicolas assumed his stumpy legs had betrayed him, which was good. No one should be near him or have a chance to talk him out of it. Looking down at his jacket, which wasn't really his jacket because he was a ghost, or lost soul or whatnot, he broke step to wipe some dust from it. If only he could wipe away his guilt so easily.

Back in the direction of the ruined homestead, there was a fierce clap of thunder. Perhaps the sky was giving him a round of applause for making the right choice?

Deities, I think some nonsense sometimes.

Perhaps he should stop invoking their name when they'd clearly forsaken him.

The faun hadn't forsaken him, though; he was still there, doing his stupid little victory dance.

'You won't have to worry about bothering me much longer,' he muttered sadly.

Now he just had to find the vehicle for his final oblivion. He didn't even pretend that he'd do it himself, but he was in an extremely dangerous place and being hunted. Vargas's men *had* to be looking for him by now. He just needed to piss them off, and *boom*, he'd no longer exist.

Finding them turned out to be easier than he'd thought. Ahead of him, he could make out four figures in the distance. From the way they walked, they definitely weren't skeletons, their movement too loose, too casual. Closing his eyes and breathing in deeply, he jogged towards them.

When Nicolas judged them close enough, he stopped and waved enthusiastically. 'Hey! Hey, you. I'm over here, you dirty sons of whores,' he cried.

The men stopped. Though he couldn't make out their features well, he knew a posture of surprise when he saw it.

Off to a good start then.

'What did you stop for?' he continued, cupping his hands to his mouth. 'Worried about getting too close in case an unarmed boy puts you all on your asses?'

He caught a faint exclamation on the wind. Not all of it, just: *'cheeky little...'*

'What's it like knowing your uncles are your dads because they were the only ones who could stand to bed your pig-ugly mothers?' he continued.

That one did it. Weapons drawn, the men charged him, shouting various unpleasant things he was glad he couldn't quite hear. His plan had worked. Death was coming for him, the final death, not this terrible in-between state.

So why am I running away?

That was contrary to his whole plan, yet as much as he wanted to stop himself, to turn and face his fate, he kept running. What a fantastic time to lose control of your body.

Entering the ruins, a thought ran through his mind. *Maybe I can find a weapon here.* What did he need a weapon for? He had no intention of defending himself or adding to his body count, which had gotten him here in the first place. Besides, he doubted another broom handle would best four men. Yet despite his wishes, he continued searching.

There was no sense anymore. No logic. Forcing himself to stop, he cried out in frustration. It seemed to echo across the plains, carrying his anguish to every corner of this world.

'Stop,' he told himself firmly. 'Just stop. It's over. Let it come. Time to pay for your sins.'

Through sheer force of will, Nicolas turned back in the direction of the oncoming attackers. Yet the minute they rounded the corner, he turned to run.

Oh shit, not again.

Once more, he went tumbling into the crater, rolling through the dust and rock, wincing with every spike of pain.

I suppose it'd be a damn shame if I died with even a little of my dignity intact.

When he picked himself up, his soon-to-be killers were already sliding down the slope towards him, chuckling at his stupidity. Now there was nowhere left to go, he knelt and awaited the inevitable.

'I don't care if the master wants you or not,' the larger of the four men snarled. 'No one calls me a dirty son of a whore. My mother was a waitress in the brothel. She promised me that's all she did.'

And that's the last thing I'm ever going to hear. Fantastic.

He began to pray. Not for himself, but for the souls of those he'd let down, those he'd brought ruin on. He hoped they were at peace. Maybe oblivion would bring him peace? The men approached. A sword was raised, and the wielder's face morphed into the visage of the faun. Nicolas lowered his head and closed his eyes. He should've protected them all. He deserved this...but he definitely didn't want to see it coming.

Above him, there was the distinctive clash of metal on metal.

His eyes shot open. The attacking blade was stopped less than a metre from his head, another sword blocking its passage.

'What in the *Deities* are you doing, kid?' Auron snapped as he pushed the attacking blade away.

What? How? But...how? And what?

He was *here*, as in really *here*. There was no see-through body made of smoke. He wasn't flesh and blood, not here, but he was solid. This was the hero as he'd looked in life.

Vargas's man swung his sword again, but by the time it was halfway up, his arm was cut from his elbow, and he was falling back from the wound across his stomach. Two of his comrades came in, and Auron danced between their weapons, felling them both before driving the tip of his blade into the stomach of the fourth with all the grace of a dancer.

'Where did you get that sword?' Nicolas asked as he looked at the rusted blade in the hero's hand.

Auron shrugged. 'I found it on the floor over there. There's loads of them lying around.'

And all I find is a broom. Brilliant.

There was a groan from the floor as the first ruffian rose. Auron frowned as he walked up and stabbed the man in the back then the hero's face became a scowl as the others got up too.

'Hey,' he shouted. 'Stay dead when I kill you.'

Another rising attacker was sent abruptly back to the ground with a slash across the chest, but as soon as he fell, he got back up.

'Oh, for Deities' sake,' Auron snapped, stabbing him again. '*Stay down!*'

'Um, you have to take their heads off,' Nicolas said.

Auron looked at him, mulled it over, then nodded. 'Heads, got it.'

Nicolas's jaw hung open as the hero's blade flashed four times. With each cut a head was parted from a neck, until all of Vargas's men had become smoke and vanished into oblivion.

Standing and admiring his handiwork, Auron nodded to himself as he threw his sword spinning into the air, catching it before resting it triumphantly on his shoulder. 'Still got it.'

Slowly, the hero turned to him, anger radiating off him like light from the sun. 'Now that's done with, I'll ask again, kid,' the hero said slowly. 'What in the Underworld did you think you were doing?'

Nicolas's mouth opened and closed but no words came out. Before things got more awkward, the hero became distracted by something. 'There's some kind of disgusting monk on the edge of the crater,' he said with narrowed eyes. 'Do I need to kill him?'

Still wordless, he shook his head. This was all too much to take in.

****

'How long have you been staring at that for?' Silva's sudden voice made them jump. They hadn't even realised she was there, let alone so close.

'A while,' Garaz helpfully answered as he finished cleaning up the area where he'd worked on Nick. In fact, he was cleaning everything within a radius of it as well, nose wrinkled in disgust. Considering what they'd heard in the past about the slobbish behaviour of orcs, it was kind of ironic.

Garaz wasn't wrong, though. They'd been staring at the chalk circle for a long time, hoping they could make them both come back by sheer force of will. So far, it wasn't panning out. They tried not to notice how pale Nick looked, focusing more on the fact he no longer had an arrow sticking out of him.

'They will return soon.' It wasn't clear if the warrior was trying to convince Shift or herself.

They didn't need reassurance. It wasn't a question of *if* but *when*. Auron *would* find Nick and bring him home. They were certain of it. Why did everyone else seem so unsure lately? Even Garaz kept eyeing the chalk circle with sadness between bouts of scrubbing. Were they the only sane person here? They would return soon then Shift could spare themselves this sort of nonsense forever. All of *this* was making their decision much easier.

'The muscle lady has a point,' the Oracle interjected, now looking more or less recovered from his ordeal. Silva's face at being referred to as *muscle lady* was a picture. 'For half an hour, you've been staring at that circle.' *That long?* 'And there's work to be done.'

'What work?'

'You need to go to Hablock,' the Oracle told them. 'And take that bloody orc with you before he cleans every surface in here.'

Why is that a problem? Because then you'll feel the need to keep it clean?

They scoffed openly at the idea of leaving. They were going nowhere. They needed to be here when they returned. 'I'm not going an—'

Garaz seemed more open to the idea as he butted in. 'What do you require?'

'Whatever has happened out there, I need answers,' the Oracle said, his voice still a little hoarse. 'These are my people, even if I never walk amongst them. And they need help. You three need to go and find out who is left and protect them. And if you could find out who did this too and readily thrash them, that'd be grand.'

'I'm staying.' They had no intention of not being here to greet Auron and Nick on their return. No number of interruptions would change that.

A large green hand rested on their shoulder. 'You can do nothing good waiting here, but you can out there.' They looked at the hand disdainfully. They'd seen what those hands could do. Shrugging off the gesture seemed to hurt Garaz, but he continued, nonetheless. 'What would Nicolas do?'

That damned phrase.

Yes, what would the out-of-his-element village boy do? He'd go and help look for survivors. Perhaps they should do it exactly the way he would and bemoan the travelling and embarrass himself at every possible opportunity too? No, that was unfair. He had a good heart. It wasn't his fault it rubbed off on people. Right now, they should've been breaking into some wealthy manor or fleecing marks in a gaming hall, but since they'd met Nick, they'd grown a conscience. Or maybe it had always been there and just needed an example to follow? Either way, it was all his fault, and they'd rectify it as soon as he returned.

'Fine,' they finally relented. They didn't look at the body, but they hoped Nick was getting a lot of rest right now, because they were going to kick his ass when he returned.

'Excellent,' the Oracle exclaimed. 'You can take the wagon. I need Cuthbert here with me. He won't mind.' From the look on his face, Cuthbert clearly minded, very much, but he kept his mouth shut. 'I think the village square is your best bet.'

Garaz raised an inquisitive eyebrow. 'Reasoning?'

'In times of peril, people go where they feel safe, usually around others and especially where there's shelter and supplies. Whatever has happened out there, I'll bet anyone left has gone to the square. Maybe you'll find someone more amenable to your stupid questions there.' That riled Garaz, which was probably not a good idea. They'd seen Garaz riled recently. It was scary.

The ghost of pain haunted their chin for a moment, a reminder of the spinning kick to the face from the toad-like creature, the faun Ro's bodyguard. For something so small, it could kick like a damned mule, and easily take on Shift, Silva, *and* Garaz.

Admittedly, half their mind had been worrying about Nick fighting the faun alone, so maybe their own battle would've gone better if they'd paid it the proper attention.

By the time the two follow-up kicks had landed, Shift had hit the deck of the freighter, hard. They'd struggled to breathe, the clearly broken rib not making that any easier. All Shift could do was watch as the toad leapt high into the air. They were too stunned to move or change form; all they could do was watch it descend towards their head at speed. Even closing their eyes would've been something, but they had to take in every detail of their fate.

Except it wasn't my fate. Not that day. But it was close...too close.

Stopped in mid-air just a handful of inches from Shift's face by two large green hands, the creature had bucked and thrashed.

A bloody impressive catch.

Their stomach heaved in discomfort as they recalled what had happened next: the tearing sounds, a feral roar, the cut-off cry of agony, and the warm blood covering their face as Garaz ripped the creature in half with his bare hands.

As the two halves of the toad were discarded, they looked up at their rescuer, ready to congratulate him on a job well done, even if there had been less brutal ways to do it. Instead they had gasped in fear. The ferociousness of the figure staring down at them was shocking. How was *this* the genial orc they knew? Red eyes were stared down at them from a blood covered face and...

No, I'm remembering it wrong. Garaz's eyes are yellow.

It was weird how the mind played tricks on you after someone kicked you in the face. But in that moment they realised how little they knew about the people they trusted with their life, a life that had been a mere second away from ending. *So close.* Another stark reminder that they didn't belong with these people. Relying on others had saved them, but it had also been the reason they'd nearly been killed in the first place.

Besides. I'm not sure if I can *rely on them anymore.*

Garaz could obviously tell what they were remembering, his yellow eyes tinged with shame as he broke from their gaze.

'I will go and prepare the wagon,' Silva informed them before marching from the room. Cuthbert's irritated expression followed her the whole way out. He must be really precious about that wagon.

CHAPTER 11

Auron stared down at him with his arms folded and lips pursed in annoyance. Only tapping his foot would've completed the picture of irritability.

'Now it seems to me,' the hero began slowly, 'that you weren't leading those men into any kind of ambush as you were firstly, unarmed and secondly, on your knees waiting for them. Based on the evidence and what I heard you shouting at them out there, it's almost like you were trying to goad them into killing you. But that can't be right, because that would be ridiculous. Wouldn't it?'

Nicolas's eyes were wide as his mouth worked up and down like a chatty fish. But still no words came out. He wasn't sure what was more shocking—seeing Auron here or how relieved he was to still be alive...or exist.

'How are you here?' he finally asked in wonder as he looked behind the hero. He was so used to being able to see through him that not being able to now was just strange.

'Don't change the subject,' Auron replied through gritted teeth.

Standing, Nicolas sank on the inside as the shock at seeing his companion, and still existing, waned and the guilt weighed on him again. Then a pressing question became clear to him.

'My parents?'

Auron's mouth dropped slightly. Not a good start. 'I don't know,' the hero said heavily. 'When we got there, your house was burned. I searched it, but there were no bodies. My hero instincts tell me they're alive, but I can't promise you that.'

'And the people of Hablock?'

'Missing, as far as I know.'

'They're dead.' It seemed like someone else, but Nicolas was saying those words. 'They're all dead.'

Auron's demeanour softened slightly. 'You don't know that, kid. If they're dead, why take the bodies?'

Trophies. Necromancy. Good eating...Etherius was full of strange folk.

'It's my fault and...' Looking at Auron, he realised that what he was about to say wasn't going to be well-received, so he let the sentence hang as he shuffled awkwardly on the spot.

But Auron wasn't letting it go. 'What did you say?'

Admitting his crime was one thing, telling it to another was much harder. Yet he persevered. 'It was my fault.'

The hero narrowed his eyes. 'And you figure this how?'

'I brought that thing down on my home. It killed everyone because of the things I did.' Saying it out loud gave his guilt more fervour. 'If it hadn't been for me running off adventuring, they'd still be alive. Hablock, my friends, my parents.'

Auron shook his head in disbelief. 'You know, kid, sometimes you say such stupid things I wish I could just slap you. But my hand would pass right through...' The hero thought for a second. The hand stung as it made contact.

'Ow.' *What was that for?* Tenderly, Nicolas rubbed his sore cheek.

'Stop blaming yourself,' Auron snapped. 'Did you put the swords in their hands? Did you light their torches? Did you open the doors for them to walk in? They are *evil*. Evil people do evil shit. It's a fact. You taking responsibility for *their* actions is ridiculous.' Auron gripped his shoulders firmly at first, but it soon softened as the hero gazed at him sadly. 'I guess you were on your knees there waiting to die because you wanted to be free of the guilt or atone or something?'

'Well, I...'

The hand struck him again. Then two hands pulled him in close and hugged him. 'Only you would try to get yourself killed because you think you're responsible for the deeds of bad men.'

As much as he knew he didn't deserve the hug, Nicolas did nothing to fight it off. 'But they were there because of me,' he whispered.

Auron broke his grip but still held him by the shoulders, looking intently into his eyes. 'What happened was terrible. Truly. But what happened to you, that isn't a guilt that you bear. It's a fire that drives you to stop more people getting hurt. These people who came after you, they're hurting a lot of innocent people. It would've been so many more without you. Take pride in the good you did and honour your parents by continuing to do good. What you were going to do...well, the easy answer isn't always the right answer. You told Silva that very thing once.' The hero gave him a warm smile. 'Besides, we'll find them.'

It'd take more than a few words to tame the wild guilt thrashing inside him, but he knew that his *plan* had been wrong. What he needed to do was get out of here and find his family, not go chasing oblivion.

'You're pretty wise on the quiet, aren't you?' He allowed himself a smile, the first since he'd been here.

'Kid, I'm not quiet about any of my finer qualities.' That was a nice piece of under exaggeration.

Yet he still couldn't let himself off the hook so easily. 'But then there's the faun, the reason I'm here. I—'

Auron rubbed the bridge of his nose and groaned. 'If you say *murder* then I'll upgrade my slaps to punches.'

'But I—'

A silencing finger stopped him in his tracks. 'Kid, you need to understand—'

'May I please interject?'

Auron gazed incredulously at Allius, who still stood at the lip of the crater, cradling his book. The hero gave Nicolas a questioning look before gesturing for the hunched man to join them. Auron looked thoroughly bemused as Allius struggled down the slope.

I can't say much. I've fallen down it three times now.

'If you'd let me talk before running off to try to die, I'd have told you that you aren't supposed to be here,' Allius said as he finally reached them.

It took him a moment to comprehend what he'd just been told. Had he heard that right? 'I'm not?'

'And you are?' Auron asked leadingly.

Allius walked up to Auron and offered his hand, which was dubiously accepted. 'I am Allius Geldheart, known as The Tallyman.' The robed man held up his book. 'This is the Book of Souls. It tells me who belongs here and who belongs in the Eternal Forest. Finding you, young man, took a while because, well, you don't belong here.'

Did he dare to hope? 'So, my soul *isn't* damned for all eternity?'

'No,' Allius confirmed. 'You aren't. In fact, I don't understand how either of you are here at all, what with *that*.' He raised his eyes to the impenetrable rolling black cloud in the sky, save for the new-looking hole in it. 'But here you are. I did try to explain, but you were bent on having those ruffians kill you.'

Okay, so some mistakes had been made. But he wasn't damned. *Yippie* to that.

'Who were your friends anyway?' Auron looked back to where the men he'd cut down had stood. Now there was no sign they'd ever existed at all.

'They were minions of your nemesis.'

Auron's brow knitted in confusion. 'My what now?'

'Vargas Quell...your nemesis.' He'd been sure that was what Vargas had said. Now he was doubting himself. Things had been crazy in the last few...however long he'd been here. His memory might've been affected.

Auron's face dropped as soon as he heard the name. 'Whoever told you that is selling you some top-of-the-line manure, kid.' The hero scoffed. 'Hang on, that ogre fondler is here? I mean, of course he'd be *here*, but you've seen him?'

'Yeah, he captured me, but I escaped during a fight and came back here and...well, you know the rest. He seemed to know who I was, though.'

'Brilliant.' Auron rubbed his hands over his face. 'That makes things a little more annoying.'

'So he isn't your nemesis?'

The hero let out a harsh laugh that echoed around the courtyard. 'He *wishes*. The only reason he makes that claim is because he happened to live slightly longer than any other bad guy I've come up against, which is usually because he ran at the first sight of me and had a ridiculous number of men around him for me to go through first.'

'So you've got history then.' It was daft to say something so obvious.

'A long one. Right up until I killed him. He was a nobleman's son who liked to play with fire. I caught him out once, and he got disowned. Ran off and formed his own gang. Fancied himself a warlord, amongst other things. Obsessed with me, of course.' Auron shook his head in dismay. 'You know, I half hope we see him so I can kill him again.' Vargas had given off the aura of someone who needed killing. The hero stopped for a moment to think. 'How exactly is old Vargas walking around here with goons? Shouldn't he be...' With his hands, Auron acted out some very graphic types of torture.

'I don't know,' Nicolas replied. 'It's insane here. There are these skeletons, and these wraiths, and—'

'*Wraiths?*'

'Yeah, that's what Vargas and his men call themselves.'

Auron snorted. 'Bit pretentious being undead and giving yourself a fancy title.'

Said the guy who didn't like being called a ghost because it was too common.

'If you would let me finish speaking,' Allius interjected impatiently. 'Then you'd know that things are a bit...squiffy down here right now.'

'*Squiffy?*' Nicolas repeated.

'There's been...ahem...there's been an uprising.'

'A what now?' Auron asked.

Allius looked around them fretfully. 'Please, I will explain all, but we can't dally here any longer. More will come.'

'So?' Auron asked, giving his new sword a lover's look.

'So, I need to get you back to Lord Sha'then so we can figure out how you both got here.'

'That's an easy one,' the hero explained. 'I was sent by the Oracle, who told me the kid's soul had been banished here.'

Nicolas looked at Auron in surprise. It was really strange seeing his eyes with pupils in them. 'You've met the Oracle?'

'Yeah, delightful chap.' The hero sniggered. 'Doesn't exactly live up to the mystic hype.' *Very true.* 'But he helped send me here to get you. He says we can slip your soul back into your body. Somehow.'

So not only was he not supposed to be here, he might also have a way back? His fortunes were turning, it seemed. But to be banished to the Underworld, apparently undeservingly, why would someone do that?

'Being banished here would take enormous power,' Allius said, still worriedly looking up at the hole in the cloud.

'Koth,' Nicolas whispered, remembering the creature outside his home and how it had reached for him as he died. At the hero's questioning look, he quickly explained what had happened.

Auron took this in thoughtfully. 'Sounds kind of like a demon host, but of a type I've never encountered.' Nicolas threw him a questioning look. 'Demons are real, kid.' Auron did like the opportunity to show his knowledge. 'They can manifest in our reality by possessing a host. The possession usually causes outward changes to the host body as it struggles to contain the demon's raw energy. Also means they burn through the body quite quickly so they can't stay on this plane of existence for too long. What you describe sounds like that. But worse. Odd, though. A demon using a bow and arrow. They're normally more of the hack and slash with claw and tooth types.'

Thank the Deities he didn't. I want some body left to go back to.

Remembering the creature, he laughed dryly. Of course he wouldn't attract a regular demon; he had to attract some form of super demonic lord, or whatever it was.

What was it Koth said to me before sending me here?

'He suffers.'

The voice in his head chilled him as much as it had when hearing it for real. So it wasn't enough that he was killed, he had to be damned to eternal torture too? He must've *really* angered someone.

The Oracle's choosing stick hadn't picked him for a task, it'd cursed him. It was the delivery of a message that had led to all...this.

'I'm sure you are cursing your luck or yourself or something like that.' Auron held his gaze. 'But at least we can change it. The robed fellow here is going to take us to Sha'then, where we can get all this sorted and send you home.'

Is there even a home to go back to?

****

They'd found the countryside strange on the wagon ride to the village square. All around them were lush, rolling green and yellow fields, which was as it should be. But in a sense, it really *shouldn't* have been like that. A terrible tragedy had occurred here, an atrocity. The sky should've been dark and pouring rain down on them whilst the ground churned to mud as the leaves withered and died on the trees. Nothing should've been normal.

The world just goes on, I suppose.

Still, it felt wrong. This was exactly why they went around thieving and minding their own business, so they didn't have to face the evil that people could do. And didn't have that evil nearly...*stop it.*

The several farms they'd passed matched the Oracle's account of things. People were just gone. There were signs of struggle, of course, so they'd been taken. But that was okay. The group had plenty of experience rescuing captives by now.

What an odd new string to my bow.

Slowly, the wagon rolled into the village square. It was deathly quiet, matching the scenes at the farms; the odd overturned cart or random item of clothing discarded in the street. It reminded Shift of the streets of Yarringsburg once the first wave of vampires had hit it.

At least there are no bloodstains.

'Who could do such a thing?' they asked sadly as they looked at buildings that should've been bustling but were instead dark and empty.

'We already know.' Well, that was new information. It was also the first time Silva had spoken since boarding the wagon. With a slight bump, the wagon came to a halt as the warrior pulled on the reins. She turned and looked back at them both. 'Yarringsburg, Sarus, Merida. It's all connected. Someone is fanning the flames, and we interfered each time. There were bound to be repercussions.'

'So when you say, *'We already know,'* you mean whatever elusive person is behind this. I was hoping more for a name and maybe a location.' It'd be nice to turn up at the door of whoever this mysterious figure was as a tiger and maul them savagely.

Except I'm leaving, so I won't be doing that.

Silva put a hand to her head. For a moment, exertion showed on her face before she slammed her fist angrily on the wagon. The horse bobbed its head in surprise at the sudden sound. 'I wish I could remember.'

'Remember what?' Garaz asked.

When the warrior turned to them properly, she looked forlorn. 'After I drowned, I told you all that I had gaps in my memory. That was...an over-exaggeration. I have one gap. Just one. Whoever my employer was. It's like there's a hole in my mind exactly where they stand. I remember Avus, the necromancer, but he was not the one. There was someone else, and every time I try to focus on their image or recall their name, it disappears, like smoke through my fingers.'

They put a hand on Silva's shoulder. The warrior looked as if a wet fish had been put there instead.

'I get it,' they said quietly. They knew well the frustration of missing memories. It was something Shift and Silva had in common. They'd searched for answers about their own past for a long time, but when none were forthcoming, and they found not even a whisper of others like them, they'd just decided to live their life and not dwell on the big question mark that was their history. Still, the yearning for the truth occasionally snuck up on them when they were unguarded. 'Though missing a single, specific memory can't be a coincidence.'

'You wish to know who you were, and I wish to forget who I was,' Silva said, shaking her head. 'But I don't think I can let this lie any longer.'

'Nope,' Shift agreed. 'There's the name of a person who has to die in your scowling head, and I'm going to need it.'

Just that one last thing then, before I return to the old life.

That thought was contrary to their whole plan. They were intent on leaving, but now it seemed they were swearing to do more stuff. Vengeance quests were no more their thing than any of the rest of this.

'I believe I may be able to help,' Garaz suggested, studying Silva's head as if it were an object of curiosity. It wasn't the usual reason people looked at Silva. Even Shift, once or twice. The warrior did have a harsh beauty to her.

After a moment's thought, the warrior inclined her head. Securing the reins, she stepped into the rear of the wagon and sat before Garaz. The orc put his hands on either side of her head and chanted. There was the usual light they'd come to expect with his healing magic.

After a few moments, Garaz sat back as if stunned. 'You do have a hole in your mind.' He was using that voice he did when he found something curious. 'Well, not a hole, per se, but a piece of your mind is locked away. I would assume some form of spell.'

Made sense to them. Mercenaries weren't the most trustworthy of folk. Why wouldn't her employer take precautions when hiring her to do their dirty work? Like aiding a potential vampire apocalypse.

'Can you break it?' they asked, confused at how eager they were to get mauling.

'It is strong,' the orc mused, looking at Silva's head as if it were a fascinating piece of art. 'But I believe with enough time I can wear away at the lock, so to speak.'

The arrow striking the side of the wagon with a sharp *thunk* signalled they had no time at all.

CHAPTER 12

'**S**o...you really don't think I was sent here because I killed that faun?'

Auron stopped walking and let out a frustrated groan. The hero turned to him slowly, giving him the full force of his contempt for the question, projected through his eyes. 'For the last damn time, *no*. The faun was bad. He kidnapped people, used children as slave labour, allied himself with a fearsome pirate, and tried to start a war. I'm sure he'd cultivated quite the list of evil deeds *before* we came across him. Oh, and he murdered a royal family. That'll be quite high on it. He deserved to die, and I hope we come across him whilst the torturers down here demonstrate the full extent of their art on him so I can enjoy the show. Now will you quit asking?'

'I did already say you shouldn't be here,' Allius mumbled loudly enough to be heard.

Maybe he'd asked more than once. Three times, truth be told. He cringed at his own insecurity. But he just needed to know that he wasn't here because he'd damned his soul. The demon thing sounded reasonable enough, but it never hurt to be sure, and Allius, well, they'd just met, and he travelled around with skeleton warriors, so Nicolas didn't entirely trust him yet.

'Listen, kid,' Auron seemed intent on hammering his point home, most likely because he didn't want to be asked again. 'The universe is quite happy with people like us removing scum like him from the face of Etherius. Not only did you avenge his previous victims, you saved all those he was going to kill. That's a good thing.'

Strangely, despite his need for reassurance, Auron's words were starting to make sense. So much so that he hadn't seen his ghostly harasser for a good while now. Yet some frustratingly stubborn part of him was still not fully convinced. Maybe it was something to do with the notion he hadn't even dared to put into words yet.

'What...if part of me *wanted* to kill him?' He'd threatened it enough on his last adventure then made good on his promise. Didn't that somehow make it worse?

Auron gave him a sympathetic smile. 'There are plenty of villains I've come across in my time that I *wanted* to kill. Vargas included. Wanting to kill doesn't make you a bad person. Every human has urges like that, as well as instincts of self-preservation that we act on. The difference with you is you wouldn't have cut the faun's throat whilst he slept or set his legs on fire to watch him burn slowly to death. And if he'd yielded during that fight you would have let him live. You're neither a murderer nor a sadist. You're human. And a human who's been confronted by some pretty nasty characters, all of whom I've wanted to kill myself. You get it?'

Nicolas had said openly the thing he'd been scared the most to voice. Yet he had, and his imaginings of Auron abandoning him in disgust hadn't come to pass. In fact, the hero had made some more sense. 'I suppose you're right.'

Auron opened his arms wide in a wholly unnecessary sarcastic gesture. 'Thank you,' he exclaimed loudly. 'Now, I'd like to get you back in your body before it becomes elderly, so can we please get moving?'

Allius looked back from ahead of them and muttered something close to, *'That'd be nice.'* Okay, so the rotund robed man was walking faster than them, but Nicolas had a lot to try to work out, and Auron probably didn't *really* care if they were caught or not. It'd just be some more villains for him to slay.

On that note, 'I thought you'd be spoiling for a fight with your nemesis?'

The word *nemesis* had just slipped out, but it got him a sharp look from Auron. 'I spent a lot of time and energy killing Vargas, who was just a regular, run-of-the-mill bad guy. Yes, I would *love* to do it again and permanently. However, my priority is to get you to safety.'

'I suppose I can see how he's obsessed with you.' Nicolas shrugged. 'He even styles himself like you.'

Auron wheeled round on him. 'Ha. He's a pale copy of the real thing. Though he's so desperate to be the evil version of me, I'm surprised he hasn't renamed himself Norua.'

'He referred to himself as *The Notorious*.'

'What a dickhead.'

'He even grew a ponytail like you.'

'I beg your pardon?' Auron scoffed, grabbing his own hair. 'This is clearly a warrior's braid. Not a *ponytail*. I'm a legendary hero, not a milk maid.'

'Sorry.'

The hero huffed and continued walking.

'You really think Sha'then will just *send us back?*' It would definitely be something he'd generally consider too good to be true.

'Well, the way I see it,' Auron began, 'we aren't supposed to be here. And if it were my house and there were uninvited guests, I'd want them gone.'

That was a very simplified way of looking at things.

'So this one time.' *How did I kind of miss this?* 'I get a call from this lord. Some goblins have moved into his summer manor and are dug in like ticks. So I get there, ready for a fight, but get told instead that the goblins are invoking squatters' rights as the house has been left empty most of the year.' The hero let out a dry chuckle.' They'd even retained legal counsel, if you can believe that. Well, it therefore wasn't my business anymore. I fight monsters, not lawyers. I mean, I kind of sympathised with the goblins. The lord used that house for two weeks out of the whole year, but it was his house, and he wanted them out.'

After a moment's silence he had to ask, 'What happened then?'

Auron shrugged. 'No idea. Like I said, it wasn't my business anymore.'

Nicolas rubbed the bridge of his nose tenderly. 'And the point of that story was?'

'No one likes uninvited guests.' The hero shrugged again.

Perhaps I can do one murder. Just one would be okay, right?

'Do you know where you're going?' he asked Allius, wishing to hurry this excursion along before he got another story.

The robed man stopped, looking almost offended by the question. 'Of course I do. It's that way.' He pointed his finger towards a part of the horizon that looked exactly like every other point on the horizon.

'But how far is it?'

Allius shrugged.

'Brilliant,' he exclaimed. 'So we could be walking for days?'

'We'll come to something eventually.' Auron smiled.

'How can you be so...'

'So this one time.' *Crap.* 'I knew this blind archer. I asked him once what made him think he could be an archer if he was blind. And do you know what he said? He said, *'If I fire my arrow far enough, I'll always hit something'.*' Auron tapped the side of his nose knowingly.

'What does that even mean?' Nicolas wanted to cry and scream; he just wasn't sure in which order to do it.

Auron scoffed as if it were obvious. 'We're the arrow. If we fire off in this direction, eventually we will hit something; a destination.'

Now for the question he dreaded asking. 'And what happened to this archer?'

'Killed himself with a ricochet. He was blind, you know.' *Brilliant.* 'But the wisdom is solid.'

He would rather follow Allius after being reassured that he knew where they were going than trust to the wisdom of the archer who'd shot himself.

Either way, they were doomed to continue walking across the seemingly endless grey plain. The only feature was the occasional rock formation, and the ever-rolling black clouds in the distance. They could've been walking on the spot for all the scenery, or lack thereof, around them changed. There was nothing, no sign of life, just the monotonous trudging onwards.

'So this one time.' *Again? I must've really pissed him off saying he has a ponytail. Or maybe this is Sha'then's torture manifested?* 'Vargas created this cave of traps just for me. It had all the classics: spiked walls that closed in on you, blow darts that shot out of holes in the wall, pit traps, a giant rolling boulder. He'd spent some serious coin and effort on this. Well, he spent the coin on the materials, but he refused to pay the guy who designed it for him. Told him to go hang for his money.' Auron rolled his eyes. 'The gentleman insisted that he required compensation, so Vargas killed his wife. Knowing he couldn't get revenge himself, the guy comes and finds me. Tells me there's a secret back door that they all used to get in and out past all the traps. Makes sense. That gnome dick's face when I appeared behind him and his goons. Priceless. He had to run back *through* the traps to escape me.'

In the many, many stories Auron had told him, he'd never mentioned Vargas once. 'Why did you never mention him before?'

The hero stopped—much to Allius's annoyance—thought about it and chuckled to himself. 'Because he wanted me to talk about him. He was always desperate for my attention. Hence introducing himself as my *nemesis*. He was a recurring annoyance, at most. It's sad that I had to waste so much energy on the guy.'

'But you got him in the end?'

'Yeah, he made it personal, and I made him pay for it.'

'How so?' It was strange to hear Auron talk about someone he'd fought on multiple occasions. Normally, his stories had a very definite conclusion.

'I won't talk about that, kid.' The hero's face was grim and his voice a whisper. 'He did something...well, it led to my death eventually. I'm sure he'd be pleased about that. Not that the arrogant filth will ever know.'

Nicolas didn't feel the need to inform him that Vargas did, in fact, know. Besides, he had a lot more questions now. Auron seemed to sense the oncoming tidal wave of inquiry. 'I think we should focus more on those buildings I can see on the horizon instead of the past.'

'If we could...' Allius interjected impatiently.

****

'*Over the side!*' Silva cried, already diving from the back of the wagon, two arrows plunking into the wood where she'd been sat.

Shift rolled over the side and onto the dirt floor as the *thuds* of arrows became far more numerous. Keeping low, they managed to duck aside just in time as Garaz's form landed heavily on the ground, nearly atop them.

Silva was beside the horse, peering in the gap between its ass and the wagon.

'Can you see them?' they asked. There had to be more than one archer. No one could reload their bow so fast.

'I can see several figures on the roof of the opposite building,' the warrior replied. 'But they keep ducking to reload so it is difficult to get an exact count.'

Another arrow struck. The horse fell to the ground with a cry. *Animals.* The poor creature had done nothing. Being able to change into any form had always given them an affinity for animals. They were definitely better than people, as demonstrated by the assassins across the street. Another arrow hit the wagon.

'We cannot stay here.' That was some great stating of the obvious by Garaz. His point was punctuated by three more arrow hits. If they kept this up, they'd run out soon enough. Maybe they should just wait? *No, that's silly.* One genius would get the idea to flank them eventually. Best not be here when it happened.

Behind them there were several buildings they could hide in, but no cover between them and safety.

'They have us pinned.' Silva looked angry. She liked a fight, and they weren't giving her one. Ironic, really, seeing as she had murdered a companion of theirs with a crossbow.

The only cover they had was the wagon, which gave them an idea. 'Silva, unhitch the horse. When you do, we can wheel the wagon back down the street toward that ugly statue in the centre. We can use that for cover then duck into one of the shops.'

Silva seemed to be on board with the idea, or at least she didn't argue as she slipped around the horse and got to work. They winced as several arrows struck horse flesh. Garaz hurled several fireballs in the archers' direction, trying to keep his head down as much as possible. They heard cries of alarm from above, but no death screams.

Shame that.

Even though the warrior had to retract her hands several times to avoid getting an arrow stuck in one of them, eventually the task was complete. They pointed to the edges of the wagon. 'Let's go.'

Garaz, Silva, and Shift each grabbed a section of the wagon and pushed it away from the horse. The orc was naturally strong, and Silva had muscles to spare, but the wagon was heavy and when it did begin to move, it did so too slowly. They needed this to go faster.

They concentrated, their skin tingling the way it did when they were about to change form. Even now, the sensation of proportions changing was strange, like waves rippling through their body. They saw their skin turn green. They had to be careful. If they shifted into too big an orc, they'd rip their clothes, and they didn't fancy dodging archers in the nude. Their arms became more muscular, and they heaved against the stubborn wood, which slowly began to move more freely. Garaz's double take when he looked back and saw an orc behind him was quite amusing, even with the raining arrows.

As the wagon wheeled down the street, the archers redoubled their efforts. The thudding of arrows was constant. *How many did they come with?* Carefully, they peered above the edge of the conveyance. It now looked like some form of ridiculous rolling wooden hedgehog. There was a cry from the building that suggested the archers were about to change position just as they reached the statue.

'Now!' they cried, bolting quickly from cover.

Silva ran at their side, Garaz throwing several more fireballs before following them, as did a trail of arrows. The statue did its job, taking many projectiles meant for them as they fled. Even then, the doorway of the store they ducked into became peppered with arrows, several too close for comfort as they threw themselves inside.

Too close.

Aware of the large, smashed windows, the trio quickly shuffled behind the shelving. Several shards of glass cut them as they crawled along the floor, but it was preferrable to an arrow in the ass. Breathing heavily, they returned to their preferred form. Their shirt and breeches were torn in several places, especially around the sleeves or any area that had filled with sudden bulging muscle, the rest of the top sagging around their body now. Shame, they liked this outfit. Maybe it could be saved with the application of needle and thread? At least it wouldn't fall off when they stood up next.

Thunk, thunk, thunk.

'Dedicated lot, aren't they?' they asked as they finally drew their sword. They had no idea what they intended to hit with it, but it was comforting to have a weapon in hand, and they were certainly motivated to use it.

'They are dedicated to dying by my hand,' Silva snarled. Great threat when they were across the street on a roof.

'Don't worry.' Shift smiled. 'Once we're out of here, we can double back around, and you can unleash a copious amount of violence on them...as long as you leave a couple for me.'

Silva inclined her head. 'I can do that...if you're quick.'

'Don't forget we need to leave one alive so they can tell us where the villagers are.' Garaz's eyes widened and his jaw dropped. 'What if it's just the surviving villagers, trying to defend themselves?'

In the rush of the attack, none of them had even considered that possibility. But it was equally as likely as them getting ambushed by the same marauders who took the villagers.

'We just have to hold off on the violence until we're sure.' Shift just hoped those precious seconds wouldn't cost them their lives.

But we need to get out of here first.

There was something strange about the store they were in. The windows had been smashed, the shelves tussled, and the contents thrown around, but nothing had been taken. It was almost as if care had gone into making it seem as if it had been looted.

What an odd thing to do?

Suddenly, the arrows stopped coming. The idea that they'd run out was too much to hope for. No, the archers were on the move, which meant that they had to be, too, but faster.

CHAPTER 13

Approaching the fortified wall—made of thick logs whose tips had been cut into sharp spikes—all Nicolas could do was wonder where they'd gotten the wood from. He hadn't seen a serviceable tree in all his time here. Did the Underworld import lumber?

Why is this the thing that bothers me about approaching an ominous camp?

There was a good chance the answer to that was simply that he'd gone insane. No one could blame him.

Along the bottom of the wall, mounds of earth had been piled up and ranks of spikes planted into it, facing outwards. And this was the place they were hoping to go and have a reasonable chat about putting his soul back in his body.

'Finally,' Allius said with glee as he began some weird shuffling run to the gate. He very much reminded Nicolas of a familiar, servants of the vampires, when they'd still existed. Maybe a few had survived. It was their master's who'd burned in Yarringsburg. Would those left want revenge?

I'm dead. What else are they going to do to me? Besides, apparently there's a queue.

'It's a camp of some kind.' Auron looked uncertainly at the gate. What if this was some kind of double bluff by Allius, and they'd just walked to Vargas's camp? Wouldn't it be nice of him to escape his pursuers just to deliver himself to their door?

'I don't like the look of it.' It was quiet. Deathly quiet. Thinking of the word *death* here sent a shiver up where his spine had once been. How had Auron coped not having a flesh and blood body all that time? He was struggling with it. The knowledge that he had none of his organs or muscles or bones... That he was just...air? What was he?

Getting home is all that really matters right now.

'Me neither, kid.' The hero ran his tongue across his teeth before he spoke. 'Stay close.'

Allius banged on the door enthusiastically. The answer came not from behind the door, but from beneath them. Even as the shuffling started, Auron had his sword in hand.

Around them, mounds of dirt rose from the ground, the earth falling away to reveal a host of skeleton warriors, planted in the ground like the most terrifying flowers in history.

Deities, these things like lying in the ground. Well, of course they would. Where else would you generally find skeletons?

Outnumbering them twenty to one, the bone warriors formed shambling ranks, cutting off their escape as rusty spears pointed at them from all angles.

Nicolas looked to Auron for guidance—fighting monsters was his favourite activity, after all. For a second, the hero's eyes widened as he looked Nicolas up and down.

'Kid.' Auron's tone was laced with annoyance. 'Back at the ruins, did you pick up a sword?'

Shit. 'Um, no.'

His companion made a disappointed groaning sound. 'Do I actually need to tell you to do stuff like that? It's pretty elementary.'

In a hostile environment surrounded by enemies, any fool would pick up a sword. Unfortunately, he wasn't just any fool, he was a special kind of capering idiot. He tried to justify it for a moment by suggesting that he had a lot to cope with right now, but he gave up quickly, realising that sometimes, he was just stupid.

'Sorry.'

With an audible sigh, Auron put his sword into the ground and raised his hands in surrender.

What is he doing? He asked the hero as much.

'Buying time. I can't fight all of these *and* keep you safe. Let's walk the path, see where it goes, and step off it if the opportune moment comes along.' How was he so calm in such a terrifying situation? Lifeless eyes stared at him, and he was glad he was no longer in a form in which he could soil himself.

Or can the dead still... Nope. More pressing issues.

'Oh, I assure you that all is well,' Allius called with a broad grin as the gate opened behind him and more skeletons emerged. 'We just have to take precautions before presenting you to Lord Sha'then.'

Using the tip of the spear, one of the skeletons indicated the direction in which they were to go, a troop of the creatures falling in on either side of them. Both Nicolas and Auron kept their hands raised. Nicolas, for one, had no intention of getting jabbed by a rusted spear tip. Who knew what he might catch?

I'm dead. What can I possibly catch that's worse than that?

The pair were marched through the gate of the camp, which revealed rows of tents. A central aisle, flanked by lines of the skeleton warriors, seemed to be the only way to go. At the end of it, in what he assumed was the centre of the place, stood a large crimson tent with black banners draped across it. From this distance, Nicolas couldn't make out the image on the banners, but given where they were, skull iconography was a good guess.

'Maybe Sha'then can help you figure out your unfinished business?' He was talking to try to drown out the terror clenching a heart that no longer beat, rather than trying to actually look on the bright side.

'I figured that out when I saw your body.' Auron's matter-of-fact tone didn't seem to match a possibly amazing revelation. 'Silva killed me, but it's the people behind this conspiracy who put my death into motion. I need to find them and finish them before I end up chasing women in the Eternal Forest.'

'Virgins?' He'd heard someone say that once.

'Deities, I hope not.' Auron's chuckle wasn't appropriate for their serious situation. 'I want women who know what they're doing.'

Hopefully that doesn't turn out to be the last thing I hear either.

Allius's chest was puffed out as he led them down the aisle, Nicolas being careful to make no sudden moves. Near the end of the walkway, a figure emerged from the tent. This was no skeleton warrior—he had skin, for starters. He was tall, ridiculously tall, and gaunt. His body was encased in black armour with, unsurprisingly, a large screaming skull carved into the chest plate, similar to the one a black helmet was fashioned into. The figure's eyes were unnerving. No pupil, iris, or sclera, just two black orbs that watched them approach. They were in stark contrast to the figure's deathly white skin.

Allius got down to his knees and bowed. 'Oh, mighty Sha'then. I have returned from collecting the soul who made it here through the barrier, and I bring him and another before your most glorious of presences.'

Nicolas's knees weakened, and not from the long walk. Before him stood Sha'then, Lord of the Underworld, usually a name whispered in such fantastic Sunday service sentences as *'If you sin in life then thy eternal soul shalt be Sha'then's plaything. To be filleted and boiled until it is raw...'* And so on and so forth.

'You managed to survive the ambush then, Shambles,' Sha'then said coldly as he bade his vassal rise with a dismissive wave of his hand.

'Ambush?' Allius asked, aghast. 'You...you mean that you used me as bait to lure Vargas out?'

Sha'then didn't deign to respond. Instead, he tilted his head slightly as he scrutinised Nicolas in a very uncomfortable way, his blue lips pursed thoughtfully. There was an unnerving flicker of recognition then the Lord of the Underworld's face contorted with rage.

'*You*!' The shout came with an accusing finger thrust in his direction, Sha'then's eyes wide, blue veins appearing on his pale temples.

Oh no, what did I do? How could I have done anything, I've only just...

Striding forwards, he covered the distance between them easily with such long legs then wrapped a gauntleted hand around Nicolas's neck like a vice and hauled him into the air. For a few seconds, he made choking sounds, before remembering that he didn't breathe.

The pale man's fanged teeth were bared like an animal about to strike. 'This is all *your* fault!'

What's my fault? We've literally just met.

'But I didn't...' he stammered despite the grip around his throat.

'Yet you *did!*' Sha'then roared, flexing the clawed fingers on the gauntleted hand that currently wasn't choking him.

As much as Nicolas wanted to look away, his eyes betrayed him, forcing him to take in every single detail as Sha'then raised his hand to strike him. But it never came, because suddenly the Lord of the Underworld had a knife at his throat.

'Put him down, now,' Auron commanded calmly but firmly.

Where did he even get that knife?

Within a second, numerous weapons were pointed at them again, yet none of the skeletons seemed willing to risk attacking. Sha'then regarded the knife at his throat with distaste. After a moment's consideration, the gauntleted hand opened and Nicolas fell to the floor in a heap, rubbing his sore neck. A second after that, the knife had been swatted from Auron's hand, flung who knew where. Guards restrained Auron as Sha-then seethed above Nicolas. '*You* sent him here. This is *your* doing.'

'What are you talking about?' The question came from Auron. Personally, Nicolas was too terrified to speak. This guy had all the markings of someone you didn't upset, yet somehow, he had.

'Avus bloody Arex is who I'm talking about.'

That name. A new rush of dread grabbed him. That was the name of the necromancer who'd unleashed the vampire horde on Yarringsburg.

'What about him?' Auron asked, sounding frustratingly casual in a very serious situation.

'That...*boy*...both of you, actually, sent him down here.' Sha'then sneered. 'But you didn't just send me a necromancer, oh no, you sent me a necromancer empowered by a ridiculous amount of stolen wizard's energy, which he brought here with him.' The Lord of the Underworld let out a frustrated cry. 'And we weren't ready for that. So what does your *friend* do? He goes and stages a bloody revolution. Suddenly, the prisoners are loose, no one is getting tortured, and I'm fleeing my own citadel. *Me*. Sha'then. The *Lord of the Underworld*.'

Every moment Nicolas reached the point where this was all too much for him, something else was dropped on his shoulders.

'And now I'm stuck fighting a war when I should be spending my time sticking sharp things into deserving souls. And it's because of *you*!'

'Actually.' *Why am I speaking?* 'I didn't send him here. Sir Eldric killed him.'

Sha'then crouched down until he was nearly nose-to-nose with him. 'I know that, *fool*. But *King* Eldric isn't here, so I can't take this out on him. You are, though. And you softened him up for the kill, so you'll do.' Nicolas had hardly done that, but he'd annoyed Sha'then enough by his mere presence that he wouldn't dare to disagree with him.

'Take them to my tent,' Sha'then commanded his skeleton minions as he rose again. 'It's playtime.'

'But, my lord,' Allius protested, only to be silenced by a withering glare from said lord.

'Shambles,' the Lord of the Underworld sneered, 'all I require from you is my tools, not your opinion.'

Tools?

****

No arrows had come for a minute or two now, but Shift wasn't about to bet a single coin that no more would if they poked their head out. The archers might be on the move, but they weren't likely stupid enough not to leave people watching the door.

They were stupid enough to miss the first shot.

Good job too. Being pinned to a wagon by numerous arrows wasn't the way they wanted to go. When they'd bothered thinking about it, they wanted to go in an ambiguous way. Like, throwing themselves into a pit to retrieve a treasure they'd dropped during a daring escape.

Yes, that'd be fun.

It was something people would argue over for years to come. Those believing they were alive would go, *'Well, they obviously turned themselves into a flying creature and swooped out of the pit.'* Whilst those who believed them dead would counter with, *'But no one saw that, and there were so many witnesses.'* The others would go, *'Maybe a fly then'*. Only to hear, *'Everyone knows they couldn't change to something so small'* as a rebuttal. But no one would ever know for sure.

And yet I may still end up dying peppered by arrows if I don't stop daydreaming. They've been shit shots up 'til now, but that doesn't mean they won't get lucky.

'What do we think?' they asked the others.

'I think we need to move quickly,' Silva said, eyeing the back of the shop. 'I assume this shop has a backdoor, but it will be covered if we wait too long.'

If we're hiding in the only shop in all Etherius without a back door that would be some truly shitty luck...and that's not the kind of luck I'm accustomed to.

'Don't reckon they've given up and gone home then?' they remarked glibly.

'Highly unlikely,' Garaz replied. 'If these are indeed the men who attacked young Nicolas, then we are next on their list. Besides, they were patient enough to wait here for us this long. That demonstrates enough will for me to believe they will not just quit now. We are as much of a danger to them as he was.'

'*Is*,' Shift corrected tartly. 'Stop declaring him dead or you and I are going to *really* fall out.'

'What if they are villagers?' Garaz said, changing the subject. 'Should we not call out to them?'

'If they are, they likely believe we are aligned with whoever took their kin,' Silva replied. 'They will shoot first, no matter what we say.'

'Seeing as they fumbled the first shot so badly when we were sitting ducks, I'd be inclined to say it's the villagers,' Shift said thoughtfully. 'But if they are, they're scared and eager for revenge. Our only option is to get out of here and find out one way or the other. After that we can find a way to talk them down. Assuming it is the villagers.'

'We won't find out sitting here,' Silva declared. 'Now come on.'

Without waiting for an answer, the warrior crawled towards the back of the shop. Shift's theory about men on watch was confirmed as an arrow hit the shelving close to her.

Shift soon followed, crawling carefully through the debris on the shop floor. Glancing back, they could make out the silhouettes of figures on the other side of the street. They were too far away to identify properly, but they were approaching carefully, bows drawn, arrows ready to loose.

If it was me out there, I'd just burn us out. Thank the Deities none of them are that smart. Speaking of burning...

'Garaz.' When the orc looked at them, Shift nodded towards the approaching men.

With a flick of his staff, Garaz sent a fireball spinning out of the door and into the street, ensuring his aim was wide, just in case they were innocents. The men scattered, only to reform when the flames dissipated.

Moving with increased urgency, the trio made it behind the counter to find there was, indeed, a back door. It offered them both hope and calamity. No one would be sure which until it was open. Standing, Silva motioned to the others to wait whilst she checked it out. The warrior placed her hand on the door's handle, and Shift braced themselves to dive aside if it opened to admit a hail of arrows. Their muscles tensed as the handle turned slowly. They exhaled at the soft click as it opened.

Carefully, Silva pushed the door open and peered out. 'Looks clear,' the warrior whispered. 'But let me be sure.'

Silva stepped out of the store, sword at the ready. Shift prepared their body to change on a moment's notice. Fast and fierce would be the pick of the day.

The warrior looked left and right, before crumpling to the ground as something was dropped on her head from above.

'Silva, no!'

Shift ran forwards thoughtlessly, focused entirely on the need to check Silva. Up until the four archers appeared around the corner. In their first real glimpse of their attackers, it was clear they were no villagers. The men wore patchy, light armour, made for fast movement, and wore expressions of men not unused to killing. Shift had seen enough varieties of bandits in their time to know what these men were instantly. Grasping the door handle, Shift went to shut it, but a moment of guilt made them hesitate. Shutting Silva out was...just shitty.

That moment was all the archers needed. Shift's reluctance must've been as obvious as anything Nick ever did, and the drawn bows were all pointed at Silva.

Sons of whores.

Biting their lip and wishing terrible pain on each of them, Shift took their hand slowly from the handle and raised both arms in the air. Shift backed into the room, and several of the archers advanced, one making sure Silva was still covered.

Maybe they aren't so stupid after all.

Hearing creaking wood behind them, they guessed correctly that some had entered through the front as well.

'Sorry,' they whispered to Garaz as they came to a stop beside the orc, whose hands were raised too.

'Never apologise for compassion.' The orc smiled.

If only sentiment made me arrow proof. I stayed with these people long enough to learn some bad habits. When we get out of this...

Preceded by a hacking laugh, a figure appeared in the doorway, walking in with all the time in the world. Thumbs hitched into his belt, the man walked to the centre of the archers, each step coming with a clink of metal from the spurs on his boots. Looking at them, the figure gave them a small salute that came with a smug half-smile emerging from beneath his long, greasy hair.

'Long time, Shifty,' greeted the gravelly voice.

Oh shit.

Chapter 14

The metal shackles were cutting into his wrists, but he'd been hung up for so long that his arms had gone numb, so there was no pain. But there was plenty of that to come. And hanging around had given his imagination plenty of time to run wild about the forms in which this would come, as it had a tendency to do. Though he doubted his imagination was anywhere near Sha'then's when it came to devising new and shocking ways to inflict pain. Still, the situation was, in the politest term he could muster, dire.

Beside him, Auron look frustratingly casual.

Who's he trying to impress?

The flap of the tent wafted aside, and Sha'then entered. 'Ah, you're still here,' he remarked with a self-satisfied grin, Allius shuffling in behind him.

Funny.

The Lord of the Underworld approached, looking them up and down with a sneer, as if they were some mouldy vegetables he'd found in his pantry.

The door of the tent parted again, and a pair of skeletons marched in, carrying a long tray that they placed on the table before standing aside.

Nicolas's eyes widened.

Laid out on the tray was a plethora of sharp instruments, ranging from the practical to the exotic. The ones that worried him most were those whose uses he couldn't immediately fathom.

And they are going in me.

All he wanted to do right now was break the chains, swat the guards aside, and shake Sha'then until he sent both him and Auron back so he could find his parents and everyone else from Hablock. But that wasn't going to happen. Instead, he was about to suffer so much pain that the whipping he'd once endured would be almost relaxing by comparison.

Sha'then mused over the tray, scratching his pointed chin thoughtfully. 'Since your friend staged his little coup, I've had no opportunity to indulge my favourite pastime. Now the opportunity is here, I find myself unable to choose which implement to start with. I'm positively giddy.' Sha'then picked up a gleaming serrated blade, turned it around in his hand and then replaced it on the table.

Oh Deities, he said 'start with.'

'You know Avus Arex isn't our friend, right?' Auron said. 'One generally doesn't upend the schemes of one's friends, kill all his lackies, and send him here.'

'I do not care,' Sha'then said dismissively as his hand hovered over one implement then the other. *Please not the corkscrew one.* 'You've made this man my problem, and I'm about to reward you for your efforts and relieve the stress of having my realm turned upside down by a *necromancer*, of all things.' The Lord of the Underworld smiled for a moment. 'You know we have a special room for them here, where zombies, like the ones they made in life, consume their flesh over and over.' His harsh, gaunt face was overtaken by a dreamy smile. 'The best part is, those zombies are recruited from sinners sent to me who happened to be vegetarian.'

That's diabolical.

'And Avus didn't make it there?'

'Oh, he did,' Sha'then snarled. 'But he used his magic to make the zombies—and there were a fair few—serve him. He fought his way out, found Vargas and his little cohort, and the next thing I know, I'm fleeing for my life from my citadel with only *this* in tow.' He gestured at Allius, who gripped his book tightly as he kept his eyes low. Nicolas highly doubted he cared for being referred to as *this*. 'I find the irony that you, the bringers of my woe, are about to suffer at my hands when you aren't even supposed be here quite delicious,' the Lord of the Underworld mused as he slashed the air with a hook scythe. 'Sending you both through the barrier must've taken great effort.'

'Barrier?' Was Auron doing his best to keep Sha'then talking?

Nicolas wasn't sure that drawing out the time before the torture was a good thing. The anticipation might be as bad as the sensation... No, that was wrong. He'd learned that lesson when he'd been tied to a ship's mast and whipped.

'The necromancer has corrupted many of the souls here to his will, either willingly or not, gaining power from every one he turned.' The Lord of the Underworld sighed. 'I could hardly allow more to come here and swell his ranks, so I put a barrier between us and Etherius—the black cloud. I sealed the place off on the assumption my victory was quick and inevitable. It has been neither. Which has given me an ample amount of built-up frustration to work out on the two of you.'

It wasn't surprising the inmates had rebelled. Given the choice between eternal torture and revolution, even he might've joined the uprising. And he assumed those sent here were less mentally stable and more inclined to violence than he was.

'So now I camp here, fighting a war whilst souls who should pass on, either way, are stuck in Etherius.' Sha'then picked up a three-pronged instrument and examined it. Nicolas tried not to imagine where the prongs went. 'But I shall prevail sooner or later, then the natural order will be restored.'

'The ship,' Auron said with a sideways glance at him.

What? There's a boat around— Oh. King Ragus's ship.

King Ragus had been the ruler of Sarus until the faun murdered him on a diplomatic mission overseas. The group had found his wrecked ship and been attacked by the zombified crew. Initially, they'd assumed it was a trap set by the faun, but he'd seemed ignorant of it. Now they knew the truth of it. It also explained all the recent talk about the dead rising everywhere.

'So they're all just stuck up there?' Auron finally appeared shaken. Not surprising, given that he knew what it was like to roam the earth, dead but never really moving on.

'Do not fear.' Sha'then laughed. 'Once this is done, I shall collect all those due me and send the rest to the Eternal Forest. You have so much more to fear in the here and now.' To reinforce his point, he picked up a long, curved hook from the table, glaring at them menacingly through the loop in it.

'And, uh, how's it going? The war?' He had to keep stalling. He did *not* want to experience that hook.

Sha'then looked at him in surprise. He guessed he hadn't been expecting that question. 'Poorly,' he finally admitted, petulantly. 'I have an army of skeleton warriors. They are good for guarding prisoners and inspiring terror, but they make a poor army in the field. Unless I have overwhelming numbers, I usually lose.' The Lord of the Underworld set his jaw indignantly for a moment. 'I sensed your presence when you entered my realm, so I dispatched my warriors. I knew the necromancer's curiosity at the barrier being broken would be enough that he'd send that idiot Vargas, so I laid a trap. I even tried to sweeten the pot with *that.*' Allius, who was sat quietly in the corner of the room, looked thoroughly hurt by the remark. 'Judging by the fact you are here and none of my warriors have returned, I take it that it didn't succeed.'

All Nicolas had seen was the giant skeleton collapsing, but that had most likely set the tone for the rest of the battle. He wanted to shrug but couldn't in his uncomfortable position. 'I didn't see. But Vargas seems a pretty good fighter.'

Beside him, Auron scoffed loudly. 'The Underworld he is! Decent amateur at best.'

'*Hey*,' Sha'then bellowed, slamming the device he held into the table with enough force that it stayed there when he withdrew his hand. 'Do not use the name of my realm as a curse word.' The hero appeared unrepentant. 'Anyway, enough of this chatter.' The Lord of the Underworld began to approach Nicolas, Grinning sadistically.

'But, my Lord,' Allius protested meekly from the corner, 'they aren't supposed to be here. The book says—'

'Silence, worm,' Sha'then snarled, coming to a halt. 'It does not matter if the book says they are supposed to be dancing atop a rainbow. They are here, and they are *mine.*' As Allius squirmed at the rebuke, Sha'then walked slowly around the table with a simple knife in hand.

All those exotic instruments, and he chooses a plain old knife?

Nicolas had no idea why that bothered him, but it was the only coherent thought in his otherwise panicked mind. His eyes focused on the blade, looking up only briefly to note the bloodlust in Sha'then's cold eyes.

As the Lord of the Underworld reached him, he grabbed the top of his shirt with a gauntleted hand and tore it from his body. His whole torso tensed in fear as Sha'then's hand pulled back, ready to strike. Behind him, the faun sat cross-legged on the table, hands resting on his chin as he watched with enthusiasm.

'You need a general.'

'*What*?' Sha'then asked, placing the tip of the knife under his chin.

Nicolas had no idea *what*, he'd just blurted out the first thing that came to mind. And now he had to somehow build on it. He cleared his throat to buy himself a second. He really hoped he could be eloquent now, because his throat seemed to be closing around the words he wanted to speak, and he only partially knew what he was going to say next anyway.

'You say your skeleton soldiers are rubbish, but that's all you have. What you need are generals to...um...lead your army. Apply a little creative thinking.'

The Lord of the Underworld seemed to mull this over for a few moments, the knife hand dropping. 'Go on,' he purred finally.

'That there is Auron of Tellmark,' he said, nodding towards his companion. 'The Dawnblade. The guy who finished Vargas Quell off. And me, I was a big part of defeating the necromancer the first time around. Who better to lead your armies into battle?'

'The kid's right.' Auron hopped down from his shackles, rubbing his wrists as Sha'then started and Allius cried out with shock. 'With the right leader, we can turn your defeat into a stunning victory, and I have a *long* history of kicking Vargas's ass.'

'How are you free?' Nicolas asked in awe.

'Kid,' the hero chuckled with a raised eyebrow, 'Shift didn't invent lockpicking, you know. I was waiting to perform a heroic last-minute rescue, but your plan is better.'

Right. Nicolas turned back to the Lord of the Underworld. 'If your current strategies aren't working, you need to do something different. And between the two of us...' He trailed off, letting the implications he'd planted in Sha'than's mind bear fruit.

'That...' Sha'then was wide-eyed as he considered the proposal. 'That actually makes some sense.' The Lord of the Underworld turned back to his desk, sweeping his black cape behind him. 'Release them...well, him.'

'Nice work, kid,' Auron whispered beside him.

As the skeleton unshackled him, Nicolas made the short drop to the floor. It turned out his legs were as numb as his arms and instantly collapsed under his weight.

How did Auron jump down like it was nothing?

Sat on the floor of the tent, he rubbed his limbs to get the feeling back into them. What exactly had he just gotten himself into?

No, he needed to focus on what he'd gotten himself out of—which was a date with that knife—and then on getting this war done so he could go home and find his family.

****

With a self-satisfied chuckle, the man ran his hand through his long, greasy-looking grey hair, removing it from his eyes with a grin to match the chuckle. 'Aren't you a welcome sight for these old eyes, Shifty.'

Deities, give me strength.

'Mace.' They spat the name, because it was a name worth spitting, much to Mace's apparent amusement.

'Same ol' Shifty. Cocky and defiant.' Mace's laugh sounded more like a wheeze as it escaped his lips.

He's so old already. Why won't he just die.

'You know this gentleman?' Garaz asked, looking as if he wanted to introduce himself to Mace using his fists. It was a common reaction to the thief lord.

'Know me? Me and ol' Shifty used to work together.' Mace chuckled. 'Until this 'un got an attack of conscience or something and double-crossed us.'

They snorted derisively. 'I didn't double-cross you. You always claimed to *'rob the rich to give to the poor.'* You just never actually gave it to the poor. I was fulfilling your oath. A *thank you* would be apt.'

That's the problem with Mace: it's all about the show, from his hollow words to those stupid metal things on his boots. It's all pathetic pageantry.

Mace rested one of his boots on a nearby shelf and looked at them with bemusement. 'And which poor soul, pray tell, did you give what you took to? What orphanage or hospital or poorhouse reaped the benefits of your thievery?'

This was uncomfortable. 'Well, I was poorer than you.'

Am I destined to become like Mace if I stay with the Guild?

Another wheezing laugh. 'Your moral high ground ain't so high now, girl.'

They took a step forward. They hated giving him the reaction he wanted but calling them *girl* was one of their triggers, and he knew it. Bow strings were drawn.

'Now, now, boys.' Mace gestured for his men to lower their weapons. 'Old Shifty's just full of hot air. *She* knows not to do anything silly or *change* into anything silly. Just a bit of impotent rage in *her*.'

Mace's men chuckled.

Okay, you want to play that game... They could push buttons too. 'Valerius told me a story or two about impotence.'

Ha.

Now it was Mace's turn to step forward. The back hand caught them right across the jaw. Of course he was wearing a glove with metal-studded knuckles. The blow hurt, but the satisfaction at getting the reaction numbed the pain considerably.

'You never did know when to shut your mouth, girl,' Mace snarled.

They spat the blood in their mouth on his boot. 'I'm not a girl, you chest of dicks. And if you think you're getting your gold back...' They shrugged. 'I spent it.'

The thief lord shook his head with a chuckle. 'I guessed that, girl. I'm not here to get money back from you, I'm here to make money *from* you. There's quite the bounty on your pretty head. And that of your orc friend and the barely armoured lady on the floor there. Between the three of you, I'm set up to retire nicely.'

'Bounty?' Garaz asked.

'Seems you got more enemies than lil' ol' me.' Mace smiled. He looked like someone's grandpa, but they knew exactly how vicious he was. 'We were approached. Told ol' Shifty would be here and offered a hefty purse to ensure you were imminently killed. The money they're paying, I'd go after a king, but with you, I get the added bonus of settling a score. Woulda had ya in the wagon, but one of the boys got a weak string finger.'

He hasn't mentioned taking the villagers. And he'd definitely brag about that. Could that have been...someone else?

Quickly, they scanned the bowmen around them. Some they recognised—the same miserable hangers-on who'd always run with Mace, cut-throat scum who'd never do any better in life because in their opinion, they were already living their best life. There were a few new faces who looked perfectly at home with the rest of the group and...

Oh.

They fought to contain a smirk as one of the group offered them a barely perceptible nod.

Hello, Mr Weak String Finger. Or maybe that wasn't the case at all?

'But it's all good,' Mace blathered on. 'Gives us a chance for this here reunion. And it means I can make you suffer a little first. That's always fun.' Yup, there it was. He did like to make people suffer. You didn't need to kill the residents to rob a manor; there were ways to do it with no bloodshed. Not Mace's style, though. That was the main reason they'd left his crew. Thievery was one thing. Thievery and a body count was something else entirely. There was a pang of guilt. They could've helped those people back then. They could've smothered the goblin anus in his sleep and saved a lot more lives. It was odd how they'd never really thought about that before. Or maybe they had, but it was buried deep down, only coming out when they'd met a certain boy who'd crawled into a vampire's nest to help them with no experience.

Nick.

Where was he now? Was Auron with him? Were they both okay? Maybe he was on his way here now to attempt to rescue them in his sweet, bungling way. The one where he actually managed to save the day regardless.

Not now. Right now, I need to focus on making sure the three of us are okay instead of dreaming about my knight in ill-fitting armour.

'I have always wondered.' *Oh, he's still talking then? Fantastic.* 'As you can change form, could you grow back a limb if someone...removed one? I think an experiment's in order, what ya reckon, lads?'

The *lads* murmured in agreement.

If I turn my arms into tentacles, how long would it take to choke the life out of you?

As pleasant as the imagery was, there were bows trained on them, Garaz, and the still-unconscious Silva. They couldn't guarantee their companions' safety and they certainly wouldn't do anything to speed up their deaths.

What to do though? I've only got a few minutes left with all my limbs attached. Think. Think, think, think.

Okay, what did they have to hand? They had an orc who could throw fireballs. Useful. They had a *can-do* attitude. Useful. They had Silva. Useless at the moment. They had an ally. Maybe useful. Mace had the numbers and bows trained on them. Less useful. There was no obvious way out of this. What Shift needed was something to tip the scales. A distraction, maybe?

They jumped forwards at the sudden and harsh sound of splintering wood. Shards were thrown across the room, and Shift threw their arms over their head to shield their neck as cries of confusion echoed from all around them.

As the chaos died down, a stunned silence replaced it. Three orcs had burst through the door of the shop...literally.

Useful? Useless?

Definitely dangerous.

CHAPTER 15

*I*t's an improvement anyway.

Now the table inside the tent had a large parchment map covering it, instead of numerous implements of pain. But as much as they'd convinced the Lord of the Underworld that they were useful, they were still in a very precarious position. Sha'then appeared indignant that he'd lost his opportunity to engage in some torturing and might change his mind at any given moment. He seemed the type who was a slave to his whims—not a good quality in someone with access to so many varied sharp objects. And also, Nicolas had just agreed to lead an army...to war.

Sha'then studied the map with pursed lips. He leant over, looking at the details as if each one personally offended him. Auron flicked his gaze from landmark to landmark, obviously studying it intently.

'The enemy has taken the Mountain of Skulls and the Canyons of Torment,' the Lord of the Underworld explained. 'The Sea of Sorrow is firmly ours, as is the Plateau of Pain, but may not be for long. The main battles are currently taking place on the Desert of Despair, which is where we are now. If we give any more ground, they'll have free rein to advance on the Cities of Sinners, and then I may as well just surrender as he will have access to thousands of souls and his power will become Deity-like.' From the look on Sha'then's face, surrender wasn't an option. 'Bad enough I lost the Citadel of Anguish, my seat of power. I will not give Avus Arex another inch.'

Despite the gravity of the situation, Nicolas couldn't help but chuckle. 'Sea of Sorrow? Canyons of Torment?' He studied the points on the map. 'Who names these places? I mean, really.' When he looked to Auron for support, the hero was making a face that suggested he'd just said something very stupid.

Sha'then fixed him with a cold glare that made his entire soul shrink. 'I do,' the Lord of the Underworld growled. 'As lord of this realm, it falls to me to name the places contained within it, which I have done to reflect

107

the theme of this land. I cannot very well have a...Garden of Tickles...in a place that's supposed to inspire *fear* and *despair*! Maybe I should call this trail here,' his finger slammed at a point on the map, 'the Rainbow Road to appease you. Or I could just remove your complaining lips from your mouth?'

He shook his head vehemently. No issue here.

Beside him, Auron sighed. It probably didn't do to insult the one who'd spared you from being tortured. But he hadn't known he was insulting him. And in his defence, they were stupid names.

'If I may continue with my briefing?'

He wasn't about to interrupt Sha'then a second time, so he nodded sheepishly.

'We know they have forces in the Caverns of Woe, here.' The Lord of the Underworld indicated a point on the map in the centre of the desert, whilst glaring at Nicolas, daring him to say something. When he was assured of no response, Sha'then continued. 'They're planning to launch an offensive to the north, breaking for the cities, and I will not have it. You two shall lead a host of my warriors into the cave network and drive these pests out, preferably killing every last one of them.'

Caves. Why was it always caves, or tunnels, or underground lairs? There were plenty of places above ground to populate. Nicolas supposed it was an *evil living in the shadows* type of thing. Mind you, it was pretty dark wherever you went here, and everything seemed pretty evil. Although, Sha'then didn't seem too bad. More of a pouty child than anything, though Nicolas imagined he'd be upset if his realm was overthrown. Then a question occurred to him. Once it was in his mind, it wouldn't leave. As much as he didn't want to ask it, he found his mouth opening anyway. 'Aren't you a...Deity? Can't you just smite them all or something?'

Sha'then's mouth did that thing people's did sometimes when they didn't like the answer to the question they'd been asked. The Lord of the Underworld shuffled awkwardly before responding. 'I am not, *technically*, a Deity.'

Well, that was news to him. There were shrines to Sha'then and everything. Plenty of worshippers would be quite upset to hear that, in fact.

'As Lord of this domain, I wield Deity-*like* power, but I am not quite...that. My power comes from the souls I hold sway over in this realm. And since your necromancer ousted me and took a hefty portion of said souls, my ability to smite anything is...lacking somewhat.'

So Sha'then had lost his power as well as his kingdom. He learned something new every day. There was a strange pang of sympathy for someone who'd just threatened to cut his lips off.

'I am still mighty and fearsome and wield power beyond anything on your mortal plain.' Nicolas hadn't asked, but okay. Then Sha'then shook his head and laughed harshly. 'Though maybe not as mighty as I'd hoped if I cannot even conjure a serviceable barrier between the worlds of life and death. Those who sent you here must be truly powerful.'

During Nicolas's brief meeting with the Oracle, he hadn't thought much of the power of the man—he'd been too overwhelmed by how little he matched up to the myth. And as for how *he'd* gotten here…Who could tell what power that creature, Koth, wielded? Not that he wanted to think about the demon at all.

I just pray that my parents are still alive.

'And our strategy is?' Auron interjected, obviously wishing to get back on task.

'Swamp them with skeleton warriors until they're all dead,' Sha'then replied bitterly. 'Anything above that…you're the generals. Good luck with them.' Dismissively, the Lord of the Underworld gestured to one of his skeletons. If the creature was offended, it gave no sign. In fact, it gave no sign of anything beyond just…standing there.

Auron didn't seem pleased with this idea at all. That made him worry. The hero turned and looked at him, but at the same time didn't really look *at* him. After a few moments of pursing lip movements, Auron finally smiled, clicking his fingers in the air.

'Hey, Sha'then.' The knowing smile was reassuring. 'The kid here told me you had a giant skeleton monster emerge from underground. Got any more of those?'

'I command a mighty and numerous host of the undead,' Sha'then replied haughtily.

Auron shrugged. 'Was that a yes or a no?'

'Yes.'

'Great.' Auron grinned. 'I'm going to need one. And the kid and I need some armour and weapons. I would prefer them not to be rusty old crap like these guys are wearing.' For emphasis, he tapped the chest plate of the nearest skeleton. A blizzard of rust flakes fell from it.

Armour and weapons? We aren't leading from the back then?

Nicolas was sure generals led from the back. Leading from the front meant violence, which meant killing. He wasn't sure he could do it, even as a necessity. He rubbed his fingertips nervously. One of the caves on the map became the faun's face, his head shaking as he looked at Nicolas in disgust.

Surely if I just keep killing bad guys, eventually it'll stain my soul, like some kind of cumulative total or something?

Either way, he wasn't sure his conscience could handle it. Yet he had to fight. If he didn't, he'd never be able to go home and save—

Quickly, he pushed the thought to the back of his mind. If he had to do this, he had to focus, and pondering what ifs would drive him crazy. All of this had him on the brink already. He was in the middle of a war. He had to concentrate on trying to survive and get home. Or he could...

'My parents, Elsbeth and Ronald Carnegie. Are they in the book?' he asked Allius, dreading the response he'd get.

The hunched man didn't answer right away, instead flicking the pages. The longer it took, the more hopeful he became. 'No they aren't,' he answered finally.

Nicolas closed his eyes, his body sagging slightly with the sudden relief. He knew this could change in an instant, so he still had to get home and find them as quickly as possible, but right now he could cry tears of joy.

That's one less question playing on my mind to distract me from what I have to do.

'I take it you have a good plan?' he asked Auron, unable to suppress his smile.

The hero smiled broadly, then looked at him in mock offence. 'Kid, I only have good plans.' Then Auron fixed the Lord of the Underworld with a determined stare. 'When we win this, the kid goes home.' It wasn't a question.

'*If* you win this for me, I suppose I can facilitate that.'

Sha'then didn't sound convincing, but even a slight hope was still hope.
****

The frame of the doorway to the general store was a ruin of broken wood. Its debris littered the floor as if the three orcs had attempted to muscle through it at the same time. Even for orcs, they were *big*. Between the three, they filled their portion of the room, the leader of the trio evident by simply being larger than the other two. The gold plating around the almost elephant-like tusks was also a dead giveaway. And the recently severed human head hanging from a rope around his neck was a nice touch. Very intimidating.

Three pairs of malicious red eyes took in the room.

'Shagraz.' Garaz's voice came out as a hoarse whisper. The orc had visibly paled as his yellow eyes fixed on the biggest orc.

The lead orc's eyes turned to Garaz, and the corners of his mouth curled into a malicious smile. 'Garaz,' he growled. 'Found you.'

Seems there's some history there.

Was this orc a friend or foe? No, that was a stupid question. Everything about him screamed foe.

Like we don't already have enough bad guys here.

'Ain't no business o' yours here, greenskins,' Mace hollered, looking decidedly less confident than he sounded.

His men had quickly repositioned themselves to cover the orcs with their bows. Shift looked at the size of the notched arrows compared to the size of their targets. The archers best be amazing shots, or very lucky, because it'd take more than one arrow to fell any of the three. Mace might have had the numbers, but the orc leader had a battle axe whose blades were the size of their torso.

'This *is* my business, humie. Gots to 'ave a word with this 'ere runt about what it means to be orky.' All that time, Shagraz had his eyes set on Garaz. Now he regarded Mace properly and with plenty of contempt. 'Stay out o' my way, and I may let you keep yer skin.'

Now, this did seem like a bad situation, stuck between two parties who meant them harm. But if you were an opportunist, as they so often were, then you could see the potential. Both sides wanted them—well, one only wanted Garaz. But they knew Mace well enough to know how greedy he was. That was something they could play on. Plus, they had a secret ally.

'I suppose you could just lose a third of the bounty and keep your skin.' They tried to make the comment off-hand, even throwing in a theatrical shrug.

'I know what you're doing.' Mace's tone was frustrated, not necessarily about the fact that they'd tried it, but the fact that it was working like a charm. It was obvious. Greed was a powerful motivator, and Mace was its bitch. The thief lord addressed the orc, 'You gotta appreciate, friend, that I got the numbers here.'

'Only 'til I kill 'em all,' Shagraz snarled.

The orc could do it. Correction: they were sure the orc was *going* to do it, regardless. These were definitely the more stereotypical orc they were used to: dumb and violent.

Wow, Garaz really is a shining beacon of his race...when he isn't angrily ripping toad creatures in half.

Mace seemed to come to the same conclusion Shift had. He raised his arm, ready to give the signal to loose their arrows. His men pulled their bow strings until they were as taut as they were going to get, and they had themselves a standoff. Which side would make the first move? And how could they antagonise the situation? Mace wasn't stupid, and still had bows covering Garaz and themselves. They'd stoked the fire; the tricky part would be getting out of here unburned.

'Try it, and you'll find yerself full o' arrows.' It was impressive how Mace was threatening someone twice his size.

No, not impressive. Stupid. But good for us, all the same.

Shagraz laughed, a deep bass sound that shook the walls. 'You fink those lil sticks will 'urt me? I pick my teef with fings bigger than those.'

As the pair traded big man talk, they tried to catch Garaz's eye. It wasn't easy. Their companion's stare was fixed on this Shagraz. In the end, they had to risk a small kick to his heel. Thankfully, doing it led to no arrow in the back, *and* it got the orc's attention. Breaking away from his staring, Garaz looked at them out of the corner of his eye, whilst they made a few gestures that they hoped translated as *'slyly conjure a fireball for a distraction.'* Slowly, the orc gave an almost imperceptible nod. They hoped he was up to this, because he certainly didn't look it. Their faith in him was continually shaken lately.

It wasn't until Garaz moved his hand behind his back and whispered under his breath that they knew the message had been received. They looked to their secret ally and gave a slight nod, which was returned.

Okay, the pieces are moving. Now we just need the luck of the Deities themselves, and we may just get out of this.

'I'll tell ya straight, orc. Get outta here while the gettin's good.' Mace was reaching the end of his patience now, his voice irate as he pointed towards the door. Good. That meant he was entirely focused on the orcs and not them.

They dared a glance towards the open back door of the shop. Silva was still laid out on the floor, with an archer covering her. But the guard was more concerned about the orcs and not paying enough attention to notice that Silva's eyes were wide open. Shift caught her eye, and Silva winked.

This is all coming together nicely.

'Maybe I will need dem arrows, afta all,' Shagraz drawled as he looked at his followers. 'I'm about to 'ave a lot o' man flesh between my teef.'

The other two orcs laughed evilly.

The pot was well and truly stirred. Now to just break this standoff. As pissed as Mace was, they knew he didn't really fancy the idea of tangling with the orcs. Their race could be brutal when provoked, and these three looked as malicious as they came. But whilst the orcs appeared dumb and angry, they also seemed to appreciate the six bows pointed towards them.

That won't do at all.

Beside them, Garaz signalled he was ready. The eyes of the bowmen supposed to be watching them were firmly on the orcs. They gave a half-smile and nodded to their companion.

In a swift motion, Garaz raised his hand, launching the fireball into the air. It had been small, anything bigger would've been noticed, but it'd do. Behind them, their secret ally leapt forward, a small knife in each hand.

Before the bowmen watching both Shift and Garaz could react, he cut the tightly pulled strings on the bows, the arrows falling to the floor limply.

As the fireball struck the ceiling of the shop, it shattered into a bright flash that lit up the room briefly, causing cries of confusion, and the twanging of bows as arrows were loosed in surprise. Feral roars of pain followed.

Time to move.

Quickly, they spun around, driving their knee into the groin of their guard, whose eyes were on his arrow lying on the wooden floor. Hard kneecap connected with soft tissue, and the man instantly crumpled to the floor, groaning in pain. The *'oof'* sound they'd elicited was satisfying.

Garaz swatted his guard aside with a vicious backhand blow that launched him from his feet, and they quickly grabbed their weapons and made a bolt for the open door, Shift hauling their secret ally by his sleeve to get him to follow.

Silva's guard was already on the floor with his head at an odd angle to his neck whilst the lithe warrior woman was using another's head to beat the door frame like a drum.

Behind them there were roars and shouts. As they passed the last piece of shelving before freedom, blood splattered across the wood.

The orcs have gone to work then.

They risked a brief glance back, but it was hard to make out any detail at all. People were moving too fast trying to get into or flee the fight. The room was filled with the din of combat, made by overlapping cries and movement and the clanging of weapons. Before they looked away, they were unlucky enough to see one of Mace's men bisected by Shagraz's axe. Nick would've thrown up at the sight. Even they were queasy.

Shift only paused in their flight to check on Silva quickly. Lines of blood trailed down one of her cheeks from where the rock had struck her. Judging by the fact that she was still smashing the same archer's head against the door frame, which now had a bloody indent in it, she was pretty sour about it.

'You okay?'

Silva nodded in response, though the warrior didn't seem completely steady on her feet. Either way, they grabbed her and ran down the alley-way, away from the sounds of carnage coming from inside the general store.

CHAPTER 16

The rhythmic thumping of two hundred pairs of feet behind him was disconcerting. Every instinct told Nicolas to run, but the skeletons weren't chasing him. They were following him. Because he was leading them. *He* was leading an army. Once upon a time, the idea of any of this would've been ridiculous, but now things like this were becoming the norm.

I don't want to think of it as marching to war. I'm marching to freedom so I can get back to Etherius and help those who are relying on me. Besides, Auron's doing all the leading. I'm just...giving moral support.

'What weapon was Vargas carrying when you saw him?' Was Auron interested or had he just noticed Nicolas's anxiety and wished to distract him from it? 'Be nice to be ready for him when we meet up. Wouldn't make a difference, of course, his soul is mine, but always good to be prepared.'

'A...um...a sword.' He tried to think back to his encounter with the warrior. So much had happened in such a short time that some of the details were still hazy, and he had to force the images into his head, though this one was easier—Vargas's impressive blade standing out from every other rusted sword they'd encountered so far. 'It had a demon-head handguard.' The memory of the leering demonic face made him shiver for some reason.

Auron's head snapped round in confusion. 'That's the sword he carried in life. He called it *Heroes' Bane*. Stupid name. How did he get that down here with him?'

All he could do was shrug. These sort of matters were way beyond him, and the rules of this place made no sense anyway.

Auron's jaw set for a second before a smile appeared on his face. 'When we face him,' the hero began with a slight thrill in his voice, 'that sword of his splits into two swords. It's one of those things that's pretty neat when you see it the first time, but every time after that it gets less and less interesting. Do me a favour, kid. Pretend you're unimpressed when you see it. It'll really upset him.'

He was sure he'd be too concerned about not getting stabbed by either of the swords to worry about acting or being impressed, but if it made Auron happy... 'Sure.' Hesitantly, he continued. 'So, I know he was a bad guy, but what did Vargas do to get sent down here?' He was definitely asking to distract himself from his anxiety.

Auron laughed aloud. 'Pick a crime, any one, and I'm sure he did it at some point. He certainly liked variety. Though his personality would've damned him to this place without the crimes.'

'And you killed him?'

'Like I said before, he overstepped, made it very personal,' Auron's face fixed in a grimace as he accessed whatever memory the question had conjured. 'Until then, he'd been a constant, yet elusive, annoyance. But after that, I made it my focus to track him down. Finished him off a month before we met.'

'That must've been satisfying.'

'I've always tried to take as little satisfaction from killing villains as possible.' Auron smiled thinly. 'There is always that...thrill for me, vanquishing evil. But it isn't because I'm taking a life as much as it's because in doing so, I'm saving another down the line, someone worth saving, or avenging someone who should still be alive. If that makes sense.' Based on the way Auron generally talked, the answer shocked him a little. 'I know how I make it sound in my stories, but to me, they're people who just need killing. Vargas just begged for it more than the rest, is all.'

'So you kill people because they need to die?'

Auron looked at him with a sympathetic smile. 'This is heading towards the faun again, isn't it?' Nicolas knew he was being repetitive, but having to fight and kill was a huge concept to get his head around. He needed to make sure he fully understood it, and the implications, or his guilt could end up turning him into a broken husk. 'The world is a violent place, kid, and a lot of people get hurt. We don't always have the option of taking every evildoer to a nice, ordered trial for execution or imprisonment. It'd be neat if we could, but what we do demands a certain amount of natural justice. Like the necromancer. What was he in the middle of doing when King Eldric gutted him? Do you think the king loses sleep every night about being a murderer? Do you think any of those who survived his rampage would trade places with him?'

It suddenly occurred to Nicolas that maybe he kept rehashing this not due to anxiety, but because he knew Auron's reasoning was working. He just had to keep hearing it to chip away at his fear of taking a life, and the ridiculous guilt about the ones he'd already taken. 'An argument could be made that I'm being a little overdramatic.'

Auron laughed heartily. 'Kid, you and overdramatic go together like a knight and his horse.' *Harsh.* 'Think on this. If you ever meet this Koth thing again, are you going to try to escort him to jail?'

If I ever meet Koth again, I'll die...again.

'A lot of murderers get sent here.'

Auron turned around in shock, as if he'd forgotten Allius was with them. Nicolas didn't like the suspicion with which his companion looked at the smaller fellow, though it was clear Sha'then had sent his servant to watch them. 'What about you, Shambles?' Auron asked. 'What brought you to this fine place?'

'We all make mistakes,' Allius replied indignantly.

Auron cocked an eyebrow. 'Is that right, Shambles?' The hero had picked up on the name from Sha'then.

'Can you not call him Shambles?' Nicolas asked. 'His name is Allius.'

Now the raised eyebrow was pointed at him as Allius smiled happily. 'Is this a *Nick Carnage* thing?'

'Well...yes.' *No sense lying about it.* 'But it *is* his name.'

The hero let out a single laugh, shaking his head. 'Kid, I love you, but you are a wagon full of issues.'

He what?

Was he flushing? No, he couldn't be. He had no blood.

Auron meant 'love' like...companions love, right? Not 'companions' companions. Friends. Of course he did. He's slept with hundreds of women of all kinds of species. He wouldn't...not with... Because I don't—

'Kid,' the hero interrupted with a smirk. 'I can literally *hear* you thinking. I meant like a knight loves a faithful squire.'

Squire? Charming.

Auron caught his eye and grinned.

I'm being teased. Fantastic.

Nicolas shook his head until he felt a small tug at his sleeve. 'Thank you for naming me correctly,' Allius whispered with pride. 'I have been treated very poorly since I arrived here, and your kindness...doesn't go unnoticed.'

He... I just assumed he was a denizen of this place because he looks... Well...um...

'So you are a damned soul then?' Auron asked. 'What did you do? Scare the local livestock to death with that face?'

'No,' Allius said with a grimace. 'I'll have you know that in life I was very handsome. And a prince. I was very sought after.'

'So Sha'then made you look like that?' Nicolas asked.

'Yes,' Allius whispered, his gaze dropping to the floor. 'I was due to be married. It was to forge an alliance between kingdoms, as was custom. Now, I understand princely duty and all, but she was very ugly and way below my standard. It was the day before our wedding, and I begged and pleaded with my father to cancel the marriage, but he wouldn't. He got very upset for me demanding it, for some reason.' Watching the hunched figure shrug was strange. 'I decided that if the princess just happened to die in her sleep, the marriage couldn't go ahead. So, I snuck into her chamber and smothered her with a pillow. Unfortunately, a servant saw me, so I had to run them down and kill them. But another servant saw that, so I had to kill them too. But then two servants witnessed that, and things were getting out of hand, so I just burned down the castle. No witnesses then. Sadly, I stood too close to admire my own handiwork, and a tower fell on me.'

'Handsome, not smart,' Auron whispered, shaking his head.

Allius sighed. 'If my father had just cancelled the wedding, none of that would've happened.'

'Um, yes,' Nicolas said uncertainly. 'Must've been very difficult for you...I suppose.'

Allius turned and beamed at him. 'Thank you. Finally, someone who understands.'

Not even slightly.

'Before the two of you get too cosy,' Auron interjected. 'I think we're here.'

Ahead of them, the ground rose into a hill strewn with hard rock faces. Even from here, he could see the black holes like giant boils on a face that led to a network of caves running through it.

Somewhere in that network of caves was an army. One that would now be waiting for them. They were hardly creeping up on it. He doubted they could if they tried, with the amount of racket the skeletons made on their march, between the rattling of bones, stomping of boots and clanking of armour. Hopefully the element of surprise didn't matter. Auron had outlined his plan briefly, and on parchment, it seemed sound enough.

But what do I know about military strategy?

Auron appeared unmoved by the looming hill on the horizon and what it represented. 'So that's it then. We'll have this done and get you home before nightfall.'

Something was wrong with that sentence. It took a minute for Nicolas to put his finger on it. 'Don't you mean *us*?'

'Hopefully.' Auron smiled. 'But most likely, this was a one-way trip for me.'

What? 'What do you mean?'

'I don't have a body to go back to, so chances are I'll be stuck here. Should be fun, plenty of evildoers to fight. I can replay some of my greatest battles. No women that I've seen so far, though.' The hero looked away thoughtfully. 'That's a conundrum. I imagine the ones who are down here aren't interested in the kind of interactions I'd be hoping for.'

How can he say that so casually?

'Why would you come here knowing you might not be able to go home?' he cried.

The hero looked at him like it was obvious. 'For you, kid. You don't deserve to be here. If I have to make a trade for that then so be it.' Auron looked him in the eye with pride. 'Despite your never ending self-deprecation, you're worth it.'

He's sacrificing himself, for me?

Even the notion that someone would do that for him was...unthinkable. For Auron to come here knowing it was a one way trip to save his soul burned through so many of the doubts Nicolas had about himself.

As irksome as the hero could be at times, Nicolas couldn't help but look up to him. And though he was technically no longer part of Etherius, he'd remained for a reason. More importantly than that, he was Nicolas's friend.

A determination was roused in him. Yes, he needed to get back to save his parents, but he'd do his darndest to ensure that Auron made the trip back with him.

****

'Where are you going?'

Shift turned to Silva. Had the head wound caused damage serious enough for her to ask such a stupid question? 'Away,' they replied finally.

'The fight is over there,' the warrior said, inclining her head back towards the shop, from which emanated a sizeable amount of banging and crashing.

'Which I thought we were fleeing from.' They shrugged. 'Am I wrong? Because I really don't think I am.'

Their eyes flicked to Garaz for support, but for some reason, the orc was staring blankly into space.

Just what we need. The one who can throw fireballs stupefied.

'Are we not going?' the archer at their side asked.

'I thought we were.' *But apparently, I'm incorrect.*

'And you think we should just leave all these villains running around?' Silva asked. The warrior's face was set in that unshakeable grimace of hers.

Well, I'm still going to try to shake it.

'They sound like they're all happily killing each other.' They found the scream that suddenly echoed through the shop door to be pleasingly supportive of their statement.

'Someone's going to be left standing,' the warrior retorted. 'That person may have information on things such as…' Silva tapped her chin thoughtfully in the very sarcastic manner Shift was normally famed for. '…who attacked Nicolas, who stole the villagers, and who sent this scum after us.'

Shift looked back towards the door and exhaled. 'Sometimes, I preferred you when you were skulking around forests ambushing weary travellers.'

'Your glibness is just an indicator that I'm right,' Silva replied firmly.

'*Fine*,' they relented. 'But I'm not going back through *that* door.' Shift pointed to it to reinforce which door they meant to Silva, just in case the head wound had knocked it from their memory. 'We go round the front, wait until everything dies down, then take out the survivors.'

Silva's lips curled in distaste. 'That is a very cowardly approach.'

Says the woman who killed Auron with a crossbow.

'Or a sensible one,' Shift bit back. 'Personally, I don't fancy ending up with a bloody head wound…or anything like that.'

'*Fine*,' the warrior relented after a moment. 'Garaz, are you with us?'

It took the orc a few seconds to realise he was being spoken to, and even then, all they got was a muttered, 'Yes.'

'So, we aren't running away?' the archer asked nervously.

'Apparently not,' Shift said, following Silva down the alley between the buildings to the main street. 'Apparently, I do the right thing now.' *For now.*

'For Deities' sake, Shift,' the archer cried. 'If I'd known that, I would've stayed in the tavern.'

Either way, he followed. Garaz, too.

Unfortunately, the fight reached the street before they did. Only seconds before, as the archer who'd been thrown through the shop window was still mid-air when they emerged from the alley. Shift winced at the thud as he crashed to the floor, his face scraping along the rough dirt road as he skidded across it. The rest of the fight spilled out after him.

First came Mace and his remaining men. Instantly, they covered the doorway, loosing arrows as Shagraz smashed his way out, obliterating anything in his path. The orc might have been big, but he wasn't stupid. Each arrow embedded itself in the clearly very dead man he was carrying.

Holding his human shield aloft as easily as one might hold a small plate, the orc grinned as the archers nocked new arrows. 'You humies 'ad yer fun. Now it's my turn.'

Shagraz's shield became a projectile as he used his thickly muscled arm to launch it at Mace's men, who'd helpfully grouped themselves together, maybe out of some sense that it would provide them greater protection.

Mace flung himself aside as his men collapsed in a heap then, with speed not in line with his immense size, Shagraz was amongst them, axe swinging wildly. The orc laughed like a child at play whilst arms and legs spun in the air around him.

I really want to close my eyes right now.

Yet they opened wider as blood covered the grinning orc's face, taking in every horrible detail of the gore-infused scene. As a hand hit the floor by their feet, Shift really wished they'd gone with the fleeing plan.

'*Garazzzzzzz*.' Shagraz's voice was a single long snarl, his blood-covered face accentuating his wild red eyes which were fixed on...drumroll...them. With a roar, the orc charged.

'A fireball would be good now,' Shift said, shaking their companion's arm. 'That way. Towards the giant oncoming orc.'

Wordlessly, Garaz raised his staff, pointing it at Shagraz. No fireball.

The ground shook as the orc bore down on them, a cloud of dust in his wake. Silva readied herself. Shift wanted to but didn't really see the point when someone right beside them ought be lobbing some Deities-damned fireballs *right now*.

'Garaz!'

Shagraz raised his axe.

'Anytime now...'

I can nearly see myself reflected in the damned orc's pupil.

'*Garaz!*'

A fireball launched from the staff, but only knocked the axe from Shagraz's hand, despite the fact that the orc was at point blank range.

'What sort of shitty aim was—'

Then Garaz was gone. Not breaking stride for a second, Shagraz careered into Garaz, tackling him and lifting him into the air to carry him into and through the wall of the nearest building. Shift flinched at the snapping of wood and the resulting crashes as the orc continued deep into the building. They rubbed their eyes as Shagraz's dust trail caught up with them.

Shift was still dumbfounded by what had happened, how close it'd been. Silva charged through the ruined side of the building in pursuit, even if the route she took to get there was scenic due to their head wound.

Shift shook themselves. *She needs help. They both do.*

Just as they were about to throw themselves after Silva, their arms were restrained, and they were pulled backwards.

'Despite this mess, I'm still gonna get paid, sweetie,' Mace purred in Shift's ear.

Reaching low without a word, Shift grabbed Mace's groin, squeezing hard and twisting their hand, and by extension, the items that hand now contained. The squeal of pain was damned satisfying, as was the crunching of bone as the grip loosened and they drove their elbow back into the thief lord's nose.

By the time they turned, Mace was on his knees, one hand on each of his abused body parts, groaning weakly. With a crack that was music to their ears, Shift kicked him squarely in the jaw, sprawling him out on the dirt floor.

'You still with us?' they asked the archer beside them, who was too pale and shaky for their liking.

He blinked a few times before finally nodding.

'Good. Watch him.' They pointed to Mace even as they charged towards the building.

Silva emerged just as they reached the opening. Though emerged was the wrong term. *Flung out* was more apt. The warrior hit the floor and rolled several times. Instantly, she tried to rise, but Shift doubted she'd be up quickly.

'Help him, not me,' the warrior snapped, waving frantically towards the building as Shift took a step towards her.

Quickly, they ran to the hole that now defaced the building. It was hard to tell with the mess of ruined furniture, but they guessed from the sawdust floating freely in the air that it used to be a carpenter's shop. Not that it mattered a damn. What mattered was Garaz.

Atop a now-broken workbench, Shagraz stood over Garaz, choking the life out of him whilst laughing like a child who'd just received a bag of sweets for completing chores. Their companion lay helplessly whilst Shagraz's hands tightened around his neck. Except he wasn't helpless.

But why he isn't fighting back is an issue for later.

Sensing the urgent need for action, Shift went to move in, preparing themselves to change into something big and mean, when their wrist was grabbed.

Dammit, one's still alive.

They'd just assumed that both of Shagraz's warriors had died in the shop. How this one was up and moving about was a miracle, judging by the arrow jutting out of its throat. Desperately, they tried to break the grip, but the green hand pulled harder, yanking their sword from their hand as he brought his cleaver up, ready to remove the arm he held.

The easiest solution seems the best here.

Grabbing the end of the arrow, Shift pulled it back out of the orc's neck, the brute hacking and stumbling forwards with the motion, blood pouring from the newly opened hole in its throat. And yet still it didn't die. Silva ramming her sword between its shoulder blades was enough to finish it, though.

Before the dead orc even hit the floor, taking Silva with it, Shift had grabbed a nearby plank of wood and slammed it over Shagraz's head, knowing there was no time left for anything fancy.

I might as well have tried blowing him a kiss.

The orc turned with a look that was forty percent disbelief, forty percent rage and twenty percent pure *'how dare you interrupt me when I'm choking someone'* indignation.

As Shagraz slowly rounded on them, Shift tried to use the broken piece of plank to defend themselves. The orc grabbed it on the downward swing before snapping one of their arms with the smallest of efforts. White hot pain ran through them as a meaty paw grabbed Shift by the neck, hauling them into the air. Clawing at the grip with their good hand did bugger all. They tried to use *actual* claws, but changing just a part of their body required more concentration and there was just a little bit to panic about right now. Besides, lack of oxygen.

They were a single second away from having their neck snapped like a twig, when Garaz finally decided to grace the fight with his presence. Roaring, Garaz slammed into the bigger orc. Thankfully Shagraz's grip broke and Shift fell to the floor as Garaz drove him back out of the store. The size difference between the two meant Garaz couldn't slam the giant orc into the floor, but it didn't matter, he was quite content to pummel him with his fists anyway.

Right, left, hook, jab, uppercut. Green fists swung wildly, each impact edging the dazed Shagraz back a little more with meaty *thwack*s. One of his two golden tusk tips was now missing.

'You do *not* hurt my companions,' Garaz snarled as he clasped both fists together. With one big swing, he brought a mighty hammer blow across Shagraz's jaw, sending the orc spinning almost full circle to the ground, before he too fell to the floor, panting.

Clutching their injured arm, Shift stumbled out of the building, breaking step only to quickly pocket the gold tusk tip they found on the floor. They ran to Garaz, reaching out to see if he was okay.

'Do not touch me,' Garaz barked at them, his eyes filled with a red-tinged fury that made Shift step back.

This is the Garaz I remember from the boat.

Slowly, they withdrew their hand, but as they did, Garaz's face softened and his breathing seemed to even out. 'Please, I need no aid. I just need to catch my breath a moment.'

They stepped back. The orc didn't seem in the mood to argue.

CHAPTER 17

For an inanimate land feature, the hills managed to look pretty threatening.

Everything here looks threatening.

But maybe this was worse, because he knew the very definite danger contained within.

Maybe Vargas has packed up and left? Maybe he decided to make a stand elsewhere? Maybe...he'll surrender?

Sometimes, he even sounded stupid to himself. They were in there and ready to fight. He could feel it. If his journeys with Auron were teaching him anything, it was how to differentiate between his usual paranoia and when something was truly wrong.

He looked at the black holes in the hill. 'They're watching us.' Knowing there were eyes on him made him shiver.

Don't do that. Do you want to bolster the enemy's confidence by standing here shaking?

'Well, of course they are.' Auron barely glanced towards the hills as he pointed troops of their skeleton army into different positions.

How is he so calm? We're about to have a battle...a battle, for Deities' sake!

Nicolas had faith that Auron knew his business, but he found himself needing reassurance. 'Have you ever led an army before?'

Auron laughed. 'No, I've always been more of a solo guy, with the odd exception. Teams...never really worked out for me in the past.' For all the stuff the hero did tell him, the stuff he blatantly didn't was the most intriguing. Auron seemed to sense his thoughts and changed the tone. 'Split reward money doesn't go very far. Plus, why have a line in an epic poem when the whole poem can be about you?' That sounded more like him. 'Don't worry, kid. The strategy is pretty straight forward. I'm confident.'

The skeletons had been arranged into three troops in a vague semi-circle facing the slopes. Their shields were interlocked in what Auron had termed a *spear wall*. Apparently, the idea was to drive the enemy from the cave then the spear wall advances, surrounding the enemy on three sides and killing them.

I hope it's as easy as that.

'Are you sure Vargas is in there?' He was the main objective of this battle. Sha'then had been certain Vargas would be here and that without the general, the necromancer's army would flounder and give him both breathing space to regroup and an opening to exploit.

'My Lord is certain he is,' Allius said indignantly. 'And his wisdom is beyond question.'

'Calm down, Shambles,' Auron said with a raised eyebrow. 'You're here to observe, not contribute. Besides, if he was that wise then he would still have his kingdom and not need us.'

His name is Allius. He didn't say it aloud. If Auron hadn't listened the first time, the second attempt would equally be doomed to failure.

The small man bristled. 'You know, one word from me and these skeletons will—'

Time to be the voice of reason.

'Allius.' Using his proper name got his attention. 'We're here to help. If we start bickering now, this battle is already lost.'

'Tell *him* that,' Allius muttered petulantly, eliciting an eyeroll from Auron.

'He's always like that,' Nicolas explained. Another heroic eyeroll. 'But he knows his stuff.'

'He'd better,' Allius grumbled. 'Because Avus Arex has many powerful servants here.'

Like...Grimmark Bear Slayer, maybe? Silva and her former mercenary partner had been working for the necromancer when he'd first encountered them. Silva, well, she'd very nearly died in their quest to save Yarringsburg. Grimmark *had* died, killed by Shift. He had to be down here; there was no way that guy was in the Eternal Forest. But Nicolas had yet to see him. If Avus had such a dangerous madman at his command, he'd certainly put him at the fore of his army. Remembering the bear-loving, hammer-wielding maniac caused his body to tense. After avoiding death at his hands on multiple occasions, he had no wish for a rematch...ever.

'Well, he's about to have one less,' Nicolas said firmly. 'Assuming Vargas is here.'

Auron raised his nose and took in a faux deep breath. 'I can smell the unmistakable scent of bullshit on the air. Vargas is in there.' What a fantastic time to act the fool. Perhaps he should tell some jokes pre-battle so everyone knew he was concentrating on the task at hand too. Auron noted his expression. 'What do you want me to say kid? I can't see through the hill. But this is the best launching point for their next move, so chances are he's here, and if he is, then he's going to die. And this time, he won't be running round commanding armies when he does.' The passion in the last part of his companion's sentence made him almost sorry for Vargas. His fate was sealed.

Auron surveyed the ranks of rusted armour-clad troops one last time and nodded approvingly. Nicolas checked his own armour. As he touched it, flakes of rust fell to his feet.

That's reassuring.

It already had several holes in it. He hoped there wouldn't be more after this. After drawing his sword, he tested it with several swipes through the air. From the look of it, it might crumble to dust on the first hit, but according to Sha'then, it was the best they had. *'What do you want from me? This is a realm of decay. That even affects the metal. If you'd like to wander the lands until you find a decent blacksmith, feel free.'* The snarky tone, he thought, had been unnecessary.

Mentally, he tried to conjure up all the training Silva had given him and the sword schooling from Captain Ramirez. Instead, he got a cluster of images of his death via various methods that appeared and disappeared at speed.

Hopefully, my muscle memory is more reliable than my regular memory.

Auron drew his own sword and circled it in his hand. 'The enemy aren't going to die by themselves,' he declared, bouncing his eyebrows twice. 'So let's get this started.' The hero stomped on the ground heavily three times. The answer was a slight tremor that passed under their feet, headed for the hills.

Is the ground visibly bulging or am I just seeing things?

As the tremor vanished completely, they watched and waited, the skinless creatures behind them standing firmly to attention. Had he not seen them march here, he would've believed them incapable of movement.

'Here we go.'

At Auron's words, he turned back towards the hill. Already, loose pieces of shale were slipping down the hillside. Then came the rumbling from deep inside the hill itself. Larger stones began to fall, throwing up clouds of dust. Soon, the whole hillside was visibly vibrating as the rumbling reached a higher pitch. There were audible cracking sounds, and some of the cave entrances disappeared under sudden cave-ins, as if they'd never been there at all.

Frenzied shadows bolted from the remaining caves, scrambling down the slopes of the hill as they were driven out of their hideaways. So far so good.

But when he looked to Auron in triumph, his companion's brow was furrowed.

'What's the matter?' Maybe he didn't want to know, but he needed to.

Auron narrowed his eyes as he looked towards the hill. 'There aren't enough of them.'

Quickly, Nicolas counted around thirty figures running in their direction. 'There was supposed to be an army here.' He didn't have any frame of reference, but he was damn sure thirty wasn't an army. 'Maybe they all died in the cave in?'

That's a wish only a genie could grant.

Abruptly, the rumbling stopped. 'Ah, crap,' Auron exclaimed, getting into a low fighting stance. 'It's a trap.'

****

Okay then. Giant orc, unconscious. Mace the asshole lord, captured. All of us, alive. I'm calling that a victory.

Though Shift had to admit it was the barest of ones. Again they'd come pretty close to death. Tentatively they moved their damaged arm. Garaz had healed the worst of it, but it still throbbed and their range of motion was impaired. They'd need to fashion a sling soon. Garaz should've seen to that, but he'd immersed himself in his sullenness again as he stood watch over the unconscious Shagraz.

Hopefully, he'll actually tie him up in a minute. Preferably before he comes to.

They wanted to suggest it, but Garaz was giving off a *'leave me be'* aura like the sun gave off light. He'd get a few more minutes then they'd snap him out of it. Nick should be waiting for them at the Oracle's cottage by now.

I hop— Know.

Silva sat watching Mace like a hawk. The handy orc healer had taken care of her head wound, but she was clearly still dazed, despite her best attempts to appear otherwise. The thief lord glared fiercely at the warrior. It was almost as if Silva was daring Mace to do something wrong, to mouth off, so she could have at him.

Let her fume a bit longer. She got hit in the head with a rock.

Besides, they had some thanks to give. When they turned, their secret ally was standing sheepishly behind them. He always pulled off that *'innocent little lamb'* expression so well—better than Nick, who most of the time *was* one. Somehow, they always had to remind themselves to look past the man's baby face. He was much older than he seemed, though his youthful appearance often came in handy during robberies.

'Rex.' Stepping forward, they embraced their old friend warmly with their good arm. The thief looked equally pleased to see them, returning the hug with enthusiasm. Parting, Shift patted him on the shoulder. 'Great to see you again.'

'You too,' he replied with a glad face. 'I thought I'd lost you after those bandits chased you near the Sarus border.'

They scoffed. 'Seriously? It takes more than a few jumped-up highwaymen to get the best of me.'

Rex mulled that over for a moment. 'True, but I can still worry.'

They pinched his baby-faced cheek. 'You're so cute when you worry.'

He swatted their hand away with a chuckle. 'And the gold...' Rex ventured.

I hoped you wouldn't ask that. 'I had to dump it. Sorry.'

Rex shrugged. 'I wasn't gutted by bandits. I'd call that a decent trade off.'

'Lucky to have an old friend turn up,' Silva said, finally tearing her eyes from Mace.

'It wasn't really luck,' Rex admitted. Deities, he even sounded young. 'I was in a nearby tavern that fronts for the Thieves' Guild. Mace came in looking for muscle. Said he's been offered this hefty bounty and—'

'Since when does the Thieves' Guild allow its members to go off hunting bounties or doing assassinations?' Shift asked. The Guild was very strict about the nature of their business. Mainly so they didn't tread on the toes of either the Bounty Hunters' Guild or the Guild of Assassins'. Doing either would be very bad for business.

Rex shrugged. 'The Guild's a mess at the moment, Shift. Something's happened. I don't know what. But there's all kinds of infighting going on. No one's taking charge and giving orders, and no one's looking when people like Mace break the rules. When he first came in, I ignored him because I do stick to our codes, but when your name came up, I knew I had to volunteer my services.'

'And Mace bought that?' they scoffed.

'Not at first, but when I told him how sad and poor I was...' Rex pouted, sticking his bottom lip out and making a mock doe-eyed expression that had netted them some very lucrative purses in the past.

'He relented, and you got the job,' they finished, clicking their fingers.

'Woulded taked you if I'd doughn you were a traidor.' Mace was having difficulty speaking with the broken nose.

He he.

One glare from Silva shut him up. She was good like that.

'I take it the early arrowshot was you?' they asked. Rex gave a mock bow by way of response. Again, they held him by the shoulder. 'Thank you. We all owe you our lives.'

Rex shook his head and raised his hands. 'You saved mine, more than once. I'm just happy I didn't have to repay the debt in gold.'

That was true. The last time they'd seen Rex, the pair had been playing a young married couple lost in the woods after being robbed by bandits. Picked up by a trading caravan that fortuitously happened to be passing, the plan had been to fleece them after everyone was asleep and make off into the night. They'd been in the middle of making a run for it when real bandits attacked the camp, and they were none too thrilled to find someone making off with what they had intended to steal. Knowing they had a better chance of getting away than Rex, they drew the bandits' attention and fled towards the border of Sarus. Turning into an otter had managed to shake their pursuers and get them across the border, but they'd lost the loot doing so. Otters aren't very good at transporting heavy bags of jewels.

No matter, they'd lived, and they were glad Rex had made it out. They were quite fond of the little grifter. Him saving them was also a big plus.

'You have my thanks,' Silva said with a nod of acknowledgement. 'Without you, we would be dead.'

'Anything for Shift.' They punched him on the arm playfully. He was almost as sweet as Nick. They took their hand back quickly as they thought of him. How much time had passed whilst they were here fighting? Had Auron returned yet? Was Nick okay?

Calm down. It'll all be well.

'What do we do with *that*?' Silva nodded towards the unconscious orc, her lips pursed with distaste.

'Leave him.' Garaz's snap was so uncharacteristic that it made them jump. Even Silva appeared surprised but made no issue of it.

At least he's doing something other than being mopey and silent.

But at the same time, what was he thinking? They couldn't just leave a dangerous orc lying around out here. Had he taken leave of his senses?

They caught Garaz's yellow eyes, ready to argue, but they had a strained, pleading quality to them. True, the orc hadn't been himself of late, but he did just save their life. That earnt him some leeway.

'Fine,' they agreed finally, to a thankful nod from Garaz.

'What about him?' Rex asked, pointing to Mace, who looked very much in a *kill everyone* kind of mood.

'Do you think he was the one who shot Nicolas?' Silva looked ready to gut him if the answer was yes.

'No,' Shift replied thoughtfully. 'If there's a bounty on us, it'll be on Nick too. No way Mace would leave his body out for the birds like that.'

'True eduff. Doe, what aboud be, darlin'?' Mace's voice sounded so funny. 'You gonna stabbe and leave be idda ditch to die?'

So tempting.

'No.' They had a much better idea. 'We're going to strip you naked and—'

The ground underfoot trembled. A rumbling noise followed it, as well as a dust cloud that appeared at the edge of the town. From the cloud emerged twenty heavily armoured knights on horseback, wearing the heraldry of Yarringsburg.

As much as they wanted to move, it wasn't the most sensible thing to go running around when the cavalry was bearing down on them. Their companions were of the same mind, so it appeared.

Thundering down the main street, the knights formed a semi-circle around them before finally coming to a halt. The lance tips pointed towards them were quite worrying.

'By order of King Eldric of Yarringsburg, you are all under arrest for the abduction of the residents of Hablock and the looting of this village,' the lead knight bellowed. 'Surrender and face the king's justice or die.'

Quickly, they looked around at the ruined village square, which now had bodies strewn around it, and considered the way it must all look to outside observers.

Oh crap.

CHAPTER 18

*T*rap. That wasn't a word he'd wanted to hear, not at all. Unless maybe it was one he'd sprung. Instantly, Nicolas was alert, scanning the horizon in all directions like some kind of overzealous meerkat. He didn't question Auron's wisdom; the hero knew his stuff. He just wished he could see where it would come from. Everything seemed the same dull grey in every direction around them.

Will it come from the left? The right? Behind us?

Frantically, his eyes darted in all directions, chasing the imagined threats in his peripheral vision.

I can't spiral now. There's going to be a fight.

It was sadly inevitable, and he had to be ready for it.

'Advance,' Auron shouted, signalling with his sword to one of the ranks of skeleton soldiers.

Slowly, the troop plodded forward in unison towards the oncoming men, spears lowered and ready. The wraiths seemed unbothered by the attack, further reinforcing that this was a trap.

'Don't we need them here?' As much as he trusted Auron, sending away a third of their force didn't seem so wise.

'I don't rate these skeleton soldiers much.' The hero was just as alert as him but managing it much better. 'Might as well have some of them kill those advancing wraiths.'

Nicolas looked back at the oncoming figures. They were the same as the warriors he'd seen with Vargas before. Now that the panic of having to flee the caves was dissipating, they were bounding towards the skeletons, weapons ready.

From his view, it was hard to tell if any of the wraiths fell as the two forces met. At least their warriors had the numbers advantage, which was the lynchpin of Sha'then's whole campaign strategy.

Failing *campaign strategy*.

'Form a circle,' Auron commanded the remaining skeletons. Almost painfully slowly, the skeletons marched into a circle, with him, Auron, and Allius at their centre.

'Oh dear, oh dear, oh dear,' Allius mumbled to himself, clutching his book to him tightly.

Can they not move faster? No wonder Sha'then kept losing.

Eventually, shields were locked, and spears pointed outwards, ready for attack. Beyond them, the battle continued; blade met blade. Wraiths turned to smoke and skeletal frames were broken apart. It seemed to be going well for them, as far as he could tell.

Beside him, Auron looked grim. 'They're toying with us. No way they should've let us get into formation like that before springing their trap. Someone's showing off.'

Someone was definitely showing off. The cloud above them bulged and pulsated, rolling thunder assaulting their ears. Large columns of black smog descended from it at four points, surrounding their formation in a pattern marking out a square. From there, the smog circled until all four points were attached to each other. Beyond the impenetrable black wall, the sounds of battle ceased instantly.

'Oh dear, oh dear, oh dear.' He didn't want to shout at Allius to shut up, but he *really* wanted him to stop doing that.

'Shut up,' Auron snapped before turning to him. 'Stay alert, kid,' the hero counselled. As if he needed telling.

What's in the cloud? Why isn't the enemy showing themselves?

When the cloud dissipated into nothing, he really wished it hadn't. They were surrounded. All around them in a circle parallel to their own was a horde of grey-skinned creatures with withered frames and dull, lifeless eyes.

'Zombies,' he whispered. Though the monsters missed the decaying, hanging-out bits he'd come to associate with that word, it seemed apt.

'Actually, they're called *shades*,' Allius corrected. 'Damned souls pressed into Avus's service.'

Another one for the list. Though it does seem like splitting hairs, really.

'This is neither the time nor the place to debate terminology,' Auron snarled, scowling at a single figure amongst the army arrayed before them.

'Well met, Nick and Auron,' Vargas said with an elaborate bow, followed by a cheeky wave specifically for the hero. 'It'd warm my heart to see you again. If I had one.'

What an asshole. Only one person gets to call me Nick.

'Screw you,' Auron snapped back.

'I'm out of your league, Dawnblade.' Vargas sneered. 'Even if my penchant *was* for male company, you'd be way down the list.'

'Shame that.' The hero sniffed, raising his sword. 'Because I have something here I'd very much like to put in you.'

Is this tough talk or flirting?

'Auron,' Vargas spoke as if he were addressing an old friend. 'Let us calm ourselves and enjoy this moment. It's you and me, back together again. Locked in our eternal battle. How has life been without your nemesis to fight?'

'Self-appointed nemesis,' the hero corrected coolly. 'And lovely.'

Vargas feigned hurt. 'Don't be like that, my friend. You know what we mean to each other.'

'I most certainly do not,' Auron replied after a drawn-out sigh. 'You always thought you were special. But you were just another guy to fight. You survived slightly longer than most, that's all. Then you made yourself my priority, and I finished you.'

The smoke coming from Vargas's ears was practically visible. 'You didn't kill me, Dawnblade. I cheated you of that.' *But Auron said he'd killed Vargas?* 'And now you're here for our final battle, and what better arena for it to take place in than the Underworld?' Vargas opened his arms wide and circled around like he was enjoying a summer meadow. 'All the time I've been here, I've imagined this, and it's almost exactly like I pictured it, right down to your denial and arrogance.' With that, Vargas clasped his hands together around the hilt of his sword, and when he pulled them apart, his sword split into two, so he had a blade in each hand. The wide-eyed maniac even shouted, *'Ha,'* as he did it.

Arguably, it was kind of impressive, but Nicolas remembered what Auron had told him so he folded his arms and put on his best uncaring expression. No way was he giving Vargas the satisfaction. The warrior's brow darkened as his theatrics turned out to be for naught.

'*Final battle.*' Auron snorted derisively. 'If you only fought as well as you talked shit.'

For a moment, it looked as if Vargas was going to charge the skeleton wall by himself, but a grey-skinned hand on his shoulder stayed him. The warrior turned, glaring in disgust at the appendage that'd dared to touch him. His demeanour changed completely when he saw the green glow in the creature's eyes. Soon those green eyes fixed on Nicolas.

'Mr Nicolas Percival Carnegie, how delightful to see you again.' The voice from the shade's mouth was that of Avus Arex. Nicolas hadn't heard him talk much, but that voice was seared into his mind forever. 'Or are you calling yourself *Nick Carnage* now?'

I most certainly am not.

'When Vargas told me you were here, I scarcely dared believe it, but here you are, in the flesh, if you forgive the phrase.'

'You've looked better.' The words left his mouth before he could stop them. Clearly, it wasn't Arex's body he was addressing. It was a good foot shorter, for starters, and missing the necromancer's rat-like features.

The shade looked down at itself. 'This is just a vessel.' Avus let out a guttural chuckle. 'I have an entire war to oversee. I didn't think I could be everywhere at once, but using these mindless creatures to speak for me changes that.'

'Why do you even have zombies?' Auron interrupted, ignoring Allius's earlier correction. 'I thought you used these *wraiths*?' The amount of sarcasm on the last word could've drowned a giant.

Vargas seethed contemptuously.

'Unfortunately, not as many of my fellow undead rose to join me as I had hoped.' Avus shrugged using his borrowed body. 'But I needed troops, so they were *pressed* into the war effort, so to speak, their souls bound to my cause regardless of their will.'

'Abominations,' Allius shouted from behind his book. 'You've perverted the dead and turned them into abominations.'

'*Silence, worm.*' The thunderous shout came from all of the shades simultaneously.

Allius cowered back behind his book.

Yes, Avus is definitely showing off.

'Death hasn't changed you then?' Auron rolled his eyes and shook his head. 'Still the same megalomaniac.'

'Please.' Avus snorted. 'I'm doing these poor souls a favour. They were doomed to an eternity of damnation before I liberated them. They may not thank me now, but they will.'

'More like you're using them as human shields.' The hero scoffed.

The shade's face contorted into a gap-toothed snarl then the light in the eyes went out. With a rumble of thunder, another column of smoke descended from the sky. This time when it ascended, Avus Arex stood before them.

Wow, he's really easy to bait.

He was just as Nicolas remembered him: a tall, rodent-faced asshole.

'I am no coward, Auron of Tellmark,' the necromancer declared. 'And you are sadly mistaken if you thought I wouldn't be here in person to greet the pair of you.'

Brave words with an army at your back. If Nicolas could get him one-on-one again... Actually, no, that hadn't worked out well for him last time. But he was different now. He had grown, so maybe... He just really wanted to punch Avus right in the face.

'Don't we feel special?' Auron chuckled.

'Not really,' Nicolas found himself saying. 'I see trash all the time.'

For a moment, Avus looked as if he were fighting back a burst of pure rage, the muscles in his face barely containing the snarl that threatened to contort his smug grin. 'Very funny, boy. But you are the same whelp who failed to best me once. Do you think it will be any different here?' The necromancer gestured with open arms to the world they now walked.

Don't let them see you riled. Don't let them see you scared.

'Well, you *have* got a few new tricks,' Auron said. 'The teleporting, for one, and the zombie mind control.'

'Not really.' Avus smirked. 'When I syphoned those wizards of their energy, I took their skills along with their power. I just didn't really have a chance to properly showcase my talents at our last meeting. So nothing's changed.' The necromancer pursed his lips for a moment. 'And they're *shades*, not zombies. It's a totally different creature.'

'I couldn't give a gnome's left bollock,' the hero scoffed.

'Nothing will change when you and I go for a second round,' Nicolas said with defiant confidence. 'I'll soften you up for Auron to finish you, just like I did for Eldric.'

More distract than soften, but either way it led to the right result.

'Let's see how mouthy you are, boy, when you aren't secure behind your shield wall.' Avus Arex gestured with a flick of his wrist, and the mass of shades shuffled forwards, moaning hungrily.

'You got your sword this time, kid?' Auron asked.

For a second, he thought Auron was joking, but the hero actually looked around to get an answer. Truthfully, the question wasn't entirely unjustified, and Nicolas checked his hand to be sure. It was there. Thank the Deities. Now just to keep hold of it. He did have a habit of dropping swords.

The shades advanced.

Quickly, he turned to Allius. 'Stay behind us.'

The scribe nodded, shrinking further behind his book.

Nicolas steeled himself. Battle was imminent.

They're already dead. This isn't murder.

****

Silva drew her sword and looked ready to slay any knight who even coughed in a way she didn't like. The warrior certainly didn't give the impression she wanted to be taken alive.

Well, she's probably wanted for quite an impressive list of crimes. I'm sure I'd have a black mark or two against me if I wasn't so damn good.

Though Shift had no doubt any last stand Silva made would be an epic confrontation that would be told throughout the ages, they didn't want to be any part of it.

'Can we all please calm down?' they shouted, ensuring they had everyone's attention before all the hacking and stabbing happened. 'There's been a terrible misunderstanding here.'

'You deny the charges?' the lead knight questioned.

'Well, yes.' Daft question. Who'd admit to it? 'We got here after the people had been taken, visiting a friend, and found, this…' With a spread-armed gesture they indicated the scene around them.

They could sense the sceptical gaze of the knight even from behind his helmet. 'And yet some of these bodies are still fresh.'

Ah.

This was going to take some careful explaining. 'My friends and I,' they made sure to indicate Rex as well, ensuring he was spared any of the knight's retribution. It was the least they could do, 'were looking for survivors when…' As much as they wanted to lie, this was a tense situation and the truth would be better, if only an edited version. '…we were attacked by these guys who're mostly strewn around the floor here. And then this group of orcs, led by the unconscious big fella there, came and killed most of them. We bested the orc and the greasy scumbag with the smashed nose. I broke his nose, by the way. Then you turned up.'

'Ridiculous!' cried the knight beside the leader. 'We are to believe you are the victims in all this when you are clearly a group of mercenaries yourselves?'

An orc, a warrior, and two thieves. They didn't look like your average missionaries. The knight had a point, but a very unhelpful one. 'We aren't mercenaries. We're just innocent bystanders.' Not entirely true, but to say any more would necessitate talking about Merida and Sarus and Yarringsburg. The tale would begin to sound very unbelievable very quickly, no matter how true it was.

'I have never known an orc to be an *innocent bystander,* as you term it.'

Wow. Can he just stop talking if he isn't going to say anything helpful?

'I am just a travelling mage, my good sir. We came to visit our friend, as they said.' Thankfully, Garaz was contributing, but he was still distant somehow.

At least he sounds eloquent enough. No talk of 'crushin' humies'.

'A travelling mage, you say?' The second knight didn't attempt to veil his sarcasm. 'Maybe your magic power is to ensure no one in any village you visit remains alive? Is that the true summation of it, orc filth?'

Garaz bristled but kept his cool.

Is he trying to pick a fight?

No matter what they said, this situation seemed destined for battle, so they gestured for their comrades to put their weapons on the ground. Surrender was the only sensible option right now. There was a great deal of reluctance—mostly from Silva, unsurprisingly—but eventually the warrior relented. It would do them good to show they were willing to cooperate.

'Excellent,' the lead knight said, taking off his helmet to reveal a wizened, reasonable face. Reasonable in this situation was a welcome thing. 'Once we have you back at the city, this will all be ironed out. If you speak true, you shall be free to go. And if you are found to be lying, the executioner's block shall await you.'

The mouthy knight turned to his leader, blatantly aghast. He removed his own helmet as if it suddenly stifled him. He was much younger, with a crown of black hair that matched his neatly trimmed beard and overacted noble bearing. 'You cannot just let them live for this outrage, this *slaughter*. They are obviously part of some bandit war party who set upon each other over the spoils of this village. We would do well to just—'

'Sir Gerran, that will be enough!' the lead knight boomed. *Good for him.* 'I have given my commands, now see to it.'

Sir Gerran said nothing more, but Shift had serious doubts that'd be the end of it.

Best keep an eye on that one.

Ensuring they kept their hands raised, Shift watched as several of the knights secured their lances before dismounting their horses. After rummaging in their saddle bags, each one approached Shift and her companions bearing thick metal shackles. Their gut instinct was to run, but this was more of a *'listen to your reason'* type situation.

At least we'll get this sorted out nice and easily back in the city. We're personal friends of the king, after all.

CHAPTER 19

The shield wall lasted only moments.

Useless bloody skeletons.

That was unfair. It was hardly their fault. The creatures couldn't exactly put much muscle behind their shields and—

What am I doing?

I know what: trying not to think about the battle. But it's here. I don't have the luxury of ignoring it.

His sword shook—though, really, it was his hand—as the wall that had promised them protection disintegrated. The shaking stopped as the battle blossomed before his eyes. It was...kind of sad. The shades had the same level of mobility as the skeletons: poor. It was like watching two armies of old arthritic men taking swings at each other. Definitely the slowest battle he'd ever been in.

But it is a battle...focus!

'You'll be fine, kid,' Auron said quietly at his side, his voice somehow carrying over the clashing of metal. 'You could hold your own before Silva, Ramirez, and I taught you. So if you can't handle some shuffling zombies, it should be embarrassment that kills you.'

Give me a chance. I haven't even dropped my sword yet.

Despite his self-deprecation, Auron's words gave him confidence. The wraiths in amongst the shades were more of a concern, but he didn't have the luxury of waiting for help anymore. It was time to take care of himself.

Great in theory.

One of the shades shambled towards him with some kind of...gardening implement. The creature raised it's weapon, but he wasn't about to allow it the first attack. Driving forwards, he thrust his sword into the creature's belly. Of course, it didn't die; the best he got was that it dropped it's weapon and moaned a bit.

Is that pain, or just a general zombie-like moan?

'Go for the head,' Auron cried as he took two of his own in one swing.

The shade groaned angrily and made to grab him. Quickly, he stepped back out of reach, kicking the creature away. It took his sword with it. By the time it'd hit the floor, Nicolas had a rock raised overhead.

But this is...was a man. A bad man, of course. Why else would he be here? But I'm here, and apparently, I'm not bad, so... Oh shit.

The shade tried to rise, and he hurled the rock, turning the undead creature's head to paste on the floor. He looked away quickly, a surge of guilt threatening to unman him at a time when he needed all the fortitude he could muster. That was only one of a vast army.

It was a monster. It wasn't a man anymore. Yet still he said a prayer for what was left of the shade's soul as it's form turned to smoke and vanished, his sword clattering to the floor.

'Kid, don't tell me you just lost your sword again?' Auron shouted, partially obscured by the veil of smoke that surrounded him, created by all the souls he was sending to oblivion.

Nicolas could barely keep track of the hero's movements as he hacked and slashed his way through opponents. The only thing he could make out was the smile of a man in his element.

He really is great.

Yet the hero was getting further and further away from him as the enemy pressed in. He needed to get to Auron. Fighting back-to-back would give them—okay, him—the best chance of survival.

Quickly, he reached for his sword, the motion arrested as a wraith's arm wrapped around his neck. 'Gotcha, boy,' the attacker snarled as Nicolas yelped.

Without thought, Nicolas grabbed the arm holding him, lowering his hips and thrusting them to the side. Using the arm as leverage, he dropped forwards, throwing the wraith over him, the attacker crashing to the ground with a grunt. His curses as he tried to scrabble to his feet were cut short by Nicolas's boot shattering his nose with a sickening *crunch*.

Did I do that? Silva's training must've...

No. No more hesitation. You're in a battle.

He grabbed the wraith's sword from the floor and hovered the tip of the blade over his attacker, who was rolling around in pain. He knew he had a chance to make the killing blow, yet his sword stayed still. The wraiths weren't like the shades, they looked exactly as they had in life, human. It was enough to make him hold back, no matter how insane it was. Instead, Nicolas turned and made for Auron. Ro pointed and laughed at his folly.

Shades shuffled into his path, and reluctantly, he dispatched them one after the other, making sure to take the head. Each soul he sent to oblivion caused a pang of regret, but his survival instinct was stronger. He'd be no good to the people of Hablock dead.

All around him was a mass of moving bodies engaged in combat. He couldn't even begin to tell who was winning. Though he had some unpleasant suspicions. Muscling his way through the last few combatants, he finally made it to Auron.

'Glad you're still alive, kid.' The hero didn't take his eyes from the wraith he was beheading as he spoke. Another came at the hero from his side, ready to kill. Before Nicolas knew what he was doing, he'd slipped around Auron and run the attacker through.

The wraith looked at the sword in his stomach and then at him, incredulous that his victory had been turned to defeat so easily. Then his features darkened and drifted away on the breeze as Auron pirouetted around and took his head.

That wasn't me. That was Auron. I just...

Inaction would be deadly here, but everywhere he looked, the shades were wearing the face of the faun, staring at him in dismay over the life he'd had a part in ending.

Why can't I ignore this? Why can't I do what I know I must?

Another wraith came at him, swinging an axe. The arm didn't complete the swing. Nicolas took it at the elbow, spinning with the momentum of his own swing, using it to turn full circle and drive his blade into the gut of his now one-armed opponent.

'Kid, stop gutting them,' Auron shouted above the din of battle. 'You know what to do!'

He made to finish the wraith, but his hand froze before he could. Frustration and guilt churned within him like the sea, raging in a storm he simply couldn't sail through. Instead, he kicked the wraith between the legs then booted him in the face to send him sprawling to the floor.

'Yoo-hoo.' Vargas gave him a theatrical bow as he appeared amongst the combatants. 'Shall we see what the lowly, squeamish squire has learned from his master?' Vargas came at him, wide-eyed with blood lust.

Nicolas intercepted the first two blows, but Vargas was toying with him, making it abundantly clear with his grin. He tried to strike back, but his own blows were expertly turned aside until he swung downwards and found his blade caught between an X made of Vargas's two swords.

'Not much then.' Vargas sneered, flicking the blades apart and cutting Nicolas's rusted sword in two. He didn't even have time to react in shock as Vargas's forehead drove into his nose, making the world tremble as if another bone monster was about to emerge from underground. He was turned roughly, his hair yanked back. Metal caressed his throat.

'Auron, look who's under my blade,' Vargas declared victoriously.

Nicolas wanted to turn away from the sword at his neck, but this was a situation in which you made no sudden movements.

Auron turned and locked eyes with Vargas in a glare that was the equivalent of a dragon opening its mouth to breathe fire. Instead of dropping his sword, the hero drove the blade into the stomach of the nearest wraith then let go of the grip and held his hands in the air.

I've let him down. He wished it had been for the first time. 'Sorry.'

'Don't worry about it, kid.' Auron half-smiled at him. 'You did good.'

'And yet still you lose.' Vargas laughed. 'And now you're at...gasp...*my* mercy.' The warrior took his sword from Nicolas's throat and looked at the blade thoughtfully. '*Mercy.* Not normally a word one associates with me. Perhaps I just cut this little runt's head off now?'

Nicolas was sent sprawling to the floor by a heavy kick to the back. For a second, it looked as if Auron was about to throw himself at Vargas, but two burly wraiths grabbed him, forcing the hero to his knees.

Vargas scoffed. 'I've always wondered what it'd be like to have you on your knees before me. And now here we are...' His voice dropped to a sinister whisper. 'And it is glorious.'

Nicolas slowly pushed himself up, sitting beside Auron, fatalism removing any fight he had left. A figure hit the floor next to them, rolling heavily before scrabbling to its knees. There was a moment of relief at seeing Allius still alive, even if it wouldn't be for long.

The forces of the enemy, victorious, closed in around them.

Defeat deflated him from the inside out as the necromancer hovered over him. Crouching, Avus ran a cold finger down Nicolas's cheek. He wanted to recoil from the touch but wouldn't give him the satisfaction.

'The boy who defeated me. After a fashion.' The necromancer shook his head slowly. 'All those years of planning laid to waste and look at the person who did it. It's embarrassing.'

'Good,' he managed to spit out through the malaise gripping him.

A wraith smacked him around the head for answering back.

The necromancer mulled this over for a moment. 'Although you didn't, did you? It was Eldric who did what you couldn't, and that all worked out very well for him, didn't it?'

What does that mean?

'Without you to distract me, I would've destroyed him with the barest of efforts. But that wasn't to be my destiny. Instead, I find myself here, bringing my vast power with me, enabling me to rule this place.'

Beside him, Auron scrunched his face up. 'I think Sha'then disagrees.'

Avus pointed his finger towards the hero threateningly. 'He can disagree all he likes. He's on borrowed time, and he knows it. Just another distraction.'

'From?' Nicolas couldn't help but ask. If he knew anything about Avus, it was that the necromancer liked a good brag.

For a long moment, Avus looked up at the large cloud swirling overhead, casting everything in twilight gloom. Nicolas sensed the incoming monologue. 'All I ever wanted was to help the world,' Avus said in a tone laced with bitterness as he got to his feet. 'I had gifts that could help people. I could show them how to cheat death itself. But instead of being celebrated, I was shunned, forced to take extreme measures to prove my worth. In the end, I knew the greater good would be served.' The necromancer shook his head with a derisive chuckle. 'All those I killed weighed against all those I could save? Pfft, the numbers would be easily in my favour. But as usual the moral and intellectual weakness of others was my undoing.' Again, his gaze went to the sky. 'Once this war is done, I shall have enough power to completely break this barrier and return to Etherius. I will create a new world, where no one can die—'

'Because they're already dead?' Auron interrupted with disgust.

'Exactly.' There was a crazed gleam in the necromancer's eyes. 'If there is no life, then there can be no death. Once they shed their corporeal forms, they shall realise the gift they have been given and worship me as a god. Because that is what I will be. Avus Arex, the God of Death.'

By the Deities, he's insane.

When Nicolas first met Avus Arex, the necromancer had wanted to be seen as a hero, averting a vampire apocalypse he'd had a large hand in causing. The guy had been pretty crazy then, but now he was an all-out lunatic. He was going to kill...everyone. Wipe out all life.

Maybe some villains do need to die.

A moment of clarity struck Nicolas like a lightening bolt. Everything he'd seen, everything Auron had said to him, Avus's ranting, it all suddenly came together to reveal a single truth; evil needs to be vanquished, by any means necessary. It was now so obvious to him that he couldn't believe he'd ever doubted it. The weight of the guilt he carried faded away as he thought of those he'd saved, instead of what he'd had to do to save them.

There was no redeeming people like Ro, like Avus Arex. The necromancer had been banished here for his sins. Had he learnt anything from that? No. All he did was plot and scheme on new ways to perpetrate evil. In this case it would be mass genocide. And the only way to stop him, to avert the death of everything, would be to finish him off for good.

A new will to fight calmed the storm of shame in him. Right then, if he had a sword in hand, he would have killed Avus where he stood, and the universe would be all the better for it.

'Are you sure one of those wizards you syphoned wasn't afflicted?' Auron asked casually. 'Because I think—'

The hero's words were cut off by Vargas's boot connecting with his chin. Auron worked his jaw for a moment before turning back and fixing the warrior with a steely gaze as he slowly ran his tongue across his split lip.

'Oh, I'm sorry.' Vargas smiled. 'Did you lose your train of thought?'

'You need to kill us soon,' Auron snarled. 'Before I rip the head off your *General* here.'

As Vargas chuckled, Nicolas couldn't help but voice a question that niggled at him. 'I assumed Grimmark would be your main general. You can't tell me *he* made it to the Eternal Forest.'

The necromancer scoffed openly. 'Oh, he's here. Of course he is. But he isn't part of my army. Not him.' Avus's face contorted in pure disgust. 'Did you know he was going to betray me?'

Betray him? What? How? Was Silva part of that?

'It's true.' Avus's face darkened. 'I was set up to fail. I planned to betray the vampires I worked with as my *allies* in turn worked to betray me. But I know the conspirators, and my vengeance upon them will be epic once I've risen from this pit. Until then, I've contented myself with Grimmark. His punishment is...suitably ironic.' A knowing smile broke across Avus's lips.

'If you've been down here since Yarringsburg, how can you be sure?' This line of questioning could be very important, if he lived. If there was some other conspiracy going on, it might trace back to this Koth. He needed to follow this road and find its end.

'I have been afforded a certain *clarity* since I've been down here.' The necromancer sneered. 'Part of me would love to spell it out for you, but I admit I like your ignorance. It's just another way I am superior to you. I will tell you one thing, though.' Avus crouched down again, leaning in close. 'I know you're from Hablock. Just as I know your friends are there now.'

He lunged forward, but the wraiths who restrained him were suddenly quicker, holding him back as Avus giggled in delight.

'Oh yes, I know where your friends are. And whilst I cannot penetrate the barrier Sha'then put up enough to enact the full scale of my plan, you two coming here has left a crack, one I think I can increase just enough for some sweet revenge. And who knows? Once my shades have consumed them, maybe their souls will come here too, and I can take a more personal retribution as well.'

Again Nicolas fought his captors, lashing out with his legs when he failed.

Why isn't Auron fighting? Why is he just sitting there?

A fist across the face ended his struggling.

Vargas and the wraiths around Avus backed away as the necromancer began to chant, his eyes becoming pupilless as tendrils of black energy coursed around his thin body. The chanting increased in speed and pitch until it was almost frenzied, foam spitting from his lips. With a cry, he threw the black energy into the sky. It struck the cloud barrier with a mighty crack of thunder, forming a swirling vortex directly above them.

'*Bring me their souls.*' The voice was no longer Avus's, but the voice of some vengeful god that echoed across the wasteland. A host of his shades turned to smoke, which rose to join the column that flowed from the necromancer until they disappeared into the vortex.

With a gasp, Avus stumbled back as the vortex closed. It looked like he'd fall completely, but a couple of his servants held him up. He was drenched with sweat, his features gaunt. After several moments, he seemed to recover, waving off his men and standing tall again.

'An effort, to be sure.' Avus's voice was hoarse. 'But for the satisfaction of killing you and your friends, I would tear apart reality itself.'

Nicolas looked up to where the vortex had only recently been.

Deities protect you. His companions might need all the blessings they could get.

****

Despite their instincts to the contrary, Shift still dutifully held their hands out, ready for the shackles to be secured around them. Their damaged arm protested the movement.

It's not like shackles are a problem for me anyway.

Still, the very idea of standing there waiting to be imprisoned was wrong. Yes, they would sort all of this out easily once they were in the city, but they didn't *want* to go to the city. They needed to be here when Nick and Auron returned. But they had no better ideas. Mace was hardly one for confessing, even if he *could* talk properly, and who knew about Shagraz? The orc hadn't exactly shown the capacity for talking in well-structured sentences so far. In fact, if the orc awoke now, it'd likely do them more harm than good.

Just as the knight was about to snap the metal shackles shut around their wrists, the ground shook violently, going from nought to nauseating in a single moment. It was all they could do to stay on their feet as the knights' horses reared with fear.

'What's going on?' It was hard to hear their own voice over the rumbling, so they doubted anyone else would hear them or had any more wisdom about the sudden occurrence than they did.

The air was filled with a loud tearing sound.

Deities, it's the ground.

Common sense told them to stay in the open during an earthquake, but as the open ground was currently cracking beneath their feet, Shift made instead for the porch of the nearest building. Though it was difficult to move in a straight line with the ground shaking beneath their feet, they pressed on, their companions following Shift's lead. Using their arms to shield their head from the loose bits of wood raining down from the building, they made it to the porch, bracing themselves in the doorway of the tavern with the others. It was the best option in a situation bereft of anything safer.

Shift's eyes widened as wide cracks broke the ground, venting gases so hot that the air instantly became thick. They choked, trying to find some breathable air. After quickly tearing off part of their shirt sleeve, they wrapped it around their face. It barely helped, but barely was better than nothing.

There was light in the smoke. Lots of light. As it cleared, it revealed pools of bubbling yellow and orange lava, which filled the holes torn in the earth. The heat was intense.

Is this how Nick's coming home, riding a wave of lava?

The knights were in chaos. Several of the horses had thrown their riders before bolting away from the carnage. A few others had been savvy enough to dismount before the same happened to them. The rest still struggled with their mounts, desperately trying to calm them. Mace was nowhere to be seen, but all the noise and activity roused Shagraz, who sat up, staring around in bleary-eyed disbelief and rubbing his chin.

With a final crescendo, the rumbling died away as if it had never been. Had it not been for the lava-filled gouges in the earth, it might never have happened at all. At least their companions were all okay.

As the knights attempted to gain some semblance of order, their ears pricked up for a moment. 'Uh, guys. Did anyone else just hear a voice shout, *'Bring me their souls?'*'

From the look on Garaz and Silva's faces, they'd definitely heard it too.

What followed was the single most ominous silence they'd ever experienced. Everyone knew something bad was about to happen—you could practically taste the evil in the air. The knights drew their swords, scanning the area warily. Even Shagraz, in the midst of so many obvious targets, appeared to be readying for whatever was coming.

There was another cracking sound.

No, not quite cracking. It was the displacement of earth. Digging, maybe? An arm burst out of the ground before them, and they gave an annoyingly girlish scream. The skin of the arm was grey and thin-looking.

'Oh no,' Garaz whispered in disbelief. 'I think I recognise the voice we just heard.'

They looked at their companion for more information, but this wasn't the time for explanations. More arms burst from the earth, more than they could count. The arms were followed by shoulders, heads, and torsos.

Why am I just standing here watching this happen? It wasn't just them, though; everyone was dumbfounded by the scene.

A lipless mouth gnawed at nothing as an undead creature got to it's feet, lifeless eyes taking in it's new surroundings.

'Zombies,' Rex cried in a voice thick with fear.

'They are...not quite that,' Garaz said curiously.

They certainly didn't have the characteristic bloody wounds or hanging out organs Shift had come to associate with the word zombie.

The wet shucking sound of Silva's sword driving through the soft flesh of the creature's head made their insides squirm slightly. 'Don't just *stand* there trying to name them!' Silva cried. 'We cannot allow those things to rise.'

Her words gave the knights a much-needed wakeup call, and they set about the rising creatures, hacking off undead limbs with vigour. Even Shagraz proved himself a team player when properly motivated, cutting through decayed flesh as if it had the consistency of wet parchment.

'What is this?' Rex wailed, his breathing ragged and his eyes wide. This not being the situation to calmly talk someone down, Shift slapped him to get him to focus.

'Zombie-ish creatures,' they shouted over the overlapping moans. 'You don't have time to be scared. Unless you want to get eaten?'

Rex suddenly pushed them aside, driving one of his knives into the top of an undead creatures skull. As it fell to the ground, Shift tried not to dwell on how close it'd been to them.

Too close, again.

By now the enemy was numerous, and rising a lot faster than they could dispatch them. Those rising at either end of the village square were beyond the reach of their attacks, forming an oncoming wall of undead creatures. Within minutes, a horde descended on whichever living person happened to be nearest, moaning hungrily and reaching out with necrotised fingers.

'We need to get inside.' They were already tentatively stepping back.

It took only moments for any of the knights to be overwhelmed. They all fought bravely, of course. But wearing such heavy armour, they were easily dragged down by the creatures, whose issue was finding an opening in which to bite. But with the knights flailing on the floor, swinging their swords wildly as they were swarmed, they had time and numbers.

'This way, quick,' they called to anyone who was listening and wanted to live.

Garaz used fireballs from his staff to immolate any undead creature that came near as they herded several of the knights, including their leader and his annoying second into the building.

'Garaz, let's go,' Shift called as the last of the knights made it to safety.

Their orc companion didn't move. Instead, he watched Shagraz, his staff pointed as if he were about to fire but didn't want to risk hitting the orc warrior.

Why does that matter? He tried to kill us.

Shagraz appeared to be having the time of his life, laughing heartily as he set about the creatures.

'Garaz, come on.' They grabbed his arm, only to have their grip flung away.

'I will not leave him,' Garaz cried, even as the creatures began to overwhelm Shagraz, several mounting his back. The orc roared as he was bitten multiple times, more piling on by the second.

Shift grabbed Garaz's arm again. 'You can't help him,' they pleaded. He couldn't just stay out here and die. 'We need you. Please.'

This time, Garaz didn't resist, but his arm was limp as if he were filled with despair. Not wasting more time, Shift dragged him into the tavern. The door slammed shut behind them before furniture was piled against it to reinforce it. Several knights were already doing the same to the windows. On the other side of the door, hungry hands slapped against the wood.

CHAPTER 20

The necromancer looked up at the sky where the hole he'd created was already sealing itself and chuckled.

That laugh. He's laughing because he's killing my friends.

Rage filled Nicolas, his vision tunnelling until there was only Avus Arex. With a burst of might, he kicked off from the floor, flinging himself towards the necromancer. There was a second where he was almost sure he was going to break the grip holding him, but instead he was hauled back, thrashing and kicking, flinging trails of dust into the air.

'Damn you, you monster!' he cried, spittle flying from his mouth,

'Can't you two hold him back for more than a minute?' Avus asked his men casually as they once again forced him to his knees.

Beside him, Auron stayed perfectly still, glowering at the necromancer.

Shift, Silva, Garaz. They've got no warning that those...things are coming for them.

He couldn't just sit there and let it happen. He had to do something. But his strength and stamina didn't match up to his drive and rage.

'Are you done with your little tantrum?' Avus asked mockingly.

In his head, Nicolas had a very clear image of himself knocking the necromancer to the floor and bashing his head in with the nearest available rock. Even a pebble would do. He was prepared to take his time. If anyone needed killing, it was Avus Arex.

'You go to—' he snarled.

'Where?' Avus interrupted, gesturing around them. 'To the Underworld? I'm already here, and I'm in charge. Anything else, child?'

He had nothing else.

'What's next?' Auron's voice was grim, suggesting that he already knew.

Avus snorted derisively. 'Part of me would love to leave you alive until I'm sure all your friends are dead so I can gloat over it, but if you two have taught me anything, it's that letting you live is a mistake. So it's time for you to die.'

Nicolas tried to think of something to do, anything. He had the will now, but was unable to use it. Every logical sense was telling him that hope was lost. Here he was surrounded by an army, about to die…again. Or die properly. He wasn't sure what it was, but he'd no longer exist, and he could do nothing to save those he loved. Just like his parents.

Black energy coursed around the necromancer's hands as Avus closed his eyes and smiled. 'Get them up,' he commanded.

Nicolas and Auron were dragged to their feet, but Allius remained on the ground. Obviously, Avus had a worse fate in store for the scribe.

Hopefully, his suffering is short.

The necromancer opened his eyes, his expression filled with satisfaction as he looked at Nicolas. 'At least I can make you watch one friend die before I kill you.'

'Before you die, I really need to know something.' Vargas stepped forward, getting right in Auron's face. Avus looked thoroughly displeased with the interruption but said nothing. 'Is it true you were killed taking a dump? Because if you were—'

The hero's answer was to headbutt Vargas right in the nose. Putting his foot on the warrior's chest as Vargas reeled backwards from the blow, Auron used it at a stepping point from which to flip himself over the two wraiths holding him. Shoving them aside, he drove into Vargas, striking him with lefts and rights. Before anyone had time to react, Auron drew a small knife from Vargas's belt and flung it.

A violent tremor transitioned from the arms of one of his captors to Nicolas's own as the knife embedded itself between the wraith's eyes. The grip on one of his arms vanished as the warrior staggered back, pulling the knife out of the socket and regarding it with a stunned expression. Seeing his moment, Nicolas kicked the wraith in the side of the knee. As he fell back, the knife slipped from his grip and fell towards the floor. In a display of hand-eye coordination and speed that stunned even him, Nicolas managed to turn and quickly catch the knife in his free hand. He plunged the blade into the neck of the other wraith holding him.

With a gasp of shock, Avus levelled his hands at Nicolas, ready to unleash his dark magic. Thinking quickly, Nicolas grabbed the guard he'd stabbed, using him as a shield. The wraith was still clinging to his wounded neck as the blast struck him, bathing him in coursing black energy, turning his body to smoke and ash. Nicolas flung himself through it, covering the distance between him and Avus in seconds.

'No,' the necromancer snapped as Nicolas bore down on him.

In those few seconds, which slowed to a crawl, more energy built in Avus's hand, which was already rising towards him. Reaching out, he grabbed it, turning the arm behind the necromancer's back and bringing the blade to his throat. The energy was unleashed, and for a moment, both Nicolas and Avus were linked as it engulfed their combined bodies.

Between the searing pain, images flashed into his mind: a memory of when he and Avus had first met and of the fighting in the tower of Yarringsburg castle. But he was seeing it all from the necromancer's point of view. Yet it was barely perceptible as his body burned, his teeth clamping together so hard they threatened to shatter under the pressure.

After a moment, or maybe an hour, the energy dissipated, and he sagged, some untapped willpower the only thing keeping him standing with the knife still in his hand. Urgently, he pressed the blade to the necromancer's throat. The squeal from Avus certainly wasn't the noise a *God of Death* made.

'Nobody move!' Nicolas wanted to shout in a commanding way, but after what he'd just endured, it was more of a shrill cry.

From atop a dazed Vargas, Auron grinned at him. Somehow, in the seconds it had taken Nicolas to grab Avus, the hero had managed to floor three wraiths yet remain in position on his self-appointed nemesis. The other three wraiths about to accost him were frozen in place, fists poised to rain down on Auron. All of them glared at Nicolas.

'Get away from him!' This time, he sounded more commanding. To put a real exclamation on his point, he tweaked the arm he held.

'You can't behead me with that knife, boy,' the necromancer snarled.

'With the proper motivation, I surely can,' he bit back. 'And you've given me that.'

'Do as he says,' Avus commanded after a grunt of pain.

The wraiths backed away, and the shades just stood there blankly. Auron rose, grinning broadly. 'Nice one, kid.' Giving Vargas one final kick in the ribs for good measure, the hero walked over to join him.

He had a man dedicated to committing genocide under his knife, and he knew what he needed to do. There was only one thing stopping him. He had no illusion that as soon as Avus died, his horde would descend upon them. How at peace he was with that notion surprised him. His life would be a small price to pay to save Etherius. Yet if him and Auron died now, there'd be no one left to save his companions, or the people of Hablock, or his parents.

And if we die here who else will stand against this Maestro and whatever vile designs he has?

Right now, they needed to live. Which unfortunately meant that the necromancer got to live a little longer. Besides, he couldn't even guarantee that he could kill Avus before his servants fell upon him. How long did it take to behead someone with just a knife? He couldn't take the risk on an uncertain outcome.

'What now?' Avus snarled in his grip.

'Now you call off that army you sent after my friends,' Nicolas growled.

'That can't be done.' Nicolas was sure Avus was lying, but this was neither the time nor the place for a protracted argument. 'So I suggest you be sensible and release me.'

He reasserted pressure on the knife tip. 'Shut up.'

There was a satisfying silence. What was better was being able to feel the shiver of fear that the necromancer let slip. It was a good question though. What now? They were in the middle of a plain surrounded by an army, albeit depleted by those the necromancer had sent to kill his friends. He looked to Auron for inspiration.

'If we kill him now, we die,' Auron whispered. 'Then we can't help anyone. As much as I hate it, I think this is one of those *live to fight another day* situations.'

'We could take him back to Sha'then?' Nicolas suggested.

'It's a long walk back kid, especially with Allius in tow.' Nicolas could hear The Tallyman's whimpering behind him. 'Eventually something will go wrong, or that lot will just charge us anyway. At the moment, none of them will make a move because we have their master under the knife, but it's only a matter of time before someone tries something. Trust me kid, once one does, the rest will follow.'

'Where do we go?'

'The caves,' the hero said quietly. 'We get to the cave network and then we run like the Deities damned wind.'

'You think I'll let you get that far?' Avus sneered. 'I'll just command them to attack you here and now.'

'No you won't,' Auron smirked. 'I have vast experience of men like you.'

'There's no one like me,' the necromancer snapped.

'Please,' Auron scoffed. 'An enemy who hides behind his army and his magic or tricks, only appearing when he is sure the odds are heavily in his favour. A man with an inferiority complex who thinks he knows better than everyone. Someone who wants to prove how superior they are to everyone around them. You are every generic villain I've ever faced, and you want to live. So shut up, or the kid will end you here and now.'

'Here's what's going to happen,' Auron declared, raising his voice. 'We are going up that hill.'

'I don't think so,' Vargas smiled, readying his swords.

'I think so,' Auron replied. The hero went to pick up a blade from the floor, but after locking eyes with Vargas for a second he withdrew his hand. Maybe grabbing the sword would have been the thing to push this delicate situation over the edge? 'Because if you don't, your master dies and Sha'then is back in charge. What exactly do you think he will do to you lot when he is?'

Vargas's eyes worked from side to side, then the warrior took a step back. Auron's threat was enough to keep him in check for now, but time was already running out.

****

They were impressed. Despite the fact that their barricades around the windows and doors of the tavern were improvised from whatever furniture they could find, they were holding. It seemed the threat of being eaten alive was the mother of ingenuity. The banging beyond their barricades was incessant.

Fighting the undead is getting pretty tiring. Maybe the next outing, when Nick and Auron are back, we can go up against some aggravated gnomes. Nice and easy to handle.

They...they can go up against aggravated gnomes. I won't be there.

Of course, there would be no next outing of any sort if they didn't survive this one first, which was easier said than done. Of the knights, there were only eight left. Most stood with grim determination, watching the shaking barricades, swords ready. A couple appeared so shocked by what had transpired that they might be of no further use. Silva was armed and ready for action, as was standard. Rex seemed nervous but holding it together. Garaz was their main concern. The only magic user in the group, he was maybe their most potent weapon, but he sat in the back of the room, withdrawn.

'What do we do now?' the annoying second of the knight troop demanded.

'Sir Gerran, hold your composure,' the leader, a man they'd learned was called Sir Darick, commanded. 'It is no time to lose ourselves when besieged by such monsters.'

Sir Gerran held his tongue but grudgingly.

Not something he's accustomed to doing, I'd wager.

'Reinforcements will arrive soon,' one of the other knights said with foolish optimism. 'When we are overdue, a troop will be sent.'

'And they will run into monsters they are as unprepared for as you were,' Silva remarked, not taking her eyes from the door.

Sir Gerran swung round, his sword pointed at Silva, who looked at the weapon inquisitively. 'You dare question our ability? We are knights of Yarringsburg, mercenary. I will not have thieves and murderers impugn our honour.'

Is this guy still trying to pick a fight? If he was, he ought to look in any other direction than Silva.

'You mistake my intent,' Silva replied coolly, though they knew she was barely keeping her temper in check. 'None could be prepared for creatures to rise from the very ground they stood on.'

'If you can call that lava-infested mess out there *ground* anymore.' Their attempt to lighten the mood fell on deaf ears.

'I thought zombies only came out at night.' Rex's voice was a murmur, his face pale. 'I'm sure I heard that somewhere.'

'I don't think the living dead care whether it's night, dawn, or day.' They shrugged. 'They're here, and we have to try to survive...*together*.' The last comment was pointed at a certain knight.

That knight took a menacing step forward.

'Sir Gerran,' Sir Darick bellowed. 'I will not tell you to compose yourself again. Like it or not, we are all in this together. Fighting amongst ourselves will do naught but serve the creatures at our door.' The banging outside the door intensified, almost as if the monsters knew they were being talked about.

'Apologies, my lord,' Sir Gerran said with contrition, albeit insincere. 'I forget myself. These are...difficult circumstances.'

'Very true.' Sir Darick nodded. 'I know you transferred to us from the king's own guard, but I expect you to remember your place. Now go and search the upstairs to ensure we are alone.'

Sir Gerran bowed and marched towards the stairs, sparing them a quick glare as he did.

Nothing like an argument to add tension to a situation where you are surrounded by zombies. They looked at Silva, and the warrior nodded that all was well. Now time for Garaz.

Walking to the back of the room, they paused only to pat Rex reassuringly on the shoulder. 'You okay?'

The young thief looked up at them. He looked terrified, but they'd been in enough situations with him to trust that he'd keep his head. 'This is all a bit *much*.'

They stifled their laugh. That was an understatement. 'Don't worry.' They kept their tone light. 'We're getting out of this. Did you see how slowly those things move?' Though they'd claimed a lot of lives already. But they weren't about to say that aloud.

'I trust you,' Rex said with a forced smile. 'I know you'll see us right.'

'Of course.' They smiled back. 'I don't like owing people, and you *did* just save my life. I'm just glad I get a chance to repay you quickly.'

Rex smiled and shook his head. 'And here was me wanting to lord your debt over you for years to come..'

'Sorry to disappoint you.' They winked before moving to the back of the room. 'How you doing, big guy?' they asked as they pulled a chair up in front of the hunched-over orc.

Garaz looked up at them and smiled wanly. 'I am as well as can be.'

But you really just wanted to tell me to piss off, didn't you?

'What was Shagraz to you?' It was a hunch, but they were sure it was a decent one.

The orc's yellow eyes met theirs for a moment. 'Just one of my people. It always saddens me when I see orcs who embody the stereotype the world has of us. We are so much more than that.'

'And what about the rest of it?' Garaz gave them a questioning look. 'Don't play with me. You have been off for a while now.'

For a second they thought the orc wouldn't answer. 'It's just the violence of this life,' Garaz sighed. 'I'm a healer, and yet I fight and kill. The toad creature. What I did...shook me.'

'What you did was save my life,' Shift said firmly. 'I'm only here because of you, so stop being so hard on yourself.' They punched Garaz on the arm. 'Was ripping him in two a little excessive? Yes. But it got the job done. For Deities' sake, don't follow Nick's example.'

The image of the toad creature bearing down on them flashed in Shift's mind. It was quickly followed by images of Shagraz choking them to death and how close the creature outside had been to killing them. Blinking, they shook their head slightly, dismissing them and the uneasy feeling that had appeared with them.

'Apologies,' Garaz said with a slight chuckle. 'I guess I got carried away defending my family.'

Family?

They had to shake that word off too. If they gave any credence to what the orc was saying, they may never leave.

'I don't think this is a coincidence,' Shift said, turning the conversation back to the matter at hand.

'I had come to the same conclusion.' They started at Silva's sudden voice behind them.

How does someone with boots so large move so quietly?

'Indeed,' Garaz agreed. 'We send Auron to the Underworld after Nicolas and then a horde of zombie-like creatures assail us. This is connected.'

For a moment, Silva and Garaz looked at each other knowingly.

'Am I missing something?' they asked.

The orc was the first to speak. 'That voice, it was Avus Arex. I am sure of it.'

Wow. The necromancer from Yarringsburg. They'd been kidnapped by his minions, including Silva, as a tribute for his vampiric allies. Though they'd helped stop his plan, Shift had never actually met the necro-mancer. But their companions seemed pretty damned sure about it, and that was good enough for Shift.

'So Nick gets attacked and banished to the Underworld, and then a necromancer sends his monsters to attack us. Could he have been behind the attack on Hablock?'

Garaz mulled this over for a moment. 'Doubtful. These poor people were taken not eaten. Besides, why not just use the creatures from the start? Why bother trying to have your thief friend, and I assume the other orcs, assassinate us?'

They'd forgotten about Mace. Where had that slippery toad gone? Hopefully, he'd been eaten and those creatures were crapping him out as they spoke.

They were in a situation, a bad one. If they were all going to get out of this, they needed to pull together. Sir Darick seemed to have a level head, but they couldn't ignore the fact that the knights had come here to arrest them, nor that Sir Gerran was an ass of the highest order. But at least their companions were in check now. That was something.

Shift's eyes flicked towards the door, where the banging and groaning from beyond showed no signs of letting up.

And we need every advantage we can get.

Chapter 21

'Maybe I'll skin you alive and let your skinless bodies wander this land for all eternity?'

'Will you *shut up?*'

Backing their way up the hillside with their hostage had been a slow process, inching their way up the slope a step at a time, their pace so slow that Allius had already scurried up to the top. What made it worse was the fact that the necromancer's army followed in their wake, dogging their every step. With every passing minute the tension grew. The attack was imminent, it was just a matter of time. And Nicolas was sure they'd get to him long before he'd managed to actually kill their master when that time came.

Hopefully we're nearly in running distance of the caverns at least.

Avus had chosen to spend their trip amusing himself by coming up with various things he was going to do to Auron and Nicolas once they were at his mercy again. Nicolas had briefly considered striking him halfway up the slope to shut him up, but the army might think he was trying to kill their leader, and right now Avus's safety was the only thing keeping them in check. Either way, Nicolas wished Avus would bloody well cut it out. At least the necromancer respected the knife tip at his throat enough not to try teleporting away or any other funny business.

'Or I could feed you to worms. That's a slow death, surely?'

'You really are a loathsome man, aren't you?'

'You think you know me, but you don't,' Avus scoffed. 'You have no idea how I got to where I am.'

'And you know what?' Auron asked. 'Nobody cares. Once you've done the things you've done, no one gives a crap about whatever tragic back-story you have. I'm sure you have your reasons for being scum, they always do. I stopped caring years ago. Like I said before, generic.'

'Ah,' the necromancer retorted. 'The soulless recourse of the arrogant hero.'

Auron seemed to take exception to that. 'I'm not arrogant. I've been doing this for so long that I've seen, heard or done most things. With that comes a certain...complacency. I'm just a guy doing a job.'

Avus let out a harsh chuckle. 'One that comes with fame and adoration and I'm sure copious sexual conquests.' Nicolas kept hoping he'd heard about all of them, but just when that seemed the case: *'Oh, listen, did you guys hear about the time with me and the seven dwarf serving wenches?'*

Auron shrugged. 'I didn't say there *weren't* benefits to my work.'

'I'm at the mercy of a naïve child and the biggest whore in the Nine Kingdoms of Man,' Avus snarled. The muscles in the necromancer's arm suddenly tensed. He was readying himself to make a move.

Nicolas dug the knife into Avus's chin. 'Yes, you are at *our* mercy.'

All thoughts of attempted escape seemed to vanish instantly.

'So this one time.' Nicolas really hoped this one wasn't going to be about his sexual conquests. 'There's this kid who gets beaten daily by the teacher at his orphanage. Guy's a sadist and decides this particular child is the object of his ire. The boy grows up and finally gets out. As you can imagine, he's a little aggrieved by his treatment and pretty maladjusted. So he goes to seek revenge. Burns down the orphanage. Ironic thing, though—the teacher who beat him was at the tavern that night. But all the orphans were home.' Auron stopped the pair and looked Avus right in the eye. 'He tried telling me his sad little backstory. I might have been sympathetic had he not killed twenty innocent children exacting his revenge. I removed his head just the same.' For emphasis, Auron drew his finger across his neck. The hero let that sink in a moment before continuing. 'So don't think you're special, just because some bad stuff happened to you. You can use it as an excuse to murder all you like, it still makes you a murderer. And I'm still going to kill you. Or maybe the kid will.'

Whatever reasoning Avus has can't justify all this death. He needs to be stopped, once and for all.

'You have to die,' Nicolas said grimly.

Avus stared at him from his peripheral vision. 'So do it,' he hissed in response. 'Please, I invite you to.' When the tip of the blade didn't penetrate his skin instantly, Avus cackled. 'I think we both know that this farce is nearly played out. Auron was right, I do want to live. But now that I've thought about it, how long would it take you to behead me with that knife? More than the twenty paces it'd take for my men to get to me?'

Oh shit.

'Vargas,' Avus bellowed. 'Take...' Nicolas drove the knife into Avus's throat. The necromancer's words became a surprised gargle, drowned out by the instant collective roar from the wraiths shadowing them.

'Charge,' Vargas commanded, and Avus's army surged forwards.

'Run,' Auron shouted.

Putting his foot in the necromancer's back, Nicolas kicked him back down the slope and bolted towards the caves. It bought them a precious second, the horde coming to a halt lest they accidentally trample their master.

Glancing back, he saw two wraiths helping Avus to his feet as the rest of the army charged towards them. The necromancer had one hand on his bleeding neck, the other was engulfed in a ball of dark energy. Almost drunkenly, Avus flung it towards them. It struck the cavern entrance just as Nicolas crossed the threshold. He skidded to a halt as he heard rumbling, looking back toward the entrance just in time to watch it cave in.

'That's a nice piece of luck,' Auron chuckled in the darkness.

****

They had an idea. It was a good idea, but they didn't like it. Mainly due to its potentially suicidal nature. For a little while, they kept it to themselves as the knights voiced various methods of escape. Most of those were variations of *charge out hacking and slashing,* and so weren't viable. They'd be swarmed in seconds. After a while, there were no more ideas, only silence. Save for the incessant banging of the damned, of course. As much as they didn't want to say it aloud, it appeared to be their only option. So they couldn't put it off any longer.

With a reluctant sigh, Shift got the attention of the room. 'Okay, every-one. We're stuck in here, and we need help, but we don't know when that will come. Our problem is, therefore, how to get help. The solution to that problem is me.' Garaz, Silva, and Rex seemed to have a clue what they were proposing, but the knights stared at them blankly. 'I can change form,' they elaborated.

'You're a witch?' Sir Darick asked, his tone equal parts scepticism and judgement.

I look nothing like a witch. But this really wasn't the time for getting their back up or lengthy explanations. 'No, but I can change shape. I propose to change myself into one of *those* and slip out of town. When I return, I'll bring a whole army with me.'

'Ridiculous,' Sir Gerran scoffed. 'You mean to slip away and leave us, the only ones who know of your crimes, to die.'

This bloody guy. Hopefully his superior is a little more sensible.

There was reluctance on Sir Darick's wizened face. That wasn't a good sign. 'Though I stayed Sir Gerran's hand for the sake of survival through unity, do not believe for a second that I trust you.' *Ouch.* 'You are responsible for raiding this village. No matter what unholy minions lie beyond that wall, I have not forgotten that.'

'Firstly, that wall isn't going to last forever.' They were fighting to keep the annoyance from their voice but only partially succeeding. 'Secondly, we didn't attack this village.'

'We received word that the village was being raided,' Sir Darick replied coolly. 'We come here and find questionable folk fighting in the streets and the villagers missing. What conclusion would you draw?'

The argument was logical but unhelpful. There was a more pressing question, though. 'Who told you this village was under attack?'

Sir Darick seemed hesitant to answer. After a moment, they figured that it wasn't because he didn't want to tell them but because he didn't know. 'Our orders came from above to investigate an attack upon Hablock. I need not know more to do my duty.'

Bluster. It clearly rankled him that he didn't know.

How do you gain the trust of someone who thinks you're a marauder?

Around them the sound of hands banging on wood was loud, almost too loud to think. 'Those things are out there, and eventually, they will come in here and kill us. I get that you don't trust me, but when I'm your only hope, you don't have that luxury. If you don't believe that I'll come back for you then believe that I will damn sure come back for them.' They indicated their companions.

The knight considered this for a moment. 'That I do believe,' Sir Darick confirmed finally. 'Tell me your plan.'

There was little to tell. Change into one of the creatures, slip out the window and run like their feet were on fire for help. It wasn't a prospect they relished, but again, it was their only hope. In truth, turning into a bird and flying for help would've been much better, but despite Garaz's healing, their arm hadn't fully recovered yet, and when you're high up in the air, you needed to be confident that both wings were up to the task.

'Very well.' Sir Darick nodded finally.

Guess who spoke up next. 'My lord, you can't trust these—'

Sir Darick silenced Sir Gerran with a look before continuing. 'However, there is an amendment to your plan. As I said, I do believe that you will return for your friends. But until you do, they will surrender their weapons and remain under guard.'

Silva looked as if she might imminently breathe fire. Shift put their hand on her arm before she could. Via a series of looks, the pair had an in-depth conversation about the sense of relinquishing weapons when surrounded by undead creatures. Eventually, Silva relented, and she handed her weapons to one of the knights. Garaz handed over his staff, and Rex surrendered his knives.

Okay then, time to be suicidal.

'Are you sure about this course of action?' Garaz asked as he stood at the bottom of the stairs beside them.

'Of course, there's no reason it shouldn't work.'

The orc put a hand on their shoulder, wishing them well without saying a word. Silva did the same. Rex looked more prone to argue, but he'd come here to save them. His whole plan would be ruined if he let them kill themselves on a fool's errand.

'I'd say that the room on the east side of the building would be best.' *Wow, Sir Gerran was actually being helpful.* 'It looks out onto the alleyway behind the building.'

They gave the knight a thankful nod. As they ascended the stairs, they tried to steel themselves as much as possible. The others would be downstairs making enough noise to attract the creatures to one side of the building, allowing the knight that came with them time to lower them down without being heard. With their bad arm, it wouldn't be pleasant, but needs must.

Stepping into one of the side rooms, they asked the knight to wait outside. Having people watch them change was kind of awkward and they tried to avoid it as often as possible. 'And don't swing your sword at me when I come out looking like one of them.' They smiled before closing the door.

The knight, a pale young lad, had nodded in agreement but not convincingly.

Alone in the room, they looked at themselves in the reflection of the tavern's glass window, already beginning to feel the change coming.

A flash of movement behind them caught their eye. Turning, they were just in time to catch Mace's fist right in their stomach. The wind driven out of their lungs, they fell forward, ending up on all fours, giving Mace a prime opportunity to kick them in the ribs. The impact rolled them across the floor. No ribs were broken, but it hurt like a bitch.

Clutching their side, still struggling to breathe, they turned to see the thief lord stood over them. They tried to change into something more skilled at brutally killing opponents, but the pain and difficulty breathing was interfering with their gift.

'Ooo fink ooo can jus break by doze an' get away with it?'

They really had to concentrate to understand what Mace was saying, which was difficult when their rib cage felt as if it might crumble to dust at any moment. What didn't need translating was the knife in his hand.

Where in the Underworld did he get that from?

It was no blade for carving cheese. This was a warrior's knife. Certainly not the kind of thing one found in a tavern room.

'Gonna cut you ub, bitch.'

Behind Mace, the door opened. 'I heard a—'

Before the young knight could finish his sentence, Mace turned and plunged the knife between the plates of his armour with the artfulness of the deadliest assassin. The young knight looked at the blade in disbelief, coughing a glob of blood onto his chin. His look turned to one of fury as he gripped Mace around the throat. The thief lord turned the knife in the wound, loosing a cry of pain from the knight, before sliding the weapon out and driving it into the stunned knight's throat. Mace lowered his dead body gently to the floor even as blood poured from the wounds.

'Wouldn do to have eddyone hear that,' Mace mumbled.

Shift had used the unfortunate distraction to get to their feet. The vase shattered as it collided with Mace's head. He stumbled backwards, arms flailing to get the debris from his face. They leapt at him, driving their fist into his cheek. Desperately, they grabbed at the knife arm, hoping to disarm him quickly. Mace was a bit quicker, driving his free hand into their ribs. This time, there was a crack. They dipped on one side with a cry, and the thief lord drove his fist into their jaw.

The world blurred for a moment. When it refocused, they had just enough time to grab the oncoming knife hand with both hands and stop it puncturing their stomach. A hand slapped them across the face. As they fell back, cold metal kissed the skin of their arm. Pain flared through their nerves.

With a sharp crack, they were driven headfirst against the wall. Again, the world blurred, everything muted for a moment. They threw a punch but were so dazed they could put no force behind it or even aim it properly.

There was a banging at the door. 'What goes on in there?'

They were vaguely aware of someone trying to enter the room, but the corpse of the young knight blocked the door. What it gave Shift was a moment's distraction to collect themselves and make sense of the world again.

Mace glanced briefly at the banging door before driving forward with the knife. At the last second, they ducked aside, slipping under his arm. With a thud, the knife tip embedded in the wood exactly where their head would've been. Now to get rid of the knife in the most efficient way possible.

They registered a metallic liquid taste as they bit down on Mace's hand. It was disgusting, but the quickest way to take the knife out of play. The thief lord cried out in pain as they quickly spat out the chunk of flesh they'd taken. The banging on the door became deeper as someone drove their shoulder against it. The corpse jigged and jerked under the force of the blows.

Their hair was yanked roughly by Mace's free hand and their head slammed against the wall twice. Each impact left a ringing bell in their head. Drunkenly, they threw a punch at him. It was intercepted, and two shots to the stomach returned for their trouble. It became hard to breathe.

Using the wall to push off, they flung themselves forwards from their doubled-over position, driving Mace backwards and to the floor, which shook as they collided with it. Again, he used their hair to lever their head back before punching their jaw.. Shift fell back onto the floor with another bump to the head.

Mace was atop them, his hands around their throat. 'You like it whed I'b od top, darlig?'

His foetid breath washed over their skin. He'd gotten too close. Now it was time to think. What would Silva do? Better yet, what would Auron do? They lashed out, driving their fingers into Mace's eyes. They didn't have the energy to put much pressure into it, but with eyes, they didn't need to. Mace practically jumped off them screaming just as the door behind them caved in with a loud crash.

Finger poke of doom. Thanks, Auron.

The world was still a swirling vortex of sensations. It was difficult to pick anything out. They managed to focus on Silva stood over them, looking down with fury in her eyes. Slowly, the warrior looked up again. 'Maybe you would like to try that with me.'

In a blur, Silva leapt from their line of sight. They were vaguely aware of the sound of multiple punches. There were also several snaps that made them wince even in their disorientated state. Each was punctuated by a high-pitched scream. There was one final crash, and then silence.

The warrior's image blurred in and out of focus above them, concern evident in Silva's hard face. 'I told you that you needed to learn how to fight.'

Their laugh came with another spat glob of blood. 'I'm okay. Thanks for asking.'

'You don't look it.' The warrior sniffed, before shouting for Garaz.

Raising their head took effort, painful effort, but they were curious.

Why is Mace stood facing the wall?

Several of his limbs were at incorrect angles to his body. In a couple of instances, bloody bones were poking through the skin. And...he wasn't really standing at all. He was impaled on the handle of the knife he'd left stuck in the wall, through his eye, if they had to guess.

Resting on the floor again, they let out a laugh that caused spikes of pain in their ribs. When Silva turned to look at them, Shift grinned at the warrior inanely. 'I love you.' They chuckled.

The confusion on the warrior's face made them laugh again.

CHAPTER 22

Usually, when Nicolas was in a tunnel, which was frustratingly often, he had Auron's aura to light the way. Not here. The hero was no longer a spirit. Well, he was a spirit, but not *that* kind of spirit. Either way, it was dark. Pitch black. He would've assumed himself alone except that he could hear the movement of Auron's feet and the nervous whimpering from Allius, which echoed around eerily.

Carefully, he advanced, testing every footstep before committing to it just as he had throughout the cavern. Thankfully, the hole the skeleton monster had made had been easy to find, being marked by the creature's remains. Still, Nicolas had very nearly fallen down it. The darkness made moving at speed difficult. And moving at speed was necessary when they were being pursued. At the moment, they seemed to be going no faster than the shades, who he was sure were busy trying to clear the entrance and come after them, if they hadn't already succeeded.

At least this tunnel leads directly to Sha'then's camp and reinforcements.

'I can't believe we're fighting the necromancer again,' he grumbled as he tried to ignore something creeping quickly over his leg.

'There used to be a time when things just stayed dead,' came the glib reply from the darkness.

'Is that not an age we can return to?'

There was a mock gasp. 'But then we'd never have met, kid.'

A big part of him wouldn't be too sad about that. As fond as he was of the hero, a lot of bad things had happened to him since he'd been in Auron's company. Somehow, even in the dark, he knew Auron's eyes were on him.

'Your life's been tough since we met. I get that. But I'm not the cause of that. Whatever this is, it's spreading across...everything. Sooner or later, it would've come to your doorstep, Word Bearer or not.'

He had no clue how Auron could read him so well, especially without being able to see him. He had doubts, many of them. But he kept them to himself. 'Let's just get out of here, shall we?'

'We need to return to the Master,' Allius whimpered. 'He'll know what to do.'

There was a chuckle in the black. 'Of course. We need to round up some more crappy skeleton soldiers to go and get killed.'

'You think he'll send us back out there?' Personally, Nicolas was more concerned about Sha'then stringing them up again for losing his army.

'I should think so,' the hero replied. 'We are all he really has. The skeletons are pretty useless, no matter how many you throw at the enemy.' A plan that hadn't worked out well for the Lord of the Underworld thus far, and showed no signs of suddenly changing. 'What I wouldn't give for some decent troops? Or just Silva. Murdering bitch she may be, but she's also massively handy in a fight.'

'Silva.' He whispered the name. Something was dawning on him. The ember of an idea...or was it? Maybe it was a silly notion. He'd keep it to himself.

'Kid, don't whisper her name like that in the dark. It sounds creepy.'

'What? I wasn't.'

'You whispered her name, I heard you.'

'Yeah, but not like *that*.'

'Glad to hear it.' There was an element of teasing in Auron's voice. 'Because you're spoken for.'

'I'm what?' What did that mean? Who was *spoken for*?

The hero chuckled. 'You two will figure it out one day.'

This really wasn't the place for stupid jokes and riddles. Especially when he had an idea.

Is it an idea? It seems silly.

Maybe it wasn't silly? He'd just talk it out and see where it led. He doubted it'd end up being the stupidest thing he'd said or done in front of Auron.

'Silva,' he began, making sure he didn't whisper it. 'Silva is a damned soul who wants redemption, right? Well, there have to be some of those here. I doubt every single soul in this place has sided with the necromancer or been enslaved by him.'

Okay, this sounds better than I thought. Keep going.

'Maybe some slipped away? If we could find them, maybe we could convince them to fight with us, somehow? They'd have to be more useful than the skeletons. Our own *wraiths*.' He wrinkled his nose at having to use the term.

There was silence. Was that good silence or bad silence? Could Auron just speak and let him know which? 'Kid,' the hero started slowly. 'That has to be one of the best ideas you've ever had.'

Oh, okay then. Pat on the back for me.

'Good luck convincing the Master of that,' Allius put in, very unhelpfully, before adding, 'But the theory is sound.'

That's a start.

'You're a ray of sunshine, Shambles.' Auron tutted from close by. Then: 'I think we're here.'

For a moment, Nicolas thought Auron mad. He could see no light...but that was just because there was none in this endlessly gloomy realm. The tunnel sloped upwards, and soon enough, he could make out the exit. He promised himself that if he ever got back to Etherius, he would be the best person he could. He would *not* end up here again.

Around the lip of the crater, marking the exit to their tunnel, was a group of skeleton warriors, spears pointed towards them.

'Easy, guys,' Auron said, holding his hands high. 'It's your fearless leaders.'

They got no warm welcome from the creatures, who didn't even help the trio out of the crater.

As Sha'then marched towards them from the fort like an oncoming storm, the clouds literally appeared to darken in his wake. 'As there are no skeletons with you, I take it that you lost then?' The Lord of the Underworld huffed audibly.

We're fine, thanks.

Though they might not be for long, judging by the fire in Sha'then's eyes.

'The necromancer trapped the trap, the shifty bastard.' Auron shook his head as he stood before the not-quite-a-Deity. 'You're lucky we made it back at all.'

'My cup runneth over with joy.' Whether it was the flat tone or the folded arms, Nicolas didn't believe him.

Allius shuffled over to Sha'then and prostrated himself before his Master.

'I see you survived, Shambles.' The Lord of the Underworld's tone matched his look. 'You were supposed to keep an eye on them so they *didn't* lose my army, worm.'

Does he have to look at him with that much contempt?

'Hey.' Sha'then spun around, and suddenly Nicolas wondered what he was doing, but he continued regardless. 'Don't talk to him like that. He couldn't have changed the outcome, and if you were *that* worried about it, you should've come with us yourself.' *While I'm at it...* 'And his name isn't *Shambles*, it's Allius. If he's respectful enough to bow before you, at least have the decency to get his name right.'

Sha'then's body was as still as one of the skeletons, his mouth wide. On the floor, Allius looked up at him as if he were some hero of old, though he might not have a chance to enjoy it if Sha'then decided to strip his flesh from his bones for his impudence.

Before anyone could react, or overreact, Auron stepped between the two. 'We haven't come back empty-handed,' the hero said. 'We have intelligence and an idea. So maybe that'll make you a little more pleased to see us.'

The Lord of the Underworld glowered silently. It struck Nicolas that Sha'then's whole persona was that of a pouty child. Someone else was playing with his toys, and he didn't like it but couldn't take them back. Maybe that meant he'd shut up and listen?

'I suppose I'd best be all ears then,' the Lord of the Underworld replied curtly. 'Seeing as I'm running out of skeleton warriors thanks to you two morons.'

'Well, firstly, Avus plans to overrun the world of the living when he's done here.' Auron left the *with you* off the end of his sentence.

To his surprise, Sha'then laughed. 'The fool. How far does he think he'll get with that before the Deities smite him? As much as they are forbidden to interfere in mortal affairs, they are bound to intercede if he tries to turn Etherius into a giant graveyard.'

The tinge of uncertainty in the Lord of the Underworld's voice didn't inspire confidence. Surely they would've gotten involved the minute Avus sent those shades after his friends? Briefly, he told Sha'then what had happened. The Lord of the Underworld's face grew paler, if possible.

'He broke through my barrier?' Sha'then seemed genuinely shaken. 'The amount of power he'd need to expend... Maybe I have underestimated him?'

'Yes, but in doing so, he depleted his forces, and maybe his strength too, if we're lucky.' Auron smiled. 'And like I said, we have a plan.'

Sha'then motioned impatiently for them to continue.

'How many of the souls down here didn't side with the necromancer or at least got away *before* he could enslave them for not siding with him?'

The question obviously surprised the Lord of the Underworld. 'I do not have an exact tally. Less than a hundred. As you can imagine, even those inmates not enthusiastic about sticking it to me felt no need to aid me.'

'Eighty two, to be exact,' Allius said, still prostrate on the floor.

'I can work with that.' Auron nodded thoughtfully. 'We're going to recruit them.'

There was a moment of stunned silence then Sha'then laughed mockingly. 'I missed out on some much-needed torture for pearls of wisdom like *that*? Just because they did not join Avus does not mean they will fight for me.' Sha'then snarled. 'Besides, they are hardly the trustworthy types. How do you propose to sway them to my cause?'

'By offering to have you redeem their souls, within reason.'

'I...you...*what*?' The Lord of the Underworld spluttered after a moment of incredulous staring. 'These people are down where they deserve to be. I won't just go around redeeming this murderer and that sadist. That's not how it works. I cannot give pardons and be lenient because someone may be of use to me.'

'You found a use for Allius,' Nicolas said, glancing at the book in The Tallyman's hand.

Sha'then frowned for a second, and Nicolas realised it was because he was trying to work out who *Allius* was. 'Oh him,' he replied finally. 'He's *barely* useful.'

For Deities' sake, man, I reminded you of his name not a few minutes ago.

'It might be the only way,' Nicolas added. 'The skeletons aren't great, and you will lose eventually if you don't. So we are...applying some creative thinking. Which is exactly what you need us for.'

'The plan is a good one, Master,' Allius said, head tilted up at an awkward angle from the floor he still lay on.

'Quiet, you,' Sha'then snapped, and Allius planted his face firmly in the dirt again. The Lord of the Underworld stroked his chin thoughtfully. 'I suppose the idea has its merits.'

'Of course it does,' Auron smiled. 'And you don't need to offer them a shot at getting to the Eternal Forest. They'd never buy that anyways. But give them a chance to make their sentences here more comfortable and I think we may be able to get a few on side.'

'Assuming they allow you to live long enough to make the offer,' Sha'then scoffed. 'Of that eighty-two, there are bound to be a few that you sent down here. In fact, in life, you were quite excellent in ensuring my torture pits were filled to the brim.'

That was something Nicolas hadn't considered. His companion had vanquished a good number of evildoers in his time, and by *vanquished* he meant cut to pieces. Suddenly, they'd exposed a hole in their plan the size of the one outside Sha'then's fort.

'So where are they then?'

Is Auron not worried at all? Perhaps I worry enough for the both of us...and Shift and Garaz.

'They've congregated away from the fighting, in the Forests of Misery.'

Of course that's what it's called.

'But I welcome you to have at them. I'm intrigued to see how you fare, and if they do kill you, I will not miss you as generals. I am quite capable of losing armies on my own.'

'Hear that, kid?' Auron's voice was thick with sarcasm. 'I think he likes us.'

'Then you certainly misheard me,' Sha'then commented dryly. Then the Lord of the Underworld cast a distasteful glance at Allius, still on the floor. 'And you can take *that* with you. If you're going to die, I'd at least like it documented for an amusing read later. Once he's finished organising getting that giant hole filled in, of course.'

Auron wasn't openly swearing at the Lord of the Underworld, but his eyes were saying a lot of bad things.

****

Garaz moved his hands away, the energy only recently built in them dissipating until they could see his large green palms again. 'Are you okay?' the concern was blatant in his tone and on his face.

That healing magic's quite refreshing, really.

Instead of answering, they just raised a thumb. The cuts and bruises were gone, but their ghosts lingered, marking where they'd been struck and beaten. They were worried about how being jumped like that would affect them.

Happens to the best of us. I bet Auron's got loads of stories of being ambushed. I already know the one that worked out worst for him.

That was a sobering thought. They cast a glance at Mace's corpse, still pinned to the wall.

Another close call. If my companions hadn't been nearby...

'Shift?' Garaz's eyes were full of worry.

Carefully, they got up and stretched themselves out, pulling out all the tweaks and twinges in their body. 'I'm good. Thanks, big guy.'

The orc didn't seem convinced but smiled anyway. 'Silva is correct. You do need to learn how to fight better.'

'Why? I'll just get slapped around until Silva comes and saves me,' they replied with a broad grin. The comment was meant in jest, but the grin faltered as their words churned up the very recent memory of their beating.

'Do not fear,' Silva said to Garaz. 'Once these creatures are vanquished, this one will be getting some thorough schooling.'

This one?

They hated to admit aloud that they needed it, so they wouldn't. But they did remember watching Silva training Nick. It wasn't something to look forward to. They'd been destined to follow but a sudden and surprising pulled muscle had delayed that...sadly.

There's a lesson to be learnt there.

'I wouldn't need to learn to fight if someone knew how to check up-stairs properly.' They ensured that their voice was loud enough for Sir Gerran to hear as he entered the room. His look of irritation was very satisfying.

'I did search thoroughly,' the knight growled in response. 'This man was obviously skilled in evading capture. As all of that *ilk* are.' The term *ilk* was blatantly being applied to Shift and their companions.

'Just thank the Deities there were none of those things up here.'

Or maybe not. If there's one person I could stand to see get eaten...

No, they weren't being fair. Yes, the guy was an ass, but Mace had a long history of evading the authorities and anyone else who hunted him. Sir Gerran had simply been outclassed. Part of them wanted to apologise, but it just wasn't going to happen.

The sudden wet sucking noise made when two of the knights pulled Mace from the wall was both distracting and nauseating. As the knights dropped the former thief lord to the floor, Sir Gerran pulled the knife out of the wall, crouching quickly to clean the blood and gore from the blade on Mace's clothes before finally finding a place for it in his belt.

Can't blame him. It is a fancy knife.

Great, now I'm jealous of Sir Aggravating.

'Does the plan still stand?'

They started at the voice. Since entering the room, Sir Darick had been so quiet they'd forgotten he was there. The knight had been stood over the young lad that'd been killed, mourning his fallen brother.

Must be difficult, so many dead in one day.

'It does,' they confirmed. 'Though maybe on the other side of the tavern now.'

The fight had been quite loud in the end, and a handful of the creatures had followed the noise. Looking out of the window, they could see them pawing at the side of the building, clawing at the wooden wall as if they could climb it. Thank the Deities their thin limbs were too weak to support their weight. One had tried, but the arms had...removed themselves...from its shoulders. It had resorted to headbutting the wall, as it couldn't slap like its foul brethren. Once the creatures noticed them watching, they growled menacingly.

Growl all you want, I'm still up here...for now.

That was a sobering thought. Soon they'd be down there, with them, pretending to be one of them. As much faith as they had in their abilities, the possibility of getting eaten was still very real.

'Well,' they said, pulling back into the room and clapping their hands, 'this isn't getting any less insane, so we'd best just get on with it. I take it the rooms down the hall were searched better than this one?'

A cheap dig, but a necessary one.

Sir Gerran rounded on them angrily, but at a brief glare from Sir Darick calmed down. 'I will check,' the knight said through bared teeth before storming from the room.

'Are you certain you are well enough to do this?' Garaz's fatherly concern was endearing.

'I am,' they confirmed. They looked back towards the window and the incessant banging. Honestly, they weren't in great shape, even after the healing magic, but proper rest and recovery was a luxury they could ill afford. Sooner or later, the creatures were getting in. It had to be now.

There was a pang of something in Garaz's eye. They were about to question it when their least favourite knight returned.

'The room's clear,' Sir Gerran reported sourly.

Really?

With a nod of good luck from Sir Darick, they left the room and walked the tavern's hall, Silva at their heels. Looked like the warrior was intent on protecting them this time.

I could kiss her for that. Maybe I should? Imagine the look on her face.

No, Shift. Behave.

The idea of being alone in one of the tavern's rooms was unsettling—not that they'd been alone in the last one—so her presence was welcome. At least Silva had the decency to turn around when they changed. Even when they were keeping their clothes on, people watching them change just felt odd, as if they were sharing a bath with them or something.

'Done,' they said as the last ripples of the change left their body. 'What do you think?'

Considering Silva's hand went to her sword the second she turned around, it seemed they'd done a good job. They looked at their own hand for a second before recoiling at the decayed greying skin upon it.

That's the last time I look at myself in this form.

'Are you sure about this?' Silva asked as they approached the window.

They wanted to say no. 'Yeah, of course. It's nice that you care,' they said glibly instead.

Silva looked at them through narrowed eyes. 'I may not show it, but of course I care. You are one of my companions.'

If Silva's opening up, she's worried. And if she's worried then...

Shut up, Shift. Positive thoughts only when you're about to walk through a horde of bitey creatures.

When they snuck a look out the window, the alley was clear. But they needed to be sure. Twice they stomped on the wooden floor. Soon enough, they heard a mass of noise below, the knights banging and shouting against the other walls of the tavern to ensure the creatures' attention was focused away from this side.

After waiting a few very tense moments, they let Silva lower them out the window. Their damaged arm complained at taking their weight, further supporting the notion that wings weren't a viable option—and that the damage had been severe. There was still a short drop to the floor, which caused a brief flash of pain in their ankles, but it was bearable. Quickly, they checked that the knife Silva had slipped them was in easy reach.

No point asking how she got that one past the knights. Hiding blades is one of Silva's better skills.

Hopefully, none of the knights' horses had bolted far. Coming out onto the main street, they saw the mass of grey bodies attempting to swarm the door of the tavern. The creatures were slowly getting the notion to properly surround the building. In the street pools of lava bubbled away as if they'd always been there, the odd fire still burning bright amongst them. Those who'd fallen, including Shagraz, had joined the undead ranks as proper zombies, not whatever the grey-skinned imitators were. None of the knights' horses had hung around, unsurprisingly, so Shift would need to search further afield for a mount.

Shuffling from the alley entrance, they made for the end of the square. The heat was fierce, and the trail ahead looked difficult thanks to the lava-spewing gouges in the earth. The stench of sulphur in the air made them fight not to heave. It was a desperate battle, but they won in the end. They spared a quick glance at the tavern. Their companions didn't have long. Already, cracks were starting to show in the tavern's wooden wall. The creatures were intent on their business, but several of the zombies turned and regarded them, probably wondering why they were going in the wrong direction, if they were capable of such thought. Shift ignored them and just kept going. Copying the creatures shambling walk was no issue in their current injured state as they made for the building on the far side of the road. Focusing on not accidentally stepping in a lava pool, they completely missed a hole in the ground that one of the creatures had emerged form. Catching their foot, they stumbled forwards.

'Shit.' The exclamation left their lips before they could stop it.

Behind them they heard an aggressive growling

Oh shit.

CHAPTER 23

With a deep sigh, he perused the rack of swords, axes, and various other weapons, all of which had a single thing in common: none of them were in mint condition. Still, beggars couldn't be choosers, and he couldn't very well go to war with a knife. So he picked up the sword that looked least likely to fall apart in his hands. It had to be a sword; he was comfortable with swords. He was starting to miss the *Dawn Blade*. That wouldn't crumble into dust in a fight.

Vargas gets his stupid custom two-bladed sword, and I have to make do with this. How is that fair?

But the *Dawn Blade* wasn't really his sword; it was Auron's. He'd just...inherited it. Beside him, the hero swung the blade he'd chosen, getting used to the weight and balance. It was still so surreal, seeing him...there.

'What was that for?' Auron asked testily.

He started. He hadn't even realised he was going to poke Auron until he did.

'Sorry,' he replied awkwardly. 'It's just weird having you so...solid.'

'Um, thanks,' the hero replied with a smirk. 'I thought for a moment you were stealing my move...again.'

When Auron, in his spirit form, had developed the ability to poke things, his first way of interacting with his environment, he'd used it offensively to save Nicolas from a hunter named Wade Le'Beck. To do this, he'd poked the hunter right in his eye, naming the move his *Finger Poke of Doom*. Apparently, naming your special move was a very heroic thing to do. It was a little lost on him. Perhaps all his companions should get a spec—

'How do you think the others are doing?' Auron wouldn't know any more than he did, and any answer would be complete conjecture, but thinking about them and knowing they were under attack by those things...well, Nicolas wasn't known for his optimism.

'They're all probably sat in the Oracle's cottage by now waiting for you to get back, with a smouldering pile of dead stupid shade things outside in the garden.'

Wouldn't make the Oracle's garden look any worse.

The answer had been quick enough to make him think the hero was trying not to think about it, and that made it less reassuring. His companions wouldn't be expecting the attack, but they were all capable. Garaz had magic, and Silva was an amazing warrior. And Shift...

'But—'

'Kid,' Auron interrupted sharply. 'What do you want me to say? Garaz is currently immolating half the horde with fireballs whilst Silva hacks her way through the other half. Shift is stood at the back making smartass remarks. Truth is, I don't know. I'm just as worried about them as you are, but I don't know. And I don't want to torture myself overthinking it. The best we can do for them now is focus on getting out of here, and we can't do that if we're distracted with worry. Head in the game, kid.'

'Sorry.' That was sage advice. He needed his head clear for what was to come. 'Yeah, they're probably sat around sipping tea.'

Auron gasped theatrically. 'Whilst we're here fighting a war of the undead? That's bloody charming, that is.'

'With the Oracle, though.' He wrinkled his nose. The old man wasn't hospitable by any stretch of the imagination. He hoped they didn't drink anything brewed in his kitchen.

The hero rolled his eyes. 'He's a peach, isn't he?'

'Oh, very much so.' Nicolas laughed. 'A truly pleasant fellow.'

'A genuinely hospitable soul.'

Suddenly, those sentences became the funniest things in the entire universe, and they both burst out laughing. Sha'then strode through the flaps of the tent indignantly, most likely summoned by the laughter. The sight of the Lord of the Underworld scowling at them with his hands on his hips only encouraged their laughing, until Auron was doubled over, slapping his knee.

'You are supposed to be in here preparing.' Sha'then snapped. 'This does not sound like preparing.'

'Relax, we're prepared.' The look of fury on Sha'then's face at being told to *relax* made Nicolas stop laughing instantly.

'My entire realm, and your world, is in danger, and my best hope is a pair of laughing buffoons.' Sha'then huffed. 'I do not see anything funny about any of this.'

'You'll see the funny side once this is done and you have the necromancer at your whim,' Auron retorted, unmoved by the Lord of the Underworld's annoyance.

That seemed to soothe Sha'then some. 'Oh, I certainly will,' he purred. 'If he would just face me, I would smite him where he stood. But the coward hides behind his tricks and his armies.'

'He's in your old keep, I take it?' Auron asked.

Sha'then sneered. 'He profanes my citadel with his presence, if that's what you mean.'

Nicolas knew the look on Auron's face well enough to know he had an idea. 'Care to share your plan?'

He half-smiled. 'This time, I'm keeping it simple. No more battles or wars. Once we recruit our guys, we'll come here, arm up, and then go straight to the citadel. Break in. Kill the necromancer and end the war. Done.'

'As easy as that?' Nicolas laughed.

'Not at all.' Auron shrugged. 'It will be a dangerous and messy business. And once it is done, Sha'then will be sending you home.'

'We will see,' Sha'then replied.

Auron rounded on the Lord of the Underworld, who was markedly taller than him. 'You will send him back,' Auron growled, pointing at Nicolas. 'He isn't supposed to be here, and you know it. The kid could be curled up in a ball crying in the corner after everything he's been through, yet he's fighting for you. When this is done, you *will* send him home.'

'As I said, we will see,' Sha'then replied in the manner of a father when his children demand to go swimming on his day of rest.

****

As curious as they were about how many were following them, they weren't looking back under any circumstances. That was when you stumbled and fell over. In that situation, the best-case scenario was that they fell into the lava and had a quick death. And they were passionately dedicated to not getting eaten or boiled alive.

They tried to listen as they carefully weaved between the holes in the road. There were definitely multiple sets of feet, but it didn't sound like the full extent of the horde.

It'd be easier to hear without all these popping bloody lava bubbles.

Quickly, they skipped over a small crack and onto the walkway on the other side of the street. Now it was safe to glance back.

For Deities' sake. How're they so close? They shuffle like geriatrics, and I'm practically sprinting.

They needed to do something to slow them down. Barging through the door of the nearest building, they tucked themselves behind the frame, drew Silva's knife, and waited.

Within seconds, a grey, snarling face stepped into the doorway.

Hey, I know that face.

It was an old *colleague* of sorts, a thief called Romero. Notorious for his greed, Romero overburdened himself on a job, refusing to leave a single coin. All well and good until the rope he was using to descend from the tower he'd robbed snapped, and his loot pile ended up crushing him. From the angles of his limbs, his moving corpse was frozen in that moment of death.

Is that my destiny if I return to thieving?

No time to consider their life choices. They pounced, driving the knife into the creature's skull. There was a moan that could've been surprise or pain...or hunger. Happiness. Anger. Who knew with these creatures? Either way, the last embers of un-life vanished from its eyes, and they booted Romero hard into those following it.

Three of the zombies were pushed backwards, falling to the floor. One thankfully fell into the lava and turned into a pool of flaming grey goo. They had no time to celebrate their victory as three more of the creatures crashed in through the shop's window.

Shit.

Glass exploded inwards as the walking corpses heedlessly hurled themselves through it, their bodies now covered in sharp shards.

Just another reason to get the Underworld out of here.

They ran towards the back of the shop, past several racks of goods, then stopped abruptly, turned, and pushed on one of the large shelving units using their good arm and all their might. Soon enough, it toppled, knocking the rest down with a series of thunderous crashes. Two of the creatures stepped aside in time. The third was a second too slow and got pinned at the waist, but it continued to struggle until it tore itself in half. The legless torso advanced down the aisle, using its hands to pull it forwards.

They made for the back of the room at speed, hurling any item they came across back at their pursuers, who were undeterred. By now, the other creatures outside were up and shuffling through the entrance.

After forcing the door open, they emerged into the alley and went to slam it shut. One of the creatures put it's head between the door and the frame, keeping the door ajar as it tried to bite Shift. It got a knife between the eyes for its trouble. But the dead weight of the creature fell against the door even as the others began to push against it, forcing Shift back as the door thrust fully open. Luckily, the shambling creatures tripped over their fully dead comrade, buying them some time they intended to use.

Shift sprinted down the street then emerged into the open fields surrounding Hablock Village Square. Luck had at last favoured them. A single horse stood grazing in the field.

Thank the Deities they didn't all bolt into the distant horizon.

The beast even had a spear attached to its saddle, which was good, because somehow the bloody creatures had caught up already. And they weren't about to leave them wandering around out here.

'Just borrowing this,' they explained to the horse as they unhitched the spear from the saddle. The horse didn't care.

Turning just in time, they thrust forward with the weapon, taking the first and fastest attacker in the head, leaving a gaping hole as they withdrew the lance. The zombie fell to the ground. Changing their grip, they hurled it at the next creature. The lance caught it in the gut before sticking into the ground, impaling the creature, leaving it writhing helplessly.

Back to the knife then.

Drawing the blade again, they got into a fighting stance, or at least a decent copy of the one they'd seen Silva use, and waited as the dead thing bore down on them.

Then suddenly it veered away.

What's it... Oh no!

Before they could react, the creature sank its teeth into the poor horse's throat. The beast reared, kicking its attacker in the head, but from the blood gushing from the wound, the damage was already done.

They reached for the horse, but it was too late. With a terrible whinny of pain, the beast fell to the floor. Its killer twitched beside it, half its head missing. The other half got a knife through it.

They stood over the dying horse, their hands hovering as they looked for some way to help, but there was none. Not true; there was one thing. Slowly, they knelt beside the animal, stroking it's mane gently and trying not to look too hard into its pained eyes. Their affinity for animals made this all the worse.

'I am so sorry,' they whispered, before putting it out of it's misery.

That poor creature. All this death and destruction...

Numb, they rose then walked over and finished off the creature stuck on the spear. There was no anger in it, no anything. At the moment, it was as if the world were on another plane, and they were just watching it from afar. They hated this part of themselves. A side effect of being so carefree and easy-going was that when something did hit them, it hit hard. And it was hitting now. Nick's death, the assassins, Mace, those creatures, near-death experiences aplenty. All the things they pushed to the back of their mind came to the fore as one, smashing Shift's defences like a mighty battering ram, leaving them open to the realisation of just how much all of this really affected them.

This is exactly why I wanted to just go. I should've left in Merida, when I had the chance.

They slumped to the ground, shaking, fighting back the tears as a choked sob escaped their lips.

No.

Punching the grass several times, they closed their eyes, forcing themselves to calm down. This wouldn't do. They didn't have the luxury of giving in and letting this take them. People were still in danger. Their friends were still in danger.

If I ever meet Avus Arex, I'm going to punch him right in the throat.

In trying to regain a semblance of self, they forced themselves to go over the events of the last few hours, to face it all. Locking it away did no good—Nick had proved that after Yarringsburg. And they didn't shy away from things because they were difficult. For a thief, difficult meant more fun.

Wait.

There was a detail in amongst it all. Something they'd noticed, but they couldn't put their finger on it. Something was off. But what?

Think.

Most of this was off. It certainly wasn't normal. But even in all that there was...what?

Think, think, think.

Mace's grinning face came to mind. In his hand, he held...

The knife. The one he used to attack me that ended up in his head.

As much as they didn't want to think about it, they focused on the blade.

It wasn't a utensil. It was a dagger. Proper, well made. Something a soldier would carry...

Trying to focus on the weapon, to recall some detail of it, wasn't easy. It'd either been slashing at them, had a head attached to it, or in Sir Gerran's belt.

...or a knight.

They sat bolt upright.

Sir Gerran had an empty sheath on his belt, and the knife fit in it perfectly.

Maybe that was normal, but he was a *knight*. They didn't just misplace weapons. And he'd been the one to search the top floor of the tavern.

An idea formed, one that wouldn't go away, no matter how much they scoffed at it. Sir Gerran had known Mace was upstairs. Sir Gerran had given Mace the knife. Sir Gerran was an assassin. And he was now in an enclosed building with the rest of their friends.

'I can't leave,' they whispered, rising.

If they were right, and they were damn sure they were, their companion's deaths were imminent. They marched back towards the village square. And the tavern that was still under siege by the undead.

This is going to be tricky.

CHAPTER 24

As much as he disliked Sha'then's naming of the landmarks that made up this place, Nicolas couldn't deny that they were accurate. Take the Forest of Misery, for example: a vast landscape filled with dead trees, their bark black and brittle and covered with aggressive thorns. There wasn't a leaf to be seen. The jagged branches looked like a wall of spears, and the single track vanished between the sharp undergrowth, giving him the impression of a dark, fanged maw, ready to swallow travellers whole.

'How quaint,' Auron remarked dryly.

The look of it wasn't even the worst of it; it was the silence. Forests ought to be teeming with life—the rustling of leaves, the sounds of foraging animals, birds calling to each other. But there was nothing. It was dead.

'It's a big forest.' He left out the term *'evil-looking.'* It didn't need saying. 'It could take an age to find anyone.'

'True, but the forest is pretty bare. Once inside, it should be easy enough to see in most directions.' The hero's brow creased for a moment. 'Or we could just ask that guy.'

Looking where Auron was pointing, he finally noticed the man hanging from one of the trees beside the entrance.

How did I miss that?

Following in Auron's wake, he approached the figure.

Oh, he's literally hanging from the tree.

A thick rope around the man's neck trailed up to the branch. Though his face looked scrunched and red due to the noose around his throat, he smiled as they approached.

'All right, lads?' His voice was strained and choked but strangely amiable.

'Are you okay?' It seemed like a stupid question, but he couldn't not ask it.

'Been better.' The man gave an almost-shrug. 'But been worse. No breathing here so can't choke to death. That leaves me just sort of...hanging.'

'Is there anyone else around?' Auron asked, again being frustratingly casual in strange circumstances.

'Oh yes, loads of us,' the man replied. 'I'll point you in the right direction if you cut me down.'

He went to draw his sword only to find Auron's hand on his, keeping the blade in its sheath. 'What're you up there for?'

The man looked sheepish for a moment. 'The others don't like me very much.'

Beside him, Auron raised an eyebrow. 'Shambles,' he said. 'Who is this guy?'

Allius puffed his little chest out as he opened his book. After flicking through a few pages, he finally came to a stop. 'This is Trax Gravin,' the little man read. 'Did a couple of murders, some robberies, several beatings, pretty standard stuff. Ah, here we go. When his criminal career didn't bear fruit, he took to grave robbing to earn a living. He died trying to break into the crypt of Sir Elias the Virtuous, who had his jewelled sword interred with him. Apparently a crypt keeper with a strong sense of justice caught him in the act and beat him to death with a shovel.'

'I take it the others are a bit touchy about grave robbers?' Auron asked. 'Seeing as they all have dead bodies of their own.'

'A little bit, yeah.' Trax chuckled hoarsely. 'So I take it you won't cut me down?'

'Sorry, fella.' Auron shrugged. 'But we need them onside, and letting you down doesn't set the right tone.'

'I get that,' Trax said. 'But I'm not going to direct you then. You understand, right?'

'Oh, of course.' Auron smiled. 'Don't worry about it. The minute I asked for directions you glanced the way we need to go.'

'Ah.'

With that, Auron and Allius walked away.

'I'm sorry for your troubles.' It was a poor sentiment, but he couldn't leave without at least acknowledging the man hanging from the tree.

'Thanks for that.' Trax smiled. 'If I ever see you again, I'll kill you.'

Oh, okay then.

Quickly, he followed Auron.

Fortunately, finding the camp took no time at all. They hadn't even really bothered to hide themselves. He supposed they didn't need to whilst the war was still going strong in the opposite direction.

As they approached the shantytown of lean-tos, Auron's stride became more confident.

'Exactly how do you intend on approaching this?' Allius asked, his little legs moving swiftly to keep pace.

Good question.

'Easy.' The hero smiled. 'I'm going to walk in with bluster and bravado.'

'Just like that?' Nicolas asked.

Auron winked confidently. 'Let me do the talking.'

No fear there. I'm staying as quiet as possible.

True to his word, Auron walked directly up to the camp, somehow unnoticed, put his hands on his hips, and declared loudly, 'All right, lads, how we all doing? Got space for some weary travellers?'

A lot of swords were drawn very quickly. Those who weren't armed balled their fists in readiness for a fight, or picked up convenient rocks. Even at a glance, this camp was full of murderers and lowlifes.

Is this plan such a good idea, after all?

An older man with thick grey stubble and the remnants of curled hair stepped forward from the rabble, scrutinising them carefully. He had an angry-looking rope burn around his neck. 'Auron of Tellmark? Is that you?'

'Vlad The Hangman Resczak?' Auron greeted the older man as if they were old friends.

'Ah, so many foes vanquished, and you still recognise little old me.' Vlad scoffed. 'I am honoured.' The Hangman gave a little bow.

Judging by the glares levelled at Auron, Vlad wasn't the only one of this lot he'd sent here.

'Dawnblade!' rumbled a heavy-set fellow with a thick jawline. 'How I've prayed for this day.'

Auron shook his head and shrugged. 'And you are?'

'I was part of Thec Shar's bandit crew.' Even from here, Nicolas could see the man's knuckles whiten as he gripped his club tightly. 'When you came upon us, I was not ready. Now I am, I shall smash your arrogant head to a pulp.'

Beside the man, Vlad rolled his eyes and sighed.

Again, Auron shrugged. 'There were, what, fifteen of you? I don't remember singular faces.' The hero then gestured to his sheathed blade. 'But now I'm unprepared, so—'

The bandit didn't even wait for him to finish the sentence before charging, really slowly because of his frame. Auron kept his hands on his hips right until the last second then he stepped to the side, drew his sword, and cut the man's head off in a motion so swift Nicolas barely saw it happen. The thug's body had dissolved to smoke before it hit the floor.

'Flawless.' Auron smirked as he returned his sword to its sheath. 'Any-one else?' he asked, folding his arms, eyebrows high.

Vlad laughed. 'Put them down, lads, unless any of you fancy meeting oblivion.'

The assembled men lowered their weapons. They didn't sheath them, though.

'So we can come in?' Auron asked.

'Just because we aren't trying to kill you, doesn't mean you're welcome.' Vlad smiled. 'And I know you didn't come to reminisce about old times. Say your piece.'

'Fair enough,' the hero replied, before raising his voice so all could hear. 'You're all down here for whatever nasty crap you did when you were alive. If I sent you here, I don't care. You deserved it. Come at me, if you like, but it won't end any better than with old cuddles just then.' *Interesting tactic.* 'Or, you could listen to a proposition that may improve your lot down here.'

That got their attention.

'Go on,' Vlad said suspiciously.

'If you hadn't noticed, there's a war on, and Sha'then needs decent soldiers. You fellows are sitting around doing nothing, so I thought I'd give you the opportunity to sign up.'

The booming laughter sounded entirely out of place in the dead forest.

Finally, Vlad recovered himself enough to speak. 'So you want us to rise up in support of our jailer and torturer? You know I've spent the last two years hanging by my neck from the side of a cliff, right?'

Sha'then loves irony then.

'I didn't,' the hero replied. 'And I don't care. Maybe now you know how your victims felt. What I do care about is getting you to fight for Sha'then and ending this war.'

'Look,' Vlad replied. 'We have no love for the necromancer. We know his plan, we've seen what he does to those who refuse him and have no wish for the same to happen to us, but you're being ridiculous asking us to just fight for the Lord of the Underworld.'

'You haven't heard the best part yet.' Vlad cautiously gestured for Auron to continue. 'Leniency for any who help end the war and destroy the necromancer and his forces.'

Again, booming laughter. 'And you have this in writing?' Vlad asked between chuckles.

'No, but *he* should show you how serious I am.' Auron turned and indicated Allius.

The laughter stopped, becoming a stunned silence. Allius shifted uncomfortably under the wide-eyed looks he was getting. Nicolas could relate. But at least they all recognised him.

'You *are* serious.' Vlad gasped. 'But still—'

'What do you want me to say?' Auron interrupted. 'That he's going to let you go to the Eternal Forest? Because with what some of you have done, I very much bloody doubt it. But I'm going to see to it that he wins this war. And maybe ingratiating yourself with the jailer of your eternal soul might be a nice idea? Or you can take your chances with Avus *Full-of-myself* Arex. If he wins, do you really think he'll be pleased with those who turned their backs on him? Maybe you'd prefer to end up one of his zombies? Or do you seriously believe he'll just leave you here to enjoy this delightful commune you've built?'

Vlad opened and closed his mouth several times. Then he looked away, stroking his chin thoughtfully. 'I think that makes a bit of sense,' he said finally. 'But what makes you think you can defeat Avus?'

'Because I have the guy with me who sent him down here.'

Now all those eyes were on Nicolas.

What? But I didn't. Yet he didn't feel the need to openly correct Auron.

Looks were exchanged, the content of which Nicolas couldn't make out. His hand tightened on the hilt of his sword.

Finally, Vlad spoke up. 'I can't make any guarantees, but I'll have a word with the other camps around here and see who's up for it.'

Nicolas got the impression that Vlad may actually be considering it, as well as some of the others around. It was hard to tell as they all looked generally so disgruntled.

****

A wind current hit, and they dipped sharply, threatening to plummet to the ground below.

Shit.

Shift flapped their wings harder, a sting of discomfort coming with every movement. Still, they dipped involuntarily, struggling hard to keep both aloft and in the right direction. Their initial thought that turning into a bird with a damaged arm would be idiotic had proven correct, but that gave them no comfort.

It's the only way.

Getting out of the building and to the field had nearly killed them; trying to sneak back in the way they came would be a thousand times worse. So they'd committed to the only course of action left, no matter how injured their arm, now a wing, was. Thankfully, it was a short distance. Besides, their companions were in there with an assassin, so time was against them.

Straining, they forced themselves into a glide, the damaged wing threatening to completely give out at any moment.

Below them, the creatures continued their relentless assault on the tavern as they opened their wings and descended towards it. The wind ruffled their feathers, and they fought hard to keep steady.

Landing on the window ledge, they let out a coo of relief.

Now to get in.

Shift's eyes closed in annoyance as it occurred to them they simply could've turned into an Aviar instead. The bird folk had wings and arms, which would've made the whole thing a crap-load easier. Sometimes that was the problem when thinking of what to change into. With numerous possibilities, occasionally, you missed the obvious.

I had a Nick moment.

After changing back, Shift balanced precariously on the ledge, the slight breeze making goosebumps on their naked body.

And maybe turning into a bigger bird so I could carry my clothes would've been sensible.

Their excuse was, panic. Sir Gerran was in there, and there was no telling what he was plotting now. So they could forgive themselves some stupidity.

It was only at the last second that they realised their next moment of stupidity: their preferred form was too heavy for the window ledge, which gave beneath them with an agonised crack. Frantically, they managed to get enough of a handhold on the broken ledge still attached to the wall, but the pain as their damaged arm took their weight nearly broke their grip. Somehow, they held firm. It wasn't much. Below them, the growling increased. The debris had caught the attention of the '*locals*'.

Great, now the creatures can see everything I have to show.

There was no time to worry about that; their handhold was growing more tenuous by the second, especially for their weak arm, and the groaning of wood under strain wasn't a good sign either. They could change again, but that meant falling for a moment. Could they change before getting within reach of the creatures? It wasn't a wager they wished to place. Reaching up with great effort, they tried the window.

Locked? What in the Underworld? We already established the bloody things can't climb.

Usually, picking a lock was a simple enough task, but this wasn't usual at all.

This needs to be quick.

Fortunately, they had another option. A handy gift from a thankful Deity that could open any lock. With a deep breath, they let go with one hand and quickly grabbed the key from the magic rope around their neck and pulled it off. Their hand was only off the ledge for a few seconds, but it was enough to tell them their arm would give out soon. Already, their shoulders ached and sweat ran down their naked back. The broken ledge was starting to come away from the wall.

No time to mess around.

With another quick movement, they reached up, pressing the key to the window lock, which clicked instantly.

Now the really hard part.

Feeling around with their feet, they finally found half-decent footholds in the tavern wall. They weren't much, but maybe just enough. Adjusting their weight, they let go for a moment, grabbing the window and forcing it upwards. Their legs slipped, but as they did, Shift grabbed the slightly opened window. The handhold was enough. With one final mighty effort, they pulled themselves up, shuffling awkwardly through the open window.

Making it over the threshold, they were about to roll to the floor, but caught themselves at the last moment. It wouldn't do to make a noise and alert people to their presence. Sir Darick seemed honourable enough, but there was no telling whether Sir Gerran had accomplices.

For a moment, they lay on the floor panting, hoping the burning in their arm would ease quickly.

That was too close.

'Why are you back?'

They put their hand to their mouth just in time to stifle the cry of surprise. Silva stood by the open doorway, sword in hand.

'Don't scare me like that,' they hissed.

'Why are you back?' the warrior asked again, before looking at them askew and raising an eyebrow. 'And why are you naked?'

'Because you haven't gotten me any clothes yet,' they replied tartly. 'And I'm back because we have a problem.'

'What?'

'If you can stop staring at me and grab some clothes, I'll tell you.'

CHAPTER 25

What are they talking about?

For a good while now, Vlad and Auron had been talking quietly. Catching up on old times, he supposed, as the group marched across the plain. Vlad was nodding a lot, so that was a good sign.

'So,' Vlad said as the pair finally broke apart. 'I have to know. Why are you here? Finally slip off the wagon of righteousness, did we?'

If it wasn't for the name, The Hangman would've appeared a genuinely pleasant fellow.

Auron rolled his eyes. 'I'm here for the kid. Some demon host massacred his village and banished his soul here. I came to get it back.'

Even though he already knew that, hearing it again stirred something in Nicolas.

For someone to come to the Underworld, for me...

'You came here for *him*?' Despite the loveable uncle appearance, every so often an edge of ruthlessness would slip out, suggesting who he used to be, or really was.

'That's what I said,' Auron replied.

'Okay then, but *how* are you here?'

'It wasn't difficult. I was already dead.'

Vlad's jaw hung low for a second. 'The mighty Dawnblade, finally laid low. Please, I must know how this happened.'

Several of his nearby men appeared to be listening as well.

If there was anything Auron loved, it was an attentive crowd. Yet it was clear from his face that this was a story he didn't want to tell. 'I got a crossbow bolt in the chest whilst I was going for a dump.'

There was a moment of stunned silence. 'You were killed...taking a crap?' Vlad asked, shaking his head in disbelief. 'I never would've called that.' Vlad chuckled. 'All the battles you've fought, creatures you've slain, traps you've crawled out of...I thought you were blessed by the Deities themselves. And you die like *that*.' The hangman looked to the others, as if to confirm that he wasn't the only one who found the notion odd. 'And who did this deed?'

'Silva Destrone.'

Vlad let out a long faux breath. 'Crazy bitch finally got her revenge then. Took her long enough.'

Revenge? What happened between those two?

'She didn't get much satisfaction from it. The kid killed her soon after.'

Vlad gave him an uncomfortably long look.

Why's Auron giving away so much?

'This whelp killed Silva Destrone?' one of the others boomed. 'We all thought you were jesting when you said he sent Avus here.'

Whelp's a bit harsh.

Auron nodded knowingly. 'Drowned her.'

That was a half-truth. She'd come back. And, technically, her partner Grimmark had knocked her into the water. He'd just dodged the hammer blow meant for him. But he didn't think this crowd would appreciate his nitpicking. Auron certainly wouldn't. So he kept his mouth shut.

'Shame, she was a fine piece of ass,' one of the men behind him joked.

'And she would've had yours if she heard you talk like that,' another sneered.

'I can think of worse ways to go.' The man shrugged.

'You did.' Another laughed. 'The pox took a month to kill you, Jacob.'

As the men chattered amongst themselves, he pulled close to Auron, as close as Allius had stayed to Nicolas since they'd met this bunch. 'Nice catchup?'

'What?' the hero asked absentmindedly. 'Oh, Vlad. Delightful guy...when he isn't hanging people.'

'Why did you tell them all that stuff about me, about Avus and Silva?' He wasn't comfortable knowing that stuff himself.

'They're all killers, kid,' he replied. 'If they thought you were weak, they would've used you to get at me. I needed them to know not to underestimate you.'

Makes sense, I underestimate myself plenty.

'As much as we're playing nice,' Auron continued, 'these are dangerous people. Vlad was a magistrate once, upheld justice and all that. But no one could really live up to his standard of justice, so he started hanging people for the thinnest of reasons. Even did little show trials. Racked up quite the body count until I crossed his path.'

'And you...' He drew his hand across his throat.

'Yup.' Auron nodded. 'A lot of people breathed easier with him in the ground. Literally.'

'Like the faun?' It was only then he realised he hadn't seen the faun in a while. Good.

'Like the faun,' the hero echoed. 'And Avus. Glad you're finally getting it.'

'This is a terrible way to learn a lesson.'

Auron looked at him for a moment. 'I wish people like me weren't necessary. Despite all the bragging and songs and the odd statue, I just want the world to be a better place. But getting there is a messy business, because like it or not, not everyone wants that. Some want to make parts of it much worse. Even for me, it took a while to accept that. The only people killing comes naturally to is the bad guys.' He chuckled. 'Several times in my early days, I nearly died because I quailed at killing at the last second.'

'So did I when the faun was choking me.'

'But you acted.' Auron's tone was almost fatherly. 'You did the right thing. The stuff after wasn't so good. But you're getting it.'

'Meeting a genocidal necromancer is a good way to learn that lesson,' he shrugged. 'Even when it comes to me and my thick skull.'

Auron patted him on the shoulder. 'Stop being so hard on yourself. You went from quiet village life to...a lot of crazy and violent stuff. You're doing great.'

His attention was caught by Vlad and his men breaking away as Sha'then's camp came into view. 'Where are they going?'

'To wait over there whilst we see the big man,' Auron replied.

By the time they entered the camp, he could already see Sha'then at the end of the row of tents, awaiting them with folded arms. As they got closer, it became clear that Sha'then had chosen to fully embrace the look of a miserable child.

'Well?' the Lord of the Underworld demanded.

No hello for us then. He might at least spare his loyal servant a 'how ya doing?'

'Our recruitment drive was a success.' Auron smiled. 'They're waiting just beyond the gate.'

'And they aren't in front of me because?'

The hero gave the smile of a parent mustering the last of their patience. 'Because they are, understandably, not comfortable just strolling into your camp. They'd like you to come out and parlay with them where they aren't surrounded by your troops.'

'Oh, of course,' Sha'then purred with thick sarcasm. 'Let me just brew up a little sweet tea for them, and I'll be right out.'

Auron exhaled loudly. 'You need their help. Stop acting like a tit.'

Sha'then was visibly shocked for a whole second before he got angry, drawing himself up to his full height, a swirling nimbus of power forming around him. 'You dare compare the manner of the Lord of the Underworld to a...to a...breast?'

'If you don't act like one, I can't make the comparison,' Auron retorted. 'Now please come out so we can take a step closer to ending this once and for all.'

After a loaded silence, the Lord of the Underworld's power vanished. 'I shall allow this insolence to pass. This time,' he said grudgingly. 'You may present my new warriors to me.'

As Auron turned, he shot Nicolas an eye roll. They left the camp, followed by Sha'then, Allius, and four skeleton guards.

'How do you do that?' Nicolas whispered.

Auron gave him a questioning look.

'How are you so good at talking people round?'

'I have charm, kid.' He smiled. 'Works as well on men as it does on the ladies. You'd be surprised how a few silver-tongued words will assist a woman out of their clothing or bring a disagreeable fellow around to my way of thinking.'

'Could you teach me?'

'Why, who do you want out of their clothes?' Auron smirked, before muttering something that sounded very much like, *as if I didn't know.*

'What? No, I didn't mean that. I meant like...' If he'd had blood to rush to his face, he would've been a red beacon visible for miles around.

Auron's smirk evolved into a smug grin.

'Is that it?' Sha'then shouted incredulously as they reached the dead trees where the new recruits waited. Vlad seemed less than impressed by the greeting, as did the twenty who accompanied him.

Weren't there a couple more?

'Where are the rest?' the Lord of the Underworld spat. 'There were nearly a hundred in that forest.'

'Eighty-two,' Allius put in.

'Silence, Shambles!' Sha'then snapped. 'I didn't ask for your wittering. You should've brought an army back with you. Those souls are hanging around doing nothing.'

'And most of them hate your guts.' Auron shrugged. 'These do, too, but you're better than the alternative.'

Sha'then looked ready to continue his ranting, but the hero held up his hands in a conciliatory fashion. 'Look, I can do a lot more with twenty good, hard men than a hundred reluctant ones. Trust me. This is a big win for your side.'

'It will be a *win* once the necromancer's head adorns a spike atop my citadel. Or maybe I'll erect a mighty monument to my victory in the centre of my realm and display it there as a warning to all who even think of disrespecting me?'

Nicolas imagined that would have a name just as silly as everything else here. The Monument of Nasty Death? The Monument of Sticking Spiky Things in Soft Places?

Ew, that last one sounded really wrong.

Though the idea of seeing Avus's head on a spike was quite appealing. Maybe he'd wave at it merrily?

Hang on...

'How can he display Avus's head?' he whispered to Allius. 'When he cuts it off it'll turn to dust.'

'You don't cut the neck,' The Tallymen replied. 'You cut across the shoulders. It's a technicality, but still achieves the same goal.'

Sorry I asked.

'Let's take it one step at a time before you start worrying about victory parades,' Auron cautioned. 'We've only just completed the first step of the plan.'.

'And what is our next step?' Sha'then enquired.

The hero feigned offence. 'You already know. Sneak into your old palace and kill Avus.'

'I was hoping for something more specific,' Sha'then replied dourly.

'Don't worry, it's all up here,' he replied, tapping his head.

I wish he'd share it with me. But he was too busy chatting to Vlad to fill me in.

'I'm sceptical,' Sha'then practically growled.

'But you won't be.' Auron gestured to his new mercenaries. 'Have a chat with Vlad and let's put your mind at ease.'

The Lord of the Underworld appeared reluctant, but finally waved his hand in what could almost be seen as a dismissive gesture. Auron called Vlad over. The Hangman strolled cautiously forwards until he was within arm's reach of Sha'then.

Auron played host and introduced the pair. 'Sha'then, Lord of the Underworld, meet Vlad The Hangman Rasczak.'

'I am aware of who *this* is.' Sha'then sniffed. 'I have been present during his tortures on several occasions.'

Vlad let out a singular laugh. 'Then you cannot blame me for doing *this*.'

Before anyone could react, Vlad swung the large club from behind his back, bringing it crashing into Sha'then's chin. As time slowed, Nicolas could see the ripples of impact extending from the Lord of the Underworld's jaw up to his cheeks as his eyes blew wide open in surprise before a dazed haze fell across them. Tumbling like a falling tree, he crashed to the floor in slow motion. Nicolas was still going for the hilt of his sword when the tip of a blade poked into the small of his back.

'Don't,' a voice commanded.

'*Vlad!*' Auron cried as the skeletons guards around them were decimated by the ambush. 'We had a deal!'

Vlad shrugged. 'Well, if it's a choice between the man who's going to rule the world and the guy who watched a skeleton shove a hot poker up my ass once, then maybe Avus isn't so bad after all.'

'You *filth*,' Auron snarled.

Nicolas was sure he'd have drawn his sword and killed Vlad on the spot had it not been for the three blades at his neck.

There was a wooden thud behind him. In his peripheral vision, he saw two of Vlad's men finish pulling the gate to Sha'then's camp closed, before barring the door.

So much for Auron's charm. How could he not have seen this coming?

On the floor, Sha'then stirred slightly, until a well-placed boot from Vlad ensured he stayed where he was.

****

'...so yeah. I think...I'm sure...that Sir Gerran is an assassin or working with them.' The way Silva's brow had darkened as they'd gone over the facts was unnerving.

'I'll kill him.' Silva's fists were clenched so tight they were shaking.

'First things first.' As much as they'd love the knight dead, there were larger matters to consider. 'He's the only one left alive who can tell us who sent him and the others. You need to get him to talk.'

The smile the warrior gave them sent a shiver down their spine. 'That will not be an issue.'

Thank the Deities she's on our side.

'The problem is the other knights,' they said thoughtfully. 'We can't assume Gerran is acting alone, but how to weed out any compatriots he may have?'

'I believe Sir Darick is true,' Silva replied without hesitation. 'He has begun to trust us enough to return our weapons and allow me to check upstairs. If he wanted us dead, he could've had his men try to kill us at any time.'

'That's a good point.'

And a welcome one. There are some people you just really don't want to be bad guys.

'But that still leaves the other six knights.'

Silva looked thoughtful for a moment, her lips pursed, and then she smiled. Not a thing they were used to seeing. 'I think I may have an idea.'

'And no one's going to die, right?' It wasn't that they didn't trust Silva, but she was the violent solution to any problem.

The warrior shrugged. 'No one who doesn't deserve it.'

That's the best I'll get.

'Okay, what's the plan.'

'I'll head downstairs. Give me a few minutes then sneak down after me,' Silva instructed.

They lifted their toga improvised from a bedsheet. 'This doesn't exactly lend itself to sneaking.'

'Turn yourself into a cat or something,' Silva responded instantly.

'I...' *Best be honest.* 'My arm's been through enough. I don't think I can face walking on all fours right now. Besides, I've only just gotten redressed. I'm pretty loath to get naked again, especially in a room full of people.'

'Why?' Silva asked, brow furrowed in confusion. 'You have an amazing body.'

'Um, thanks.' Were they blushing? 'But still. I don't really want a load of knights checking out everything I have to offer.'

'Maybe if Nicolas were down there—' Silva cut off her sentence abruptly.

Their hackles rose. 'What?'

What's he got to do with anything?

'Never mind.'

Is she stifling a laugh?

Before they could question the warrior further, she turned and slipped out of the room. They had no intention of letting her off the hook that easily, but the conversation would keep...for now. Pulling up their toga, they followed her.

As they reached the end of the hall, Silva was at the bottom of the stairs.

'Is all secure?' The voice was Sir Darick's. 'You were gone a while?'

'I was just being thorough,' Silva replied. 'The noise was nothing.'

Carefully, they crept down a few steps, just enough to see Garaz and Rex sat together in the corner of the room. As they watched, Silva walked past the orc, tapping him gently on the hand as she did. It was smooth. Only someone really studying her would've seen it. Garaz looked at the warrior quizzically then looked straight at them. The quizzical look became a perturbed one. All they could do in their awkward half-crouch was give him a little wave and a look that hopefully said, *be ready.*

Slowly, the orc rested his hand on his staff, which lay on the table beside him.

Success. Now to find out what Silva's plan—

'Everyone, weapons on the ground!' Silva cried from a position they couldn't see.

What followed was a general uproar. They ran down the stairs to find Silva holding Sir Darick around the neck, knife to his throat. Around him, four of the knights had their weapons drawn and were shouting challenges. Garaz had his staff in hand and Rex had his knives, but neither seemed to have any idea what to do. Outside, the banging intensified.

What is she doing?

'I said drop your weapons,' Silva commanded, jostling Sir Darick roughly.

'What is the meaning of this?' the knight commander cried. 'I trusted you.' Then Sir Darick looked at them, wide-eyed. 'Why are they back? What treachery is this?'

'That's what we aim to find out,' they said, trying to make it sound like they were in control of a situation they had no clue about.

'We do?' Garaz asked.

'Drop your weapons,' Silva demanded slowly. 'This is the last time I shall ask.'

Sir Darick looked like he wanted to rip the warrior's head off with his bare hands, but he had to appreciate the knife at his throat. 'Do it,' he said reluctantly.

'What's going on, Shift?' Rex asked nervously.

They gave him a look that hopefully said, *just follow my lead.* A big ask in this situation, granted.

The knights all lowered their swords to the floor and stepped away from them, hands held high. Instantly, Silva dropped the knife from Sir Darick's throat and took a step back. 'They're fine,' she said simply.

The knights' swords were in their hands again in a flash, but Sir Darick held up his hand to stay the attack.

Thank the Deities for curiosity.

'What, may I ask, was *that* about?' the old knight asked as he ran his hand over his neck to check for blood.

'We had to be sure that your knights were honourable,' Silva replied. 'They all lowered their weapons when commanded.'

'*That* was your plan?' they cried. 'That doesn't mean a damn thing.'

The warrior looked slightly annoyed that she had to explain this. 'If any of them were assassins, they would've taken the opportunity to start a fight and kill us.'

'Assassins?' Sir Darick cried. 'You stick a knife to my throat and call my men assassins? You question their honour?'

'Just the one,' they replied. 'But we had to be sure of the rest.'

'What?' Sir Darick asked.

'Sir Gerran is in league with the assassins,' they explained. 'He knew Mace was upstairs and gave him a knife to murder me. Ever since we met him, he's been trying to pick a fight. He wants us dead, because he's an assassin.' They looked at Sir Darick. 'You said yourself that he only just joined your little band.'

'But he has been a knight for many years,' the knight commander replied coolly. 'He is a knight of Yarringsburg, and his honour is beyond reproach.'

'Ask him,' Silva suggested. 'Call him from guarding the back door and see if we're right.'

'He's guarding the back door?' they asked. That explained why they couldn't see him. Made sense for Silva to make her move when he wasn't in the room.

'He tried to pick a fight with me, and Sir Darick sent him out,' Silva replied.

'That's pretty suicidal.' They chuckled. 'What did he do? Look at you funny?'

'He asked if we could trust the *wench* who'd been sent to get help,' Rex interjected. 'Silva said she'd gut him if he ever called you a wench again.'

They gave Silva a big smile. 'That's sweet.' For a second, they thought the warrior's cheeks coloured slightly.

'We shall see about all of this *now*.' Sir Darick looked quite formidable when he was angry. 'Sir Gerran,' he shouted, 'come here at once.'

There was no answer.

'Sir Gerran?'

Silence.

'Sir Hector,' the knight commander called. 'Where's Sir Gerran?'

This time there was an answer: the low moan of the grey-skinned creatures that began to pour into the room.

CHAPTER 26

This plan had always had the potential to go horribly wrong, and lo and behold, it did.

Why didn't I see this coming? I was so proud of my stupid idea.

In hindsight, the gaping flaw in the plan, like a giant's footprint in a field, was obvious: trusting people who'd been sent to the Underworld. They were, by the very fact that they were here, untrustworthy.

And now, because of him, they were once again prisoners, being marched across this grey pit of a land.

Oh look, there's a couple of rocks. Let me guess, they're the rocks of despairing hopelessness and torturous...torture. Stupid place.

He couldn't look directly at Auron for two reasons. Firstly, because by his actions he'd once again doomed a friend, just like he had his parents and his entire village. And secondly...

Why is he so damn calm? Just one bloody frown, that's all I ask.

In all fairness, the hero had frowned plenty for half of the trip, when Sha'then *didn't* have a sock in his mouth and was spitting the most vivid descriptions of what he was going to do to Vlad and his men. Nicolas never realised before that simple words could nauseate him. He was *way* better at it than Avus. Even the sock didn't deter the Lord of the Underworld, who for the past hour has been *'mm-mmmmm-mmmm-mmm'*ing his giant black heart out. Nicolas wished Sha'then was free to enact his threats; Vlad and the knaves that followed him deserved nothing less. He'd happily do it himself. The idea of giving Vlad a thrashing was a very tempting one.

Maybe he'd get the chance when they reached...wherever they were going. They certainly weren't heading back to the forest, but the general featurelessness of this place made it difficult to tell much else.

Would it kill Sha'then to put up a signpost or two?

There was, however, a ruined building ahead, one they seemed to be heading towards. One of the walls was a pile of dusty bricks over the floor, and the windows were filled with jagged shards of broken glass. Could he maybe break a piece off and cut his bindings with it?

'Hail, weary travellers.'

Great, it's Vargas.

The warrior stepped from the shadow of the house, beaming expression tarnished by the lumps on his face where Auron had previously gone to work on him. Beside him was one of Vlad's men from the forest.

What?

'I like what you've done with your cheek,' Auron said as they got closer. 'You're pulling off the 'swollen jackass' look perfectly.'

Vargas's face dropped as ten of his men emerged from the house.

'Don't trust us?' Vlad asked, gesturing to the newcomers.

'We're in the Underworld.' Vargas laughed. 'Who trusts anyone here?'

'Naïve village boys, that's who,' Nicolas muttered to himself.

'Stop beating yourself up,' Auron scolded, giving him a sideways glance.

Vargas put his hand to his ear as he stepped towards Nicolas and Auron. 'I'm sorry,' the warrior said, feigning contrition. 'Did someone say beating up?' With that, he swung his fist, striking Auron right in the stomach. The hero stumbled back a few steps, grunting with the impact of the blow, before standing straight again, eyes daring Vargas to take another shot.

The warrior snorted, and even Nicolas could see he was ready to accept the challenge when Vlad interrupted. 'Always a pleasure, Vargas.'

Vargas unclenched his fist and put the beaming smile back on his face. 'Vlad Rasczak, it's been an age, you old dog.'

'And yet, I already feel like it wasn't long enough,' Vlad retorted. The tone of the voice indicated humour, but there was an undercurrent of truth to it.

Vargas feigned insult. 'But here you are now, with presents. Almost makes up for the time you tried to hang me.'

'They're for your master,' Vlad added with a stony face.

'*Partner*,' Vargas corrected quickly.

Beside him, Auron chuckled. 'Oh, here we go.'

Vargas looked past Vlad and glared at Auron. 'Problem, Dawnblade?'

'No problem.' The hero sniggered. 'I just wondered how long it would take for you to get put out by being second fiddle to Avus.'

Vargas wagged his finger at Auron. 'You aren't going to get me like that, Dawnblade. I know what you're doing.'

'Of course you do.'

'It won't work.'

'Of course it won't.'

Instead of continuing to protest, Vargas drew his sword, much to Auron's amusement. Vlad's arm impeded the warrior's progress. 'For your master,' he repeated.

For a moment, this looked like it'd get really ugly, but Vargas sheathed his sword and held up his hands. 'We'd best go and see him then.'

Vargas walked over to Auron, smiled at him, and struck him in the gut again. As Auron doubled over, Vlad frowned at him.

'Whoops,' Vargas said insincerely.

Auron, for his part, said nothing. He simply rose, dusted himself off, and stared at Vargas until he walked away.

'Are you okay?' Nicolas asked.

'Pfft, of course,' the hero scoffed. 'The day Vargas Quell throws a serviceable punch is the day I see an eight-foot tall dwarf.'

Nicolas found his mouth working up and down. There was a lot of outrage in his head and only one mouth to fire it out from. 'How can you make jokes at a time like this?' he snapped in a harsh whisper—they were still surrounded by armed men. 'We're prisoners, on our way to death without even a drop of hope left.'

'Kid,' Auron said with a half-smile, 'there's always hope.'

For some reason, the hero gave Nicolas's hands a pointed look, with the slightest of nods. He looked at them himself. They were just his same pale hands, with the addition of a pair of rusted metal shackles.

If they had a half-decent blacksmith down here, he'd make a fortune.

But that couldn't be what Auron was alluding to. He was about to ask for some clarity when the tip of a sword under his chin got his undivided attention.

'The only hope you have,' Vargas whispered in his ear, 'is that I'm not bored when it's time to kill you and decide to have a little fun.' The warrior stood back and raised his voice. 'Now get moving.'

As they moved out, now flanked by Vargas's men, the warrior stuck out his leg as Sha'then passed, tripping the Lord of the Underworld. The big man fell hard. Allius scrabbled over to help him up, only to be batted away. There was a lot more *'mmm-mmm'*ing as Sha'then rose. He looked as if he were about to break his bonds and tear Vargas apart, until the flats of two swords rested on his shoulders next to his neck.

'Problem?' Vargas asked. He waited for a moment for a response from a man who couldn't speak. When none came, he made a big show of how unthreatened he was by casually sheathing his sword and pointing down the road. 'Move.'

More tedious walking then.

Nicolas had no idea how time worked here, but it didn't seem *right*. Had they been here hours? Days?

Years?

What has happened in all the time we've been away?

That was a ridiculous notion. There was no going back now. They were going to die...again...more...properly? All those people in Etherius he'd let down...

They'd only moved a few feet when Vargas stopped and began to laugh, his men joining in on some joke that confused Nicolas. Finally, the warrior turned, shaking his head at what Nicolas assumed were his own antics. 'You idiots really think we're going to walk all the way back there?'

Vlad rolled his eyes at the theatrics. 'So what then?'

Vargas's face broke into a smug grin. 'Normally Avus wouldn't do this, but I guess he's getting excited now the war's won.'

Before Nicolas could even yelp, the black cloud consumed him. It was everywhere, smothering him, consuming him. Vaguely, it felt like his body was in motion, but he was stood still. Where was he? Was he to be trapped in here forever? There were no walls, but the world definitely seemed to be closing in on him.

As quickly as it appeared, it vanished. It took him a moment to regain his equilibrium. He could see everyone else now, and *something* else. Before them towered a mighty castle. Judging by the fact that it was black and had either spikes or skulls on every conceivable surface, this was Sha'then's seat of power. The glowering of the Lord of the Underworld seemed to confirm this. Ranks of wraiths and shades stood in neat columns before it, awaiting them. Hundreds of voices chanted the name of the necromancer in unison. The shades just gurgled.

Part of him wanted to try to struggle free, to throw off the shackles and fight for his life. But when he looked at his hands, the metal looked too strong. There was no hope. Would he know what oblivion was like when he was there, or would he just not exist anymore? He laughed to himself. He was already halfway there. He was already dead; this was just...the icing on the cake? No, really bad analogy. The final shovel of dirt on his grave? That made more sense. There'd even been a low point after his arrival when he'd courted this. Not now.

He'd never have the chance to save his friends and family, and Koth, and this Maestro he'd mentioned would go unpunished for their crimes. And for all the crimes they would commit after this. Maybe his companions would finish the task? Provided they survived the shades.

'You having some kind of *last moments* internal monologue, kid?'

Looking up, he saw Auron half-smiling at him. 'How can you be so calm? We're about to die.'

The hero laughed. 'Kid, there are mathematicians in the finest universities who couldn't total up the number of times I've been about to die. I'll worry about it when the sword is in my gut.'

'Or the crossbow bolt in the chest?' That was harsh. He was stressed, and it slipped out.

'Touché.' Auron's bemused expression showed no offence taken. Thank the Deities for that. This was all bad enough without offending his friend.

The hero changed the subject. 'What do you think that's all about?'

Following Auron's gaze, he saw a large podium had been erected just before the entrance to the keep. It was difficult to make out the detail from here, but it looked like a throne sat atop it.

'Showing off,' Nicolas answered dryly.

The path to the podium was paved with a row of lit torches with black flames dancing wildly. From the throne, Avus Arex watched them approach with steepled fingers. His face broke into a wide grin as he stood.

'Welcome to my seat of power,' he greeted, arms wide. 'The Citadel of Anguish.'

Judging by the stifled noises coming from behind the sock in Sha'then's mouth, he had thoughts on this. If only he were free, maybe he could smite the necromancer. That'd be quite handy right about now.

The Lord of the Underworld, Auron, Nicolas, and Allius were marched up the carpet and lined up before the throne, being forced to kneel due to the boots striking them in their back of the knees. Avus walked down from his podium with a regal swagger.

'There is a simple joy in life that comes from having one's enemies prostrated before you.' The necromancer laughed as the ranks of wraiths around them watched in silence.

Oh no, they were in for a lot of preening and boasting. *Maybe oblivion would be nice after all?* At least it'd be quieter.

'The last obstacles to my conquest of this realm have been overcome.' Avus looked towards Vlad. 'And I have you to thank for this. Your sins, and those of your comrades, turning your back upon your new master, are forgiven.'

'You are too kind,' Vlad replied, with just a little irony in his voice.

'I am now the undisputed ruler of the Underworld,' Avus proclaimed, to the renewed chanting of his minions.

'Are you, though?'

Avus looked at Auron with distaste. Within moments, Vargas's sword was at the hero's neck, the warrior looking expectantly at the necromancer, waiting for the command.

'What do you mean?' the necromancer asked with a raised eyebrow.

'I mean that as long as he's alive, you're really master of nothing.' A nod of Auron's head indicated Sha'then.

'Do you not think I will take care of that imminently?' Avus purred.

'Do what you like,' Auron scoffed. 'But you didn't beat him.'

'Of course I—'

'He was brought to you in chains by someone who didn't work for you. Doesn't count.'

What's he doing?

Auron seemed intent on pissing the necromancer off as much as possible. With his every word, Nicolas was sure their deaths were becoming just a little slower and more painful.

'Doesn't set a good example for your army, having someone else do your dirty work.' Auron shrugged. 'I expect you'll even let Vargas finish him. You aren't man enough. I get it.'

No, he was goading Avus. Why? Okay, yes, the necromancer had an inferiority complex that dwarfed some mountains, but surely...

'Get Sha'then up and untie him,' Avus commanded with a sneer.

Oh, maybe it is just that easy.

The Lord of the Underworld was hauled to his feet. His shackles were removed and so was the sock from his mouth. The whole time, he glared at Avus Arex. 'Usurper,' he hissed once he'd finished removing pieces of sock fluff from his tongue.

'Arrogant creature,' Avus snapped back. 'Too stupid to see who the real master is. Well, I shall show everyone. And then there will be no more dispute about who rules this realm.'

Sha'then seemed keen to accept the challenge. 'Choosing to face me was a mistake, worm.'

Avus let out a single harsh laugh. 'The only worms here shall be those that feast on your corpse.'

Auron and Nicolas were pulled aside to make space for the upcoming duel.

'You think Sha'then can win?' Nicolas asked quietly.

The hero turned to him and raised an eyebrow. 'The Lord of the Underworld verses a jumped-up necromancer. This should be pretty straight forward. I plan to enjoy the show.'

Should it? Was that how these things worked? In his experience with adventuring so far, nothing proved to be as simple as expected. But he supposed Auron had experience and therefore must know better than him.

'And once I crush you, all shall bow before me.'

Oh wow, they're still tough talking.

'Just die!' Sha'then roared as he thrust forward with his hands. Beams of black energy shot from his fingertips, coming together into a large lance of energy that flew towards the necromancer.

Avus held his forearms together and the lance struck a wall of energy, dissipating it. Instantly the necromancer dropped his shield and launched several balls of black magic towards his opponent. Sha'then blasted three of them from the sky and created his own shield to intercept the final two.

With a roar, Sha'then took the energy he'd been using to protect himself and raised it above his head, forming it into a mighty spear, which he launched towards Avus. With a flick of his wrist, the necromancer changed the spear's trajectory, causing it to instead strike the citadel, turning a gargoyle that had been minding its own business into a pile of falling rubble.

Avus's hands worked feverishly as he flung daggers of dark energy towards the Lord of the Underworld, who blasted them aside with a mighty wave of his arm. One struck the ground by Nicolas's foot.

I don't think this is going to go the way Auron thinks.

Furiously, Sha'then thrust his hands forward, unleashing two more lances towards his enemy. Avus waited until the last second, then clapped his hands together, forcing the beams into one which he somehow then managed to catch. Holding Sha'then's power before him, he added his own to it, swirling his hands around to make it grow before firing a mighty wave of magic at the visibly shocked Sha'then.

The Lord of the Underworld got his shield up just in time, but the attack was relentless. Between the flashes of power, Nicolas could just about make out the strain on Sha'then's face. Slowly, the Lord of the Underworld was pushed backwards by the force assailing him. Yet his shield held.

But for how long?

Out of the corner of his eye, Nicolas caught Allius moving closer to Sha'then. The hunched man was putting all his might into swinging the heavy book on the chain around his wrist in circles, gathering speed and momentum. Then he struck.

Sha'then stumbled as the book struck him in the back of the head, and his power waned. It was only a second, but it was enough. Avus's energy blasted through the opening, sending sprays of Sha'then's magical shield flying in all directions as it shattered it like smashed window. The Lord of the Underworld was knocked from his feet, a large rend torn in his armour as his smoking body was thrown through the air, to roll across the dirt with audible thuds.

'What did you do?' Nicolas cried at Allius.

The small man let his book dangle from his wrist as he looked at his former master's smoking body. 'He should've respected me, I was a prince once,' he said to no one in particular. 'And my name isn't *Shambles*.'

'Victory.' Avus, looking completely spent, barely managing to stay on his feet as he raised his arms. The chanting of his name renewed with vigour.

'I am the *Lord of the Underworld*.' The necromancer's voice was shaky but filled with triumph. 'The *God of Death*.'

'Huh.' Auron was slack jawed. 'That's not the way I thought that was going to go.'

A couple of minions helped Avus to his throne. They nearly had to carry him. Despite his obviously weakened state, the necromancer grinned with glee. Another couple hauled Sha'then to his feet and shackled him again. The Lord of the Underworld looked barely alive. The skin beneath the hole in his armour was charred and angry. The minions had to drag his unconscious form.

After a few moments to compose himself, Avus spoke again. 'Take Sha'then to my throne room and these other two to the dungeons. An execution such as theirs requires something grander than being blasted outside my keep.'

There's a giant throne and an honour guard. What's not grand about that?

He got half an idea that Avus was stalling so he could recover. Not something you want to admit in front of the troops. Not that it mattered to him; he and Auron were doomed regardless.

Then the necromancer turned his gaze to Allius. 'There is room in my new court for one such as you. Come and take your place at my side.'

Though he held Nicolas's gaze with sorrowful eyes, Allius walked up the steps and stood beside the throne.

An arm grabbed him and dragged him towards the keep.

****

Two of the knights fell within moments of the creatures shambling heedlessly into the room, swarming their victims. One of them died from sheer forgetfulness, his muscle memory betraying him as he stabbed his attacker in the stomach, forgetting that destroying the head was the only way to fell them. The creature made him pay for his mistake. The others fought bravely, but the sudden press of bodies made it hard for them to swing their swords.

'The stairs, go,' they shouted, grabbing Rex just before a grey-hand could.

They made it to the stairs, Rex in tow, with Garaz following closely behind. Silva and the knights fought a desperate rear-guard action. Several were cut off by the creatures. Cries of anguish followed them up the stairs.

'Come on!' they cried from the top of the landing.

Sir Darick was the first to reach them. The knight looked pale and shaken.

'Silva, move it.'

The warrior beheaded the creature assailing her and charged up the stairs. Hands grabbed at her legs through the bannisters and missed, barely. The knight behind her wasn't so lucky. There was a great crash as metal armour collided with wood. Silva turned to go back for him, but by the time she'd turned, the attacking creature had already found a weak point in the armour around the neck and bitten deep. Even as he died, he pleaded for rescue—right up until his last word was abruptly cut off, his life leaving his body.

At the end of the hallway there was a window. Even as they made for it, they began to change. Their body elongated and their skin became rough bark. Lengthening their legs as they were running was disorientating. They nearly banged their head on the ceiling as they became accustomed to their new height. Thankfully, their improvised toga didn't tear. Just.

They yanked the window open and scrambled through it, turning as they did and clinging onto the side of the building with long wooden fingers. 'Climb down me,' they bellowed in a deep voice. 'But do *not* yank my toga off.'

Thankfully, the tree-folk—what were they called? It was definitely tree-something. Or was it forest-something?—were really tall, which meant their companions would only have a short drop to the ground after climbing down.

Rex went first. He was slight so it was easy, save the uncomfortableness of having someone shimmy down your back. Sir Darick was slightly worse, the hard edges of his armour catching them several times. Even though they had bark for skin, it was surprisingly sensitive. They winced each time a piece flaked off.

Garaz was the worst. They had to put all their willpower into their grip as the weight of the large orc was loaded onto them. They tried not to let the exertion show as they'd made enough jokes about his size in the past. He'd get a complex.

Silva was, unsurprisingly, last. But also the quickest at shimmying down. Just as the growls of creatures reached the window, they let go, dropping to the ground with a thud before changing back to their preferred form, toga thankfully intact.

As they ran out into the street, their pursuers threw themselves from the window with abandon, thumping to the ground to rise again and continue their pursuit. But the majority of them were still inside the building.

'Garaz, do me a favour,' they said as they looked at the decayed bodies falling from the window. 'Burn that building down.'

'With pleasure,' the orc snarled. His muscles tensed as he raised his staff above his head. His green lips worked furiously as he whispered whatever spell he was about to unleash. Then, taking his staff in both hands, he thrust it forward, and a giant fireball flew towards the tavern. Upon impact, there was a bright flash, a thunderous boom, and a concussive wave as the tavern blew apart. They threw themselves to the floor as shards of wood flew through the air. When they looked up, one wall of the building was missing, black smoke and flame pouring from it. There was a strained creak, and slowly, the entire building toppled forwards, almost in slow motion. Putting their hands to their ears, they winced as it collapsed to the floor with a thunderous crash, the once blocky tavern now a pile of burning rubble.

'Is everyone okay?' they asked to affirmatives from all their companions.

Garaz was using his staff to push himself back to his feet, his body a lighter shade of green and his eyes sunken. 'I think I may have overloaded that one.'

They looked back at the destroyed building. 'No,' they corrected. 'I think that was about right.'

Around what was left of the tavern, several creatures who'd been thrown clear by the blast began to rise.

'Allow me,' Silva said, advancing on them.

As the warrior set about the last of the undead, they doubled over, trying to catch their breath, trying to fight away the shaking in their body. Beside them, Rex was doing the same thing.

'You okay?' they asked.

Rex looked back at them with raised eyebrows. 'I will be, as soon as I find a wizard who wipes memories so I can forget all of this crazy shit.'

They laughed heartily then straightened and watched Silva finish the last of the creatures. As its head left its body, the eyes glowed green for a second.

That's odd.

CHAPTER 27

As they were paraded past the throne, Nicolas kept his head down. What was there to look up at? The preening necromancer who'd beaten them? The guards marching them towards a door framed by skulls that most likely weren't carved from stone? The still-smoking body of Sha'then? The smell of burnt meat in the air painted a clear enough picture to not have to see it first-hand. Though it was impressive that the Lord of the Underworld had lived after taking that blast.

He was aware of the necromancer's eyes on him, and the glee of his gaze. He wouldn't meet it, wouldn't give him the satisfaction. Avus was the key, yet he remained out of reach. If he could just get to him...

If he breaks the barrier between the Underworld and Etherius, millions will die, only to rise again as his mindless slaves.

And here he was, chained. Powerless to do anything about it.

Something changed. At first, he couldn't tell what, but he knew in which direction to look. He gazed up at Avus, and the necromancer was sat bolt upright in his throne, his face set in some incredulous half cry as he gazed wide-eyed at the sky.

'Impossible,' he spluttered finally.

'What?' He didn't want to speak, but something in the necromancer's expression made him ask.

Avus turned to him, eyes wide with disbelief. 'Your damnable companions,' he cried. 'They defeated my shades.'

Yes.

'Nicely done, guys,' Auron said, looking into the sky.

Avus slammed his fist on the arm of his throne. 'We can't have that,' he snarled through bared teeth, turning to stare Nicolas right in the eye. 'Don't worry, boy. There's plenty more where they came from.'

Raising his arms, Avus Arex chanted feverishly until the scene with the vortex played itself out again. When it dissipated, a portion of his army had vanished.

'That ought to do it,' the necromancer sniffed weakly before half-falling back into his throne. Avus was looking paler by the moment. The necromancer could barely sit upright in his chair. Allius began fussing over him, helping him straighten.

Filthy traitor.

There was pain in his hands as he clenched his fists so tightly that he nearly broke the skin. His friends had survived, just for that madman to try to kill them again. Without thought, Nicolas broke from the group and bounded up the steps towards Avus, who tried to raise his shaking hand to blast him back.

I don't need a sword. I'll beat him to death with my bare hands.

Closing the gap, he raised his fists as Avus's attacking arm recoiled, attempting to shield him from the oncoming onslaught.

A hand gripped Nicolas's hair, yanking him backwards and throwing him down the stairs. He grunted with each step he hit on the way down.

Rolling to the ground, he recovered himself just in time for Vargas to reach the bottom step and kick him in the head. The world spun as his body rolled across the ground. He should've been dizzy, dazed, disorientated, but rage was fuelling him, and he kicked himself from the ground, charging the smirking warrior. Just before his own blow landed, Vargas's fist cracked him in the face. A flash of pain moved through his cheeks like a wave. His vision switched off and came back on again just as suddenly, and at the perfect time to witness the punch to his gut on its final approach.

'Oof,' he cried as hard knuckles drove into his soft stomach. He fell to his knees, groaning in pain.

'Very, very stupid,' Vargas informed him with a wagging finger, crouching beside him.

Well, I've been stupid already, might as well go with it.

With one burst of speed and strength, he headbutted Vargas right in the nose. Though the strike disoriented him, he was aware of Auron's gleeful laugh before he was dragged from the floor by multiple pairs of hands.

As the guards held him down, Vargas scrambled to his feet, delicately probing his nose. It didn't look broken. *Shame.* The warrior drew his sword and advanced. With a cry, Vargas lunged forwards.

'Enough,' Avus commanded.

Nicolas opened his eyes to find the tip of the blade hovering just in front of his face. At the end of the hilt, Vargas's pupils were tiny enraged black suns. It didn't look like he fancied obeying that order.

'I said *enough*,' the necromancer repeated pointedly, before adding, 'Would you just take them away already?'

With blatant reluctance, Vargas sheathed his blade. After once again rubbing his nose tenderly, the warrior looked directly at him and slowly drew his finger across his throat, eyes wide.

'I think you've made a friend, kid,' Auron said glibly beside him.

'Worth it.' Well, if this was to be his end, at least he'd gone down fighting.

****

The smell of cooking decayed flesh was so aggressive that they wanted to remove their nose, but at least it meant the creatures were dead. Those not charred to death by Garaz's mega fireball, or crushed by the falling building, had been handily dispatched by Silva. Which gave them a moment to relax. They'd rather not have done so amongst a load of lava pits, but beggars couldn't be choosers. Again, they tried to ignore the slight shakes in their body.

I don't panic, and I'm not about to start now. Nick isn't coming back to some jittery, shaking mess. That's his role in the group, and he can keep it. It'll give me something to laugh at next time.

The thought of that made them actually laugh.

'Care to share the joke?' Garaz asked.

Shift stared at him for a moment, thinking on all that had happened. 'I was going to leave,' the said finally. 'After Nicolas returned I was going to just slip away.'

'You *what*?' The display of emotion from Silva caught them by surprise. 'Why?'

Standing at the edge of doing some introspection made them squirm slightly. 'Because I thought it was the right thing to do, to go back to my old thief life and be where I thought I was supposed to be. I kept coming up with excuses, like Garaz's change in mood, as proof that I didn't know you and should leave.' It sounded hollow as they said the words aloud. 'But I don't think it was that at all. I was scared. I'm not used to near death experiences...'

'Bullshit,' Rex snorted. 'I've been there for several.'

'Yes,' they admitted. 'But it's never been that close before, or frequent. I...I'm certainly not used to having people around to care for and who care for me...'

'That sounds more...'

'Will you shut up,' they snapped at Rex. 'I always thought I was better alone. But I'm not. I'm better with you, doing what we do, as dangerous as it is. I don't think I truly understood how much we looked out for each other. When I knew you were all stuck in that building with Sir Gerran...well. Like Garaz said, we're family.' They allowed themselves a smile as they tried to end their little speech on a lighter note. 'Beside,

I certainly don't want to end up like Mace. And if I go back to the Guild there's a good chance that'll happen.'

Shift's words surprised even them. They hadn't even realised they'd firmly changed their mind about leaving. It'd just...happened. But they were going nowhere.

I think I'm actually lucky to have these people around me.

Garaz still looking deathly pale, smiled warmly. Silva's mouth was even curled slightly, almost threatening a smile.

'Family then,' they said as they stood, needing to be somewhere else now they'd been much more open than they cared to be.

Shift walked over and leant against the cart beside Sir Darick. They weren't sure how old the knight was, but right now, he looked every day of it. 'I'm sorry,' they said.

The knight's mouth became a thin line before he spoke. 'They were all good, honourable men.' The old man let out a harsh laugh. 'I've been in battles where I haven't lost so many men. What is becoming of our world, that such *insanity* should occur?'

'You'll calm down in a minute,' they reassured him. 'They're defeated, we won. Let's just rest a minute and get our heads right.'

'Wise counsel,' the knight nodded.

Then it's back to the Oracle's unliveable cottage to see Nick.

Deities, did they look forward to seeing him.

They kicked off from the wagon and slowly approached one of the bubbling pools of lava at their feet. The thick molten liquid had no more place here than the zombies. Would the touch of Avus Arex forever taint this land now, or would the lava dissipate eventually?

Oh, for the chance to punch Avus Arex in the face.

Hopefully, Nick and Auron had done that repeatedly.

The molten liquid was so mesmerising that they cursed aloud as a sword appeared at their throat as if from nowhere.

'All of you stay where you are,' Sir Gerran commanded as he turned Shift around, keeping them between himself and their rapidly rising comrades.

'Unhand them,' Garaz demanded.

'Before I *unhand* you,' Silva threatened.

'Sir Gerran, stay your sword,' Sir Darick commanded, his own blade in hand.

The knight scoffed, spitting on their ear a little as he did. 'I shall do no such thing, because I am in control of this situation.' The blade of the sword dug into their neck to emphasise his point. Maybe they should've feared this man, but really, they just wanted to beat the sense out of him. 'Drop your weapons,' Sir Gerran snarled.

Though reluctant, Garaz dropped his staff. Sir Darick then threw his sword to the ground, and Rex his knives. It was only Silva who took more convincing, which meant another kiss of that blade at their throat. Was that blood running down their neck?

Oh, he's going to get it now.

'So what's next?' they asked.

'What is next is that I finish my mission,' the knight replied smarmily.

'I knew you were an assassin.'

'It shouldn't have gone this way,' Sir Gerran snapped back. 'Mace and the orcs should've been enough to take care of you. We certainly picked people who had vested interests in seeing you dead. They would've naturally turned on each other by the time we arrived. Then it would all have been neat and tidy. Village gets pillaged and all the perpetrators killed each other because that's just what marauding scum do. Anyone who survived...well, let's just say they wouldn't have made it back to the castle.' Venom dripped into the knight's voice. 'But no, you wouldn't die. Instead, you survive even those abominations and forced me to take extreme measures against you.'

They were getting the impression the knight was getting desperate, and considering they were under his sword, that wasn't good at all.

'Who sent you?' Sir Darick challenged. 'You are a knight of the realm. You have betrayed your sacred oaths, you...you...knave. You honourless cur.'

Whoa, calm down with the cuss words, grandpa.

'Oh, I stand for something much bigger than a single realm,' Sir Gerran replied. 'Unfortunately, you will not be present to see our great works unfold.'

'Do we at least get the satisfaction of knowing who you work for?' Garaz asked as they winked at the orc, just to let their companion know they had the situation well in hand.

'I shall give you no satisfaction,' Sir Gerran snarled. 'I'd sooner die.'

As you wish.

Concentrating hard on changing a single part of their body, Shift dropped their weight, and kicked off from the ground, though with legs sturdier than their usual ones. The force of the motion caught Sir Gerran off balance, and they both fell backwards, the sword swinging away from their neck. The knight landed directly in the pool of lava behind them, and they landed on top of him with a painful thud.

Quickly, they stood up, using the flailing knight's body as a stepping stone to jump to firm land, even as Sir Gerran screamed, the back of his armour melting, combining with the lava, and cooking him inside the uniform his betrayal had tarnished. Unable to free himself as the lava slowly consumed him, all he could do was thrash and cry for help that would never come. The screams became less and less human by the second. Eventually, only a pair of legs, slowly sinking with the rest of the body, showed from the molten liquid.

'Disgusting,' they said. 'Though I do suddenly have a craving for roast beef.'

'I take it from that remark that you are well?' Garaz chuckled.

In truth, I'd rather not smell cooked meat again, but it wouldn't do to sound squeamish.

'I'm better than him,' they replied, pointing to the tip of Sir Gerran's boots as the lava finally sucked them under. 'And I'll be even better when we get back to the Oracle and see Nick and Auron.'

Garaz laughed again. 'Your optimism is truly a force of nature.'

'It gets pretty tiring sometimes,' Rex chimed in.

He was about to get a witty retort when their concentration was broken by a nearby cracking. The ground next to them bulged before a rotting hand appeared, clawing at the air. And it wasn't alone.

They huffed loudly and threw their head back. 'Oh, piss off. Not again.'

Judging by the numerous limbs they could see, and the growing amount of indents in the earth, there would be a similar number to the last wave, if not more.

I only want two people to come back from the Underworld. Instead, I get hundreds.

'We cannot have a repeat of what just happened,' Garaz said.

Wise fellow.

'We need to move,' Silva said.

'No argument here,' they said. 'Back to the Oracle's cottage. Let's go.' It was the most logical place to hole up.

Quickly, they jogged towards the edge of the village square, dodging appendages that emerged from the ground, their companions on their heels.

'Is it close?' Sir Darick asked between huffs and puffs.

'Kind of.' They shrugged. Briefly, they glanced back at the old knight; their answer didn't seem to encourage Sir Darick, who shed his armour as he ran. A pretty good idea. They needed speed right now, not durability. Behind him multiple bodies were rising to their feet.

Reaching the edge of the town, Silva turned and set herself in a stance, sword drawn. 'I will stay and cover your escape,' she declared.

'No, you bloody won't,' they cried as they passed her. 'What has Nick told you about suicidal last stands, especially unnecessary ones?' Damned woman seemed bent on seeking a glorious death. That wouldn't atone for her past sins any quicker. Plus, they didn't want Nick to come back only to find out they'd lost one of their own. Especially one whose muscular physique he seemed entranced by on occasion.

Maybe she should stay? One less thing to distract him...

They stopped and turned, realising the damnable woman wasn't budging. 'Move it, Destrone,' they cried, 'Or I'll come back, pick you up, and carry you. You fancy the indignity of that?'

Shaking her head, Silva sheathed her blade and followed them out of the village square.

Breaking into the open countryside, they ran down the tracks between the cornfields, which were completely indifferent to their plight. Deathly moans followed in their wake. They glanced back; a horde of creatures was shambling after them.

Okay, we've all been through a lot and are pretty tired, but they aren't even running. How are those bloody things keeping pace?

They were tempted to ask Garaz to throw some more fire, but the orc still looked spent from the giant one earlier, and any slowing now might cost them. Deities, they were tempted to shift onto four legs and make for the horizon, to the Underworld with their damaged arm, but they weren't leaving their companions behind. Not again...never again.

Are they actually gaining?

Deities damned things had no right to be so fast. Regulating their breathing, they put all their effort into their legs. They just hoped they could keep this pace up.

As tired as they got and as painful their legs became, the gnawing death on their heels kept them running. Every time any of the group slowed, their pursuers would cry out and renew their charge. They were glad Sir Darick had removed his armour, or he would never have been able to keep up with them. Even without it, he looked pale and near death from the exertion.

By the time the edge of the forest surrounding the Oracle's cottage was in sight, they could barely run in a straight line. Every so often, their tired legs betrayed them, causing them to veer off or stumble a little. None of their companions were faring any better, though thankfully, no one had fallen. But they were all slowing, and the creatures behind them didn't have to worry about issues like cardiovascular fitness. Whatever unholy magic animated them ensured they didn't tire. The gap was closing.

'We need to turn and fight,' Silva said between laboured breaths, and she was arguably the fittest of all of them.

'The heck we do.' They scoffed. 'Have you seen how many of them there are? They'll swarm us in an instant.'

'If we go on much longer, we will just fall down and they will be on us anyway,' the warrior countered. 'At least if we make a stand now, we have some energy to give a decent account of ourselves.'

'You both make good points,' Garaz added. Be nice if he actually picked a side, for once. Preferably theirs.

'I'm all for keeping going,' Rex chimed in, face nearly beetroot red. 'I know I'm new and everything, but in this situation, I feel like I should get a vote.'

Good old Rex.

'We don't all need to stay.' Even as he said the words, the thumping of Sir Darick's boots behind them petered away to nothing.

Turning, they saw the old knight with his hands on his hips, puffing and panting. Slowly they came to a halt just ahead of him.

'What's going on?' Garaz asked.

'Keep going,' Shift said between laboured breaths, before addressing Sir Darick. 'What are you doing? This is no time for a breather.'

'I think I've run as much as I fancy,' Sir Darick said with a tired smile. 'As your friend says, they will be on us soon. Please allow me to buy you what extra time I can.'

They wanted to argue, to go back and grab him and drag him with them. There'd been enough loss already, but he had a determination in his eyes that even Silva would be impressed by.

'You're an honourable man.' They gave him a solemn nod of respect then made to catch up with the others, yet unable to tear their gaze from the knight. Sir Darick nodded. 'That was all I ever aspired to be.' Slowly, the knight turned and trudged back towards the oncoming horde of the dead, blade at the ready.

As they crossed the threshold into the forest, they heard a battle cry and snarling. Whispers of hacks and slashes reached their ears for a few moments until they were abruptly cut off. An agonised scream followed shortly after.

Enjoy the Eternal Forest, Sir Darick of Yarringsburg, you valour-filled old goat.

CHAPTER 28

The inside of Sha'then's citadel continued the outside's skull and spike fetish. The pillars were carved into the likeness of numerous humanoid figures, crying out in pain.

No wonder he's the way he is.

Not to mention, someone must be making a fortune crafting skull furniture for vampire lairs, pirate ships, and places like this.

Under guard, Nicolas and Auron advanced through the grand entrance hall, passing numerous statues of figures in agonised poses. The sound of dragging feet followed them. Behind the pair, Sha'then was being returned to his seat of power in the most undignified way, his body limp and drool hanging from his mouth. Thin trails of smoke still danced around his body.

In the centre of the hall was a stairway whose bannisters were fashioned like long serpents. Sha'then was taken up the stairs, whilst Nicolas and Auron were herded into a side corridor, a long and horrifying one. At regular intervals, there were alcoves set into the wall that looked like they ought to have closed doors in front of them.

Oh Deities, no.

Suddenly, he realised what they were: torture chambers. Each contained various devices even more sadistic than the old-looking ones in the entrance hall. The worst thing about these was that they'd obviously been occupied not that long ago. The walls and floor around them were covered in dried blood. It was hard to imagine people doing things that could be deserving of such punishment.

Surely there must be some terrible evil in the world to necessitate this?

Vlad and several of his men walked along with Avus's guards. The older man's head twitched as if he were recalling terrible memories.

Who exactly did the hangman hang?

He didn't want or need to know. His betrayal here was enough to let Nicolas know what kind of man he was.

Selling us out to that scumbag necromancer. If I was free...

Nicolas jumped at a scream of pain from one of the alcoves they passed. It was still occupied. As much as he didn't want to look, morbid curiosity drew his gaze towards it. A thick see through door cut the room off from the rest of the hallway, and a good job it did too. Inside the alcove was a large naked man, his body ravaged with scars and bites. Pieces of flesh hung from his skin like leaves hang from a tree. The man cried out again as claws as thick as Nicolas's arm cut into his back.

Slowly his eyes were drawn up to the creature the claws belonged to. It was reminiscent of a bear, but a horribly mutated one. Though the top of the creature was covered in shaggy hair, it's belly and legs had none, exposing thick muscles covered in red tinted skin. Tusks sprung from the end of the creature's snout and it had a row of spikes across it's back. It was primal and furious as it set about it's work, mauling it's helpless victim, picking him up in it's jaws and launching him across the length of the alcove, where he flopped, right beside where Nicolas stood. As he watched, the claw marks on the man's back were already beginning to knit themselves back together.

He can't die. The creature will just keep butchering him, forever.

What manner of man deserved that? He stepped back as the man looked up at him.

'Grimmark?' Nicolas cried.

The warrior frowned, and then a look of recognition crossed his torn and rent face. The damage should've made it hard to identify him, but he'd never forget the face of someone who'd tried to beat him to death with a hammer on a bridge...twice.

There was pain in the warrior's remaining eye, and not just physical pain. Despite their past, Nicolas found himself wanting to put Grimmark out of his misery. But there was no way he was getting in there with that bear.

'Guy who loves bears being mauled eternally by one.' Auron chuckled. 'How ironic.'

It was true that the mercenary had some weird fetish for the animals. The head of his hammer had even been fashioned into the shape of a snarling bear's maw. The thought of that hammer brought back memories of the thing approaching him at speed, and he shivered.

Nicolas hadn't even realised he'd stopped until he was shoved hard from behind. 'Keep moving,' commanded the wraith—one of the eight escorting them, with Vlad and two of his men bringing up the rear.

'I've had about enough of this.' Auron sighed before his shackles dropped to the floor with an echoing clang. Even before the guard beside him registered what the discarded shackles he was looking at meant, Auron had drawn the wraith's sword from his sheath and plunged it into his ribcage. The next guard was about to cry out in alarm a second before the sword was yanked from his comrade's stomach to take his head off in a single clean cut.

Time did that strange slowing down thing it did whenever he was in a fight. Another guard fell to Auron's stolen sword. In his peripheral vision, he saw the guard beside him begin to draw his blade. Swinging in a full circle with his hands clasped together into one fist, he brought them down on the back of the guard's neck. Even as the wraith began to crumple, Nicolas kicked at his knee, turning his stumble into a full-on fall. Just moments after the guard hit the floor, Nicolas brought his boot down on his head.

Two of the other wraiths moved to join the fray—cut short when they were stabbed in the back by...Vlad's men.

What's going on?

By that time, Auron had done his thing and the rest of the wraiths had vanished. Vlad finished off the one at Nicolas's feet. The hero threw his sword in a circling motion in the air, catching it with his opposite hand. 'And that, gentlemen, is how it's done.' His look of smug satisfaction stopped when he looked at Nicolas. Then Auron raised a quizzical brow. 'Kid, why have you still got your shackles on?'

What sort of daft question is that? Does he think I'm Shift? 'Because...they're locked on my wrists.'

Now both Auron's eyebrows rose, and he pursed his lips. Beside him, Vlad shook his head and chuckled. 'You do know those aren't locked, right?'

What's he talking about? Of course they're... He pressed the clasp and the shackles fell to the floor. They hadn't been locked.

'Deities, kid.' Auron sighed.

How am I the idiot here? 'You could've told me.'

'I did tell you.'

'*When?*' he cried.

'When we were outside.' This seemed really obvious to Auron but not to him. 'I gave you the nod. You know, the *your shackles aren't locked* nod?'

That was what that had been? 'How was I supposed to know that?' He wasn't the idiot here. He was reasonably sure of it. 'I'm not schooled in the interpretation of various nods.'

'I'll add it to the list of things you need to learn.' Auron chuckled. 'I did wonder why you didn't undo them when you took your run at Avus. Very silly, by the way.'

'So you and Vlad planned all this then?'

'Not all of it, exactly.' Auron shrugged.

'And you didn't tell me because...'

'I needed it to look real. That's why I had Sha'then jumped. If he and Allius didn't look so aggrieved, Vargas would've guessed something was off and not presented him to Avus. It was all about keeping up appearances. Same with you. I couldn't really risk you giving the game away. You're quite easy to read.' That stung, but he could hardly argue with the logic. 'If it makes you feel better, sorry for keeping you out of the loop.' He knew the apology was hollow, but somehow it did actually make him feel a little better.

'The idea was to get Sha'then in front of the necromancer so he could smite Avus,' Vlad said as he shrugged awkwardly. 'That's the bit that didn't go exactly as planned.'

'I may have overjudged the power of our overthrown monarch.' This time, Auron did seem a little more contrite, before his mouth curled in annoyance. 'And the loyalty of a certain scribe.'

'Just a little.' It was a cheap dig, but he'd just been made a fool of, so the pettiness slipped out.

'And that's okay, kid,' the hero replied in a way that completely stole his thunder. 'Just means we have to think on the fly. I'm good at that.'

Nicolas gestured for him to continue.

'So, it won't be long until old Avus has had a nice sit down and is ready to kill Sha'then. He'll probably drain his power to recharge,' Auron said thoughtfully. 'When he does, Etherius is going to be flooded with the dead, and all life will end. We can't allow that.'

Yes, a great summation of events but no clue how to stop them.

'Whatever plan you come up with next, it'd best be good, Dawnblade, because my men and I are very close to walking away and leaving you with this mess,' Vlad warned.

Auron looked aghast. 'My plan is simple and genius. Kill Avus Arex.'

'Oh, just like that?' Nicolas and Vlad asked at the same time.

'He has an army surrounding him,' the Hangman added as he looked testily at Nicolas.

Auron paused for a second then a large smile crossed his face. Nicolas did not like that smile. 'The army won't be a problem when the kid here goes and gets that bear on our side.'

There's more than one bear here, right?

Because the only one he could see was the giant slavering beast tearing strips off Grimmark. His eyes went from the half-dead mercenary to the mighty creature killing him. 'You have to be kidding me.'

'Nope.' Auron grinned. 'I want you to go and work your magic on it, like you did with the creatures in the Big Boss's arena.'

He thought back to that time. The dwarf gangster had used a Deity's stolen power to create strange hybrid creatures to fight in his arena.

Nicolas had released them to keep the guards distracted whilst he rescued his companions. The creatures had shown their gratitude for their freedom by not mauling him to death.

'This...this is a completely different situation,' he stammered. 'Those animals were held captive.'

'And does he look happy to be in that cage with Grimmark?' Auron asked as the beast roared. 'I wouldn't be. He's probably a prisoner too.'

Probably could mean the difference between his limbs being attached to his body and not. Yet the hero looked at him with the utmost confidence. Where was he getting this faith from that Nicolas was now some kind of demon bear whisperer? A minute ago, Auron had been bashing him for not realising that his shackles were unlocked.

'Go on, kid.' The hero gestured towards the glass. 'Just give it a try.'

'Why can't you?'

'Because you're non-threatening.'

Oh, come on. He had his moments. He'd knocked out one of the wraiths, hadn't he?

'We don't have much time,' Auron added impatiently.

Looks like I'm doing this then.

With no small amount of trepidation, he approached the glass separating him from the cell. As he reached it, the bear ceased its attack and looked up, snarling. Its breath frosted the glass, which Nicolas wasn't entirely sure could contain it if it chose to come for him.

'Um...hello there.' He had no idea what he was doing. 'My name is Nicolas Percival Carnegie.'

'Did the boy just formally introduce himself to a bear?' Vlad whispered behind him.

'He does that,' the hero confirmed. 'I've been trying to get him to take on a more heroic name, but he won't have it. Yet.'

'Oh, like what?'

'Get this...*Nick Carnage.*'

There was a moment of silence. 'That's a good name. Solid and fearsome,' Vlad finally replied with an impressed tone. 'Many enemies would soil themselves at the sound of that name.'

I don't want to be responsible for soiled undergarments.

Nicolas shot them a glare. While he was trying to negotiate with some kind of demonic bear was not the time to start questioning his preferred name.

Turning back, he nearly jumped as he found the creature much closer to the glass than it had been, studying him intently. On the ground, what was left of Grimmark moaned softly. How long had he been in the room with that thing? He looked into the eyes of the creature. Probably best not to refer to it as a *thing.*

But how to approach such a beast? He supposed the direct way was the best. 'I know you're trapped in there as much as he is, and I was wondering if you'd like to get...out.'

Oh Deities. Maybe it really likes it in there.

The bear was silent. He was going to take that as a good sign, as only moments before it had been growling softly at him.

'I'm willing to let you out on two conditions,' he continued, hoping this was actually going as well as he believed it to be. 'The first is that you don't kill us. The second is that you help us get revenge on your captors. After that you can go...roam the world. Whatever you fancy, really.'

The bear was still silent. It was unnerving. Though he hardly expected it to suddenly go, *'Oh, well, that does seem like a fine offer. I'd be more than happy to assist you in exchange for my freedom.'* On the other hand, he had travelled with a talking chicken once...

Does it even understand me? Perhaps demonic Underworld bears don't understand the common tongue?

He was just about to turn and give up when the creature made a sound not dissimilar to a grunt. Using its snout, it pointed to Nicolas's right. There, on the wall beside the glass, was a touch plate. It seemed the bear was agreeing to help them, but the potential for imminent mauling couldn't be ignored.

'So, we have an accord?' he asked nervously.

The bear grunted again. It didn't sound massively committal to him.

'Just get on with it, kid,' Auron shouted impatiently behind him.

Trying to keep his hand steady, and failing, Nicolas touched the plate. It gave beneath the pressure. There was a flash of green energy, and the glass was gone, and so was their only protection. Cautiously, the bear padded out of the cell, until it was nearly nose to nose with him.

It could take my head off with one bite.

The animal's eyes looked at him, looked *into* him, it seemed. There were several tense moments of silence then the creature bowed its head slightly. Though it still seemed mighty angry, it had also agreed to help.

Well, how about that?

He began to turn away from the cell when a voice called him weakly. 'Boy.'

Hesitantly, he approached Grimmark and knelt beside his broken body. Half the warrior's face was missing, but nerves and muscles were already reconnecting, ready for the next round.

'Please,' Grimmark's hoarse voice pleaded. 'End it.'

What? How dare a man who'd repeatedly tried to kill me ask for mercy?

'End it. Please,' the warrior begged. 'I've led a terrible life, boy. I deserve my punishment. I see that now. For what it's worth, I am sorry. For you and for all of it. I just...I don't want to exist anymore.'

Something about Grimmark's eyes and words were so compelling. Could he do it? An arm touched his shoulder and pulled him aside.

'This one's mine,' Auron said firmly as he stood over Grimmark. 'He betrayed the Hall of Champions. If anyone should finish him, it's me.'

Grimmark let out a single pained laugh. 'You're right, Dawnblade. Let our rivalry end here. Once and for all.'

Auron drew his sword and granted Grimmark's wish.

****

Panting, unsure how many more steps their legs could manage, they broke from the tree line into the clearing. Beside the door of the cottage, Cuthbert was rising. He didn't look pleased.

'Where's my wagon?' he snapped as they got close.

Huh, he can speak after all.

'Well?' the driver insisted. 'Where's Gerty?'

Gerty? Please tell me he didn't name his wagon.

Answering him was difficult whilst running, and once they stopped, the group needed to take a moment to soothe their burning lungs. Maybe more than a moment.

'It...got...shot...with...arrows... Sorry,' they managed between gasps.

'And you just left her there?' the driver raged. 'What about my horse?'

Judging by his reddening face, Cuthbert could read the story in their faces.

'*Cuthbert*,' the Oracle shouted as he opened the door. 'What's all the hollering about? I'm trying to rest.'

The Oracle turned and looked at them all with a raised eyebrow. 'What happened to you lot?'

'They lost my wagon,' Cuthbert snapped, eyeing them as Silva eyed anyone she was about to enact violence upon.

'Oh, shut up about your bloody Gerty,' the Oracle snapped back. 'What's going on? Why do you look so... Oh.'

The Oracle was looking past them. Turning, they saw the first of the creatures emerging from the tree line, snarling in triumph as they realised their prey had stopped.

'Didn't fancy leading them anywhere else then?' the Oracle asked testily as he shuffled over to his door. He ran his gnarled hand along the frame, chanting softly to himself. As he did, runes they hadn't previously noticed illuminated a glowing blue. The air around them became static. A blast of wind from behind tussled their hair. When they looked back, a wall of blue energy rose around the circumference of the clearing.

'Impressive,' Garaz murmured in awe, as he did when something magical fascinated him.

The Oracle almost treated that as an insult somehow. 'I'd be pretty daft to live in the middle of nowhere undefended, orc.'

The advancing creatures threw themselves against the barrier, but though they could see through it, it was as solid as any wall. Held at bay, they beat upon it furiously, flashes of energy coinciding with each strike. The only issue was that a handful of them had entered the clearing before the barrier had risen.

'Cuthbert, take care of them,' the Oracle said with a dismissive wave of his hand.

Glaring, the wagon driver reached behind him and drew a staff with a thick curved blade at either end. Stomping away like an upset child, he muttered to himself, 'Damned wagon-losers. Loved that wagon.'

'I thought he was just a driver?' Garaz asked as the man set about the creatures in a way that would likely impress even Auron. Silva certainly seemed taken with it.

'Wagon driver, butler, bodyguard, he does a lot of things.' The Oracle shrugged. 'Mostly he just drives the wagon. Can't stand the miserable blighter for too long.'

As Cuthbert flipped over the head of an oncoming creature to bisect the one behind it, they wondered if maybe he wasn't wasted as a driver.

'How long will that hold for?' Silva asked. The way she looked at Cuthbert and her envious tone suggested she was unhappy that he got to have all the fun. In their opinion, he was welcome to do as much fighting as he pleased. Shift had officially had enough of the creatures.

The Oracle gave an unhelpful shrug. 'Don't know. Never tested it.'

Maybe testing it for the first time against a horde of the undead wasn't the greatest idea. But the barrier of rippling blue energy looked sturdy enough. A grey head suddenly flew across their eyeline, distracting them from the shield. They glanced to the side then instantly looked away from Cuthbert's gory work. He seemed intent on cutting each creature into as many pieces as possible. Unfortunately, even after they looked away, they could still hear wet hacking.

Hopefully, he's working out all his anger about Gerty on them.

But to more important matters. 'Where's Nick?'

For a brief second, they caught a glimpse of a human emotion from the Oracle other than aggravation. 'He hasn't returned yet,' they replied solemnly.

Nonsense. Absolute nonsense.

They'd been gone for ages. They'd fought assassins and the undead, and they'd been naked on a window ledge...of course, he was awake by now. Shift stomped towards the door of the cottage then shoved inside through the amalgamation of disgusting smells that waited to greet them. There, on the table, was Nick, lying just as he had when they left.

'Nick? Nick?' *Why is he playing such a stupid game?* 'This isn't funny, Nick.' *After all we've been through, this is in really poor taste.* 'Can you get up now?' *We don't have time for games.* 'Will you get up? The undead are outside.' *Infuriating village boy.* '*Nick!*'

It was only when large green hands rested on their shoulders that they realised they'd been shaking Nick's body and noticed how limply his head hung. Why was that? They'd been gone ages. Auron must've found him by now.

'He's not there,' Garaz whispered softly. 'I believe Auron may have failed.'

They threw off the orc's hands and rounded on him. 'Oh, that's what you *believe*, is it? Well, I choose not to believe it. I can't write him off as easily as you.'

There was hurt in Garaz's yellow eyes. 'I want him back as much as you.'

They guffawed. 'If you did, you wouldn't be stood there telling me he isn't coming back. Silva, talk some sense into this guy.'

The warrior's head was hung low, her face set grimly. When she did finally look at them, she shook her head slowly. She was just as stupid as Garaz. 'Okay then. Rex. You don't know what's going on, but just nod and agree with me that he's coming back.'

The young thief's mouth worked up and down as he shrugged.

Why wasn't he just agreeing? They'd told him to agree. This was ridiculous. 'You know what? I'm not giving up on him.' And apparently, they were alone in that. After jumping on the table, they straddled him and shook him again. '*Nick? Nick?* Wake up right now. *Nick?*'

The eyes didn't open. They were sick of this stupid game. They slapped him. Once. Twice. Three times. They'd beat the stubbornness out of him if they had to because he was waking up.

They wiped wetness off their cheek. *Stupid cottage has a leaky roof.*

Behind them were distant voices. 'Whatever dark magic is animating them, it's interfering with the barrier.'

'How long do we have?'

'They're already starting to push through.'

'Close the door. Barricade the entrances.'

'What's the shapeshifter doing?'

'Never bloody mind that, Cuthbert, just barricade the sodding door.'

'There, in the window.'

'I've got it.'

'Hold the door. Deities, these things are strong.'
'I may have a spell for—'
'Side window! Side window!'
Why is this stubborn ass not waking up?

CHAPTER 29

The bear crashed through the giant double doors, and he began to slip. Desperately, he grabbed the creature's fur to hold on, hoping it wouldn't be angered by how tightly he pulled as he turned his head away from the shower of splinters that struck him. Just in case no one had noticed the giant demonic bear that'd crashed into the room with a scrawny guy hanging from its back, the beast gave out a mighty roar that shook its whole body and threatened to jiggle him loose. The bear was huge, and if he fell, it'd be a nasty one. As the bear quieted, he quickly scrambled to a more secure position on the beast's back.

Whose stupid idea was this?

He knew the answer to that: the bear's. Once free of its cage, the monster had been quite insistent, lowering its side to him so he could mount it. His reluctance was met with a snarl that clearly translated from bear to common tongue as, *'If you don't climb up on my back, I'll tear your head clean off.'* Not much of a choice, really.

Maybe it thinks this is the best way to honour our bargain? I'd rather a handshake...pawshake...whatever.

His companion had provided no help. Instead, Auron had watched enviously as the bear rose with Nicolas on its back. Though it hadn't upset the hero enough to stop him laughing as the bear bounded off and he was thrown from side to side.

How am I still even on it?

The room they'd abruptly entered—a large antechamber leading to Sha'then's throne room—was filled with shades. The creatures all stared at him and his mount blankly.

A little surprise would be nice. I am riding a war bear to battle.

He tried to ignore the tinge of excitement at the last part of that thought.

Slowly, the shades shuffled forwards, maws opening. Decayed hands clenched around the weapons they carried.

'Shades,' Nicolas cried as Auron, Vlad, and the rest of his men filed into the chamber behind the beast. 'A lot of them.'

'Meh.' The hero shrugged. 'We have a war bear.' Auron then looked up at him impatiently. 'Get it stuck in then.' Interesting how he assumed Nicolas had any control over this beast.

Looking back towards their objective, it really did seem like a lot of enemies, and they were getting closer.

This isn't getting any more sensible, is it?

Wincing, he carefully tapped the bear with the heel of his boots. The creature turned its head so one eye could glare at him as it snorted in irritation. 'So, do you, maybe, want to...go then?'

Like I could insist if it decided not to.

Luckily, it definitely wanted to. With a low growl, the monster launched itself forwards with such speed that Nicolas nearly rolled right off its back, again. He righted himself just in time to be sprayed in the face with limbs as the bear literally tore a path through the shades.

As the bear advanced towards the door at the far end of the room, like the unstoppable force of nature it was, the shades' eyes glowed one after the other, each managing to speak a word before the bear tore it to shreds. 'Very...clever...Nicolas...' Each green-eyed creature spoke in the voice of Avus Arex. 'But...I...have...more...where...they...came...' It was really frustrating trying to follow a conversation when the person speaking was killed every other second. '...from.'

The bear crashed through the back of the ranks of shades just as even more filed into the room, as well as a fair few wraiths. At the bottom of the small flight of stairs before the door, which was framed by a giant leering skull, Nicolas finally jumped down. It took him a moment to regain his land legs after struggling on the bounding creature.

'Have you got this, Vlad?' Auron asked as he looked at the advancing horde.

'That depends.' Vlad chuckled. 'Kill the necromancer quickly, and we will be fine.'

'I don't think either me or the kid are in the mood to draw this out too long.'

He was right about that.

Nicolas moved around to the bear's head. The creature stared at him. Slowly, he raised his hand, holding it in the air until the monster nuzzled his snout into it. Gently, he stroked the mighty beast. 'Thank you.'

The bear grunted before turning and roaring at the oncoming horde.

For a giant monster bear, it's quite sweet, actually. Definitely handy.

As the beast charged back into the fray, he stepped towards the door next to Auron.

'Ready, kid?' the hero asked him.

It was an easy answer. He knew exactly what he had to do. Avus Arex had to die, once and for all. The necessity of what needed to be done removed all doubt or inaction from his mind. There were too many lives hanging in the balance to not act decisively. Evil had to be vanquished.

'Yes,' he answered simply but firmly.

As Auron pushed the heavy door open, Nicolas turned to the faun, who shuffled awkwardly next to him. 'Haven't seen you for a while.' The faun said nothing. 'You need to go now,' he told the tormenting spirit. 'And never come back.'

Without agreement, the faun simply ceased to be there, and a weight inside him lifted. There would be no more shying away from getting his hands dirty. Especially in the next room when the fate of the world was at stake.

Ready to do what he must, he slipped into the room after Auron, the sounds of battle, and the roars of a demonic bear, echoing behind him.

The chamber was filled with pillars on which countless names were written. Maybe they were the ones Sha'then had been particularly fond of torturing? From the throne at the back of the room, which was surrounded by a row of large spikes, Avus seethed at them. Even from here, Nicolas could see the necromancer's knuckles turning white as his fingers dug into the armrests of his unsurprisingly skull-themed throne. Whoever specialised in making this skull furniture must've been able to retire after doing this palace.

'Just in time to see my ultimate triumph, Nicolas,' Avus sneered, flanked by Vargas and a handful of wraiths.

'If I recall, the last time we were in a room together was just before another of your *ultimate triumphs*,' he replied. 'How did that work out for you?'

'Your tough talk's getting better,' Auron whispered beside him.

The necromancer shot up from his throne. 'As I recall, you were defeated and nearly dead before I was stabbed in the back.'

'All I know was that I walked into that room and back out. You ended up here.'

The last time they'd met, he'd been a different person. Even as he'd resolved to kill the necromancer last time, there'd been conflict. Right here and now, he was sure Avus Arex had to die, once and for all.

'Once I have drained this fool dry,' the necromancer indicated Sha'then, who hung limply above the room, dangling from chains that held his arms, 'his barrier will fall, and the world will be mine.'

'No, not letting that happen,' Auron interjected with supreme confidence.

'You think you and your little sidekick have got what it takes?' Vargas laughed from beside the throne.

'Yes,' Nicolas and Auron said in unison.

Nicolas glowered at the warrior. How dare Vargas call him a sidekick? It was belittling, mean and...accurate.

Avus jumped down from the throne walked forwards until he was directly beneath Sha'then. 'This will be different from last time, young Nicolas.' The necromancer smiled. 'Last time, you didn't face a god.'

One of the necromancer's hands reached towards them. Dark tendrils of black energy swirled between his fingers as he bared his teeth in a preening smile. 'Die.'

Nicolas tensed, preparing himself to dive aside, wincing slightly at the idea of hitting the floor. But the bolt never came. Instead, the energy faded until it was nothing. Avus's eyes bulged as he looked at his hand.

'Oh dear.' Auron sucked his teeth. 'Performance issues?'

'I...what...I...' It was nice to see the necromancer lost for words.

'My friend, Garaz, taught me something about magic.' Nicolas smiled. 'It's not an infinite resource. Overusing it can drain you. You may have been juiced up on those wizards you syphoned when you got down here, but you've been using your magic a lot lately. Overthrowing the Underworld. Your little trick with the shades. Cracking Sha'then's barrier to send your minions to Etherius...twice. Teleporting people around. Your little duel with the Lord of the Underworld. I think you're spent. No death bolts for you for a while.'

Avus stared at his hand as this realisation set in. Then he looked up at Sha'then. If he managed to drain the Lord of the Underworld, it would be an instant recharge for him, maybe a permanent one. He bet the necromancer had enough juice left for that.

Good job I'm not about to let that happen.

'Get them,' Avus screamed at his wraiths as the six guards charged forwards. Beyond the advancing bodies, the necromancer raised his arms in the air and began to chant.

'Stop Avus, kid,' Auron told him. 'I've got these.'

The hero threw himself forward, intercepting the first of the attackers. Metal clashed as two swords met, Auron letting his parrying blade come around his head to strike down on the attacker's neck. It didn't completely take the head off, just made it...very loose. Nicolas slipped to Auron's side, batting away a spear that stabbed at him. He didn't have time to play clashing blades with the wraiths. In his peripheral vision, he saw the spearman turn to pursue him, only for the tip of Auron's blade to explode from his stomach before the sword moved on to its next target.

After rolling under a blow meant to behead him, Nicolas scrambled to his feet and bolted for Avus, vaguely aware he was being chased. Letting his instincts guide him, he turned on his heel, swinging the blade and removing the hand mere inches away from grabbing his hair. Kicking his attacker away, he briefly spied Auron finishing off the wraith he was fighting before picking up the discarded spear from the floor and throwing it into the back of another wraith charging at Nicolas.

He spun back around. The way to Avus was clear. And not a moment too soon. Already, tendrils of black energy snaked from the necromancer's hands, reaching up towards Sha'then.

No.

Again, time slowed to a crawl as he closed on the necromancer, but at the same time, he could see Vargas closing on him. He had neither the skill nor time to match swords with the warrior. Every second he delayed was a second Avus had to complete his spell. And when that happened, all was lost.

As their paths intersected, Vargas swung his sword. Nicolas didn't stop; he didn't even slow. Instead, he threw himself forward, Vargas's blade barely missing him as he landed in a roll, to a cry of anger from the warrior. As his body unfurled, Nicolas pushed hard off the floor, flinging himself forward. His shoulder struck Avus right in the gut, sending the necromancer flying backwards, with him in tow. The ground was hard and ungiving as it came up to meet them, but Avus took the brunt of the impact, Nicolas rolling off of his opponent unharmed. As he got to his knees, Nicolas locked eyes with the snarling necromancer. As Avus's gaze flicked behind him, a small sadistic smile creased the necromancer's lips.

What...

There was a clash of metal directly behind his head. Spinning around, he saw Vargas's sword suspended in the air only a foot from his head. Auron's sword had abruptly intercepted it.

'Tut-tut,' the hero said, wagging a finger at Vargas, before pushing the warrior back a few paces.

Nicolas took Auron's hand and was hauled to his feet. 'When you're fighting, opponents don't just come from in front of you,' Auron scolded him. 'Be mindful of what's around you.'

'We were running out of time,' he retorted. 'I had to stop the necromancer.'

'Yeah, and good job,' the hero replied. 'But I didn't come down here and do all this to lose you at the last moment.'

Funny, it was the last moment. This was it. The two of them facing Vargas and Avus. The necromancer growled as he rose from the floor. 'You...are ruining my work,' Avus cried at them. 'Again.'

'In about two minutes, you won't have to worry about that anymore,' Auron threatened.

'Two minutes?' Vargas scoffed, returning to his master's side. 'I'm your nemesis. You think you can take me that quickly after all our battles, our epic encounters?'

'Pfft. You never won one.' Auron shrugged. 'And I did kill you.'

Vargas visibly shook with rage. 'Liar!' he spat. 'I killed myself.'

'What?' *But Auron said he'd killed Vargas?*

'Oh yes,' Vargas cried. 'Once my God had abandoned me, your friend there had me cornered and beaten once and for all. I knew my time was nigh. And I wasn't going to give him the satisfaction of taking my life, so I took my own. I cheated you of your victory, Auron, and you know it.'

'Did you, though?' Auron laughed. 'I put you in a position where you either killed yourself or I killed you. Either way, you died because of me. And therefore, I killed you.'

Vargas seemed to weigh this up for a moment before he screamed in frustration. 'I can kill you, Dawnblade. I can do it. I know it.' His hands wrung the hilt of his sword, and it seemed he and his sanity were starting to go in separate directions. 'You don't understand. My God didn't abandon me completely. He ensured I had *Heroes' Bane.* He knew you'd be here and he knew I would be the one to finally defeat you, the right way, not with some crossbow bolt.'

'If you could've defeated me, you would've long ago.' Auron snorted. 'What you can do, is spare me the insane ramblings. Though you have more of a chance of boring me to death with them, than you do of killing me with *that*.' He dismissively gestured to Vargas's blade.

'To think that our epic saga finishes here, in this place.' The warrior looked around him in wonder, fully immersed in whatever delusion had gripped him. 'Glorious.'

'To think that you need two swords to be half as good as me.'

'We shall see.' Vargas smiled dementedly. 'Let this be our final battle.'

'Deities, please,' the hero replied with an eyeroll.

Vargas took a step forward and slowly brought his sword down in front of him. Then he did that thing where he made it two swords. He circled both blades in the air with wide eyes before bringing them in front of him. Crossing the blades, he then repeated the process.

Beside him, Auron scoffed. 'You want a sword pose-off? Now, I'm not one for posing, but I can't just stand here and watch that shoddy display without showing you how it's really done.'

Auron isn't one for posing? Since when?

The hero circled his own blade in a fast figure of eight. Every so often, he would throw it in the air and catch it with the other hand. His weapon was a blur as he continually changed grip—then it went behind him, then over his head. Finally, the blade came to rest in front of him, pointed at Vargas. Auron looked like he'd barely exerted himself as he winked at his self-declared nemesis.

'If you're quite finished?' Nicolas asked.

Auron half-smiled. 'I think I've made my point.'

Vargas's sullen face suggested that he had.

'I take it you want Vargas then?'

'Oh yes. You okay with the necromancer?'

'Oh yes.'

'Good. Let's go kick their heads in.' Auron put his free hand out towards Nicolas, who shook it firmly. The pair advanced.

Avus reached behind him to the throne and drew a black metal sword which, judging by the skull iconography on it, had been Sha'then's. It was a lot bigger and more impressive than the rusted blade Nicolas carried, but the necromancer wielded it like someone unused to holding a sword. Plus, it was clearly too big and heavy for him, requiring a two-handed grip. That might even things out nicely.

As the furious clashing of swords rang out to his side, Nicolas jumped backwards to avoid an amateurish swing from Avus. For a moment, it looked like the sword would carry the necromancer in a full circle. Seeing his chance, he jumped in with a downward cut. Avus managed to arrest his sword's motion just in time, instead bringing his weapon overhead to intercept the attack. As the swords met, Nicolas's was overwhelmed by the superior blade. The shock of the impact travelled up his arm to his shoulder painfully, forcing him to put some distance between himself and Avus.

'Who needs skill when you have the better sword?' the necromancer gloated as he advanced.

Nicolas sidestepped the stab to his gut, countering with a slice to the neck, which the necromancer ducked just in time. Nicolas grunted as Avus Arex's bony shoulder drove into his sternum. Stumbling backwards, he saw the sword coming towards him at speed. Instead of trying to parry it, he simply continued to fall backwards to the floor. A rush of wind passed by him as the attacking blade sailed overhead.

After rolling to the side, Nicolas stood quickly. Lying on the floor was the worst place to be in a sword fight. He brought his guard up just in time to fend off another blow. Another painful jink to his arm came as flakes fell from his blade. He let the swords slide apart and kicked the necromancer away. Briefly, he caught a glimpse of Auron and Vargas fighting, their swords moving impossibly fast and their faces set in expressions of grim determination.

Nicolas and the necromancer continued to dance. Dodging and attacking and parrying. Avus was starting to look tired wielding the bigger sword, but he still had the bigger sword. With a cry, the necromancer charged him again, swinging the sword high. Knowing he had little time to dodge it, Nicolas raised his own sword, which shattered upon impact with Avus's blade. Sprinkles of rust fell across his face as he instinctively stumbled back from his destroyed weapon, which was probably the only thing that stopped him being bisected. As it was, the tip of the blade cut down his brow and caught his cheek. Pain flared as he quickly brought his arm up across his eyes. Getting rust flakes in them now would be deadly. His cheek was wet with blood.

Blinking furiously, he saw the necromancer stand tall before him, sword at his side. 'It seems I am the only one with a sword now, young man.' Avus chuckled in faux sympathy.

Nicolas held what was left of his blade, which wasn't much. The sword had been almost decimated by the blow, leaving him with the hand guard and hilt. Be a shame to waste it. With all the strength in his arm, he threw it at the necromancer's face. The hilt hit Avus between the eyes, causing him to falter and giving Nicolas an opening.

Charging in, he grabbed Avus's sword hand, controlling the wrist as he pushed the elbow from below, locking the arm out to a grunt of pain from the necromancer and causing him to drop his weapon, which Nicolas promptly kicked away. He then stepped back to avoid a punch as Avus lashed out in frustration.

'Stupid boy,' Avus cried, removing his robe and throwing it to the floor. Nicolas had forgotten how skinny he was, but at the same time, his lean frame had muscle. 'If you want to settle this in a fist fight again, then so we shall.'

Nicolas balled his fists. 'Whenever you're ready.'

With a cry, the necromancer leapt at him. Nicolas ducked below the punch aimed at his jaw, driving first a left then a right into Avus's stomach. An uppercut to the jaw followed, which sent the necromancer reeling backwards. As he pressed his advantage, Avus recovered too quickly, dodging his hook punch and driving his fist into Nicolas's face. Blood ran freely from his nose as the world shook for a moment. Thankfully, his nose didn't break.

His focus on his injuries was enough of a distraction to allow the necromancer's fist to catch him in the jaw. Stumbling back, he brought his forearms up in front of his face to guard against the flurry of blows that came next. Avus came on with fury and clearly wasn't going to let up. He needed an opening. Inspiration struck when he thought back to their last fight. Swinging upwards with his leg, he aimed a kick directly at the necromancer's testicles.

Instead of landing the blow, two hands intercepted his ankle, gripping it firmly. Apparently, he wasn't the only one with a good memory. 'You did that last time, boy,' Avus spat gleefully. 'Have you learned nothing since then?'

'One or two things.' Pushing his single foot off the floor, Nicolas swung his leg up, kicking Avus in the side of the head. The grip on his other leg loosened instantly. When he landed on his back on the stone floor, Nicolas drove both feet into the necromancer's knees. As Avus growled in pain, Nicolas rammed his foot between his enemy's legs and rolled backwards to a standing position as Avus stumbled forwards, clutching his groin. With a cry, he charged, driving his shoulder into the necromancer's stomach, lifting him from the ground and carrying him across the room. Coming to a sudden stop just before the ornate throne, he shoved the necromancer off him with all his might. Avus flew through the air until his body was impaled on one of the large spikes adorning the throne. The necromancer looked in horror at the giant point protruding from his chest, before his body weight caused him to slide down it slowly.

As Avus struggled feebly to remove himself from his impalement, Nicolas approached him slowly. Somehow, the horrendous injury was doing nothing to remove the confident glint in his eye. 'You think this is enough to stop me, boy?'

'I was hoping not.' Giving in to the anger welling inside him—at this place, at his parents and home being taken from him, and at Koth—he rained fists down on the necromancer. '*Ahhhhhhhhhhh!*' he cried as his knuckles collided with flesh again and again.

When he was nearly spent, and Avus Arex's face was a mess of broken skin and swollen tissue, Nicolas staggered back over to Sha'then's sword. It took two hands and a lot of grunting to lift the blade. Resting it on his shoulder, he returned to the necromancer.

'You think you have the will to kill me?' Avus spat. 'You were hesitant last time, we both know it. You are no killer.'

'You've taught me a lesson in necessity. I should thank you for that,' Nicolas replied grimly. 'There are people like you who simply can't be allowed to go on. If I have to get my hands dirty to stop them, then so be it.'

For a moment, Avus stared at him in horror then he laughed. 'Silly boy, you should know by now that I am eternal.'

'Just shut up and die.' He sighed.

The sword swung in an arc, perfectly on target. Avus Arex's shocked head fell from his shoulders. As Nicolas watched the body and head turned to smoke. But instead of vanishing, as all the others had, the smoke came together into a single ball of energy. Maniacal laughter filled the room as it rose through the ceiling and vanished. Maybe he truly was eternal, just as he'd claimed?

I'll just have to keep killing him until it sticks.

A grunt of frustration behind him made Nicolas remember that there was another fight going on in the room.

'Ha,' Auron cried as he sent the second of Vargas's swords spinning across the floor. 'Told you I was better.'

The warrior looked at his empty hands. 'Maybe this wasn't our final battle after all, Dawnblade. But don't worry, we shall meet again.'

Auron sighed and reached for his belt as Vargas turned to flee. With a deft flick of the wrist, the knife spun through the air, burying itself in the back of Vargas's neck. Even as Vargas hit the floor, Auron was above him. The last thing Nicolas saw before Vargas's body turned to smoke was the incredulous look on his face.

'And stay dead this time,' the hero spat.

'He was already dead,' Nicolas noted. 'He couldn't hear that.'

'I know.' Auron shrugged. 'But it's always good to say something after you kill them. Gives you a sense of closure.'

'Fair enough. Nice work with the knife.'

'Throwing knives are the best, kid. You should always keep one handy.'

'I'll remember that.' Nicolas smiled. 'Speaking of closure. Hadn't we better cut him down?'

Hanging in the air, Sha'then stirred drunkenly.

'I...I'm sorry, my lord. I'm so sorry. So sorry,' Allius, who they hadn't even realised was in the room, shuffled towards Sha'then on his knees. 'I made a mistake. Please forgive me. Please.'

It was pathetic in the extreme.

Slowly, Sha'then's lolling head rose, and his pained eyes rested on his treacherous servant, becoming filled with a fury that could've burned an entire world to ash. 'Run,' he snarled.

Nicolas had never seen Allius move so fast. It wouldn't be fast enough.

****

The cottage was rapidly filling with the shambling dead. The improvised barricades at the windows hadn't held and neither had the door. With a hefty swing, they cracked the stool they held across the attacking creature's head. As it fell to the floor, Rex deftly impaled its head with his knife. But the room was shrinking.

The defenders were pressed back towards the table upon which Nick lay. Even the Oracle used his stick to keep a snapping jaw from his flesh. For every one they slew, two more appeared. The room shrank again.

We're done. Being killed by zombie-like creatures in a cottage in the middle of nowhere while mounting a brave last stand is a pretty decent way to go. But there's no one here to spread the tale.

Ducking down to retrieve their lost sword on the floor, they swung it at the latest attacker. Instead of taking off the head, the blade lodged in an undead shoulder. With a cry, the creature surged forwards, knocking them back to the table. As they fell back, they caught glimpses of images. Garaz with a zombie on his back; Silva furiously keeping two at bay; Rex stabbing and slashing feverishly; Cuthbert with the shaft of his stick in a snapping mouth; the Oracle, cursing and cussing. Each was fighting desperately to stave off the inevitable.

At least I get to die surrounded by family. And a couple of moody bastards.

The world came back with a bump as they hit the floor. Within a second, the zombie was atop them. They grabbed its throat, desperately trying to push it away, but the creature kept coming. Any second now, their grip would give, and the undead thing would be upon them.

The creature suddenly shook violently, its eyes rolling back in its head. They could see the exact moment the walking corpse became an empty husk again. As it fell forwards, a literal dead weight, they pushed it aside and rose. The same thing happened throughout the room.

Each of their companions looked around cautiously, waiting for another trap to be sprung, waiting for their new found hope to turn to dust before their eyes. But nothing came. The creatures were gone.

The Oracle poked one contemptuously with his stick. 'Cuthbert's going to have his work cut out cleaning this up.'

The wagon driver sighed loudly but said nothing.

'So, that's it then?' they asked tentatively. That seemed the wrong turn of phrase. They'd actually been through quite a bit. And their heroic last stand had turned into victory. But not because of anything they'd done. That was weird.

Oh, here we go.

The earth shook around their feet, pots and plates smashing on the floor. Something was happening outside. They ran towards the door.

Outside, a ball of black energy emerged through the grass. At about the height of a man, it stopped, just hovering there.

'I, Avus Arex, am eternal,' the ball declared. *Oh, it speaks?* 'I cannot be killed. I have transcended both life and death. I shall be reborn, and once I am, I—'

The bright flash made them cover their eyes. The ball was engulfed in a burst of orange and yellow flame. There was an inhuman death scream that faded to a whisper and then to nothing as the last fragments of the ball turned to flaming embers.

Beside them, Garaz blew on the tip of his still-smoking staff. 'Odious fellow,' the orc snarled.

CHAPTER 30

You'd think that someone whose kingdom had just been rescued from the brink would be happy. Instead, the Lord of the Underworld looked as if that kingdom had been returned to him with a steaming pile of dung atop it, as he belligerently rubbed his wrists. Without a word of thanks, he stomped past Auron and Nicolas, breaking stride only to collect his sword from the floor before taking his place upon his throne.

Sha'then struck the hard stone once with the tip of his blade, the sound resonating out like the ringing of a temple bell, before declaring, 'The Lord of the Underworld is restored to his seat.'

'And you're welcome,' Auron muttered.

Sha'then's head turned towards Auron sharply. 'What was that?'

Nicolas looked at Auron, shaking his head slightly.

Don't repeat it. Don't repeat it. Don't repeat it.

'I said, *you're welcome.*' Sometimes, Nicolas wondered whether Auron enjoyed upsetting the wrong people.

The Lord of the Underworld's lips curled into a snarl. 'I still have to clean this place up. There are thousands of souls to put back in their proper places, traitors to hunt down, punishments to be devised,' he said flatly. 'Excuse me if I don't shower you both in hugs and kisses.'

From him that would be a form of torture.

'At least you won,' Nicolas pointed out.

'I suppose there is that,' Sha'then conceded grudgingly.

'Speaking of which,' Auron interjected, 'it's time to send the kid back now.'

Sha'then raised an eyebrow. 'Why?'

That...isn't good.

Auron's face dropped. 'Because he helped you save your kingdom.'

'And do I come across as a particularly grateful or merciful person to you?' the Lord of the Underworld asked. Again, not a good answer.

'No, you don't,' Auron admitted. 'But you seem like one who likes revenge.'

'Which is why he should stay here,' Sha'then sneered. '*He* is responsible for this.'

Nicolas could definitely argue the logic of that.

'Hardly,' Auron snapped back. 'But those who were, those behind Avus getting that much power are still out there. Down here, you can't do anything about it. But *he* can. And believe me when I say that his heart will be in it. And once he's done his work, they get to come down here so you can do yours.'

Sha'then steepled his fingers and thought on this. Finally, he rose from his throne. 'I will do this,' he declared. 'But understand this. Putting a soul back in a dead body is…unprecedented, no matter how it has been preserved. I cannot guarantee that it will work nor that you will be truly human again. Are you sure about this?'

That sounded ominous. But he was never going to save his family down here. 'Please send us back.'

'*Us?*' Sha'then asked with a raised eyebrow.

'Yes, he comes too.' Nicolas pointed to Auron, just so it was completely clear. He didn't want to accidentally end up with Vlad.

'Kid, you don't—'

'Yes, I bloody well do,' he interrupted. 'You came down here to save me knowing it may be a one-way trip. Well, I'm not having that.' Nicolas looked back at Sha'then. 'You want me to succeed? Then I need him to show me how to do it. He's my mentor. I can't do it without him. I just can't.'

The Lord of the Underworld looked unamused. 'I am not accustomed to bargaining with souls in my kingdom. Nor do I care for it. I should torture you both for letting me be beaten.'

'But without it, Avus would have won.'

'He may have—'

'*Would have* won.'

Sha'then sighed laboriously. 'Very well then, but only because you two irritate me so, and I don't want you around. At least Auron will be easier to send back as he is a disembodied soul.'

This guy's sense of gratitude was very underwhelming.

'Wait a second.' As Auron looked at him, undoubtedly wondering why he was delaying, Nicolas threw himself at the hero, embracing him. 'Thank you. For coming for me.'

After a few moments, he felt Auron's hand on the back of his head. 'You deserved no less, kid.'

As the pair parted, Auron held out his hand, and Nicolas shook it. It might be the only time he ever would.

'If you two are quite done,' Sha'then snapped impatiently.

'What about us?' At the back of the room, Vlad and his men had filed in. There were fewer of them and some looked much worse for wear. In the doorway was the head of the giant bear, sniffing the air slowly.

'I have a lot of work to do, and my skeletons have proven inadequate for many tasks,' Sha'then declared. 'You shall now be trustees in my service. Your first task shall be to hunt down Shambles. I need to repay him for striking me.' Vlad nodded happily as Sha'then dropped his voice so only Nicolas and Auron could hear. 'And once they are done, I shall have them back in my torture pits. I owe nothing to murderers and rapists.' As nice as Vlad seemed, Nicolas got the impression he still had this coming.

The Lord of the Underworld looked past the pair again and raised his hand. The demonic bear padded into the room, it's approach to the throne only pausing to give Nicolas a growling nod. It finally came to a halt beside the throne, then tilted it's head upwards. Sha'then began to scratch the beast's neck.

'And you are going to be my new favourite pet,' Sha'then purred. 'Your mighty claws will bring roaring, bloody death to my enemies. Yes they will.'

The bear answered with a satisfied grunt, clearly enjoying getting smoothed.

I hope Allius is fitter than when we first met. He will need to be.

'Who knew he had a soft side, after a fashion?' Auron asked with a chuckle. 'Do you think...'

Before the spirit could say anything else, black energy engulfed Nicolas.

****

Nicolas's eyes shot open, and he gasped. Deities, it was good to breathe again. Then, when his nose registered the air he was breathing, he hacked and coughed violently. Rolling to the side, he only realised he was on a table when he fell from it. He got his legs under himself just in time.

There are corpses everywhere.

His legs struggled to take his weight. How long had he been out for?

Are we in the Oracle's cottage?

Ah, that explains the smell.

He reminded himself to wash his clothes later; that table was likely very unsanitary.

Oh, my shirt's ripped.

For a moment, he started at the sight of the giant demonic handprint on his chest, but as he watched, it faded away to nothing.

Nicolas wheeled around suddenly, aware that someone was directly behind him.

'Is that you?' Shift asked, face emotionless.

They appeared to be wearing just a bedsheet. He wanted to ask, but all the sudden sensations he was feeling again were too overwhelming. He needed to get his head straight before he went asking questions about people's attire.

Quickly, he checked himself over. 'It appears to be.' He shrugged.

'Good.'

To his surprise, Shift grabbed his head and kissed him fully on the mouth. The kiss was passionate and seemed a little angrier than he would've expected, though he had no experience of kisses to compare it to. After the first seconds of surprise, he let himself fall into it. It was…nice.

Once they pulled back, Shift's brow furrowed again, and their eyes evaded his for a few moments. Then Shift fixed him with their gaze again and slapped him hard across the face. 'Never again, Nick.'

Never again what? The kiss or the nearly dying?

Tenderly, he rubbed his stinging face. They could certainly swing when they needed to. He looked up just in time to see Shift storm out of the cottage.

'I am so glad to see you alive, my friend.' He was still trying to process the kiss when Garaz wrapped his large arms around him with enthusiasm, hauling him from the floor. He struggled a little in the grip but finally returned the hug. 'I have no intention of kissing you,' the orc whispered before releasing him.

He was still disorientated by it all as Silva approached him. He raised his hands defensively as she lunged forwards, until he realised that she was hugging him too. It was quick and firm. As the warrior released her grip, she coughed awkwardly, before patting him on the shoulders and walking away.

Have I come back to the right Etherius?

'Lucky kid,' the Oracle commented with a derisive snort.

'Why are there dead bodies everywhere?' he asked.

'We have had quite the adventure.' Garaz smiled wearily.

Before he could ask more, Shift's head appeared in the doorway. 'Out here, guys.'

Proceeding into the sunlight, he realised how glad he was to be alive. The sun was bright, and every breath was now a blessing. And it seemed he wasn't the only one who'd been blessed. On the grass before him was Auron, back in the familiar ethereal form they knew him best, sat upon a horse of the same makeup, smiling broadly.

The spirit beamed as he dismounted. 'He gave me Mare back. Well, the spirit of Mare, at least. Maybe Sha'then was a little more grateful than he let on? Or more dedicated to revenge.'

'How is that possible?' Nicolas asked. 'Your horse wasn't in the Underworld. I don't think we even saw any horses there at all.'

'He probably has a little sway over the nicer side of the afterlife too, but I don't really care. I've got Mare back.' Considering Auron had just been returned to his undead form, it was nice to see his beaming smile.

'Wait,' Shift said. 'You call your horse *Mare*?'

'Yup,' Auron replied. 'That's her name.'

'Why?' Shift asked cautiously.

The spirit's features broke into a wide grin. 'Because a stallion rides her.'

That's just wrong. And terrible. But also something only Auron would say.

Shift wrinkled their nose. 'That's disgusting. And stupid.'

'Many a fair maid has disagreed.' Auron winked theatrically, before his face dropped slightly and he added, 'Oh, and I got this too.' From the side saddle, the spirit drew a bright blade. 'I'm less impressed with this. What am I going to do with a spirit sword that can't stab anything?' To illustrate his point, he walked to the wall of the cottage and poked the sword through it. Auron looked like he was holding a wet fish as he stared at the blade half sticking out of the wooden wall. Then he withdrew it and shrugged. 'A gift is a gift, I suppose.'

Nicolas chuckled to himself. It was good to be home.

Home.

He wasn't, though. This wasn't his home anymore. They'd taken it from him. He'd lost everything.

'Nicolas?' Garaz asked at his side. 'Are you okay?'

Involuntarily, he found himself sitting on the grass. 'Not at all,' he whispered quietly. 'Everyone's gone. I have no family anymore.'

'Nonsense, kid.' Auron looked at him with sympathy. 'We're your family.'

Nicolas looked at those around him and let out a single laugh. What an odd assortment of people he'd found himself with. He didn't even know who the young guy hanging around at the back was.

Nicolas thought over everything that had happened and everything to come. A determined realisation came to him. 'I have work to do.'

'What work?' Silva asked.

'I have to get them back. My parents, everyone.' His fists balled up. 'And I have to make those responsible pay for what they've done and prevent them from doing worse. I've learned my lessons. It's time to walk the path I seem to keep ending up on.'

Not as a chosen one. This is all just terrible coincidence.

'*We* need to make them pay,' Auron corrected.

'You are not alone,' Garaz added.

'We are at your side,' Silva said firmly.

'Come whatever.' Shift's green eyes were sad as they looked into his.

Maybe I do have some family left after all.

Nicolas had no idea what would come next. But he was happy that he'd be facing it with them. Hopefully, wherever he was right now, the Maestro had just experienced a shiver of fear.

Because I'm coming for you, you bastard.

Realising what that would require, he turned to Auron and Silva.

'I need you two to train me,' he said quietly. 'Really train me. No more bumbling around. If I'm going to do this, I need to do it properly.'

'Kid,' Auron began with a beaming smile, 'I thought you'd never ask.'

Epilogue

He knew he was dreaming the instant his eyes opened. Everything around him seemed normal, and his real life had become so unreal. He was in his bed, in his home, so this was definitely a dream. That was all gone. He hoped he didn't see his parents here. Every time he dwelt on them, he couldn't help going over their possible fates.

Though at the same time, I hope they are here.

Something told him he needed to go downstairs. Maybe this wasn't a dream. Maybe it was a memory? Was he about to repeat what had happened with Koth in his mind? Perhaps he was stuck in this moment forever, playing it again and again in an endless loop? It occupied his waking mind, so why not his dreams as well?

He got to his feet and walked to the door of his room. His hand hovered over the handle for a moment. He was afraid of what was beyond that door. But he knew he had to face it, so he gripped the handle and opened it.

As he moved down the stairs with trepidation, a voice greeted him. 'You're awake.'

The rage boiled in Nicolas instantly, his hands clenching to shaking fists. *'Get. Out.'*

From the dining table, Avus Arex looked up from his drink. 'Is that any way to treat a guest?' He had no right to play hurt, after everything he'd done.

'You aren't welcome here.' He stomped down the stairs and over to the table, ready to have his third go at beating the necromancer senseless.

Avus seemed unconcerned by his rage. As he went to pick up his glass again, Nicolas slammed both his hands on the table. *'GET OUT!'*

Avus sat back, smirking at him. 'You know this is a dream, right?'

'I don't care what it is.' He was about ready to throw himself across the table and beat the necromancer to a pulp. 'I want you gone.'

With a sigh, Avus looked at his own hands. 'I will be soon.'

The sorrow in his tone caught Nicolas by surprise. 'What do you mean?'

'I'm not a dream.' Avus half-smiled. 'I'm a remnant, a part of me left behind to pass on a message to you. When you took me hostage by the hill, it occurred to me there was a chance you might kill me. When the energy passed through us, I left this little *note*, just in case I lost. As we are having this conversation, I doubt I need to ask how things turned out.'

'You're dead.' He couldn't hide the pleasure in his voice, though it shamed him. 'Really dead this time. No coming back. Oblivion.' *Thank you, Garaz.*

'I will be once this last piece of me fades.' Avus shook his head slowly. 'All my potential wasted. My great works ruined.'

'Spare me your sadness. You were a monster.'

'That,' the necromancer raised a finger, 'is a matter of perspective.'

'Please—'

'Contrary to what you believe of me,' the necromancer interrupted, 'I only wanted to help the world. To show how my gifts could help. Did I do some terrible things? Yes. But in service of a greater good, of...'

Slowly, the scene around them began to shimmer. Nicolas was shocked, more so that Avus seemed to share in his surprise. He'd assumed the necromancer was in control here, but maybe not? The walls of his house melted into a garden he'd never seen before. What sorcery was this? Just beyond him, a young lady with beautiful long blond hair picked flowers for a basket.

'Oh.' Avus's face dropped, his lips trembling.

The lady sat on a nearby log and fastened some of the flowers into a chain, which she placed around her head, humming a melodious tune the whole time.

'Do you mind if we linger a moment?' Avus asked him quietly, his eyes betraying deep hurt as he stared at the young woman.

'What is this?'

'A memory,' the necromancer told him, his brow furrowed. 'One of mine. Why it should be here I don't know. Maybe I wanted to see her one last time before the end?'

'Who is that?'

'Helene.' The name came out as a hoarse whisper. 'My love.'

Nicolas scoffed. 'You had a love?'

Avus seemed hurt by this. He looked down at himself and laughed. 'I wasn't always...this, you know. There was a time when I was much more, because of her.'

Flower crown on her head, the lady rose and twirled, arms outstretched, and eyes closed, enjoying the world around her.

Despite wanting the necromancer gone for good, curiosity got the better of him. 'What happened?'

'She died.'

'I'm sorry.'

Not half as sorry as Avus was, judging by his expression. Nicolas had some experience losing loved ones recently, and as much as he didn't want to sympathise with the necromancer, he couldn't quite help himself. 'How did she die?'

Avus looked to the side. 'Do you see the house there?'

It was a small, rustic cottage with a thatched roof. 'Yes.'

'That was our home.' Avus smiled at the dwelling. 'I was a young healer at the time. I would lock myself away in there and study whilst she was out in the garden. Making people better was my obsession. She loved the garden, loved being outdoors. I wish I'd spent more time out there with her.' He paused before continuing. 'One day she came in. Something had stung her. I never found out what. Initially, we thought nothing of it. Then she got sick. And she kept getting worse. I did everything I could to heal her, used my magic until I was exhausted, dug up every healing herb I knew, but nothing touched the sickness. As she got worse, she began to...waste away. By the end, there was barely any of her left. She wasn't the woman I'd known anymore. And then she was gone, and my world had no more light.'

'That must've been terrible.' He'd seen imagined images of his parents' deaths a lot lately, and that had been bad enough.

'That was the day.' Avus let out a harsh laugh. 'That was the day I became obsessed with raising the dead. That day I was set on the path to become what you know me as. If I couldn't heal the living then by the Deities, I would cheat death itself. I could help them. I could stop people dying. Maybe bring her back in the process.'

'Do you think she'd be happy knowing what you did to return her?'

Avus scoffed. 'You think I'd care. She'd be back. I'd wipe out cities for that.'

'You nearly did.'

'Until you stopped me.' The glare from the corner of the necromancer's eye chilled him. 'Which brings me to why I'm here.'

Finally, a point.

'There's a tavern in Yarringsburg called the *Merry Ogre*. It was there I met those who helped me in my scheme, those men in the shadows. Go there and ask for Alric Tavish. He was the one who came to me with the plan and provided me with the tools to enact it.'

Now it was Nicolas's turn to scoff. 'And you're just helping me out of the goodness of your heart.'

Avus laughed harshly. 'Not at all, boy. I'm telling you this because I want you to die. You're going against them, and they *will* kill you. I'd like to know I at least had a hand in your death before I'm gone completely. Hopefully, they'll get all your thrice-damned friends too.'

However spiteful the necromancer was being, he had just given Nicolas a lead, and he intended to follow it. Whoever these people were, they were going to pay for everything they'd done.

For a moment, Avus looked as if he wanted to ask something. Nicolas gestured for him to spit it out. 'I know I have no right to ask this of you.' The necromancer coughed awkwardly. 'But can I stay a few minutes more?'

Nicolas was asleep so he wasn't going anywhere. Avus may have been insane and vile and needed to die, but that didn't mean he couldn't be compassionate to his foe before he finally faded from existence. If it had been his parents...well, he could understand the fulfilment Avus would get from that. As terrible as the man was, Nicolas found he couldn't deny him.

Sitting on a nearby log, the pair watched Helene saunter about the garden. The necromancer viewed her with adoring eyes. Nicolas hoped one day he'd have someone to look at, and who looked at him, that way. Unconsciously, he brushed his lips and then his cheek.

Nicolas wasn't sure exactly when the last essence of Avus Arex faded away, but he was gone seconds before the garden and Helene blurred into a ball of greens before vanishing forever.

'And don't come back this time,' he muttered.

He found himself longing to be awake. They had a man to find.

Alric Tavish.

ACKNOWLEDGEMENTS

And that was it, the book I like to term *the end of the beginning.'*

Nicolas is in it now. No more dipping his toe in and out of adventuring. Now it's time for the series to really get going.

And what a way to get to this point?

As soon as I decided to bring back Avus Arex, I knew I was going to have a lot of fun writing this book. I was a little uncertain about the multiple perspectives at first, but I'm really happy with how this turned out. In fact, I'm really happy with how the whole series is turning out. I'm getting great feedback from people (someone even referred to themselves as my fan the other day...I was not prepared for that, I can tell you, but it meant the world to me), which is the whole point of writing these books...for people to enjoy.

I can tell you now, as I work hard on the first draft of book 9, that there is plenty of story still to tell!

Thank you for continuing to follow my work. You are the reason I publish these books and will continue to do so. (It's safe to say I definitely have the writing bug now).

Though as usual, I am nothing without the team behind me. Firstly I have to give a shout out to Dani, my amazing editor. Her feedback polishes my work up into the book you just enjoyed. She is also really fun to work with, including a Mrs Doubtfire picture in the editing notes when I accidentally wrote 'hoovered' instead of 'hovered.' She gets my vision for the series and helps me tell these great stories.

Then there is my mum, Christine, who's brilliant hunting down of those damned elusive typos ensures that there aren't too many 'Hoover/Hover' issues in the text.

And what is a book without a beautiful cover (it's how we judge our books lol). Once again Miblart did a fantastic job, creating a stunning cover that wowed me the minute I saw it. Sometimes seeing pictures of the threats that Nicolas faces almost makes me feel sorry for him. I can't let myself do that though, or I'd stop putting him in danger, and no one wants to read a book where he has a chilled day in the garden.

I take it you've read enough of my books by now to know that I use Kickstarter to fund these books. It is a fantastic platform for indie authors like myself and I am grateful to every one of my Kickstarter supporters, who continue to believe in my work, and all the associated exclusive swag I throw their way!

Getting these books published is hard work, but so rewarding. And I hope you enjoyed this little Dawn of the Dead meets Dantes Inferno tale of mine.

Let's see what Nicolas does now he isn't fighting against his adventures in book 5.

Until then,

Keep adventuring!

Andrew

About the Author

Andrew Claydon has an imagination, one full of variety.
Sometimes it's funny, sometimes it's adventurous, sometimes it's shocking, and occasionally it's outright strange...but it's never boring!
Andrew is a UK author who grew up loving fantasy movies such as Conan, Krull, Beastmaster and Willow. The epic worlds and battles of swords and sorcery therein inspired him to create his own fantasy worlds, adding to them his own brand of irreverent humour; because sometimes it's good to chuckle in between sword fights!
He wants to inspire the imagination of others, just as he's been inspired; with dashing heroes, epic quests and vile villains.
So reader beware, you aren't just opening a book, but a doorway into Andrew's imagination. It'll be a strange journey, but an entertaining one!
When he isn't writing, he loves to read sci/fi and fantasy novels. It's one of the things that inspires him to write himself. He also enjoys playing Warhammer 40,000 and is a keen wrestling fan.
He has degrees in both history and psychology, as well as black belts in several martial arts.
When he isn't creating vast fantasy worlds and populating them with good guys and bad guys to run around fighting each other, he works as a supported employment coordinator, helping others to try and achieve their aspirations.

Subscribe to my newsletter for the latest publishing news (and get a FREE prequel novella) at: www.andrewclaydonauthor.com
Or follow me on social media:
Facebook: Andrewclaydonauthor
Instagram: @authorandyc
Tiktok: @authorandyc
If you enjoyed the book, then please leave a review with your preferred retailer and/or Goodreads.
Reviews are really important to indie authors to help them get their work out there and create more amazing books for avid readers like you.

If you do take the time to leave a review, thank you.

Also By

Chronicles of the Dawnblade Series
The Simple Delivery
Strange Companions
The Odd Sea
Wrath and Wraiths
Trail of Death
Demons and Disorder

Novellas and short stories
A Grudge is Born
The Gathering
Don't you know who I am?

www.ingramcontent.com/pod-product-compliance
Lightning Source LLC
Chambersburg PA
CBHW061807190726
48289CB00007B/2100